IDOL

VIP SERIES

KRISTEN CALLIHAN

LIBBY

I found Killian drunk and sprawled out on my lawn like some lost prince. With the face of a god and the arrogance to match, the pest won't leave. Sexy, charming, and just a little bit dirty, he's slowly wearing me down, making me crave more.

He could be mine if I dare to claim him. Problem is, the world thinks he's theirs. How do you keep an idol when everyone is intent on taking him away?

KILLIAN

As lead singer for the biggest rock band in the world, I lived a life of dreams. It all fell apart with one fateful decision. Now everything is in shambles.

Until Liberty. She's grouchy, a recluse —and kind of cute. Scratch that. When I get my hands on her, she is scorching hot and more addictive than all the fans who've screamed my name.

The world is clamoring for me to get back on stage, but I'm not willing to leave her. I've got to find a way to coax the hermit from her shell and keep her with me. Because, with Libby, everything has changed. *Everything.*

For Cobain, Bowie, and Prince —rock idols who helped shape the soundtrack of my life. They were taken from us too soon.

ABOUT THE AUTHOR

Kristen Callihan is an author because there is nothing else she'd rather be. She is a RITA award winner, and winner of two RT Reviewer's Choice awards. Her novels have garnered starred reviews from Publisher's Weekly and the Library Journal, as well as making the USA Today bestseller list. Her debut book FIRELIGHT received RT Magazine's Seal of Excellence, was named a best book of the year by Library Journal, best book of Spring 2012 by Publisher's Weekly, and was named the best romance book of 2012 by ALA RUSA.

You can sign up for Kristen's new release at

 @Kris10Callihan

 KristenCallihan

www.kristencallihan.com

ALSO BY
KRISTEN CALLIHAN

AUTHOR NOTE

To see where you're going sometimes you have to look at where you've been. Killian and his band have their own idols who helped forge their sound. To that end, most of the music mentioned in this book is not of this past decade, but older. Some of you might discover new songs, and some of you—like me—might take a trip down memory lane.

Also, Collar Island, where Libby lives, is a made up location. Mainly because, that way, I could shape the place and the people who live there with impunity. However, if you're curious about how it might look, Bald Head Island, NC is the closest equivalent.

Thank you and happy reading!

Love,

Kristen

Prologue
KILLIAN
The Past

Music can be your friend when you have none, your lover when you're needy. Your rage, your sorrow, your joy, your pain. Your voice when you've lost your own. To be a part of that, to be the soundtrack of someone's life, is a beautiful thing.

—KILLIAN JAMES, LEAD SINGER AND GUITARIST, KILL JOHN

THE ANIMAL IS A TEMPERAMENTAL BEAST. It can love you one moment, then hate you the next, and you never know what side of it you're going to see until it's upon you. If it hates you, there's nothing to do about it but endure and hope you survive without being completely shredded until you can safely make your escape. But when it loves you?

Damn, but it's the best feeling on Earth. You crave that time with the Animal. Live for each encounter. It becomes life. Your purpose. Your entire world. And because you become so dependent on it, you come to hate it a little bit as well.

Love. Hate. No down time. No middle ground. Just highs and lows.

It's out there now, waiting for me. Growling with a slow, gathering rumble. I feel it in my bones, in the subtle charge that lights the air, and in the tremble beneath my feet.

My heart rate begins to rise, adrenaline already kicking in.

"You ready to dance with the devil?" Whip asks no one in particular. He's chugging a bottle of water, his free hand tapping an agitated rhythm on his knee.

Devil, Animal, Mistress—we all have our name for it. Doesn't matter. It owns us, and for a time, we own it.

The roar grows louder, followed by a *thump, thump, thump.* My name. It's calling for me.

Killian. Killian.

Panting, I rise. A shiver licks over my skin, my balls drawing tight.

I answer its call, and a wave of sound and sheer energy crashes over me as I walk into the light.

Hot, blinding.

The Animal screams. For me.

And I am the one who controls it. I raise my arms, walk up to the mic. "Hello, New York!"

The answering cry is so loud, I rock back on my heels.

A guitar is placed in my hand, the smooth neck both a familiar comfort and an adrenaline kick. I settle the strap over my head. Whip's drums start up, a pulsing beat, and my body moves with it. Jax and Rye join in, their riffs weaving an intricate pattern. Harmony. Poetry of sound. A scream of defiance.

I begin to strum, my voice rising. Music flows through my veins. It pours out of me like lava, igniting the air, inciting a riot of eager screams.

Power. So much power. The Animal responds, its love so potent that my dick gets rock hard, the hairs on the back of my neck lift. Everything I am, I put into my voice, my playing.

In that instant, I am God. Omnipotent. Endless.

Nothing—*nothing*—on Earth gives a charge like this. Nothing compares. This is life.

But that's the thing about life; it can change in an instant.
All it takes is one instant.
For it
to all...
End.

LIBBY
The Future

"THERE'S BEEN SO MUCH WRITTEN about your involvement with Killian James. But you and James have been rather closed-mouthed about the topic." The reporter gives me a slight but encouraging smile, her blue hair slipping over one eye. "Given last night's performance, would you care to offer us a little bite?"

Curled up on a leather-and-chrome hotel room chair, my back to the New York City skyline, I almost smile at the question I've heard about a thousand times now.

But training kicks in. A smile would convey either acquiescence or that I'm being obnoxiously coy. I don't want to give up a "little bite," and despite what critics say, Killian and I have never been coy. We've just never wanted to let the public in. The Killian I knew was mine, not theirs.

"There isn't much to tell that the world doesn't already know." Not really true. But true enough.

The reporter's smile has an edge to it now—a barracuda searching for blood in the water. "Oh, now, I'm not so sure about that. After all, we don't know your side of the story."

I resist the urge to pick at the cuff of my white cashmere tunic. God, the sweater—hell, my underwear—cost more than I would have spent in a year before *he* walked into my life.

I turn my head and catch a glimpse of water bottles nestled

in a silver ice bucket: a dark green bottle, one that's gold, another bedazzled with crystals. Earlier an assistant proudly proclaimed that the green one, supposedly from Japan, cost more than four hundred dollars a bottle. For water. Suddenly, I want to laugh. At the craziness of my life. For going from tap to designer water. For the fact that this penthouse suite is my new normal. And then I want to cry. Because I would have none of this without him. And not a single fucking bit of it has any meaning without him to share it. Emptiness threatens to swallow me whole. I'm so alone right now that part of me wants to grab this woman's hand just to feel contact with another human being. I need to talk. I need to be heard. Just once. And maybe, just maybe, I won't feel like I'm falling apart anymore.

I take a breath and flick my gaze back to the reporter. "What do you want to know?"

The Present
LIBERTY
1

There's a bum on my lawn. Maybe I should use a better term, something more PC. Homeless person? Vagrant? Nope, I'm going with bum. Because I doubt he's actually homeless or without means. His current state seems more a choice than a situation.

The big black-and-chrome Harley that's smashed into my poor front fence is proof enough of some wealth. Fucker tore the hell out of my lawn on its way down. But it isn't the bike's fault.

I glare at the bum. Not that he'd notice.

He's sprawled on his back, arms akimbo and clearly down for the count. I might wonder if he's dead, but his chest lifts and falls in the steady pattern of deep sleep. Maybe I should worry about his health, but I've seen this before. Too many times.

God, he stinks. The cause of his stench is obvious. Sweat soaks his skin. Vomit trails down his black T-shirt.

My lip curls in disgust, and I swallow rapidly to keep from gagging. A snarl of long, dark brown hair covers his face, but I'm guessing the dude is youngish. His body is big but lean, the skin on his arms firm. Which somehow makes him all the more depressing. Prime of his life, and he's fall-down drunk. Lovely.

I pick my way around him, muttering about drunk-driving assholes, and then march back with hose in hand, taking careful aim. Water shoots out at high speed, hitting its target with a satisfying hiss and splatter.

The bum jerks and rears up, sputtering and flailing around, searching for the source of his torment. I don't let up. I want that stench gone.

"Get off my lawn." Because he's filthy all over, I aim lower, drenching his pants and crotch.

"Mother fucker!" He has a deep voice, and it's raw. "Would you fucking stop?"

"Yeah...no. You smell like shit. And I sincerely hope you did not actually shit yourself, bud, because that is a seriously low point to come to."

I draw the jet of water up his lean body to his head. Long, dark hair whips in all directions as he sputters again.

And then he roars. The sound rings my ears, and really ought to put the fear of God in me. But he's too weak to stand. One muscled forearm swings up, though, slapping the wet hanks of hair back from his face.

I get a glimpse of dark eyes blazing with confused rage. Time to wrap this up. Letting go of the spray nozzle, I lower my weapon. "Like I said, get off my lawn."

His jaw ticks. "Are you fucking insane?"

"I'm not the one covered in vomit and laid out on a stranger's property."

My lawn bum glances around like he's just realized he's on the ground. He doesn't spare his clothes notice. Seeing as they're soaked to his skin, he's probably well aware of their state.

"Here's a tip," I say, tossing down my hose. "Don't be such a cliché."

This gives him visible pause, and he blinks up at me, water running in rivulets over his cheeks and into his thick beard.

"You don't know me enough to slap a label on me."

I snort. "Literally fall-down drunk, crashing your bike—which I somehow doubt you actually ride other than on weekends. Over-long hair, a face that hasn't seen the business end of a razor in weeks—again, probably because you want the world to believe you're a badass." I glance at his arms. Strong, ropy with muscles. "The only thing I don't see are tattoos, but maybe you've got 'Mom' plastered on your butt for color."

An indignant sound leaves him. Almost a laugh but too full of anger to fully get there. "Who *are* you?"

It's impressive, the layers of disdain he manages to get into that one question. Especially given the state I found him in. Humility certainly doesn't stick to this guy. Unlike his smell, unfortunately.

"The person whose land you fucked up. I'd slap you with a bill, but I don't want to come too close to the stench." Wiping my wet hands on my jeans, I give him one last glare. "Now go on and get before I call the police."

It's safe to say I'm worked up now. I march back up the long drive to my house instead of walking with quiet dignity as I'd planned. But it feels good; my pace is freeing. I've been so quiet these past few months. So contained.

So maybe I have something to thank Mr. Arrogant Drunk for.

However, my charity does not extend to him following me. Which he does. I see him rise in my peripheral vision. He wobbles, then steadies before peeling off his shirt and slapping it to the ground.

A strip show. Great.

I pick up my pace, cursing that my driveway is so long—at least two hundred feet from curb to doormat.

Another movement and he's flung a boot my way. I glance back, slightly alarmed. And there go his pants. Six-feet-something of sinewy, pissed off, naked male starts stalking up behind me. There are the tattoos I'd guessed at. Or rather, one massive one of swooping, intersecting lines that covers his upper left arm and torso.

I concentrate on that instead of the heavy length of his dick hanging between his legs, swaying like a pendulum with each step he takes toward me.

I glare over my shoulder. "You come any farther up my drive and I'll shoot you."

"You would have a shotgun, wouldn't you, Elly May," he snaps back. "Talk about a cliché. All you need is a pair of overalls and a piece of straw to chew on."

I can't help myself, I spin around. "Are you calling me a country bumpkin?"

He halts too. Hands low on his hips, utterly unashamed of his nakedness, my lawn bum stands there, glaring at me like he owns the world. "Are you saying you aren't, Huckleberry Pie?"

Heat swims over my skin. I stride right up to him—well, not too near; I'm still afraid of the stench. Up close, I can admit that he isn't bad looking. Past all the scruff, bloodshot onyx eyes, and pasty morning-after complexion, he has blunt but even features, and lashes long enough to make a girl envious. This just makes me angrier.

"Listen, buddy, stalking a woman while naked can be construed as an act of sexual intimidation."

He snorts. "That speaks volumes for your sex life, Elly May. But don't you worry. Even if I had the slightest interest in doing you, I have a nice case of whisky dick working, so nothing's getting up right now."

"Happens a lot, does it?" I wrinkle my nose, refusing to look down. "And you talk about *my* sexual deficiencies."

A glint comes into his eyes, and I could swear he wants to laugh. But he smirks instead, his lip curling in annoyance.

"Give me an hour and some coffee, and then we can talk about it all you want."

"Next thing you know, you'll be demanding breakfast too."

A cheeky smile lights him up. "Well, now that you mention it..."

"You know what pisses me off the most?" I snap.

His thick, dark brows scrunch up as if he's confused. "What?"

He actually says it like he hasn't heard me right, not as a response to my question. But I answer him anyway.

"You could have hurt someone else. You could have hurt me, or some poor soul along the way, with your drunk-ass driving." Grief sinks its fingers into my heart. "You could have destroyed lives, left people behind to pick up the pieces."

He blanches, those ridiculous lashes of his sweeping his cheeks as he blinks.

"You want to kill yourself?" I snap. "Do it some other way —"

My voice dies as a snarl leaves him, and he honest-to-God bares his teeth at me. He takes a hard step in my direction as though he might actually come at me, but he halts himself. "Don't you dare...You have no fucking clue what I've... " His face goes gray as he glares down from his great height.

We stare at each other while he kind of just sways there, all pasty and trembling, his anger so near the surface that his eyes shine with it.

It's that pain-filled rage that snares me, distracts me from the warning signs.

"You don't know..." He swallows convulsively.

Only then does it occur to me that I'm in trouble. I leap back, but it's too late. My lawn bum hunches over and hurls. All down my front.

Shock roots me to the spot for an agonizing moment. Then

the smell hits me anew. I force myself to look up, face my tormentor. A thousand curses race through my head but only one sentence gets past my clenched teeth.

"I hate you."

KILLIAN

USUALLY WHEN A WOMAN tells you she hates you with a cold, dead look in her eye, she makes an effort to avoid all further contact.

Not so with Elly May, she of the water hose from hell.

Okay, I did just yack all over her, so she might have reason to hate me. Very good reason.

I haven't apologized to anyone in years. A small voice in my head is telling me I should do it now. But the whisky still sloshing around in my head is drowning that voice out. Shit, everything is sloshing right now—the ground, my brain, my blood. My ears are ringing.

I'm going down. I know I am. Vague surprise registers as my tormentor steps forward, not away, and wraps her arms around me. Holding me up.

Good luck with that, honey.

I hear her curse, feel her knees buckle under my weight. We fall down together. I think I laugh. Not sure. It's all fading. Exactly what I want.

THE WORLD IS A BLUR. Water blasts my face. Again. Mother fuck, that's annoying.

Sputtering, I try to wipe my face, but my arms aren't working right. Everything is rubbery and heavy.

"Stop flailing, you complete pain in my ass," snarls a girl.

Elly May. I don't care if her voice sounds like vanilla cream over ice, she's the devil. A water devil. Maybe hell doesn't burn. Maybe it's perpetual drowning.

"You're not going to drown," she says, spraying me again.

I sputter, spit out a mouthful of water that tastes of vomit and whisky. I can't see a goddamn thing past the deluge. "What is with you and water?" I manage before another round hits me.

"It has this magical ability to wash away filth," she drawls as her hand rubs over my chest, not in a soothing way, but hard, as if she's trying to remove my skin. Soap bubbles. It smells like grapefruit and vanilla. Girl soap.

"Yes, soap. Water and soap cleans," she continues, as if I'm an infant. "I know. Crazy, right?"

Sarcasm. I'm an expert on it. When I'm not so drunk my eyes refuse to open, that is.

Hard hands move to along my scalp. Fingers snag in my hair.

"Jesus, when's the last time you brushed this mop?"

"Birth. Now lay off. Let me up."

"You have vomit in your hair. I'm getting it out."

I let her wash me, her voice drifting in and out as she bitches. She's never gentle. Doesn't matter. I can't handle gentle anyway.

I am dried off, tugged along. Everything still spins. Dip, sway, spin. No matter what I do to get away from it, I still hear the rhythm of life.

"I don't hear anything but you babbling," she says, her face a fuzzy halo above me.

Below me is soft. Cool sheets. Heavy blankets.

She rolls me on my side, shoves pillows behind my back. "You barf again, you're on your own, buddy."

Always am, honey.

KILLIAN
2

The pillow beneath my head is...fucking fantastic. I mean, it really is. Like a squishy cloud or something. Which is weird. Why am I getting a hard-on over a pillow?

This oddball thought wakes me up enough that I open my eyes. Sunlight burns, and I wince, squinting for a second. The room is white. Whitewashed wood-paneled walls, white sheets, white curtains drifting in a soft breeze coming through an open window.

I press my face against the cool pillow that feels like a cloud and take a breath. There's an axe of pain splitting my skull. My mouth is burnt toast.

On the bedside table sits a tall glass of some red drink. It's filled with fresh ice, the glass beaded with condensation as if someone just brought it in. Next to it are four clear, blue pills and a note:

For the criminally stupid.

Despite the fact that movement makes my stomach heave, I snort. Memories of my hostess's sharp tongue and rough hands rush in. I ignore them—because I really don't want to remember how drunk I was—and pick up the glass.

The drink smells vaguely like a Bloody Mary but also of something sharp and citrus. I don't want to taste it, but that axe is driving deeper, and I'm thirsty as fuck.

It goes down hard, me gagging along the way, the pills I take with it almost getting stuck in my throat. The concoction is fizzy, which is a surprise. I'm guessing it's Bloody Mary mixed with ginger soda and lemons—but hell, maybe there's arsenic in it too. By the time I finish, I kind of enjoy the taste and feel like I just might live.

I lie on the white cloud bed, smell the touch of sea brine in the air, and listen to the wind chimes. Until the banging of pots and the slam of a cabinet door snag my attention.

Elly May.

If her name really is Elly May, I'm going to laugh my ass off. But Elly May sounds more like a sexy, hay-riding chick. The kind that will milk you dry then offer up her pie. My Elly May is far from that.

Yesterday was fuzzy, but I remember her all right: Frowning face. Foul mouth.

I hear it again in the form of a muffled "fuck" and another slam of a door.

Grunting, I sit up, taking a few breaths as the room spins. I'm buck-ass naked and have to smile at that. Most interesting shower I've had in a while, and I didn't even get off.

It takes an eternity to stand and even longer to reach my clothes. I find them neatly folded on a chair and smelling of Tide. My grandma used Tide. I shove my clothes on and head for the door.

I've been sleeping in the back room of an old farmhouse, apparently. I don't remember what the outside even looks like, but inside is kind of spare country with plank floors and faded furniture.

There's a nice, well-used Martin acoustic leaning against an entire wall of bookcases filled with old LPs. She must have a couple thousand records. Outside of a few deejays I've met, I haven't seen anyone own actual vinyl records. They give the room a musty smell.

So, I'm dealing with a guitar-playing music lover. Please, God, don't let this chick be some sort of Annie Bates psycho. But then I remember the way she glared at me last night. I doubt she's my number-one fan.

I follow the noise and find her in a kitchen, a big square room with one of those classic farm tables that can seat twelve in the middle of it.

She ignores me as I sit at the table, my moves slow and pained. Fuck this shit. I'm not drinking that much again. Never. Again.

In the silence, I watch her stir something in a pot on the stove like she's trying to beat whatever it is into submission. She is definitely not a hot bumpkin. No Daisy Dukes on this chick. Her plump ass hides under ratty jeans with holes in the knees as she stomps around in heavy black boots better suited for my bike—the bike I'm pretty sure is wrapped around her fence. I don't remember crashing and haven't got a scratch on me. The will of the universe is a strange thing. Why it brought me to her of all people, I don't know.

My hostess moves to turn off the stove, and her profile comes into view. Long, straight hair the color of wet sand, gray eyes, and an oval face that should be all soft angles but somehow looks sharp and hard: Elly May is kind of plain. Until she opens her mouth.

Then it's one long stream of colorful bitch.

It's been years since I've had a female berate me for such an extended period of time. If the dousing of ice-cold water hadn't shocked me yesterday, that tongue lashing surely did the job.

Yeah, she has a mouth on her. Though she isn't using it now. I find that more unsettling.

"Hey." My voice sounds like cracked glass. "I, uh, thanks for…ah…" I swallow. "Well, thanks."

And people call me a poet.

She snorts as if she's thinking the same. I silently will her to fully turn and face me.

And she does, her expression pinched with disgust. "You drink what I left you?"

"Yes, ma'am." I salute, fight a grin.

She just looks at me, then grabs a bowl and fills it. Her boots thud as she stomps over and sets it before me. A blob of lumpy white stuff stares back at me.

"It's grits," she says before I can speak. "I don't want to hear any crap; just eat it."

"You always this sunny?" I ask, taking the spoon she's thrust in my face.

"With you? Yes." She gets her own bowl and sits far away from me.

"'And though she be but little, she is fierce.'" While Elly May might have a juicy ass, she can't be more than five foot three, and is small boned.

Her scowl takes on epic proportions. "Did you just quote Shakespeare?"

"Saw it on a tattoo," I lie, because it's fun to tease her. "There might have been something before that." I scratch my bearded chin. "Something like… 'Oh, when she is angry, she is keen and shrewd!'"

"Never saw that part on a tattoo," she mutters, giving me a dubious look before taking a bite of her grits.

I give her a bland, innocent look, and then we eat in silence. The grits are good, taste-wise. The consistency, however, isn't exactly helping my nausea.

"The drink was helpful," I say to fill the silence. I once thought I'd love silence. Turns out, I fucking hate it.

"My dad's old hangover cure."

A timer dings, and she gets up. I smell the biscuits then, and my mouth waters. Like a hungry dog, I track her movements as she pulls the tray from the oven and puts the golden mounds on a plate.

As soon as she sets the plate on the table, I'm on them, my fingertips burning, my tongue smarting. Don't care. They're too good. Heaven.

She watches me, her lips slanting as if she's stuck between a smile and a scowl. She's got nice lips, I'll give her that. Cupid lips, I think they're called. The kind that, while small, are shaped like a kiss.

"Want butter with that?" she asks.

"Is that a real question?" I manage between bites.

She gets up, grabs a jar that I find out is filled with honey butter—damn, that's good—and gets us each a cup of coffee, adding cream to both without asking if I like it that way. I usually take it black and sweet, but I'm not complaining for shit right now. Not when she might take away the biscuits if I do.

I swallow another bite of heaven. "What's your name?"

I can't keep calling this girl Elly May. Then again, I'm just passing through, so it's not like it really matters. But I want to know just the same. Grumpy or not, she's taken care of me when I'd have called the cops in her position.

She sets down her mug and looks me in the eye. "Liberty Bell."

I'd wonder if she's fucking with me, but the militant expression on her face says she is completely serious.

"That's…patriotic."

She snorts and sips her coffee. "It's ridiculous. But my parents loved it, and I loved my parents so…" She shrugs.

Loved. As in past tense.

"You alone then?" I wince as soon as the words come out, because she tenses, her soft gray eyes going hard again.

Liberty pushes back from the table. "I had your bike towed this morning. I'll take you to town so you can sort it out with the mechanic."

I stand too, fast enough to make the floor tilt. "Hey, wait." When she pauses to look at me, I've got nothing. A first. I run my hand over my tangled hair and remember her washing it. "Don't you want to know my name?"

Hell, it's the last thing I want to give. But it irks that she's already rushing me out the door. And damn if I know why that bothers me.

She looks me over, a slow inspection that makes my skin itch and swell. It isn't a hot look. It's judgment. And I'm clearly found lacking. Another first.

Her hair sways, catching the sunlight as she shakes her head. "No. No, I don't."

And then she leaves me with a cup of cooling coffee and a plate of biscuits.

LIBERTY

I'VE BEEN ALONE TOO LONG. I don't know how to act around people anymore. Especially not this guy. Yesterday he was disgusting. Drunk and too far gone to function. I should have left him on my porch, called the police, and cleaned myself up while they hauled his ass away.

But I couldn't. Not all drunks are bad. Some are just lost. I have no idea what this guy's issue is. I only know that, when faced with the decision, I hadn't the heart to leave him.

So I dragged him to my bathroom and washed him clean. There was nothing sexual about the act. He stank something awful and was so butt-drunk, it was all I could do not to wring his thick neck for being so reckless.

Not to mention I was pissed to have to give my bed up to the idiot. No way was I going to be able to haul him upstairs to the guest rooms.

But now, in the light of day, I am at sea when it comes to my drunken bum. His presence in my house is immense. As if a mere room could never contain him.

Presence. My mom used to say there were those who just *had* it. I never understood what she meant until today. Because even though he's fumbling his words and clearly hung-over, this guy vibrates with vitality. It permeates the air like a perfume, soaking into my skin and making me want to rub myself all over him just to get a little bit more of that feeling— as if by being near him, I, too, might be something special.

It makes no sense. But then life rarely makes sense to me.

And now that he isn't piss-ass drunk and filthy, I can see the beauty of him. His body is long and tight with a sort of rawboned strength of sinewy muscles and sharp movements. His hair is still a tangled mess, falling down to his shoulders and the color of rich, dark coffee. A thick, unkempt beard covers most of his face, which is…annoying. Because it hides too much.

But what I can see points to an attractive man. His nose is bold, a bump along the high bridge as if he once busted it, but the shape fits his face. Prominent cheekbones and what looks to be a stubborn chin under all that fuzz give him an air of pure masculinity.

His eyes, however, are downright pretty. Framed under the dark slashes of his brows, they shine like obsidian.

How could a person not be swayed? Those eyes tracked my every move around the kitchen earlier. Unnerving me.

I shoved food at him just to make him look away. He hadn't, though. Even as he inhaled my biscuits like a man starved, he watched me. Not in a sexual way, though, more like I was a mess he'd inadvertently walked into. The irony made me want to laugh.

Now, I just want to get away from him. Talking about my parents reminds me why I should hate this guy—this drunk-driving stranger who took not only his life but the lives of everyone he shared the road with into his unsteady hands. My life will never be the same because of a drunk driver, and I have little respect for those who do it. Even if they quote Shakespeare and have cheeky, somewhat cute smiles.

Not looking back, I get my keys. He's not far behind though, his boots clomping just as loudly as mine, echoing in the front hall. He's got a fresh biscuit in hand and is chewing on the remnants of another. I refuse to find that endearing.

"You really don't want to know my name?" he calls.

I grab my sunglasses. "Why is this bothering you? It isn't as though we'll ever see each other again."

His frown grows. "Seems like common courtesy."

"After that shower, I think we're past basic etiquette."

Oddly, this makes him smile, and when he does? Oh boy. It's like the sun breaking through storm clouds, all brightness and open joy. I'm fairly blinded by it and have to blink and look away.

"See, that's my point." He gestures toward me with his biscuit before taking a huge, grunting bite. "You've seen me naked—"

"Don't talk with your mouth full. It's disgusting."

He keeps chewing. "You've washed my cock—"

"Hey, I didn't get anywhere near your dangly bits, buddy."

That grin of his wraps around his food. "In my mind you did. And you washed my hair. You can't wash a man's hair and not know his name. That's just bad juju."

"Juju?" I try not to laugh as I head for the door. "You're still drunk."

"Clear as a crystal, Libby." He's right behind me, dogging my steps. "Now ask my name."

I stop short and turn, and my nose meets the center of his chest. The contact ripples through me like a vibrating wave. I step back and tilt my head.

He gives me a slightly smug, completely antagonistic look. But his voice drops, sweet and cajoling. "Come on, ask."

God, that voice. I've been trying to ignore it because it's the kind of voice that can pull you under, make you lose your train of thought. Low and deep and powerful. He talks, and it's a melody.

He's staring at me now, waiting, his dark gaze expectant. It sets off a slow *thud, thud, thud* in my chest. I haven't stood this close to anyone in a good, long while.

Swallowing, I find my voice. "All right then, tell me."

But he doesn't speak. He freezes as if he's caught and is suddenly wary.

"You're kidding me, right?" I laugh, not really amused at all. "You bug the hell out of me to ask, and now you pull a Rumpelstiltskin?"

He blinks as if shaking himself out of a trance and then glares. "Don't worry, your firstborn is safe from me." He sucks in a breath and thrusts out his hand. "Killian."

I eye that hand of his. Big, broad, the fingertips and top edge of his palm are calloused. A musician of some sort. Probably a guitarist. I run a thumb over my own rough fingertips. He's waiting again, his brows knitting as if I've insulted him by not taking his hand.

So I do. It's warm and firm. He gives me a squeeze strong enough to bend my bones, though I don't think he knows how hard his grip really is. Definitely a musician.

"Pleased to meet you, Liberty Bell." His smile is nice, boyish almost, beneath his thick beard. Earlier, I thought he was in his thirties. But now I'm guessing he's more my age, mid-to-late twenties.

I let his hand go. "I wouldn't call our meeting a pleasure, exactly."

"Oh, now, you have to admit I have great aim." He gives

me a nudge as I roll my eyes.

"Let's never speak of that again."

"Speak of what?" His tone is light as he follows me outside.

I head toward my truck, but he stops me with a touch to my elbow. He's focused on Mrs. Cromley's house across the way. Mrs. Cromley died six months ago, and her nephew, George, took over the place. Haven't seen him yet, but I know he's a forty-something with a wife and kids. I doubt he'll move in; the house sits at the edge of nowhere, and our little island of the tip of the Outer Banks doesn't even have a school.

Then again, Al's Grocery van is idling out front, and two big boxes are on the porch. Killian looks around, taking in the rolling grass turning toasted brown as fall sets in, the crest of the hill, and the small sliver of blue where the Atlantic Ocean crashes to the shore.

Killian scratches his jaw as if his beard itches. "That house over there. That George Cromley's place, do you know?"

A sinking sensation pulls at my gut. "Yeah," I say slowly.

Killian nods and catches my gaze. His smile is just as slow and smug as usual. "Then I guess I won't need a ride into town after all, neighbor."

KILLIAN
3

I told her my name, and she didn't recognize me. It's been so long since someone my age looked at me as if I were a total stranger, it's oddly unsettling now. And ain't that fucked up? I've roamed far and wide to get away from fans, from people kissing my ass and wanting something from me. And now that I've crossed paths with a girl who clearly would just like me to go away? I'm irritated.

Snorting, I take a sip of scalding hot coffee and lean back in my old-fashioned rocking chair. From my seat on the porch, I have a good view of Liberty's house. It's a two-story, white clapboard. The type you'd see in an Edward Hopper painting. Driving past, you'd suspect a little old lady was inside rolling out pie dough. I bet Liberty makes awesome pie, but she'd probably brain me with the roller for pissing her off before I even got a taste.

The scar my bike slashed along the grass is an ugly reminder of what I did the other night. Driving drunk. That isn't me. I'd been the one to keep the guys in check. Keep them away from falling victim to the hard stuff—from becoming clichés, as Liberty put it.

Something strong and ugly rolls in my chest. All my efforts hadn't helped Jax. Images of his limp body flash before my eyes in vivid color: graying skin against white tiles, yellow vomit, green eyes staring at nothing.

My teeth clench, my fingers aching from the force of my grip on the mug.

Fucking Jax. Idiot.

Hurt makes it hard to breathe. My body twitches with the need for motion. Go somewhere else. Keep moving until my mind is blank.

A slam of a screen door has me flinching, and hot coffee spills over the rim of my mug.

"Shit." I set it on the floor and suck on my burnt finger.

Across the way, Liberty stomps down her porch steps, heading toward a high-fenced-off vegetable garden. A smile pulls at my lips. The girl never just walks. Wherever she goes, it's like she's embarking on a mission of doom.

She moves through a patch of sunlight, and her hair turns the color of brown butter. I have the urge to capture the moment, write down a lyric. Panic at the thought has me rising and pacing.

I should go into the house. And then what? Lie on the ancient couch covered in ugly blue roses? Drink the day away?

Crates of my stuff have arrived. Including three of my favorite guitars. Scottie, the rat bastard, sent those along even though I never asked for them. Does he think I'm going to compose? Write a song? No fucking way. Shit. I have no idea what I'm doing here. Scottie's grand idea of me hiding out on an island almost nobody has heard of is stupid. That's what I get for listening to him while I was drunk.

Maybe Scottie has psychic abilities, because my cell starts ringing. And only a handful of people have this number. My eyes are on Libby kneeling between rows of green things when I answer the phone. Only it isn't Scottie.

"Hey, man," Whip says.

I haven't heard his voice for nearly a year. The familiar sound is a kick in the head. I sag back into my chair. "Hey." I clear my throat. "What's up?"

Jesus, don't be about Jax. My fingers go cold, blood rushing to my temples. I take a deep breath.

"Is it true you're slumming it somewhere in the wilds of North Carolina?"

I let out a snarl. "Is he okay?"

There's a pause and then Whip curses. "Shit, man, I wasn't thinking. Yeah, he's fine." Whip makes an audible sigh. "He's a lot better. Seeing a counselor."

Good. Great. Nice that Jax has called to tell me as much. I rub my hand over my face, closing my eyes. "So what's going on, then?"

"Just been thinking." Whip's voice goes distant. "We've all been scattered to the four winds. And...hell, just wanted to talk. See where you were at."

Jax is the one who scattered us. He broke us that day, as effectively as if he'd thrown a boulder into a window. And while Jax and I usually played the roles of mom and dad in the group, Whip has always been the anchor, our glue. He'd throat-punch me if I said it to his face, but Whip is also the most sensitive. I know he's hurting.

I glance over at Libby again. Her plump ass sways as she pulls on weeds. The sight almost makes me smile; she'd hate knowing I'm watching her. I find my voice then. "Have you talked to the others?" I ask Whip.

"Been hanging out with Rye. We've come up with some material."

This is new. It's usually Jax and I who write. I sit up a little straighter, trying to focus. I need to be supportive. I know this. But it's hard to muster any enthusiasm. Even so, I say what needs to be said. "You record anything I can hear?"

"Yeah, sure. I'll send it to you." Whip pauses, then causally adds, "Maybe you can fine-tune it. Give us some notes."

I don't know how I feel about this. I'm not pissed. I like

that they're composing. But something rolls inside of me: avoidance, the desire to get away, and with it, the need to end the call.

But Whip isn't finished. "Or maybe come back and work with us."

I'm on my feet again, walking to the porch screen. I rest my forehead against its fragile wall. "Not yet. But soon, man."

"Yeah. Sure." Whip sounds about as sincere as I do.

"I'll be in touch," I say. It may or may not be a lie. I haven't picked up my guitar in nearly a year, and have no desire to try now.

"Right."

The silence, when he hangs up, rings in my ears. I don't know how to be myself anymore, don't know how to be part of Kill John. How do we go on? Do we do it without Jax? With him? And all the time looking over our shoulders for fear he'll try it again?

Part of it isn't even about Jax. I'm tired. Uninspired. It makes me feel guilty as hell.

Though I'm on a porch, the walls press in on me, taking my air. I should go inside, do...something. My feet take me the opposite direction, off my porch and straight to Liberty.

She's hunched over a row of herbs and doesn't look up when I lean my wrists against the top of the fence, which is at chin level. I watch her work, not minding the silence. It's amusing the way she ignores me, because she doesn't do a good job of it. Her whole placid, I-don't-give-a-fuck-that-you're-here expression just tells me she very much gives a fuck. Only she doesn't want to.

I grin at the thought. There's something so *normal* about it all. "You know, I've had girls on their knees before me plenty of times. But they usually do it with a smile."

She snorts. "I'd be more impressed if you were the one used to being on your knees. I like givers, not takers."

Jesus. I can just imagine her, plush thighs spread wide, using that bossy tone to tell me what she likes best as I eat her out. I shift my hips, drawing them away from the fence. No need for her to see the growing bulge in my pants; I'm not entirely sure if I'm attracted to her or have suddenly become a masochist. "What about give *and* take? You down with that?"

Even as I joke, a twinge of guilt hits me. When was the last time I gave, anyway? Because she's right; I got lazy, sat around like a king having girls suck me off while I thought up song lyrics or planned the next album. Reached a point where I did not give a ripe grape what those girls did or where they went once I got off.

Liberty glares up at me now. "What exactly are you doing here anyway? Don't you work?"

God, I want to laugh at that. I bite my bottom lip. "Don't you? Isn't it, like, a Tuesday?"

"It's Wednesday, and I work from home, thank you."

"Doing what?"

"If I wanted you to know, I would have said."

"Are you a deejay?"

"A deejay?" She gapes up at me. "Are you serious? Where would I even play? At the church?"

I actually flush. I don't think I've flushed with embarrassment in my entire life. Glancing up at the sky to see if any pigs are flying around, I mutter, "You have all those records."

"Ah." She gives me a tight nod. "Those were my dad's. He was a deejay in college."

"It's an impressive collection."

"It is."

"And the guitar?"

Her shoulders hunch. "Also my dad's."

Now I know how reporters feel when they interview me. I empathize. This girl has me beat on evasive maneuvers.

"You're really not gonna tell me?" I don't know why I'm pushing this. But her determination to shut me down amuses me.

"Guess not." She pulls out a pair of scissors and snips off bunches of sage, thyme, and rosemary. My grandma used to have an herb garden. A small box set up in her kitchen window back in the Bronx. When I was a little kid, I'd beg her to let me cut what she needed, and she'd remind me not to bruise the leaves.

I shake off old memories before they choke me. "Fine. I'll just leave it to my imagination." I scratch my chin, now beard-free and smooth—damn thing itched too much to keep in this heat. "I'm gonna go with phone-sex worker."

Libby tucks her herbs in her basket and leans back on her heels. "That's just ridiculous. Do I sound like a phone-sex worker?"

"Actually? Yeah." I clear my throat because I can practically hear her cream-and-ice voice doling out demands. "Yeah, you do."

She scowls at that, her eyes finally meeting mine again. Whatever she sees in my expression has her frown deepening and her color rising. She quickly turns back to her gardening. "I've got work to do. You gonna stand there watching all day? Or maybe there's a bottle you'll be wanting to find your way to the bottom of."

"Cute. And no. No more binge drinking for me."

She makes a dubious sound.

I should go. I glance back at my house. It sits like a lump against the land, all forlorn and silent. That ugly itch feeling rises within my chest again. I have to fight not to scratch at it. Libby isn't looking, though; she's yanking weeds. Sighing, I clear my throat. "Can I help?"

LIBBY

HE'S NOT LEAVING. I'm not sure what to do with that. It kills me to be inhospitable to him. With every short word I throw him, I can feel my grandma rolling in her grave. I was raised to be polite above all things. But Killian sets my teeth on edge for a whole host of reasons.

I'd expected to see him again, sure. We're neighbors after all. But I didn't expect him to immediately seek me out and want to remain in my company. And though I haven't been welcoming, that doesn't seem to bother him. He kind of reminds me of those boys in grade school who get a kick out of tugging girls' pigtails.

And the bald truth is guys who look like Killian simply don't bother with me. They never have. So why now? Is he bored? Slumming?

Whatever the case, I'm both unsettled by his presence and annoyingly curious about the guy.

Killian, on his hands and knees, weeding, should be diminished in size. If anything, he seems larger now, his shoulders broader as they move beneath a faded Captain Crunch T-shirt. His coffee-dark hair falls in tangles around those shoulders, and I have the urge to offer him a haircut. I don't mind longer hair, but Killian's is just a hot mess. I swear the man doesn't own a brush.

But he has shaved. The sight initially threw me because I'd been expecting that backwoods beard when I heard his voice earlier. But instead of a fuzzy face, I was greeted by the smooth, clean sweep of his jaw, a stubborn chin, and a big, dimpled smile. How is anyone supposed to resist that?

"How did you learn the difference between weeds and plants?" His black velvet voice envelops me, but he doesn't look up from his task. The little furrow of concentration between his brows is kind of endearing. "Because it all looks the same to me."

"My grandma taught me." I clear my throat and rip at a particularly tenacious weed.

"Grandmas are good like that."

I can't imagine him hanging around a grandmother. Or maybe I can. She'd probably serve him milk and cookies and chastise him about taking better care of himself. I point out another weed. "Eventually it gets easier to spot them."

"If you say so." He doesn't sound too happy but keeps working.

We're silent again, going about our business.

"Top-secret spy?"

I jerk my head up at Killian's question. "What?"

He waggles his dark brows. "Your job. Still trying to figure it out. You a spy?"

"You found me out. Now come with me." I incline my head toward the house. "I have something to show you inside."

White teeth sink into his plump lower lip. "Unless it involves spanking, I'm not going."

I snort, despite myself.

"Sex-toy tester?"

"Ah. No."

"Erotica writer?"

"Why are all the options suddenly sex-related?"

"Because hope springs eternal."

"Better hope I don't accidentally, on purpose, nut you."

"All right, all right. Home shopper?"

"I hate shopping."

"Yeah, I can see that about you."

My head jerks up. "What's that supposed to mean?"

He shrugs, completely unrepentant. "A girl who stomps around in worn out Doc Martens isn't usually the type to squeal over a new sale."

I sit back on the heels of said Docs. "Okay, I'm not big on fashion. But that doesn't have to mean I'm not a shopper."

"You just said you hate shopping. Like, *just* said it."

"Yeah, but you shouldn't be able to tell simply by looking at me."

His nose wrinkles as he scratches the back of his neck. "I'm confused."

"Maybe I'm addicted to buying dolls. Maybe I have a whole room of them at the back of the house."

Killian gives a full-body shudder. "Don't even joke about that. I'll have Chucky nightmares for months."

I think about a room of dolls staring at me and shudder too. "You're right. No dolls. Ever."

He winks at me. I have no idea how he manages to do it without looking like a smarmy ass, but it's cute instead. "See?" he says. "Not a shopper."

"And you are, what? A detective?"

He sits back on his heels too. "If I was, I'd be a pretty shitty one since I can't figure out what you do."

We stare at each other, his dark gaze drilling into me, waiting. It's surprisingly effective, because I swear, I'm starting to sweat.

"Fine," I blurt out. "I'm a book cover designer."

He blinks as if surprised. "Really? That's...well, the last thing I'd have guessed, but totally cool. Can I see your work?"

"Maybe later." I go back to weeding, though really, I'm hacking the same spot over and over. There isn't anything left but a dark scar of soil. Smoothing a hand over the cool earth, I eye him. "And what do you do?"

He's good; he barely flinches before covering it with a wide and easy smile. "I am currently without employment."

I'm about to ask what he did before, but something brittle and pained lingers in those coffee-colored eyes of his, and I don't have the heart. Yesterday he was drunk on my lawn. I don't think life is going his way at the moment, and I have no desire to pick at that wound.

He covers the silence by pointing at a green vine. "Pull this?"

"No. That's a tomato vine."

It becomes apparent that Killian isn't comfortable with long silences. "So was this place ever a working farm?"

I'd think he talks to hear himself, but he looks at me with genuine interest every time he asks a question. I take a moment to look at the land around me. Collar Island is part of the chain known as the Outer Banks. While the northern end has a town and multiple grand vacation homes, the southern tip—where my grandma's house is located—is fairly isolated. Nothing but a few scattered houses and waving green and tawny grass, surrounded by sandy beach and vivid blue ocean.

"Back when my grandparents were young," I say. "They farmed rotating vegetable crops. Same with the owners of the house you're staying in. Now I just attend to the land nearest the house and let the rest grow free."

"Beautiful place," Killian admits. "Kind of lonely, though."

Can't say much to that. So I merely nod.

We go back to work. Which is good, fine. Until Killian reaches behind his head and pulls off his shirt to tuck it in his back pocket.

I've already seen the man naked. But that was different. I was too pissed and too busy trying to get him clean to fully notice the particulars. Now he's in the full sun, his tan skin already glistening with a fine sheen of sweat. He's lean and strong, his muscles a work of art. The massive tattoo that covers his left shoulder and torso is actually a vintage map of the world, like a spread-out globe.

"You looking at my art, Libs?" He sounds amused.

I meet his eyes and find them glinting, those ridiculously long lashes practically touching his cheeks. No fair that a dude has such pretty eyes.

"I am. I figure you put pictures on your body, it's fair game for anyone to study them."

His grin is quick, devilish, the little dimples on the sides of his mouth going deep then fading with his smile. "Didn't say I minded." He sits back on his heels so I can see it all.

Unfortunately, I find myself wanting to study his lower abdomen, where the muscles are like stepping stones leading the way down to Mr. Happy.

Damn it. I am not attracted to this guy. Nope. I'm just undersexed and need to get me some. Soon. But *not* with Killian. I cannot forget how I met him. Alcohol addiction is my hard line in the sand; it destroyed everything I loved.

Ignoring my inner argument, I take in his tattoo. It's done in clean, sure lines, more of an impression of the globe instead of being heavy with detail. And it is beautiful.

"Does it have any meaning?" I ask. "Or was it for fun?"

Killian tosses a dark lock of hair back from his face. "Started off as a way to cover up a mistake."

He leans in, bringing the scent of clean sweat and heady male pheromones with him. Hell. There really isn't any good way to describe that fragrance other than delicious and addictive. I brace myself as he points to a spot above his nipple where there's a compass rose. "I wanted to cover a name. Darla."

"Love gone bad?"

He gives me a wry grin. "That would at least be romantic. But no. It was high school graduation. Me and..." His face goes blank for a second, a haunted look flashing in his eyes. But he blinks, and it's gone. "My friends and I got wasted and hunted down one of our other friends who was practicing to become a tattoo artist. I was the guinea pig."

"And he put 'Darla' on you?"

"Yep." Killian sits back and starts to weed again. But he's still grinning.

"Who was Darla?"

He laughs. "That's the thing; she was just a name he thought would sound funny. I might have kept it. But, shit, it was ugly—all lopsided and fucking loopy." Killian shakes his head. "Looked like some third grader did it."

I can't help but laugh too. "Nice."

Killian's expression goes soft, his gaze running over my face. His smile grows.

"What?" I ask, thrown by the gleam in his eyes. It makes my breath catch.

"You're pretty."

He says it so matter of fact, I snort. "You sound surprised."

Killian leans in just a little. "Truth? I am. You've been scowling at me so much... Ah, there it is again. Glaring hate-fire at me." The calloused tip of his finger traces the top of my cheek, and my lower belly clenches in shock. His voice grows thoughtful. "But when you smile? You kind of glow."

"Like a light bulb?" I retort, trying not to duck my head.

His brow quirks, his eyes glinting with suppressed humor. "Fine. You're radiant. That clear enough?"

Words stick in my throat. It hits me that a man has never called me pretty before. Not once. How could that be? I'm not ugly. Objectively speaking, I know I'm pretty, or can be. I've had multiple dates, a boyfriend briefly in college. I've been hit on before, sure. But I've never been complimented in such a simple, honest way. The knowledge sinks into my skin like an itch, and suddenly I don't want Killian to look at me.

My spade plunges into the earth with enough violence to send soil flying. "So how did this Darla tat go away?"

Killian frowns down at my spade for a second before he eases back to his usual cheekiness. "My mom was so disgusted with it, she gave me the money to get a new one to cover it."

"I'd have thought she'd want you to get it removed."

"Naw." He tugs out a weed. "She didn't object to a tattoo, just that it was poorly done. And there'd still be a scar. Mom isn't big on scars. Anyway, I got the compass rose. The map came later." He glances down at himself. "Kind of like, 'Hey, Kills, here's the world. It's all yours if you don't fuck it up.'"

The regret in his voice, though he's clearly trying to hide it, hits something in me. I take a breath, my gaze wandering to the clear blue sky overhead. The world. I've seen so little of it. Just this small blue corner of North Carolina and the slightly bigger swath of land when I went down to Savannah for college. Twenty-five years old, and I'm a hermit of my own making.

My chest closes up, and I have to fight to breathe. I have an overwhelming urge to run into the house and curl up in my nice, cool bed where it's dim and silent.

"This is surprisingly relaxing," he says.

Killian's comment catches my attention.

"What? Weeding?"

He glances at me from under the fans of his lashes. "Yep. I like doing something constructive." Killian stops and rubs the back of his neck. "You got any fences to mend or wood to chop? Something like that?"

"You need hard labor to forge you into a better person?"

"Yeah." He smiles. "Yeah, I think I do."

"And you want me to...what? Mr. Miyagi you?"

His laugh is a rolling wave, deep and warm. "Fuck yeah. Paint the fence. Sand the floor."

"And when you're done, we can go down to the sea, and you'll balance on one leg."

"Shit, that would be epic." Killian spreads his arms wide, doing a half-assed crane move. It does nice things to his torso, which I promptly ignore.

I stand instead, dusting the loose soil off my knees. I grab my basket of veggies. "Come on, then. You can mow the law if you're really serious. That's about as Mr. Miyagi as I can get right now."

Killian hops up with ease. "Killian-san ready for duty."

I roll my eyes, pretending that I find him annoying. But I don't. And that scares me.

KILLIAN
4

I'm mowing Libby's lawn. Sadly, that isn't a euphemism for something more pleasurable than pushing an old mower back and forth over her vast and rolling yard. Out here in the hot sun, my muscles moving and sweat trickling down my spine, I realize I haven't had sex in months. Six to be exact. I haven't gone that long without sex since I started having sex. What really freaks me out is that I haven't missed it much.

During my travels, I met plenty of hot women ready and willing to rock my world. *Willing* isn't even the right word. They were desperate to fuck me. It isn't arrogance that makes me say that. It's the truth. They knew who I was and did their best to be the girl who would blow me so away I would take them with me. Same old story for the past eight years. Fame equals dick chasers.

Pushing the mower, I think back on all those women. God, some of them really did rock my world. The things they let me do, that they did to me, were unreal—as close to a high as I could get when not on stage. But it always ended as soon as my dick went limp. Eventually, sex with groupies became almost another form of masturbation. The excitement had long since faded. No matter how good a chick's technique, she never saw me as anything other than a means to an end. And those girls never expressed an opinion that contradicted my needs. I could send in a roadie, tell the groupies he was part of the band, and they'd fuck him raw too.

I used those women just like they used me. Pump, dump, and go. Soulless encounters.

Is that what Jax felt? Soulless? Off kilter?

For the first time in years, I feel like I'm walking on solid ground. And I'm doing nothing more than yardwork. Libby gave me the side-eye when I asked to do more, and I made a joke out of it. But I was completely serious. I feel good. I want more of that— more of knowing I'm as normal and human as the rest of the world.

Pulling my shirt from where it's tucked in my back pocket, I wipe the sweat from my brow and head for the big barn-like garage at the back of the property. The lawn is done. It's not perfect—my lines are slightly askew.

I'm stretching out my shoulders when Libby appears on the back stoop. She's holding two tall, icy glasses of lemonade. She meets me halfway, and I barely get out a heartfelt "thanks" before I'm gulping my drink down. Cold. Fresh. Perfect.

I'm beginning to think this girl will never give me anything that isn't fucking sublime. Then I catch a glimpse inside the shed and nearly choke on my last mouthful of lemonade.

"You have a ride-on mower," I get out while sputtering on my drink and glaring at the John Deere that would have cut my work time to less than an hour.

Liberty, the little she-devil, just shrugs, taking a dainty sip of her lemonade. "Would Mr. Miyagi have let Daniel-san use a power sander? I think not."

She lets out a surprisingly girlish squeal when I launch myself at her, catching her around the middle, and haul her onto my shoulder.

"You spilled my drink, fuck face," she shouts, but she's laughing.

Thank God. Because I really didn't think about the consequences when I acted. I rarely do. But I don't want to piss her off or freak her out. Grinning wildly, I spin her in a circle and give her juicy ass a slap.

She really squeals then, her feet kicking at my thighs, her hands beating my butt. "You will die for that, mister."

"Might as well enjoy myself then," I shout over her protests and slap her ass again. Jesus. I need to stop because now I want to grab her round, firm butt and give it a squeeze. Maybe slip my fingers in between the crack and... *Down, boy.*

I'd blame the heat and my lack of sex life, but I'm not sure. There's something oddly appealing about prickly but oh-so-plush Libby.

Reluctantly, I set her down and brace myself to be nutted. She swats my arm instead, her face red as one of her tomatoes.

"Jerk," she says without heat. "I have a total head rush now."

"Ah, those are the best." Before she can totter, I touch her elbow just enough to steady her. Now that she's not in my arms, I'm oddly hesitant to make contact again. Only yesterday we were at each other's throats. And now I want to touch her as many times as she'll let me.

"You're crazy pants, you know that?" Her scowl is kind of cute.

"I've been told as much on occasion."

"Not surprising." Libby rakes her fingers through her hair, and the sun glints off the strands. "I was going to offer to take you to the beach—"

"We're going." I try to grab her hand but she evades me this time.

"I don't know..."

"Liberty," I warn. "Don't make me toss you over my shoulder and haul your little ass there."

"Yeah, right. I bet you're all bark too, buddy."

I step close, so quick that I neatly pin her to the side of the shed. We're not actually touching but she goes still anyway. I take advantage and lean in until our noses nearly bump. "Oh, I bite, babe. But you'll like it."

It then occurs to me what I'm doing. And that she smells like sunshine and lemons and brown sugar. Alarms start going off in my head, shouting *danger* and *step the fuck back*. But I can't stop myself from looking at her lips. Mistake. Big fucking mistake.

They're pink and soft and parted, as if waiting to be taken. Heat surges to my cock, and I have to physically brace against the urge to thrust my hips forward. What the fuck? I'm losing it.

Proof that this is a bad idea comes by way of Libby pressing those pretty lips together. "I bite back, Kill, and you won't like it."

I give her a big, fake-ass smile. "So you say. Now get your suit on or I'll bug the shit out of you all day."

She rolls her eyes but thankfully turns toward the house. "I'll pack a lunch."

God, she's gonna feed me. I'd like this girl just for that. But I've got to hold myself together. Because she's not the type to fool around with. Any guy with half a brain can see that. She might be hard on the outside, but it feels more like a brittle shell. Christ, she reminds me of Jax in that way. The thought cools me. Maybe I should tell her to forget the whole thing and just go by myself.

But then she pops her head back out the door. "Get in here. I got stuff for you to haul."

Like that, I'm hooked again. There's just something about her I can't ignore. I push off the side of the shed and bound to the stairs. "As long as you don't forget lunch, I'm all yours, Miss Bell."

LIBBY

THE SWATH of beach near the house is narrow, butting up against wild dunes. I set up my blanket, umbrella, and chair while Killian looks on, as if perplexed.

"It's like you're getting ready to camp," he tells me when I take the cooler from his hand and plunk it in the shade behind my beach chair. "You gonna pull out an air mattress next? The kitchen sink?"

"I like my comforts. And I'd rather not crisp in the sun like a tater tot."

Killian snickers. "I'll be the tater."

I pull off my tee and ease out of my jean shorts. "You do that. But don't come crying to me if you burn. I'm not rubbing aloe on your back." *Lie.* I'd be far too happy to rub him.

"You will, Libs." His voice is oddly faint, distracted. "You're all bark, babe."

"Babe? That's no way to get me to…" I glance up to find him watching me. Not leering, but definitely looking.

And I have the urge to pull my top back on. My black bikini is made for comfort rather than sexiness, and it covers as much as my bra and panties would. But I'm not used to a man seeing so much of me. I'm not ashamed of my body—though I wouldn't cry if I suddenly had a smaller butt and bigger boobs. I'm a B-cup, so I don't have to wear a bra every day, and I'm not exactly filling it out when I do. Something tells me Killian has seen his fair share of spectacular boobs. It annoys me that I fear I'll be found lacking.

I catch his gaze, and the air around us seems to take a pause. Killian's dark eyes narrow, his expression hooded. I wonder what the hell he's thinking, and my heart starts to pound, little zings of heat going haywire low in my belly.

I don't know how long we stand there, looking at each

other as if we're strangers who happened upon each other on this beach. It's probably only a few seconds, but it feels like an eternity. Then he blinks, cutting that cord, and makes a pretense of looking all around the beach. We're alone here. Though, far in the distance, a few people are walking along the shore.

"I'm going for a swim," he says. "Want to come?"

"You don't want your sandwich?" Something in my chest squeezes tight because he's kind of twitchy now, as though he wants to take off.

Killian eyes the cooler and lets out a breath. "Right. Forgot about that."

He plops down next to me on the beach blanket, close enough that his thigh nearly brushes mine, and I can feel the heat of his body. He's got nice legs, muscular and dusted with dark hairs, his skin already deeply tanned.

I shouldn't be noticing his damn legs. I shouldn't be fidgeting with plates.

"You come here a lot?" he asks.

"I visit the beach almost daily."

"With your friends?"

I wipe my hands down my thighs. "No. By myself."

He takes a bite of his sandwich, his gaze on the sea. "No friends?"

God, the man is like a bloodhound. Or an annoying rat, chewing away at all my weaknesses. With that lovely image floating before my eyes, I set my sandwich down. "Not much of a social life here. Most of my friends are online." And when was the last time I talked to any of them? It's a slap to the system to realize I haven't emailed anyone in months. And no one has emailed me either.

I'm not shy. But I am an introvert. Going out has never been my thing. But when did I grow so isolated? Why hadn't I noticed? Or cared?

"Anyway, I like my privacy, doing my own thing…" My neck tightens, and I take long gulps of my lemonade.

I have no idea what Killian is thinking. He just nods and eats his BLT in neat but big bites. A sigh of contentment leaves him before he peers down at the cooler, a little frown between his eyes.

"Here." I pass him another sandwich. "I packed you three."

His grin is quick and wide. "I knew it. All bark."

I won't smile. I won't. "Eat your sandwiches."

"I see that smile, Libs."

"I can take back the food."

He grabs the third sandwich and sets it on his lap, hunching protectively over it as he wolfs down the second one. "You grow up here?" he asks me after swallowing a huge chunk.

"No. I grew up in Wilmington. The house was my grandmama's place. She left it to my parents when she died, and they left it to me." There. I said it. And it only hurts a little. A dull pain, like a boulder crushing down on my ribs. "I was living in Savannah, but after… Well, I just wanted to go home. This was the closest place to it for me."

Killian frowns, but his voice is gentle. "When did they die, Libby?"

I don't want to answer. But silence is worse. "A little over a year ago." I take a breath. "My mom and dad went out to dinner. Dad got drunk but drove anyway."

I can't tell him that my dad was always drunk in those final days, missing a lifestyle he'd vowed to give up when my parents had me. Was I the cause of my father's bad choices? No. But some days, it sure felt like it. I swallow hard. "He crashed into a family van. Killed the mother in that van, himself, and my mom too."

"Fucking hell."

I try to shrug and fail. "It is what it is."

"It's fucked up, honey."

Nodding, I search through the cooler for another lemonade.

"Liberty?" His voice is so soft and tentative that I immediately still and lift my head.

Killian squeezes the back of his neck, his jaw bunched. But he doesn't look away, even though it's clear he wants to. "I... Fuck..." He takes another breath. "I'm sorry. For the way we met. For tearing up your lawn and puking on you." His cheeks redden, which is kind of cute. "But most of all, for forcing you to take care of a drunk driver."

He flicks a few grains of sand off his knee. "It was fucked up. And I'm not that guy." His dark eyes are wide and slightly haunted. "Or I wasn't until recently. I just...had a rough time lately," he finishes with a mumble before frowning at the sea.

"And you turned to the bottle." It isn't my place to criticize. And I try to make my voice gentle. "It never works, you know."

He snorts. "Oh, I know." He glances back at me, and his lips curve on a bitter smile. "I failed spectacularly at that experiment in oblivion."

"If you'd failed," I say softly, "you'd be dead."

Killian blanches. "I guess you're right," he says in a thin voice.

We're quiet for a moment, the crash of waves and the cries of gulls filling the air. Then I hand him his sandwich. "I'm glad you didn't." *I'm glad you're here. With me.* But I don't have the courage to say that.

He shakes his head as if laughing at himself, but when he meets my eyes, there's a lightness in his expression. "I'm glad too, Liberty Bell." Killian leans in and peers at me. "We cool now?"

He sounds so hopeful—and a bit unsure—that the last

vestiges of anger toward him leave me. I fear that too. Anger is a wall I've built to protect myself. I know this. What I don't know is how to protect myself from hurt without it. But I want to try.

I find a smile. "We're cool."

LIBBY
5

We're friends. I don't know how it happened. I was all set to hate Killian, but he's wormed his way under my skin with embarrassingly little effort. Maybe because, as the days pass, he never really leaves. Somehow he's around for breakfast the next morning, then ends up hanging out with me all day until it's night again. Or maybe because I've sunk into a pattern of enjoying his company and then waiting until he returns to me. I swear, I seem to be waiting for him even in my sleep, my thoughts consumed with all things Killian—what is he doing? What's he thinking now? When's he coming over again?

The annoying thing is that I was perfectly content before he came. My life had a pattern and was comfortable. Reliable. Now, it's anything but. Everything is driven by this push of anticipation for *him*.

I tell myself it isn't really my fault. I don't think there's a person on Earth capable of resisting the man. Killian is a peacock in a world of sparrows. He catches the eye and holds it. Oddly, it isn't even about looks. Killian's features are bold and strong; he's good looking, sure, but not extraordinary. And yet he is, because whatever makes Killian *Killian* lights him up and draws people in like a candle in the dark.

Proof positive I'm not the only one affected? Grumpy old Mrs. Nellwood is currently beaming at Killian like he's her favorite grandson, even though he's rifling through her store and making a general ruckus.

Killian has dragged me away from work and into town. I hate going to town, but he whined and pouted, then grinned and poked at my ribs until I agreed to give him a ride.

"You're not gonna make me walk all that way, are you, Libby?" he'd said with that lopsided smile of his, the one that causes little crinkles to form at the corners of his dark eyes. "It's got to be, what? At least a mile. Maybe two."

"You're a fit young man. You'll survive."

"I'm new to the area. I could get lost. Next thing you know, I'm half-starved, and in my weakened condition, I could be eaten by wild, rabid bunnies."

"Bunnies?" I hadn't wanted to laugh but did anyway. "Of all the animals, you go with bunnies?"

"Have you ever looked in a bunny's eyes, Libs? They're just waiting for their chance to dominate. Why do you think they're always so twitchy?"

"Because they're freaked something's going to eat them for dinner?"

"Nope. They're plotting. It's just a matter of time before they make their move. Mark my words."

So here we are, in Nellwood's General Store, Killian all but hopping from shelf to shelf, intent, it seems, on touching everything. "Oh, shit," he drawls. "Look at this, Libs."

He picks up a red trucker hat and tries it on. "What do you think?"

Of course he looks good in it. Even with his long, tangled hair. In truth, he's like a hot trucker. It doesn't help that his faded black Star Wars T-shirt clings to his chest and displays his tight biceps with loving care. Disturbed fantasies involving a big rig and a truck stop parking lot fill my head, and I have to give myself a mental slap to focus on the question at hand.

His grin is one of goofy happiness, and I can't help but

smile back. "It's totally you. In fact, you really should buy one in every color they have."

Killian points at me. "You're getting one too."

"Yeah, no."

"It'll protect your skin from that sunburn threat you keep going on about."

Behind the counter, Mrs. Nellwood titters. "So sweet, looking out for you. Liberty, dear, who is your young man?"

My man? Gah.

Under the brim of his hat, Killian's dark brows waggle, though he manages to keep a straight face while he does it.

"This is my new neighbor..." I glance at him and realize I have no idea what his last name is. Good God, I've let a virtual stranger into my life. And become way too attached to him at that.

Killian doesn't look at me, so he's oblivious to my panic as he steps to the counter and extends his hand. "Killian, ma'am. I'm renting the Cromley place for a few months."

Mrs. Nellwood preens, her white bun trembling. "Welcome to Collar Island, Mr. Scott."

Killian frowns as if confused. "Mr. Scott?"

Mrs. Nellwood's pale blue eyes are shrewd. "I thought a Mr. Scott was the name on the rental agreement. Was I mistaken?"

Killian's back stiffens in surprise. He clearly hadn't understood the busybody nature of a small town. But he recovers quickly and gives her the full force of his charming smile. "Mr. Scott handled the rental for me. I was traveling at the time."

It's strange. Watching Killian, I get a sense he's telling the truth, and yet he seems oddly unsettled. Maybe he's like me and values his privacy. I don't blame him. I've spent every summer of my life here. Still I'm treated like an outsider and an object of curiosity.

I hide a lot since I moved in permanently. The idea that they're just waiting for me to slip up and spill my innermost secrets sets my teeth on edge. I hate small talk, always have. Hate the awkward, too-tight effect it has on my skin, my throat. I'm better off on my own. Which is why I rarely come to town.

Killian is paying for his things—a mountain of candy, chips, soda, knick-knacks that no one ever needs, and the hat —when the bell over the door rings and a group of girls enter on a wave a giggles.

They look about sixteen, and it occurs to me that I've really been hiding away for a long-ass time, because I don't recognize a one of them. At the counter, Killian shifts his weight so his back is to the girls. I wouldn't have noticed except my attention, apparently, is always somehow on him.

He thanks Mrs. Nellwood with a quick, tight smile then hustles over to me. He doesn't actually move quickly, but each step he takes seems laden with the intent to get the fuck out of here. Fine by me.

The moving mass of teenagers has hit the makeup aisle, and much squealing has ensued. And they've definitely noticed him. The girls keep whispering while glancing at his back, which isn't surprising. Killian is tall and well formed. A hot stranger. He might as well be bait on a hook for the local female population.

I am surprised, however, when Killian takes my hand and tugs me outside. Not surprised that he wants to leave, but that he does it in a way that makes it look like we're a couple. In silence, we walk down Main Street, and all I can think about is the rough yet warm feel of his hand in mine. His hold on me is secure but easy, his stride slowed to match my shorter steps.

Jesus, I need to get a grip. I can't have a crush on this man. We've already set up a pattern in our relationship. He teases, I sneer. The idea of him finding out I'm attracted to him makes my insides twist. I'd never live it down. Never.

"That was a cool place," he says, breaking me out of my panicked thoughts.

"I don't think I've ever heard Nellwood's described as 'cool.' But if you liked it, that's all that matters."

Glancing down at me, his dark eyes flash with good humor, though the lines around his mouth are still tight. He gives me a little nudge as we walk along. "How very magnanimous of you, Libby."

That's the other thing. Despite his general I'm-a-wayward-bum appearance, Killian has clearly received a fine education. Better than mine, if I had to guess. I want to ask him, but every time we touch on anything remotely personal about him, he withdraws.

"Oh, hey." He stops and faces me while digging around in the bag. "Got you something."

"Hell, no," I blurt out when he lifts up a matching trucker hat, this one in purple.

"Now, Libby, don't knock it 'till you try it."

Before I can make a run for it, he slips the hat onto my head. He's standing so close it's almost an embrace when he lifts his arms to adjust the brim. Close enough to draw in the faint scent of soap on his skin. Close enough that a soft flush of heat washes over me, and I struggle not to lean in to him.

"There," he says. "You look…"

He falls silent. The sound of my own breathing, and his, grows loud in the quiet. Flustered, I look up. He's biting his lower lip in concentration, those strong, white teeth making little dents in that lush curve.

Eyes the color of hot coffee meet mine, and my heart gives a great *thwump* in response. A tremor goes through my middle, my body heating so swiftly, I'm surprised I haven't broken out in a sweat. I want to look away, but I can't. He stares at me as if confused, his lips parting slightly.

My own lips seem to swell, blood pulsing through them. I want to press them to his and ease this strange ache. I don't move. Desperately, I try to think of what we were saying, where we are.

I clear my throat. "I look what?" My voice is a croak of sound.

Killian blinks, his dark brows knitting. He licks his lower lip, and I almost cave. When he speaks, his deep voice is a rumble. "Cute," he says. "You look cute in that hat."

The gentle touch of his fingertips brushing back a lock of my hair has me shivering.

"I thought your eyes were gray," he says, still not stepping back. No, he's leaning in, his breath a soft caress over my lips. "But they look green now."

The observation gives me the strength to break eye contact. I take a big step back and look away, a kick of pain hitting my heart. "I have my mom's eyes. They change color depending on the light. Gray, green, blue." I don't want to think of Mom's eyes. Or that the only way I can see anything close to them now is to look in the mirror.

Killian touches my elbow. His expression is somber. "They're beautiful." He looks as though he's about to say more, but then the group of girls come out of the hardware store in another wave of giggles.

Killian tenses. I look their way and find them staring at us. No, not us. At him. Heads bent together, the girls peer at Killian and frown.

I'm about to frown back at their rude asses when Killian gives the brim of my cap a playful tap. "Come on, little trucker, we've got snacks to eat."

He takes my hand again, tugging me along. The simple fact that he never looks their way makes me believe he's trying to avoid interaction.

"Do you know one of them or something?" I ask as we

hustle toward my truck.

"Who?"

"Don't play stupid. It isn't a good look on you. You're walking away from that group of girls like your balls are on fire."

"Sounds painful." He shudders. "In fact, never ever talk about my balls being on fire again. Add that to our 'Nope' list."

"Killian, those girls. Do you know one of them?"

"I'm twenty-seven. Why would I know a bunch of teenage girls here? Or anywhere? That would make me some sort of creeper."

"I don't know why. But they were looking at you as if they knew you. And you're clearly avoiding them."

"Now who's playing detective."

I stop short by the passenger door to my pickup truck. His hand slips from mine, but he turns to face me. His scowl is dark. I glare right back. "Tell. Me. What's going on?"

He deflates then. "All right. Just...get in the truck, will you?"

I gesture to the door, since I'm the one driving. He growls low in his throat and wrenches it open, tossing his snacks into the cab.

It isn't until we're almost home that he speaks. "Okay. No, I didn't know those girls. But I think they might have recognized me. Or they were trying to place me." He frowns and rubs his chin. "I shouldn't have shaved."

"Who are you that those girls would recognize you?" Jesus, is he some infamous criminal released on a technicality? "Is Killian your real name?"

I sound a touch panicked, and he gives me a measured look. "Yes, it's my real name."

The truck sways as we drive over a divot.

Killian braces his arm against the dash. "Look, can you pull over while we talk about this? I'd rather not end up in a ditch."

"Fine." I ease into the next pull-off that leads to a public beach. The Atlantic stretches out to the right of us, a dark swath glittering with sunlight.

Killian squints into the sun. "My name is Killian James."

I stare at him, trying to place why that sounds so familiar. And then it hits me so hard I think I gasp. I must, because he turns to face me, his eyes wary.

Killian James. Lead singer and guitarist for Kill John. The biggest fucking rock band in the world. Oh, God, I want to laugh. Just lose it right here and now. Of all the men fate has to put in my path. A rocker. And not just any rocker—one of the biggest stars of our generation.

"You have guitarist's hands," I say faintly, as if that matters.

His brows quirk as if he fears for my sanity.

"When you shook my hand, I noticed the callouses," I add, still kind of dazed. Jesus, Killian James is in my car. "And I wondered if you were a musician."

He glances down at his hands, then nods. "Yeah. I am." He barks out a laugh and shakes his head.

Heat invades my cheeks. I feel utterly stupid for not recognizing him. On the heels of that comes resentment of him hiding it from me. Because why the hell would I recognize him? I barely go on social media. I know his voice, his songs, but his face? Not so much. And no one expects a rock god to drop on their lawn. Drunk and disorderly, at that.

"Why are you here?" I grind out.

He leans back against his headrest. "Jax. I couldn't deal..." He bites his lips, his cheeks flushing dark.

Jax. The lead singer for Kill John. Now this story I know. Mainly because it was on the actual evening news. Last year, John Blackwood, Jax as the world calls him, tried to commit suicide by overdosing on sleeping pills. It was public and ugly. And from the little I heard of it, his attempt had broken up the band.

"Killian..." I reach out, but he edges away, curling in on himself.

"I found him, you know?" He stares at nothing. "My best friend. As close as brothers. I thought he was gone. After that... We were broken. Nothing felt real or solid anymore. And I needed to get out."

"The drinking?" I ask softly.

Dark eyes meet mine. "It was the anniversary of his attempt. On the way here, I pulled over at a bar." He shakes his head. "Wasn't thinking right. Wasn't thinking at all."

My heart aches for him. "I'm sorry about your friend. That you're hurting."

He nods but still frowns at the road before us. "So now you know."

Silence fills the car. I want to stare at him. I can't help it.

Killian Fucking James. In my car.

I'm not one of those fangirl types who learns the stats of her favorite band members and follows their every move. But I love music. It is personal to me, part of my life and my heritage. I have all of Kill John's albums. It hits me that, aside from seeing shots of Jax on the news, I have no clue what the rest of Kill John's members look like—they never put their faces on the album covers. I want to ask Killian about that. About a million things.

But I don't. I turn on the car and pull out onto the road. "Come on, we'll snack. And later, I'll make you my grandma's famous chicken and dumplings."

I swear I hear him release a breath.

When he talks, he's his old, charming self. "Sounds like heaven, Liberty Bell."

TRUE TO MY PROMISE, I cook Killian chicken and dumplings, and I bake a peach pie for dessert. Cooking helps ground me. I need it tonight. Bumblebees have taken residence in my belly, bumping around and fighting for supremacy in that small space. I find myself putting a hand against my abdomen throughout the evening, trying to settle them.

I don't know how to act anymore. Why on Earth is he here with me? When he could hang out with anyone. Seriously, I'm hard pressed to think of a rich and famous person who'd turn him down. Me? I'm prickly and private and plain. A fairly boring woman who all but hides out in her house. These are facts. It annoys me that I question my worth. But I can't shake it. I don't understand him.

For his part, Killian is quiet tonight, as if he's tired. He doesn't leave, though. He calmly sits at my kitchen table and watches me with hooded eyes.

It makes me more nervous, and I find myself jumping up more than once to get this or that.

I do it again, and Killian snorts.

"What?" I ask, meeting his glare.

He points an accusatory finger at me. "You're acting weird."

I freeze in the act of topping off his already full cup of coffee. "Shit." I wince and sit down. "I am. I totally am."

"Well, stop." His jaw clenches as he tosses down his fork. "It's pissing me off."

"I'm sorry." My hands lift in a helpless gesture. "I don't mean to. It's just, I keep thinking it." He's Killian James. In my kitchen. Mind. Blown.

He stares with eyes that seem to see right through me. Hurt clouds those dark depths too. "Not you, Liberty," he says in a low, raw voice. "Okay? Just... Not you."

My heart pounds in my chest. "W-what do you mean?"

Killian braces his forearms on the table, his expression tired. "You Google me yet?"

"No." Annoyance colors my tone. Sure, I'd been sliding into this side of ridiculousness, but I'm not that bad. "I figured you'd tell me about yourself if you wanted to."

He gives me a tight sort of smile-grimace, as if he wants to lighten the mood but can't. "My mom is kind of famous. She was a top model. Her name is Isabella." His lips twitch. "She *only* goes by Isabella."

"That Isabella?" I say, gaping.

He gives me a sidelong look. "Yeah, that one."

Isabella Villa, famous supermodel and second-generation Cuban American. She is gorgeous: perfect golden skin, high cheekbones, luminous dark eyes, and glossy raven hair. Killian has her eyes, her coloring, her charisma. He must have inherited his bold features from his dad, because Isabella's are as delicate as a doll's.

"Her image was everywhere when I was in high school," I say.

He rubs the back of his neck, his nose wrinkling. "Yeah. Try being a teenager and all the guys have your mom's picture hanging in their lockers."

The iconic image of Isabella wearing a diamond bra and panty set with white angel wings fluttering behind her as she struts the catwalk comes to mind. I'm not even into women, and I found those pictures irresistible. "Bet you got into a lot of fights."

A smile creeps into his eyes. Just barely. "You have no idea." Laughing darkly, he shakes his head. "Thing is, she's a good mom. Loving, if a little flighty."

"And your dad?"

"Killian Alexander James, the second." He gives me a wry look. "I'm the third. My dad is a hedge fund manager. He met my mom at a Met fundraiser, and that was it for him. They were good parents, Libs. Well, as good as they could be. But they were also busy and traveled a lot. My grandmother took care of me most of the time. She was great, you know? Took no shit, always kept me grounded, made me do chores, learn how to cook, that sort of thing."

"She sounds lovely."

Killian nods, but he's not focused on me. "She died about two years ago. I still miss her. She was the one who encouraged me to start the band. Hell, encouraged all of us to keep at it. We'd practice, and she'd listen. Even when we sounded like shit, she'd praise us." His gaze draws inward, and a frown pulls at his mouth. "When our album went platinum, she was the first person I went to see."

He stops talking, just scowls at the scarred kitchen table. And I find myself reaching for him.

At the touch of my fingers to his, Killian looks up. "She fluttered around the apartment she practically raised me in, dusting off the seat for me, running to get me coffee and *pan*. My *abuelita*," he hisses, leaning in. "Like I was the fucking president or something."

My fingers twine with his cold ones. "I'm sorry, Kill."

He holds onto me, but doesn't seem to see me. "I sat there on the old chesterfield sofa I'd peed on when I was two, while she tittered away, and I knew my old life was over. I'd never be the same. That no matter what I wanted, there would be a dividing line between the world and the person I'd become."

"Killian..."

"It's not all bad, Libby. I'm living the dream." His lips pinch. "But it gets fucking lonely sometimes. You start wondering who you are and how you're supposed to be. And I think...shit, I know that's why Jax couldn't handle things."

His eyes meet mine then. "I didn't want to tell you who I was because you looked at me like I was just another guy."

"More like you were a pain in the ass," I correct with a watery smile.

"Yeah," he says softly. "That too."

"Okay, so I got a little...starstruck. But I still think you're a pain in the ass."

"Promise?" The worry in his voice, his eyes, has me squeezing his hand again.

"My dad was a studio guitarist," I tell him. "Played backup in recording sessions for a lot of huge bands in the nineties." Killian jerks up in surprise, but I forge on before he can speak. "My mom was a backup singer. That's how they met."

"Hell, that's awesome."

"Yeah, they thought so." I still do.

The sun rose and set on Mom and Dad. They'd do a duet, and joy would flood me. Music has always been a part of my life. A way to communicate. Silence entered my world when they died.

Emptiness threatens to pull me under. I focus on the present. "Thing is, Dad was always around famous people. He never gave it much thought. It was talent he respected—and a good work ethic. But one day, David Bowie came in for a session, and my dad literally fell off his seat. Couldn't play for shit, he was so overwhelmed. Because Bowie was an idol to him."

Killian chuckles. "I can see that."

"You ever meet anyone you'd been a fan of?" I ask him.

"So many," he admits. "Eddie Vedder was a big one. I think I grinned like an idiot for an hour. He's a cool guy. Down-to-earth."

"Well, there you go. You're my Bowie, my Eddie Vedder."

I start to pull away, but he gives my hand a little tug, and I finally see the twinkle in his eyes. "You like me better than Eddie."

"Whatever you say, hon."

But he's right. I'm beginning to think I like him more than anyone.

———

KILLIAN ASKS for a second slice of pie as we spread out on the floor and sort through Dad's old records. I'm determined not to act like a nut anymore.

We listen to Django Reinhardt, one of my dad's favorites.

"You know he only had use of three fingers on his left hand," I tell Killian as we bop our heads to "Limehouse Blues."

"One of the greatest guitar players of all time," Killian says, then pulls out another album from the stack I've set on the rug between us. "*Purple Rain*. Now, talk about a fucking brilliant guitarist. Prince was a monster, just so…effortless but with such badass soul."

Resting my head in my hand, I smile up at him. "You ever seen the actual album?"

His dark brow quirks. "No."

My smile grows as he slips the record out of its sleeve and his eyes go wide. "It's fucking purple!"

The way his deep voice almost squeaks makes me laugh. "Yeah. I had the same reaction when I was eight and found it. My dad totally yelled at me when he caught me using it as a tea tray for my dolls."

Carefully, Killian tucks the purple record back into its sleeve. "I think it's awesome that you grew up with music that way. My family appreciated it, but not with the same consuming love I had."

I hum an acknowledgement but sorrow holds my tongue. Life has been so silent since my parents died. Too silent. I never really thought about how I turned my back on the simple joy of loving music, and how badly that has affected me.

I'm so distracted by my own thoughts that I don't see Killian reach for the black file box until he's already opening it.

"No, don't—" My words die as he lifts up the battered ream of paper.

His gaze darts over the first page. "What's this?"

Kill me now. Just take me out back and shoot me. Heat pushes through my flesh with a thick, uncomfortable fist. "Nothing. Just scribbles."

I make an attempt to grab the stack, but he easily evades me by sticking out one of his freakishly long arms and holding my shoulder with his freakish strength.

"Hold up." A smile starts pulling at his lips, and he uses a thumb to riffle through a few of the top pages. "These are songs." Dark eyes flick up to meet mine. A twinkle of surprise lights his expression. "Your songs."

"How do you know they're mine—"

"You put your name on the top of each."

I flop back on the floor and cover my eyes with my forearm. "They *were* private."

Silence greets me, but I don't dare look. I'm so exposed now. Worse than being naked. Getting naked with Killian would at least result in pleasure. This? Torture. I swallow hard and grit my teeth.

The floor creaks, and I feel his warmth. His touch is gentle as he lifts my arm from my face and grins down at me. "These are fucking great. Why are you embarrassed?"

"You just read the equivalent of my diary. Why wouldn't I be embarrassed?"

"You're right. I'm sorry."

"Funny, you don't look at all sorry."

He bites his bottom lip, clearly trying to rein in his glee. "Well, when I stumble across a diary like this?" He holds my stack of songs a little higher. "How could I be? It's like finding a unicorn."

"Into unicorns, are you?"

"Ha. Stop deflecting." Killian crosses his legs before him and keeps flipping through my songs like a geek who's found a long-lost chapter of *The Lord of The Rings*. "Why didn't you tell me you wrote songs?"

I lurch up and snatch them from his hands. "It's something I did when I was younger. A hobby." Something my parents made quite clear was a dead end.

"The last one is only a few years old." His expression pinches as he watches me put the songs away and close the file box lid. "It's nothing to be ashamed of, Libs."

With a sigh, I press my hands on the box lid. "I know. Honestly, I haven't thought about them in a while. Okay, after you told me who you really were, they did enter my mind. But I didn't want you getting any ideas."

"Ideas?"

I can't look at him. "You rightly called me out on getting weird on you. No way was I about to say, 'Oh, hey, I wrote these songs!' Like some lame sales pitch. I wouldn't do that to you, Killian."

"Libs." He touches my arm so I'm forced to meet his gaze. "I'd never think you were doing that."

I nod. "At any rate, it really isn't a big deal. It was for fun."

His frown doesn't ease, as if he still wants to ask a whole host of questions I don't want to answer.

Panic clutches my chest. "I'm serious. Can we please drop this?"

Killian takes a deep breath. "Okay, Libby."

He glances around, at a loss. I'm there too. But before it can get any more awkward, he shrugs and returns to picking through the records like nothing happened.

I'm so grateful, my vision blurs before I blink it clear.

"Oh, man, *Nevermind*." He holds up the Nirvana album and flips it over to read the back. "God, I remember when Jax and I discovered the Seattle Sound. It was like this beautiful rage and perfect disdain. The power behind it, like a fucking wave of sound that crashed into, sent you tumbling." He grins wide. "We'd listen, study, then make these horrendous attempts to copy it."

Lying on my stomach, I rest my chin on my palm. Inside, I'm still a bit shaken, but talking about legends is easer. Comforting, almost. "You didn't copy it. You found your own voice."

Nirvana had "Smells Like Teen Spirit." Kill John has "Apathy"—our generation's battle cry. "Apathy" drives just as hard and fast as "Teen Spirit" but there's more pain in it, less rage. A question of why we're here. A song of loneliness and feeling useless.

"When my parents died," I tell him quietly, "I listened to 'Apathy' on a loop for a week straight. It made me feel...I don't know, better somehow."

Killian's lips part in surprise, his gaze darting over my face. "Yeah?" His voice is soft. "I'm glad, Libs."

He reaches out as if he's afraid I'll bite. But he's a brave one. The tips of his fingers trace my cheek. My lids lower as he speaks, low and rumbly. "Had I been there, I'd have wanted to give you comfort."

Warmth swells in my belly, spreading outward. I'd have wanted him to give it. I clear my throat and force my eyes open. "So it was just you and Jax at first?"

Killian sets his hand on his thigh. "Yeah. We grew up together and then both went to the same boarding school. We met Whip and Rye there."

I have to laugh. "I can't picture you in a boarding school."

Killian makes a goofy face. "I was a right saint, you know. Good grades. Followed the rules."

"So how did you become a rock star, then?"

He ducks is head, shaking it a bit. "I don't consider myself a rock star. I'm a musician. I've always loved music, loved making music."

"If you love to make music," I ask him, "why are you here? Why not in a studio?"

His expression shuts down. "You don't want me here?"

I want you any way I can get you.

"Here is the least likely place anyone on Earth would expect you to be." I peer at him. "Is that why? Are you hiding?"

He snorts. "Jesus, Libs. What's with the inquisition?"

"It's not an inquisition," I say calmly. "It's a legitimate question. That you're agitated only means I'm picking at a nerve."

Killian lurches to his feet, his glare cutting. "Most people would stop picking."

"Yeah, I'm annoying that way." I stare at him, unwilling to blink.

He huffs out a breath, his hands linking behind his neck. "I don't feel it, all right?" His bare feet slap against the floor as he paces. "I don't want to sing. Don't want to play. It's just...a void."

"When's the last time you tried?"

He spreads his arms wide in an annoyed appeal. "I don't want to try right now. I just want to be." He pauses, glaring at me over his shoulder. "Is that okay with you? Am I allowed to just be for one freaking second?"

I stare at him for a long moment, then slowly rise. "You can be anything you want. It's whether you're happy that's the question."

"You're one to talk," he shoots back, stalking toward me. "Tell me right now that you aren't hiding from life in this old house. Jesus, you're a young woman living like an old lady. You won't even let us talk about your hidden talent. I honestly wouldn't be surprised if you'd rather I thought you pedaled porn."

A slow shake starts deep in my belly, cold and hard. "I don't want to fight with you," I say quietly. "I just want you to be happy. And I don't think you are."

"Yeah, well, right back at you, babe."

"Okay, now I'm pissed."

He huffs, his hands on his hips as he glares down at me. "Thanks for the update. I didn't notice."

"Fuck you, Killian."

His jaw pops as he grits his teeth. "You know what? Fuck it. Here's the truth: I wasn't happy—until I met you."

I literally rock back on my heels, nearly blown down by his candor.

His hands fist as he takes a step closer. "I've been here for nearly two months. I never stay in one play that long. And why do you think I'm still here? The scenery? No. It's you I don't want to leave."

"I...I don't. You shouldn't..." I swallow hard. No, no, no. Never fall for a musician. Isn't that what Mama always said? They'll break your heart the way they're always looking over their shoulder for the next gig.

Killian's mouth twists. "That too real for you? Shocker."

I wince at the bitterness in his tone and try to speak calmly. "What you do, how you've affected the world, I can only dream of what it must be like."

He snorts again, but I talk over him.

"I have your albums. I've heard you sing. There's so much life in your music. God, people would kill to have that talent, that power to convey so much emotion. And I..." I shake my head. "Hiding here, or behind our friendship... I can't pretend that's right, Killian. I wouldn't be a friend to you if I did."

He's silent for a long moment, his expression stony. Then he gives a short nod. "Understood." He looks around as if he's suddenly woken up and doesn't quite know where he is. His gaze slides over me, not holding on. "It's getting late. I'm gonna head out."

Before I can say another word, he leaves. And it takes everything in me not to shout for him to come back.

KILLIAN
6

I stay away from Liberty for the next few days. Not sure what to do but keep my distance until I cool down. She hit below the belt when she basically spoke the truth—damn it. The worst was when she claimed she didn't want me using her as an excuse to stay.

Excuse? The last thing I view Libby as is an excuse to hide. I'd been a breath away from kissing her when she'd looked up at me, her eyes wide beneath that ugly trucker hat. Hell, I've wanted to kiss her for days. Every time I look at her. Normally, I wouldn't hold back, but nothing about my relationship with Libby is normal.

I don't spend time with chicks. I don't spend time with anyone. It's writing-composing, practicing, recording, touring, fucking, sleeping. Same old record spinning round and round. I used to hang out with the guys, but that tapered off once we went Platinum. No free time and too much attention on us when we were in public took care of that.

I'm a twenty-seven-year-old, multimillionaire singer-guitarist in the biggest rock band in the world, and I have no earthly clue how to have a relationship with a woman. I could laugh. But I don't find it funny.

Because I want Liberty Bell.

Hell, I knew I was in trouble when she stripped down to

that plain, black bikini, and I got instant, demanding wood. I swear she's trying to hide behind the clothes she wears, because her body is banging. She isn't model perfect; I've done model perfect, a lot. And at some point, bodies just become bodies. Attraction is a whole different beast.

Liberty's plump-but-firm ass, narrow waist, and perky little breasts just do it for me. Jesus, her tits. They'd fit the wells of my palms perfectly, those sweet tips pointing up, just begging to be sucked.

That day at the beach I'd wanted to get my hands and mouth on them so badly, I'd almost run off into the ocean so I didn't jump her.

So, yeah, I'm in trouble. She got starstruck over who I am, and while I know she still likes me for me, when I try to see her stepping into my world, I fail. Not because she wouldn't fit. But because everything I know about Libby tells me she wouldn't want to. When she lets her guard down, I see that she's into me too. But she's fighting it, throwing up walls almost desperately. What's a guy supposed to do with that?

So I've put some distance between us in the most literal way I can.

My bike is back from the shop, and I took a long drive along the mainland coast—staying at cheap motels, driving when I get up, eating when I get hungry. It's beautiful, calming. Lonely. I miss her. Which is weird since I only really just met her. But I know her. After weeks of hanging out, I know all sorts of Libby things.

I know that even though she makes the best damn biscuits in the world and perfect peach pie—food that will have me moaning in pleasure—Libby likes to snack on ramen noodles slathered in BBQ sauce and butter, which is some truly disgusting shit. I know that she loves Scooby-Doo cartoon movies and actually gets freaked out during the "spooky" scenes.

And she knows me. She knows that Britney Spears was my first concert, not The Strokes as the public believes—though how I wish that were true. She knows I hate beans, not because of the taste, but because I can't stand biting into the nasty skins surrounding them.

We know each other. We can talk about anything, or nothing. It never gets old or boring. Libby is my resonance; when I'm in her vicinity, I'm suddenly amped up, with everything moving at a different frequency. And I don't care if that's sappy. It's the truth.

I can't stay away any longer. If all I can have of her is friendship, I'll have to take it.

It takes me all day to get back home. When I turn down the long shared road toward our houses, the sky is fading to smoky blue shot with coral pink. My house sits dark in the shadows. Golden light streams from Libby's window, hitting the lawn. Her silhouette moves past the kitchen window, and I imagine she's cooking something awesome.

My bike nears the fork in the road, one way taking me to her, the other to my house. I want to go to Libby so badly it's an actual, physical pain in my chest and gut. I want to sit in her kitchen that smells of comfort food, hear the slam-bang of her pots and pans as she talks about nothing in particular, and watch the efficient way she moves in her space.

I want that.

I turn toward my house instead. And it hurts.

After a shower, I grab a beer and slump in the big rocking chair on my porch. I find my cell sitting on the little side table. I left it behind on purpose. Five missed calls from Scottie, and a text: **Jax is ready. Get your ass back to NYC.**

Well, for once I'm not ready. I text him back so he'll stop bugging me.

Tour doesn't start for over a month. We have time.

His response is immediate.

Guys want to get back into it. They're asking me to book a few earlier shows.

Fuck. Part of me is annoyed that they didn't call me themselves. But I haven't exactly been communicative. And we all know that the best way to get any of us to do something is to sic Scottie on our asses.

Rubbing my neck, I think of what to do. Libby is right; I can't hide forever. But I'm not ready to leave. Not yet. I send Scottie a final text: **I'll call you in a few days.** Then I turn off the phone.

The night is muggy, the beer icy. Over the hum of the cicadas comes the sound of a guitar. It's an acoustic version of The Black Keys' "You're The One." It must be a new recording because I haven't heard it before.

Then I realize—it isn't a recording. It's live. Libby is playing that guitar. Of course it's Libby, the girl raised by musicians, who writes songs of poetic beauty and hides them away like a dirty secret. Of course she'd hide this from me too.

I want to be irate, but her sound distracts me. The hairs on my forearms rise as I sit up. She's good. Really good. Her style is easy and smooth, not the hard, tense drive of mine. More folk to my rock. But I appreciate the fuck out of it.

My fingers twitch with the desire to pick up my guitar. For the first time in months, I want to play. Fuck that, I *need* to play, be the rhythm to her lead, or the lead to her rhythm. Find out what she can do.

She eases into Sinead O'Connor's "The Last Day of Our Acquaintance." It's an older song, not heard much anymore. But Rye developed a huge thing for O'Connor after he saw her "Nothing Compares 2 U" video during some '90s rockumentary, and it was all we could do to get him to turn off her music. I'm pretty sure at this point his dream girl has a shaved head.

Memories of Jax chucking a salami sandwich at Rye on our

tour bus after the five-hundredth playing of "Mandinka" run through my head, making me smile. And then Liberty begins to sing.

The beer bottle slips from my hand. *Holy. Fuck.*

Her voice is melted butter over toast. It's full of yearning, soft and husky. Need. So much need. And pain.

I'm on my feet before I know it. I go into the house and pull my acoustic Gibson from its crate. The neck is smooth and familiar against my palm. A lump fills my throat. Christ, I'm close to crying.

Get a grip, James.

My fingers tighten on the guitar. From the open door, Liberty sings about loss and separation with a rasping defiance. That voice guides me, sends my heart pounding.

She doesn't hear me approach or even open the door. Her eyes are closed, her body curling protectively over the guitar. That her voice has so much power in such a restrictive position is impressive. But it's the expression she wears, lost yet calm, that gets to me.

She feels the music, knows how to phrase it and own it.

I'm hard just being close to her. My balls draw up when she hits the last power refrain, her voice coming down like an anvil, and I swear I can't breathe. It's like the first time I sang on a stage and felt the world open up with possibilities.

I think I fall a little in love with Liberty Bell in that instant.

She notices me then and gives a yelp, abruptly killing the last note. "Jesus," she says when she finds her voice again. "You scared the life out of me."

You're bringing me back to life.

The thought runs through my head, clear as glass. But I don't say that. I can barely find my voice at all. I stand there like an idiot, my chest heaving, gripping my guitar as if it's a life line.

A flush rises up her neck and over her cheeks. She ducks

her head, as if she's ashamed. No way in hell am I letting her hide.

"Beautiful," I croak past the lump in my throat. "You're beautiful." I know with an eerie calm that I'll never see anything or anyone more stunning in my life. Everything has changed. Everything.

LIBBY

MY HEART IS STILL TRYING to beat its way out of my chest after the scare Killian gave me. But it's slowly calming, and on the heels of that comes something that feels a lot like mortification. Killian has caught me singing, balls to the wall —or whatever the female equivalent would be.

A few days ago, I heard him take off on his bike, and when he didn't come back that night, or the next, my heart squeezed and my stomach sank. I might have thought he'd left for good, only Killian tacked a note on my front door before he left: *Gone roaming for a while. Don't do anything I wouldn't do—at least not without me.*

It simultaneously hurt that I was so easily left behind and pissed me off that he didn't bother saying goodbye in person. But I'm not his keeper. And I clearly can't make anyone stay in my life. So I went back to business as usual, trying to ignore the yawning pit in my stomach, only to discover that my "usual" was now empty and quiet, too quiet.

To fill the void, I played my guitar and sang. Every night. Something I hadn't done in months. It made me think of my parents, and that hurt too, like a wound scabbed over that you keep picking despite the pain, or maybe because of it.

And now Killian is back, filling my porch doorway and lighting up the room with his presence. He's here. My own personal magnet. His pull is so strong, I have to fight not getting up and running to him. Fight not grinning like a fool even though I'm still hurt. But I want to grin, so badly. Because He. Is. Here.

It sets everything right again. And yet it puts my world off kilter as well.

The way he's looking at me... Hell, it lights me up, sends sparks and flares along my nerve endings.

Beautiful. He called me beautiful, his dark eyes roaming over me as if I was his reason, the only reason.

I sit frozen under the force of that stare. He isn't wearing his usual playful smile. He looks almost angry, desperate.

His fingers tighten around the neck of the guitar until his knuckles turn white. "Play with me, Liberty."

I should have expected that—he's holding his guitar, after all—but I didn't, and the request is a sucker punch to the throat.

A strangled sound escapes me. I can't perform in front of Killian James. While I'm comfortable with Killian the man, Killian the musician intimidates me. His vocals are the stuff of legend—strong, clean, and powerful with a rawness that hooks into your soul and gives it a tug. He sings, and you feel he's doing it just for you, taking your pain, frustration, joy, rage, sorrow, and love and giving it a voice. And while I know I can sing, I'm an amateur.

Killian's eyes go wide as he takes a step closer. "Please."

He stands in the center of the room, still clutching the neck of his guitar as if it's the only thing holding him together. But it's me he watches, the lines around his eyes tight, his chest lifting and falling with deep, quick breaths.

He wants this. A lot. I suspect he needs this. Whatever his reason, he's been pushing his music away. But he wants to let it back in just now. To deny him feels akin to stomping on a spring bloom fighting its way through the cold winter earth.

I lick my dry lips and force myself to tell him everything. "The first time I tried to perform for someone other than my parents was for the fourth grade talent show. I was set to play 'In My Life' by The Beatles."

Killian starts to smile, but I shake my head. "It was no good. By the time I got on the stage, I was shaking so badly, I thought I'd faint. I just stood there, staring. And then I heard someone snicker. I ran out of there and fucking pissed my pants backstage." A pained grimace pulls at my lips. "They called me Piddy Bell until senior year."

"Fuckers." Killian scowls. "And I have it on good authority that Jax pissed himself during his kindergarten's holiday play. On stage."

My hand caresses the smooth curve of the guitar body. I love this instrument. Love playing it. How can that be when it's also linked to so much fear and humiliation? "Second time I tried to play on stage was in college. Open mic night. Didn't even make it out there. I threw up behind some amps and ran out."

"Babe..."

I hold his sad gaze. "I quit, Killian. Quit trying. Quit dreaming. And part of me is ashamed of that. But part of me is relieved. My parents were happy. They didn't want that life for me. Said it was too brutal."

Killian's jaw works as he grinds his teeth, and when he speaks, it's almost a growl. "When did they tell you that?"

"From the beginning. I just didn't want to believe them at first."

He nods as if I've confirmed something for him. "And then they were there to say, 'We told you so.' Had you tuck away your songs and focus on other things."

My fingers clench my guitar neck. "It wasn't like that."

But it was. That burns too.

Killian's gaze doesn't waver. "You wrote those songs, tried

to play for others, because you love music, just as I do. It's in your blood whether you want it there or not."

"Yes," I whisper, because I can't lie to him when he looks at me like he's seeing my soul.

Killian takes a step closer. "Play with me. See how good it can be."

"I don't..."

"I will never laugh at you," he promises fiercely. "Ever. I'm your safe place, Libby. You've got to know that."

Some deep tether in me sags a little, giving me room to draw a deeper breath. I swallow my fear. "What do you want to play? One of yours?"

His tension seems to release on a breath, but his nose wrinkles. "Naw. Feels pretentious asking you to sing my songs. Let's do something classic. But fun." He bites his bottom lip, his brows knitting, until he lights up. "You know Bon Jovi's 'Wanted'?"

I have to grin. Were my dad alive, he'd be moaning over Bon Jovi being called a classic. But I can't fault Killian's choice. It's unexpected, yet I see the possibilities. The song can work well on an acoustic and without drums to back it up. And it's a duet of sorts.

"'Dead or Alive'? Yeah, I know that one." I adjust my strings, fiddling with the tone. And then I pluck the first few notes, the old but familiar twang making me smile.

Killian makes a happy sound as he pulls a chair close and starts to do his own adjustments. Good Lord, just the sight of his big hand and long fingers moving along the frets, his forearms, corded with muscles and flexing, makes my mouth dry. Killian holding a guitar is the stuff of both my dirtiest fantasy and my most girlish daydreams.

My heart is pounding, anticipation and nerves running through my veins. I can't believe I'm about to play with him. Sing with him.

He glances at me, his dark eyes glinting. "You take the lead."

"What?" My stomach drops. "No. No way. You're the lead guitarist."

He chuckles. "Not tonight. You lead. We'll harmonize the lyrics, but you take the first verse."

After a few minutes of working out who will sing what, we agree to start. My hands are so sweaty, I have to rub them on my shorts before I can hold my guitar.

Killian's voice is a soft purr of encouragement. "This is gonna be fun, Liberty Bell. Just let go, feel it."

Taking a deep breath I start. And fumble. Blushing, I power through it. *The music. Just feel the music.*

Okay. I got this.

I begin to sing—wobbly at first, but stronger when Killian smiles wide and nods, encouraging. I close my eyes and think of the lyrics. It's about a musician, world-weary and jaded. Lonely. A man who's been reduced to nothing more than entertainment for the masses.

And it hits me. I open my eyes, look at Killian. My heart hurts for him. But he doesn't seem to notice. He's listening to me sing. He comes in with the rhythm, picking up the second verse. Then he sings.

Killian's voice is a wave of sound that sweeps over the room. It's the difference between singing in your shower and finding yourself in a concert hall.

I stumble a chord progression before getting a hold of myself. *Feel the music.*

So I do.

And we sing, just enjoying.

Killian is a generous musician, letting me lead, propping me up when I stumble. Occasionally he changes things up so I'm forced to follow, but he does it with a smile, daring me to step outside my safe box and risk. It's like a dance, playing with him.

And I grow bold, putting more emotion into my voice. I become that lonely but proud musician.

Our gazes clash, and energy licks through me, so strong it prickles my skin, pulls at my nipples. Joy unfiltered surges through me, and I smile even as I sing with all my heart. He grins back, his eyes intense, burning like dark coals. It makes me so hot, I want to toss down my guitar, throw myself in his lap and just take. It makes me want the song to never end.

He picks up singing the refrain, and that deep voice sinks into my bones, runs like liquid heat up my thighs. God, he's beautiful. Perfect.

With fluid grace, he hits a guitar solo, his lids lowering, his strong body rocking. All of his sinewy muscles tense and flex, but he's loose, so loose now, totally into the song. It's like sex, watching him let go. And I throb.

The song ends too soon. I'm left panting, sweat coating my skin.

We stare at each other for a long minute, a dull roar swooshing in my ears as if my body can't quite come down from the high.

"Jesus," I finally rasp.

"Yeah," he says, just as raw. "Yeah."

I'm shaking when I set my guitar down and run a hand through my damp hair. "That was..." I take a hard breath. "How can you give that up?"

The fire in his eyes dies, and he ducks his head, carefully setting his guitar aside as well. "Everyone needs a break now and then."

Fair enough. I'm still shaking. "I feel like I've run a sprint or something."

"It's the adrenaline." His lips quirk. "Happens when you make good music. And, Liberty Bell, we made some fucking good music just then."

Heat invades my cheeks. "It was you."

"No," he says softly. "It was us." He glances at the guitar by my side. "Want to go again?"

Do I? I'm not sure. It feels dangerous in a way, addictive. Once I give in, will I be able to go without?

Killian looks at me with calm eyes, and yet he's leaning in, his body tight. Waiting. I can't resist him. I'm beginning to think I never will.

I pick up my guitar. "Sure. You know Pearl Jam's 'Indifference'?"

Happiness gives his dark eyes light. "Again with Eddie?" He shakes his head, but his dimples are out. "Fight it if you must, Libs, but you know you like me better."

I more than like him. That's the problem. "Any time you want to play one of your songs, just let me know," I tell him blithely. "And then I'll reassess."

The long fall of his hair hides his eyes from me as he strums out a few chords, but there's a smile in his voice. "Maybe someday soon."

Those words sound a lot like hope.

KILLIAN
7

It's the middle of the night when three things happen: my room lights up with a flash of lightning, followed by a tremendous crash of thunder, and Libby screams bloody murder. I lurch up from a full sleep as if yanked, my balls crawling halfway up my ass in fright, my heart threatening to beat out of my chest.

For a bright, sharp second, I sit panting, my eyes wildly searching the darkened room, trying to figure out what the fuck is going on. Then I remember the scream. Libby.

Another round of lightning and thunder brings on another scream. The fact that I can actually hear her screaming all the way in my house is enough to stop my heart.

"Jesus." Terror mixed with rage has me leaping out of bed and reaching for the only weapon I have, my Gibson. It's not much, but it's solid, and I will bash the fuck out of anyone who hurts Libby.

I race out of the house and into a storm so violent, I can barely see. Icy rain lashes at my skin as I run, my feet pounding through sandy mud puddles.

I nearly face-plant when another spectacular flash of lightning arcs through the night. But a desperate wail from inside Libby's house has me charging forward.

"Libby!" I don't hesitate kicking her door in. Darkness

greets me. Libby is still screaming, and the sound shreds me. My bare feet slap over the floorboards as I run to her room.

I scream too—a fucking beast of a roar, adrenaline and sheer rage lighting me up. I swing the Gibson over my head like a club, ready to caveman-bash someone's head in, only to stop short when I finally enter her room.

Libby is sitting up in bed, her eyes wild, screams pouring from her. Nobody else is there.

For a second I just stand, guitar overhead, my hair dripping, my chest heaving. Then my wits return, and I slowly lower the Gibson.

"Libby?"

I don't know if she can hear me over her cries. They're coming faster now, and she's rocking back and forth. The sound unhinges me, cuts into my heart. All the hairs stand up on my body as if in protest. This isn't natural.

"Libby." I set the guitar down and ease toward her. "Baby, stop."

She doesn't hear me. I don't think she sees me.

Night terrors. It hits me like a brick. Mom told me I used to have them, and she said it was almost impossible to soothe me when they hit. I don't remember them for shit, but she told me it was awful. I fucking believe her now.

Ignoring Libby's frantic shrieks for the moment, I go to close the front door. When I return to her room, she's still going at it, but I head for her window, which she's left cracked open. After closing it and the drapes, I move to the bathroom and turn the light on, leaving the door open just enough to give her bedroom a bit of illumination yet not tear her out of sleep.

Maybe it's the light or the diminished sound of the storm, but Libby suddenly takes a deep breath and then sobs.

"Libby?" I whisper, walking slowly. "Baby doll?"

Her body shudders, and she blinks. Another rasping sob

leaves her. "Killian?" Her voice is toast. "What are you doing in my room?"

I approach her like I would a ticking bomb. My heart still hasn't calmed, and I'm starting to shiver. But I focus on her. "You were screaming, Libs. I thought you were being attacked."

She puts a trembling hand to her forehead, blocking me out. "I...the storm..." She curls in on herself, clutching her legs to her chest.

I can't wait any longer. I sit next to her and draw her close. She's covered in sweat and like a furnace in my arms. "It's okay, Libs. I'm here."

"Jesus." She rests her clammy hand on my arm. "You're soaked. And freezing."

I secure my grip on her because she's warm and soft, and, yes, I'm fucking freezing. But the truth is I need to hold her right now, need to feel the physical proof that she's safe and solid.

"Don't know if you noticed," I say with false lightness, "but it's raining cows and chickens out there."

Her snort buffets my skin. "Cows and chickens?"

"This here is farm country, Libs," I drawl. "Ain't no cats and dogs filling these skies."

I can feel her smile against my chest. "We're more about produce than cows. Did you see any falling tomatoes?"

"I might've been slapped upside the head with some flying arugula. It was too windy to tell."

As if to punctuate my words, a gust of wind slams into the windows, and the whole house seems to rattle.

Libby snuggles closer, and her warm hand smooths over my skin. "And you ran out into this veggie storm without getting dressed?"

"It sounded like you were being murdered," I grumble. "What was I supposed to do?" Hell, I'm pretty sure I'd walk through fire to get to her if she screamed like that again.

"So you charged into a possible murder attempt armed with a guitar and naked." She stiffens. "Are you naked? I can't remember."

"But you remember the guitar?"

"I thought you were going to brain me with it."

"Nice. Some thanks I get for my mighty heroics."

"Let's focus on the important part here. Please tell me you aren't naked."

I grin. "I won't tell you that." I have on boxer-briefs, but it's fun to tease.

Neither of us moves. Me, because I'm pretty much frozen solid. And Libby? Despite her professed fear of my nakedness, she wiggles against my side, like she's antsy.

"You're fighting the urge to look down and check, aren't you?" I say in the dark. My dick stirs, like he knows he's about to become a conversation piece and wants to look his best.

"I've already seen the goods, Kill." So very deadpan.

I give her shoulder a squeeze. "Which means you know exactly how good they are."

Well, not exactly. She's seen me at my worst. My dick twitches again as if to protest this injustice and demand another viewing. I tell him to calm the fuck down; it's not going to happen.

Already Libby is pulling away, her body stiff. "You should dry off. Your skin is like ice."

"Yeah." I run a hand through my wet hair. I'm shaking, which can't be good. But I don't want to go. I have to, though. I'm no longer needed. Swallowing back a sigh, I stand, noting the way she turns her head so she can't see. Adorable. I know she wants to check. I fight a shiver. "I'll let you get back to sleep then."

"No," her voice is almost a shout, and I halt.

She doesn't look up, but her hand lifts, imploring me to

stop. "Could you...I mean, you can dry off in my bathroom, maybe? And just..." She makes a choking sound. "I mean, it's raining."

A smile pulls at my lips. "You want me to stay, Lib?"

God, please let me stay. I'm so damn cold. And my bed is empty.

"Yeah," she whispers.

I almost dive under the covers right then and there. But I can't. "Libby, babe, I gotta be honest. I'm not naked, but all I have on are boxers. I might wake up with morning wood. Hell, I might get contact wood too." I'm actually in danger of getting hard just being in bed with her. "I don't want you kicking me in the nuts if I do."

The corner of her cheek plumps on a grin. "Killian can't control his dick. So noted."

"Oh, I have excellent control. I am the master of—"

"Your teeth are chattering," she butts in blandly. "Just dry off and get in the damn bed."

She doesn't have to say it twice. I hustle my ass into the bathroom and scrub myself down with a towel. Five seconds later, I'm sliding under the blankets and wrapping myself around warm, sweet Liberty.

LIBBY

KILLIAN IS ice cold when he gets into bed with me, and yet it's all I can do not to fling myself against him. The night terror still sits upon my heart, sending tremors through my body. For the first time in years, I didn't wake up and find myself alone in the dark. A lump swells in my throat at the thought of Killian charging into the storm, armed only with his beloved guitar.

At my side, he shivers and burrows under the blankets. I

fight a smile as I help him cover up. His feet find mine, and I yelp.

"Crap, you are cold." It's no small thing to help warm the ice blocks his feet have become.

"Didn't know how cold I was until you mentioned it," he mutters, then sighs as I tuck the blanket around his neck.

I should be unnerved that he's lying in bed with me, our noses almost touching. But I'm so glad he's here that I can't think of anything else. The storm is raging outside, each boom or crack making my back tense. But here, with Killian, I feel secure.

"I'm in love with your pillow," he says conversationally. "Have I told you that?"

"No." I fight to relax, but the tremors in my belly won't die down. "Weirdo."

He sighs again. "It's just so fucking comfortable. Why is it so comfortable?"

"It's a memory foam and gel pillow. I paid two hundred dollars for it. Don't judge. My bed is my sanctuary."

His eyes are dark stars in the night. "Why would I judge? I'm all for spending quality time in bed." White teeth flash. "In fact, I'm going to order a case of these babies in the morning."

I start to laugh, and then, to my horror, a sob bursts out.

"Hey," he croons. "Hey, come here."

Killian pulls me close, tucking me under his chin. I feel the shape of him against my belly, but for once I don't think of sex. He's like an anchor, a solid wall between me and emptiness. His arms are strong, and he holds me tight.

It's been so long since I've felt the basic human contact of a hug, I come completely undone.

I can't stop the great, ugly sobs that come out of me. "I'm just so...alone. They're never coming back. And I know, I'm an adult, I shouldn't be freaking out like this. Plenty of people don't have parents. But they were the only ones who knew the real me. And now there's no one else."

"There is," he whispers fiercely. "You have me. You *have* me, Liberty."

But for how long? And in what way? I can't ask. I'm too far gone. The stress of waking up in another dark storm, the loneliness, all the shit I try so hard to ignore crashes over me. I cry until I can't cry any more. It's messy and loud. And he holds me the whole time, stroking my back, murmuring nonsense words in my ear. He is warm and smooth and alive.

I fall asleep at some point, worn out and weak. When I wake up, it's morning, and I'm alone. My throat is sore, and my eyes burn. The bedroom is hot, the air heavy and oppressive. I stumble to the bathroom and wince when I catch sight of my puffy eyes and blotchy skin.

A cool shower does a lot to revive me. I brush my teeth and put on a tank and shorts. My wet hair keeps me fairly comfortable, but it's too hot. And too silent. I realize the power is out and sigh, shuffling my way to the kitchen.

I stop at the sight of Killian's broad back as he stands before my counter. Shirtless and wearing army green shorts that cling to his trim hips and tight butt, he moves with grace. I take a moment to admire the way the muscles on his back bunch and flex beneath taut, tan skin, and how his long bare feet flex when he shifts his weight to grab a couple of forks. Weird that I notice his feet, but seeing them seems intimate somehow.

He must feel my stare because he turns and gives me a soft look. "Hey. Power is out. I made fruit salad—if you can call chopped peaches, oranges, and one banana fruit salad—because that's all there was."

He's adorable. Still, I hover by the kitchen entrance. I think of how I lost my shit last night. No one has seen me that way since I was a kid. Not even my parents. Maybe he gets my embarrassment, because he sets down a big bowl of roughly chopped fruit and holds out a fork.

"Today, we shall eat from the trough. Later we shall play Fun with Water Hoses." His gives me a cheeky smile. "You have no idea how much I'm looking forward to payback."

"Yeah, I bet." I take a bite of sun-ripe peach. "Never mind the fact that I was performing a community service."

"Don't worry, Elly May. I'll be kind. Ish."

We grin at each other like idiots, and then his phone rings, the muffled sound coming from his pocket. His smile fades as he reaches down to turn it off.

"You're not even going to look and see who it is?" I ask.

He shrugs and stabs a peach chunk with his fork. "Don't need to. That's Scottie, my manager's, ringtone."

"And you don't want to talk to him?"

"Not particularly." He spears another piece of fruit like he's hunting game. "He just wants to talk business and…" Killian gives me a large, kind of fake smile. Anger and irritation flicker in his eyes. "I'm on vacation."

"Well, all right then." I try for teasing, but my mouth is stiff.

A lead weight settles in my gut. His manager wants him to go back. That much is clear. No matter how much Killian wants to enjoy his vacation, real life is still waiting for him. And eventually, I'm going to lose him to it.

"Thanks, by the way," I rasp, hating the soreness in my throat.

He shakes his head. "It's a horrible fruit salad, babe. And we both know it."

"No, I mean for being there… Here."

Killian looks at me for a moment, his brows drawing close; then he rests his hand over mine. It's warm and heavy, his grip gentle but strong. "Thanks for letting me."

Jesus. I'm in danger of clinging to his hand and blubbering. I need to get a grip. I lift up a slice of mangled orange. "You know, it's ideal to include at least a little of the fruit with the rind."

His lips twitch. "How about the seeds, Martha Stewart? Are they okay?" He flicks one at me before I can answer.

As I prepare to launch a banana in retaliation, relief eases the tightness in my chest. This, I can handle.

LIBBY
8

Usually after a storm, things cool down; the land gets to breathe a bit. Not so here. Heat settles like a thick blanket, smothering everything in its wake, turning the world humid, heavy, and slow. With the power out, there's not a thing to do but wallow. Even going to the beach is useless. The full summer sun scorches the sand, and as soon as you leave the ocean, you're baking, sandy, and miserable.

I settle for lounging on the porch's sleeping couch, the shades lowered against the sun, and every now and then stealing a lump of the rapidly melting ice I've filled my cooler with. Cotton shorts and a thin tank is all I can manage, and for once, I'm grateful for my small boobs because it means I can comfortably go bra free.

Or maybe not. I'm all too aware of the ribbed fabric clinging to my damp skin, outlining my shape. But what can I do? I'm not willing to suffer this heat any further by putting on more clothes, so if Killian happens to get an eye-full, so be it.

He isn't looking at me anyway. He's sprawled out on the floor, plucking away at his guitar, and taking sips of the lemonade I fixed. The slow twang of his guitar lulls me, and I drift in and out.

"If the power doesn't come back on by tomorrow," Killian

says, pulling me from my daze, "we're going to a hotel in Wilmington."

I don't bother opening my eyes. "It'll come back on."

He makes an annoyed noise. "We should have gone this morning."

"Didn't know it would take so long then. Besides, the sun's setting. It will get cooler."

Killian hums, which might mean an agreement or the vocal equivalent of an eye roll. I don't care. I'm too hot.

And the heat is getting to me. I should be listless. But I'm not. I'm restless. The thick, heavy heat has settled on me, too, caressing my skin, drawing my attention to it. I'm aware of the way my chest rises and falls with each breath. Perspiration trickles down my spine, and the ice I'm slowly rubbing over my sternum melts in rivulets that slip between my breasts.

But it's not the weather. Not really. It's Killian sitting across the way, wearing nothing more than a pair of low-slung shorts and a sheen of sweat on his toned chest. It's the deep, rolling sound of his voice, so gorgeous it pulls at my nipples and touches that achy spot between my legs.

I shift, hating the heat that throbs there, luscious and needy. I have to fight the urge to arch my back and thrust my nipples outward, calling attention to them. Begging.

Killian sings a low, soft song I've never heard before. I focus on the lyrics. It's about a man, aimless and jaded, finding solace in a woman's smile. It's about sex—lazy, languid sex— that goes on for days.

I want to tell him to sing something else. And yet I don't want him to stop.

But he does. He stops and starts, and I realize he's composing. Tingles run over my skin.

"New song?" I murmur when he pauses, messing around with a chord progression. He's been writing since he sang with me a few days ago. And it's been a thrill to witness.

When a song hits him, it comes hard and fast. But he needs feedback, someone to work through it with. He'd told me that role had been Jax's. Only Jax isn't here, so the task falls to me.

After the second song he composed, I'd become attuned to this need. And so I sing the refrain now, softly, feeling out the words. "It's good. But maybe 'thirst' instead of 'lust'?" I sing it again, testing the lyrics.

Silence.

And then his voice comes husky, rough. "Beautiful."

I turn my head. His gaze burns into me, those dark eyes glossy with heat. My stomach dips and swirls.

He doesn't look away. "Your voice is so fucking beautiful, Liberty Bell. Like sex on Sunday."

A shuddering breath leaves me.

God, I'm stripped by that dark gaze. And it feels good.

"You should use that," I rasp past the lump in my throat. "'Like sex on Sunday.' It's a good lyric."

Killian huffs. "Take the compliment, baby doll."

"Baby doll?" I glare up at the ceiling. "You're trying to annoy me, aren't you?"

"Honestly? It just slipped out."

Shocked, I look back at him. He doesn't flinch but returns my stare as if daring me to protest any further. Doing a stare-off with Killian isn't easy. His eyes are too expressive. One little quirk of those sweeping dark brows conveys entire sentences. We have a conversation without saying a word:

Go on, tell me how you don't like having a nickname.

I don't.

Liar. You love it.

How would you like to be called baby doll?

It depends. Are we naked in this scenario? Because you can call me anything you want then.

Okay, I probably imagined that last exchange. That's the other problem with staring at Killian; I become too aware of how hot he is. I have no defense against that. His chiseled features, especially that slightly pouty bottom lip, have all my thoughts drifting to sex.

Maybe he knows this because he suddenly chuckles, low and lazy. "I won," he drawls and plucks the B string on his guitar like a victory note.

I roll my eyes and try not to smile. "Go on and write your song, pretty boy."

"Tell me more about how pretty I am, and I will. Use specific details."

He catches the ice cube I throw at him and slips it between his lips, sucking it with a teasing hum of enjoyment. The muscles low in my belly clench in response, and I have to shut out the sight by closing my eyes. God, that mouth. It'd be cold now. And my skin is so hot. I lick my dry lips. "You're procrastinating."

He huffs but then plays a few chords before stopping again. "You were right."

I crack open an eye. "About?"

He's focused on his guitar, idly playing the song he's been composing. "I have been hiding away."

The confession falls like a stone in a pond. The ripples of it wash over me, and I sit up just to gain some footing.

Killian shakes his head slowly. "I see that look, Libs. I didn't mean I was using you as a distraction. But I have been avoiding going back. After I found Jax, everything felt like a lie." His hand smooths over the curve of his guitar. "Playing with you, I remembered. Music is real."

"Always will be," I rasp, then clear my throat. "I'm glad you remembered."

His fingers tighten around the guitar neck, his body leaning forward as if he's about to rise. "You woke me back up, Libby. You have to know that."

I have no idea what to say. I duck my head, the heat and

humidity getting to me. "You would've found your way without me. Music is too much a part of you to be denied for long."

"Maybe." He doesn't say anything for a long moment. When he finally talks, his voice sounds pained. "I have to go back."

My fingers dig into the couch cushion. "When?"

"We're going on tour in the fall."

One small sentence, and I'm ripped open. It isn't easy keeping my reply even, but I manage it. "It'll be good for you guys. And your fans will be so happy."

"Happy," he says. "Yeah, I guess they will be." Killian scowls at some distant point and runs a hand through his hair, only to have his fingers snag in the long strands. He mutters a few choice words before leaning back against the chair he's sitting in front of.

"I can cut your hair." *What am I saying?* I'll have to get close to him to do it. Not smart. But the tension between us is all wrong, too thick and awkward. I don't know if we're fighting or about to combust.

Maybe he thinks the same, because he frowns a little. "You know how to cut hair?"

"Cut my dad's. Still have the scissors." *Shut up and get while the getting's good.*

Killian sets down his guitar. "All right. That'd be great."

He sounds as strained as I feel. Such a stupid idea. But I'm stuck in it now.

———

I GO to get the scissors while Killian pulls up a kitchen chair to sit on.

His big, lean body is as tense as a guitar string when I return. In the light of the sinking sun, his skin is a deep honey-gold, shadows playing along the dips and valleys of his muscled torso. My steps slow as though I can draw out the inevitable by taking as long as I can to stand before him. But I can't avoid this without saying why I want to. And there's not a chance of me doing that.

I'm all business as I set down my scissors, comb, and a stiff brush for flicking away small, cut hairs. Killian's dark eyes track my moves, his expression far too controlled. Does this bother him too? It appears to. But for the same reasons? Or maybe he's worried I'll make a move on him?

I want to laugh. When did it get so complicated?

"You want to wear this so hair doesn't get all over you?" I ask, holding up a plastic cape I brought with me.

He gives a shake of the head. "I'm too hot already."

True that.

I clear my throat. "What style would you like?"

He looks at me as if I've spoken in Greek. "Style?"

"Ah, yeah. That's kind of important, since it affects how you look."

He shrugs. "Do what you want."

I lift my scissors. "So...mullet." I nod. "You'll look hot. Very nineteen-eighty-five. Maybe I can persuade you into a mustache as well."

"Har." His nose wrinkles. "Fine. Cut it short."

Really, it's like pulling teeth.

"A Channing Tatum maybe?"

One dark brow quirks.

"You know, Magic Mike?"

Killian flashes a grin. "Of all his movies, you pick that one? Shocker."

"Shut up." Slapping his shoulder, I move around to the back of his head and try to comb out the tangles. "You totally acted like you didn't know who he was."

Killian snorts. "Know him? We've hung out a couple of times. Just wanted to find out how *you* saw him."

"Well, now you know. Half naked and gyrating."

Though I can only see the crest of his cheek, I know he's making a face. I find myself grinning. Resting my hand on his warm shoulder, I lean around to catch his eye. "You never answered."

He stares at me for a beat, then blinks and clears his throat. "Hack it off."

"Channing it is."

There it is again, that regal expression of disdain he manages so well when offended, his dark brows lifting just a touch, his nostrils pinching as if he smells something off. "You're giving me the Killian James cut, babe, and don't you forget it."

I go to work on the back of his hair. "Arrogant, aren't we?"

"A man who names his hairstyle after another man isn't much of a man."

Long locks of silky, mahogany hair fall to the floor. "If you say so."

We fall quiet, which is a mistake. Because now I can't help but notice how close I'm standing to him, or the feel of my fingers threading through his heavy hair, and my breasts hovering by his temple when I move to his side.

I should be immune to Killian by now. I really should. But aside from last night's freak-out, I've never been this near him for a sustained amount of time. The heat of his skin has a scent —indefinable but luscious. My mouth waters, and I have to swallow hard so I don't drool on him like some creeper. His breathing has a rhythm and sound that holds my attention.

Agitation. I hear it. I feel it. Agitation surrounds us. It messes with my concentration, and I find myself hacking at his hair, cutting fast and loose. Luckily, he's asked for a short style, and I can fix what I've done. Biting my lip, I focus on my task and ignore him.

Or try to.

The more I cut away, the more his strong bone structure is revealed. Killian looked damn fine with long hair. Short? He's a work of art. With his high cheekbones, squared-off jaw, and strong nose, he'd almost look too hard if it wasn't for his pretty eyes.

My mouth twitches as I think about telling him he has pretty eyes. He'd hate that.

"What's so funny?" His husky voice snares my attention.

"Nothing." I carefully shape around his ears.

"*Libby…*"

He won't let this go. He's like a tick that way.

"I was just thinking that you have pretty eyes," I mutter, face flaming.

He makes a gurgled sort of sound. "You flirting with me, Libs?"

I don't meet his gaze. "Stating a fact. And you know they're pretty."

Those dark eyes watch me as I finish the basic shape of his haircut. "I know nothing," he says softly.

Our gazes finally meet. We're about a foot apart, and the air between us is hot and damp. It's a struggle to breathe, a struggle not to look away. In the background, evening cicadas hum. Killian swallows hard, searching my gaze for some sign. I don't know what to say. Every memory of all the awkward, bumbling encounters I've had with attractive men surges forward. I'm utter crap at this stuff.

Blinking, I stand straight and run my fingers through his hair. I've left it a little longer at the top. "I just have to shape this bit and you're done." My voice sounds thick and uneven.

"Okay," he says in a voice just as rough.

I frown at myself as I trim. This exercise in torture needs to end before I do something stupid. I step between his thighs to finish off the front of his hair. Mistake. He's now only inches away from my chest.

Killian's shoulders go stiff. I swear he stops breathing. Or maybe I do. Silence falls over us just as the cicada song ends. Neither of us moves or says a word.

And then everything changes.

It doesn't matter that it's barely a graze of his fingers against my shirt, the second he touches me, my body tenses, then vibrates like a tuning fork struck. I pause a beat, breath halting before escaping in a silent rush. The scissors hesitate then snip through his hair with a loud *snick*. The tips of his fingers gently press against the dividing line between my shorts and shirt, holding me steady as I sway a little.

I close my eyes for a second. I could move away, tell him to get off. But I don't. That small yet significant touch sends heat and need throbbing through me, and it feels so good, I almost whimper. I swallow hard and continue to cut his hair, less steady now but determined to finish the job well.

Neither of us acknowledges the fact that he's touching me. We don't say a word when his fingers slowly move up under my shirt, seeking bare skin. But, Jesus, I feel it, and my knees threaten to cave.

Idly he moves, as if he's simply enjoying the feel of me. As if I'm his to touch.

I can't pretend anymore. The scissors clink when I set them down.

Killian tilts his head back to stare up at me. There's something almost defiant in his expression, and I can't meet his eyes.

"What are you doing?" I whisper, heart pounding.

"Touching you." Gently he strokes my skin, and he sighs as though in heaven.

"Why?" I croak, because I've lost my damn mind, apparently.

Killian's tone stays soft, almost thoughtful. "It's all I think about lately, touching you." A low sound leaves him, as if he's laughing at himself. "Can't seem to talk myself out of it any more. Don't want to."

My hands shake, my breath growing uneven as he slowly, softly, plays along the curves of my waist. His gaze burns, zeroes in on my breasts that tremble right before his eyes. My nipples harden, wanting more of that attention.

He lets out a soft exhale, barely a sound, but I'm so aware of him now, it's as loud as a bomb to my ears. "You ever think about it?" he asks, a whisper. "What it would be like? You and me?"

"Yeah." It's a breath of sound, because I've lost the ability to talk. But he hears it. A gleam lights his eyes, his grip tightens a fraction, and he pulls me forward.

As if I've been waiting for it, I straddle his thighs, coming into contact with a considerable hard bulge. I want to grind myself against it but settle for resting on it now. Killian grunts low in his throat and slides me closer, holding on to my hips as if he's worried I'll run away. Not a chance.

For a second we just breathe, staring at each other as if trying to figure out how we got here. Killian looks me over, his expression relaxed but intent. Then he cups my cheek. His hand is huge, the skin rough. I want to kiss each callus. But I don't move.

He touches my lower lip with the tip of his thumb. His gaze rests there, thoughtful, as he brushes his thumb back and forth. My lips part, my breathing light and agitated. I want him to kiss me so badly it aches. But he doesn't.

His fingers trail down my neck, sending shivers along my skin. And he watches the path his hand takes. When he reaches my collarbone, he stops. His gaze lowers and a sound rumbles in his chest. It's greedy, impatient. He cants his hips, a slow roll as if he's already inside of me.

"You've been teasing me all day with this thin excuse for a top," he murmurs, his voice dark and rough. I whimper, wiggling on his lap, so hot I can barely stand it. He cups my ass and, with little effort, hauls me up higher as he slides farther down in the seat.

The chair creaks in protest. Killian spreads his thighs wide, cradling me in his lap. I hold on to the hard curves of his shoulders.

Dark eyes roam. His breath gusts over my skin, his mouth so close to my aching nipple. "Barely covers those sweet little tits. You gonna show them to me now, Libby?"

God, his voice. It's heated toffee, sticky and rich, coating my skin. It's black magic, taking command of my body. I sway a bit, wanting to press myself against him, fighting for just a little longer because anticipation aches so sweet.

"You like me looking at you, Libby?"

I can only make a strangled sound.

"Yeah, I think you do." His fingers twitch on my side, his gaze hot and needy on my breasts. "Lower your top, baby doll. Show me what I've been dreaming about for weeks."

The sound of my own whimper turns me on. Beneath me, his erection pushes against my ass. I take a shuddering breath and slowly reach for the strap on my shoulder. The thin cotton slides easily down my arm. I shrug off the other side and the top slithers over my chest like a caress.

Killian's breath turns choppy, his lips parting as if he needs more air.

The top reaches my hard nipples and clings, holding there.

We both go still. Heat licks over me, and I arch my back, lifting my breasts high. The top falls away.

Killian groans, long and deep. "Fuck yeah. So fucking gorgeous." Soft lips brush one swollen nipple. "I knew they would be."

He runs his parted lips back and forth, caressing me while I shake. The tip of his tongue flicks out for a quick taste, and my entire body jolts.

A hum of enjoyment rumbles in his chest. "You like that?"

I twitch as he idly peppers my breast with gentle kisses and his big hands run over my back. "Yes," I whisper.

Killian hums again then angles his mouth and sucks me. I groan, arching into it. And there's no more talking. Just Killian paying homage to my nipples. Killian cupping my small breasts in his hands, gentle, and not so gentle.

He stays content there, sucking and licking, pinching and nipping, like it's his favorite thing in the world. And I pant, grind myself against his hard cock, the seam of my jeans digging into my sensitive flesh, and wanting to come so badly I have to grit my teeth.

"Killian." It's a whimper of need.

He hears it and lifts his eyes to mine. I'm so undone, I don't notice his hands moving until they're in my hair, tugging me to him. We meet in the middle, our kiss deep and messy but right to the heart of it, as if we both knew how it would be, as if we've been here before.

And yet every touch of his lips to mine, every slide of his tongue in my mouth is this new, brilliant white and searing hot thing, sending a jolt of feeling straight through me. Every time.

I fall into his kiss, sinking deep, needing more, more, more. I'm hot, sweaty. His body is a furnace, and I only want to get closer, skin to skin, slick and sliding.

My arms twine around his neck, my fingers combing along his newly shorn hair. The press of my aching breasts to his firm chest has us both groaning. He grips my shoulders, holds me tight.

I don't know how long we stay there, making out like teens in the dark. Long enough that I grow dizzy, my body one big throb of want. Long enough that my jaw aches and my lips swell.

When he finally pulls back, it isn't far. His lips brush mine as we breathe light and fast, both of us trembling.

"We should have been doing this all along," he says against my mouth.

"All day long." I touch his jaw, lightly kiss his swollen lips.

His eyes flutter closed, long lashes touching the crest of his checks. He turns in to me, running the tip of his nose against mine. "I knew it would be so good. I shouldn't have held back the first time I wanted to kiss you."

"When was that?" Everything feels languid, hot, slow. His touch, mine. I nuzzle his neck, drawing in the scent of his skin.

He smiles, small and smug. "When you threatened to shoot me."

"I hated you then."

A low hum vibrates in his throat. "You found me irresistible. You would have caved."

"I would have bitten you."

"Bite me now."

That husky whisper has me moving, seeking his lips. I nip his lush bottom one, tugging at it gently, and he groans, drawing me in, slipping his slick tongue along mine. "Tell me you want this too, baby doll."

"Want what?" I can't think, my head is heavy, my limbs fumbling.

His dark eyes meet mine. "Everything."

My finger shakes as I trace the dark line of his brow. His lids lower, his head tilting to follow my touch. I lean in, kiss the corner of his eye. "Only with you."

KILLIAN
9

Libby weighs next to nothing in my arms, but my knees are weak as I stumble into the bedroom. I barely see where I'm going. I can't stop kissing her. God, she tastes good. I don't ever want to stop.

We tumble onto the bed, me protecting her fall and bracing myself over her.

But she's a greedy girl, tugging me down, wrapping her lush legs around my waist to grind herself against my cock. I love it. Love the way she kisses me like she's starving for it. Love the way she strokes my skin with a strange mix of tenderness and possession.

It is not bullshit or bluster to say I've been adored by millions. I've been pursued by countless women. But I have never felt as wanted as I do now. Being on stage is addictive, but it's nothing compared to this.

My fingers fumble on the snap of her jean shorts. She lifts her sweet butt to help me pull them off. We're both panting. It's too hot to be doing this. I couldn't give a fuck. No way am I stopping. I want her so badly right now, I can barely see straight.

Her shorts fly over my shoulder, and I kiss my way down her slick body, pausing at her tits, because they need to be worshiped just a little bit more. I could spend all night here.

But I've caught a glimpse of what waits for me.

I can't get there fast enough, settling down on the bed and gently spreading her legs to make room for me. Heat licks over my skin, and my balls draw tight. "Oh, God, you have such a cute little pussy."

Her head wrenches up, and she glares at me down the length of her body. "Do *not* call it *cute*."

"But it is," I croon, placing a soft kiss on her pink bud, loving the way it jumps under my touch. I hum in satisfaction. "So fucking cute."

She plops back onto the pillow, her voice weak. "Fine. Whatever."

I know she loves it. Every dirty word that comes out of my mouth gets her wetter. I stroke my knuckle along her swollen lips, watching her glisten. My voice is low and rough. "We're going to have to work at getting my cock in here."

She whimpers, her hips canting, trying to follow my touch.

I push my own hips against the bed. "It'll be so tight, this little pussy."

Jesus, I almost come right there. My breath whooshes out, and I'm slightly dizzy. I lower my head. A groan tears out of her as I gently suckle her clit. Hell, I moan too because she tastes like butterscotch, rich and sweet and fucking perfect.

Everything gets hazy, thick and dark. I'm so hot my skin prickles and shivers. There's nothing but me and the feel of her against my tongue, the sounds she makes—little whimpers—and the wet suck and slide of my mouth. My palms grasp her plush thighs, hold them steady as she writhes.

"Killian...God."

I pull back from my feast, loving how hot I've made her, and give her a smile. "For you, I'll answer to both."

A cute growl escapes her. She's quick, grasping the back of my head and tugging me close. "More."

I chuckle, low and pleased. "Yes, ma'am."

And when she comes on my tongue, my fingers pumping deep inside her snug box, it's gorgeous. She puts her whole body into it, arching off the bed, tits pointing skyward, her slim body glowing and damp.

She falls back, weakly grasping the sheets. "Fuck."

"Soon, baby doll." I'm scrambling to get my pants off because I need to be in her.

Libby lies prone, gazing at me down the length of her body. And I pause to take it in. My breath catches in my throat, and I can't help running my palm down her thigh. "Look at you, all open and wet for me. And so fucking beautiful it makes my heart hurt."

Her breasts tremble as she giggles. Giggles. I made my reclusive girl giggle. "Just your heart?" she asks.

"Oh, my dick hurts too." I palm it now. I'm so hard it's weighed down. No give to it at all. "It needs a hug."

Her smile is sunshine, spreading warmth over my skin. "Come here," she says.

And I'm done.

The bed creaks as I shove my shorts down and kick them free. My arms are unsteady, fucking shaking, as I lean over her. My dick pushes against her entrance, and she gazes up at me. When our eyes meet, my throat closes. "Libby."

She touches my cheek but then frowns. "Wait."

I freeze. I think my heart stops cold. I want to beg at this point, but I manage to speak without cracking. "What is it?" *Please don't tell me you've changed your mind.*

She gives me a weak smile. "Aren't you forgetting something?"

Something? I have no clue. My dick is doing all the thinking now, and he is pretty much yelling, *let me in!*

Her brow lifts. "Condom?"

Reality is a long crash down. I stare at her blankly before groaning long and pained. "Mother fucker."

LIBBY

SOME SICK PART of me wants to laugh at Killian's agonized expression. But mainly I want to sob. Because it's clear he doesn't have a condom.

His head sinks to my shoulder as he sighs. "Shit. I haven't… I haven't needed them for a while."

Call me a jealous slag, but warmth fills my chest. "Me either."

He gives me a squeeze. "I didn't plan this. I mean, I've fantasized about it constantly, yeah. But I didn't think it would happen tonight."

This endears him to me even more. I wrap my arm around his broad shoulders and kiss his cheek. "I know." If I had any sense, I'd have stocked up on my own.

"I'm clean," he says, almost hopefully. "Never gone without a condom before. Test regularly. I should have said all that before."

"I am too." I wriggle a little beneath him, because he feels so damn good against me. The tip of his cock is broad and hot. It actually hurts not having him push into me, I want it so badly. "But I'm not on birth control."

He sighs and, as if he can't help himself, rocks his hips just a bit. That thick, wide head nudges me. We both make a noise of want. I close my eyes, lick my swollen lips. "Killian…"

"Just the tip, baby," he whispers, half laughing-half groaning. "I swear, I'll be good."

I laugh too. Not much, though, because I'm tempted. But he doesn't push it.

His body trembles, his muscles locked tight. "I'm going to the store."

"The power is out. It'll be closed."

Killian whimpers, his cheek resting against mine. "I'm going to cry."

I snort, but I empathize. I want to cry too.

"I'm serious," he grumbles as his body shakes. "Full-out man-baby bawling." With a groan, he rolls off me and flops onto his back. Naked and glistening with sweat, he's so beautiful, I have to grip the sheets to keep from jumping on him.

Breathing deep, he rests his forearm over his eyes. "Just give me a minute. Or sixty. Or kill me. That might be better."

"Drama llama." I laugh and then launch myself at him.

He catches me with an *oof*, his arms going around me instantly. I kiss his damp neck, licking a spot—salty, tasty Killian—and he groans. "Libby. You're really going to kill me."

"Mmm…" I kiss my way along his jaw. "Just because we can't fuck doesn't mean we can't do other things."

His hands slide down my back, possessive, hauling me closer. "Don't say *fuck* in that sexy voice of yours. I might come right here and now."

I nip his chin. "I wouldn't mind."

He scowls, nipping me back. "I would. It would be humiliating." He smiles a little. "At least before I got you off."

"You already did. Thoroughly." I kiss his lips, soft, slow, then pull away, loving that he follows, wanting more. I give him another one. "Let me get you off now."

His hips nudge against my belly, that thick cock jumping. "It won't take much." He nudges again, a little more insistent. "Just put your mouth on it. Give it a little lick. I'll blow like a fucking canon."

I smile as I skim my lips down his chest. His hands slide into my hair and cup the back of my head, not pushing, just holding me. His abs twitch, those tight muscles clenching. I could touch him for days.

My tongue dips into his little belly button and he groans, his body stretching taut. But when I move lower, his head jerks up. "Libs, wait—"

He shuts up as I come face to face with his cock. And gape like a frightened fish.

"Uh…" I say. And then I remember a joke I once heard in college. About Killian. One of the girls at a party had called him Don't Kill-Me-an. Because, as she had laughingly explained, groupies claimed his dick was so thick and long that a girl was in danger of being split in two. I don't want to think about Killian and other women. At all. But the evidence is staring me right in the face.

He lifts up on his elbows, which does lovely things to his abs. He's panting faintly, his chest gleaming in the evening light. "Yeah, about that."

I hold up a shaking hand to silence him. "Just…let me get acquainted."

Because his dick? It's big enough to need its own name. Maybe its own address. Sure, I've seen it before, but he was hanging limp and cursed with a severe case of whisky dick at the time. Now it's hard as iron and thrusting upward as if begging to be stroked.

I oblige the beast, gently running my hand over its silky, hot length, and it twitches, nudging against me. He has a beautiful dick, tawny colored, well-shaped, and straight, the tip wide and smooth. Beautiful. And on steroids or something. Because it's just…

I wrap my fingers around it, and my sex clenches. I can imagine this meaty girth pushing its way into me. It'd be rude work, filled with raw grunts and deep groans. I clench again, giving him a squeeze. So very firm.

"We'll go slow," he rasps, almost desperate as I slowly trace the wide, round crown of his cock.

"Yeah, we will," I mutter.

"And you don't have to— Oh, fuck, that's good," he groans as I lean over him and suck on the fat tip. It fills my entire mouth, the crown fitting into the curved roof. And I groan too, because it is *so* good sucking on him. Better than anything has a right to be.

Killian mutters rough curses, makes pained, pleading noises as I work him, sucking and stroking—because there is no way to take all of him in. I'm so turned on, I can't be still. Just the sight of him, his strong arms stretched overhead, hands wrapped around my wrought iron headboard, his abs bunching, his hips rocking, sends heat rushing through me. I suck him deep, lick around the weeping head.

His dark brows knit, his lips parting as he whispers my name again and again. His thick thigh slides between mine and pushes hard against my aching sex. I groan against his cock.

We come together, Killian filling my mouth, me riding his thigh with shameless abandon. I stay with him until he softens against my tongue. He's panting hard when I release him and rest my head against his firm stomach.

His hand smooths over my hair. "I'm dead," he whispers, then hauls me up, wrapping me in his arms. His lips find mine. "You've killed me."

I stroke his damp temple. "Good. Then I can have my way with you all night. And you won't be able to protest."

"Do your worst. I'll just lie here and take it."

We might not have the damn condoms, but he keeps me well satisfied for hours, until I fall into a dreamless sleep, Killian's strong body pressed against me. Even as I fall, I want to hold on, stay awake. Because being this happy cannot be real. It can't last. Can it?

KILLIAN
10

The pillow beneath my head is…fucking fantastic. I mean, it really is. Like a squishy cloud or something…

I've been here before. In this bed. On this pillow. I fully wake in a rush of memories. Kissing Libby. Touching Libby. Libby making me fall apart and then putting me back together.

Her head is resting on a pillow next to me; her gray-green eyes meet mine.

And my chest floods with warmth. "Hi."

Her voice is soft and slightly rough. "Hi."

We're wrapped up in each other. I hadn't noticed before now. It feels natural, where I'm supposed to be. I touch her cheek and thread my fingers into her hair to pull her closer. I kiss her softly, and she opens to me on a sigh. It would be so easy to roll over her, part her legs, and sink it.

If I had a condom.

"Would I look like a total dog," I ask against her lips, "if I left you here and went to get condoms?"

I feel her smile. "Well, it's Sunday so—"

"Don't," I growl, nipping her lip. "Don't fucking say they're closed on Sundays."

She sighs, kissing me back. "Not saying it won't make it any less true."

"Mother. Fuck." I lean back a little. She's smiling at me, her golden brown hair falling into her eyes. I ease a strand behind her ear. "Fuck that, I'm driving off the island."

"I'll wait right here."

But I don't go. I kiss her some more, run my hands over her curves because she's soft and warm. And mine.

"What's it like?" she murmurs between kisses.

"Being with you?" I nuzzle her neck. "Fucking perfect."

Her chest vibrates with a chuckle. "No. Being on stage. Performing in front of all those people."

Resting my head in my hand, I look down at her. A lot of people have asked the same thing. I've never really cared. But with Libby, a lick of excitement runs down my spine. Because I can see her up there under the hot lights, her voice owning the air. It would be beautiful. "The Animal is like nothing else on Earth."

"The animal?"

"That's what I call the crowd." I run my fingertips over her arm. "It's a living thing, Libby. More than just individuals, a whole entity. You can feel it swelling up around you. It's like..." I bite my lip trying to put the feeling into words. "How do you feel when you sing?"

She blinks in clear surprise, and her cheeks flush pink as she thinks about it. "I don't know... Sometimes it's the only way to get all the pain out of my soul. Other times, it's like I'm flying."

"Exactly," I say, stroking her side. "Now imagine it at full throttle. You're flying at supersonic speed. And all that energy just lights you up, until you're hotter than the sun."

"It must be something." She's gazing up at the ceiling as if picturing it.

"The rush is addicting." I lean down and kiss the tip of her nose. "Almost as good as sex with you."

Her pink lips quirk. "We haven't had sex yet."

"Don't remind me." I find that fragrant spot on her neck

that makes her shiver. "Fooling around with you is better than anything I've done before."

It's the truth. Shocking, and yet it fills me with a strange relief, as if I've been wandering forever and finally come home.

Libby cups the back of my head, holding me to her. Idly, her fingers move through my hair. I close my eyes in pleasure, and her voice comes out soft. "I used to..."

"Used to what?" I prompt. That fine blush grows, chasing down her neck. I follow the heat with my fingers. "Libs."

She takes a quick breath and talks in a rush. "I used to dream about what it'd be like performing at a concert."

I rise up on my elbows. She tries to avoid my gaze, and I touch her cheek. "You have the talent. Why didn't you try?" Why is she hiding here? This place is slowly suffocating her. She has to know this.

Libby shrugs a shoulder, her attention focused on my tattoo. "I'm a homebody. Hell, going to class in college was adventurous for me. And my parents..." She shrugs again, turning her head to the side, the pillow cradling her cheek. "Well, what they had to say about the life wasn't entirely complimentary."

"Warned you away, didn't they?" I can understand that. There's a lot of shit in my world. Still, it pisses me off. They had to know she had talent, that she was curious to see where it could lead. And they stomped it down before she could even try.

She pushes out a self-depreciating breath and glances at me from under her lashes. "They'd flip their shit if they knew I'd taken up with you."

"Are you with me?" I ask carefully. If I have to fight ghosts, I want to know now.

Warmth floods my chest as she reaches up and traces my eyebrow. "I'm in this bed, aren't I?"

"Fuck yeah, you are." I kiss her mouth because I have to taste her again.

She makes a hum of pleasure. "I'm torn between demanding you go get those condoms and keeping you right here."

My hands roam lower, filling themselves with her plump ass. "If it wasn't for my blue balls shouting at me, I'd be all for staying right here."

"Talk to you a lot, do they?"

I grin against her neck. "Yes. Right now, they're saying, 'If we don't get acquainted with Libby's pretty pussy, we're going on strike, and we're taking the dick with us.'"

She laughs. "That doesn't sound good."

"It's a bluff. They'll cave in a heartbeat. Besides—" I lift my head and grin. "My dick had decided never to leave your side."

"Goof."

"Only for you."

Our peace is broken by a sudden slamming on the front door, followed by a familiar feminine bellow. "Killian James, get your trashy butt out here before I call the baby daddy police on you!"

I freeze, horror prickling my skin, as I stare down at Libby.

She's gone still beneath me, her eyes wide as saucers.

Then they narrow. "I'm assuming you know the person trying to knock my door down?"

I give her a weak smile. "Yes. That's Brenna James. My cousin and all around pain in the ass."

Said pain in the ass is still pounding on the door and bellowing my name. If it wouldn't upset my Aunt Anna, I'd kill the little brat.

Libby glances toward the door and back to me. "You knocked up your cousin?"

"Ha." I glare at her and reluctantly pull away. "You're a

riot." Grabbing my shorts off the floor, I haul them on and button them. "I'm letting her in before someone actually does call the cops. It's happened before."

When I'm greeted with silence, I turn and find Libby frowning at me. My back stiffens. "You're not seriously questioning this." I take a step back toward her. "Because I'm all for getting in that bed and demonstrating, in thorough detail, how you're the only woman in my life."

"*Kiiiilliaaaaan!*"

I swear Brenna's screech could raise the dead.

"I think we'd have an audience," Libby deadpans. She hasn't moved from her spot. Less than five minutes ago, I was in there with her, warm and content. I'm cold now. I want back in.

"I don't care." Libby's faith in me is more important. I need it.

I move to unbutton my shorts when my cell starts playing "Welcome to the Jungle." Fucking hell. The pest is calling too.

Libby bites her lip but then bursts out laughing, a low, rolling sound. "Go open the door. I've gotta meet this girl."

My shoulders drop, and I smile. "Your funeral, baby doll."

"Killian Alejandro James! I just got a bug in my mouth, and it's all your fault!"

Libby snorts. "Sounds more like yours."

Shaking my head, I go to let the beast in.

LIBBY

DESPITE MY TEASING, I don't want to go out and meet Killian's cousin. I'm not even sure why. All I know is dread lies like lead in my stomach. This feels like the end, the happy little bubble that Killian and I lived in burst by the arrival of his relative.

The way his body jolted, his face freezing in horror, when he heard Brenna for the first time, knocked me clear out of Lust Land. For one heart-wrenching moment, the words *baby daddy* hung in the air, depriving me of mine. The pain had been so all-consuming, I'd wanted to vomit.

This doesn't bode well for me. Do I trust Killian? Yes. He's too impulsive, forthright to hide another woman from me. I don't think he's capable of that level of deceit. I don't think he'd bother, truth be told. Killian says and does exactly what he wants.

The problem lies with me; I'm half in love with a man who will drift through my life like smoke in the wind.

I hate that my hand shakes as I apply mascara. Scowling in the mirror, I toss the wand down. *Fancying up to impress another woman. New low, Liberty. New low.*

Voices in the living room create a hum in the air, punctuated by the higher-pitched comments of Killian's cousin. Just how many people are out there?

I turn the corner and stop short.

Killian stands, hands low on his hip, face twisted in a scowl, as he talks to what could arguably be the most handsome man I've ever seen. I mean, wow. Glossy black hair, aqua eyes, tan skin—dude could be David Gandy's twin. Dressed in a pale gray suit, he looks like he stepped off a runway in Milan and jetted over here for a chat. He also appears to be about as pleased as Killian.

"The fact that I am in this backwater burg ought to tell you how serious this is." His British accent is as crisp as his suit. "Playtime is officially over, Killian."

"Funny," Killian drawls, low and irritated. "I don't recall putting you in charge of my life."

One cool brow raises. "It would have been the day you signed a contract allowing me to manage your band. More to the point, it would be when you bid me to get Jax back to work as soon as possible."

Killian winces at that, glancing off, his jaw hard.

"He's ready," the man says. "They all are. Now you want to put that off and threaten the ground I've gained because you're dipping your wick—"

"Don't go there," Killian snaps. Color paints his cheeks. "Not even a little. Understood?"

They glare at each other like it's high noon, and I decide to show my face.

As soon as I enter, the tension snaps. Killian's hard expression gentles. "Hey. I was wondering when you'd get out here."

He holds out a hand, and I walk across the room, too aware of Mr. Stunning and Brenna James watching me. I don't like being on display. Ever. And this feels like some odd test.

Because Mr. Stunning's scrutiny bores into my skin like a laser, I glance at Killian's cousin instead, who had been half hidden by the wing chair she's sitting in.

She's nothing like I imagined. I'd expected some punk girl version of Killian. But I don't see a family resemblance. She's tall and pale, with a smattering of freckles over her snub nose, and has hair the color of amber honey. It's pulled back in a sleek ponytail.

Just like Mr. Stunning, she's impeccably dressed, poured into a navy suit with a pencil skirt. Her sky-high heels are metallic, rainbow-colored snake skin, which ought to look ridiculous, but even I'm envious. I've never seen Louboutins in person, but the red soles make me think that's what they are.

She peers at me from behind red cat-eye glasses. I resist the urge to stand straighter. Wouldn't matter. Good posture isn't going to change the fact that I'm in ratty cutoffs and a ribbed white tank. I'm a country mouse who's walked into a den of lions. In my own damn house.

Killian grasps my hand in his warm one and tugs me to his side. "Libby, this is my manager, Mr. Scott, or Scottie as we all call him."

The handsome man, who is even prettier up close, gives me a short not. "Miss Bell."

So he already knows my name. He does not appear pleased.

Killian inclines his head toward Brenna. "And you've already heard the pain in the ass."

Brenna rolls her eyes and stands to cross the room. "He's just pissed because I know where he hides the bodies."

"Just be thankful you aren't joining them," Killian says easily. His fingers steal under the edge of my shirt to caress bare skin. Mr. Scott's gaze follows the movement, and his lips thin.

Flushing, I ignore this and smile at Brenna. "Anyone who can make Killian move that fast is okay in my book."

"Ha!" Brenna wrinkles her nose at Killian. "See? I'm useful."

Killian snorts but gazes down at me. "Brenna does our PR."

"Pleasure to meet you," I say to both Brenna and Mr. Scott. It isn't precisely true, but I don't want to alienate the people in Killian's life. "Can I get y'all anything?"

"Thank you, but no." Mr. Scott gives me a smile that could freeze water. "We were just leaving."

He glances out the window. It's then I notice a small moving truck and guys packing up Killian's things. A guy walks out, carrying one of Killian's guitar cases.

Panic hits me, and Killian holds me closer, as if sensing my fear.

"I'll meet you over there in a bit," he tells them.

Mr. Scott nods and, after bidding me a brusque "good

day," leaves. Brenna is slower, giving Killian a kiss on the cheek and me a weak smile.

"We'll meet again, I'm certain," she tells me.

My nod is wooden. I mutter some sort of farewell, but I don't really know what I'm saying. Blood whooshes through my head, muting out sound. My heart is in my throat.

The silence they leave us in is pained and complete.

Killian clears his throat and tries to wrap his arms around me. I draw away.

"You're leaving."

Sunlight slants through the windows and over Killian. Bathed in that golden light, he looks surreal. The chiseled planes of his chest and abs, the strong lines of his face, the dark power of his eyes—all of it highlighted in sharp relief. Part of me marvels that I've touched every inch of that body, that I've kissed his lips, taken him into me.

It doesn't feel real anymore.

He stares down at me, and I see the pain in his eyes. Do I seem as fleeting to him?

"I don't want to go," he says, small, flat, final. "But Scottie has booked a couple of early shows before our fall tour. And the guys all want to do it." He runs a hand over the bristles of his short hair. "I'm the outlier."

"This is the first time you all will be together since…" I bite my lip.

"Jax," he finishes for me. "Yeah."

He shifts his weight onto one foot and then back to the other, as if his body is warring between staying here and heading out the door. I'm being fanciful, I know, and yet I also know he's torn. I can see it in his pinched lips and pleading eyes.

"Well then," I say slowly. "You need to join them."

He blinks as if I've sucker-punched him. I don't know what else he expected me to say. He has to realize I'd never keep him from his life.

When he speaks, his voice is rough, as though he's been yelling. "I thought I had more time. I *wanted* more time."

I've suffered no illusions that this summer was anything more than Killian's escape from reality. It doesn't stop me from hurting, though. But I don't let that show. "That's the thing with endings in real life. You never really know when they're going to happen."

"Endings?" His head snaps up. "Is that what you think this is?"

I frown. "Isn't that what you're trying to tell me? Goodbye?"

"No!" He tugs me against him and holds on tight. Anger tightens his features. "You want to get rid of me, you're going to have to try harder, baby doll."

Unable to resist, I smooth my hands over his chest. Beneath his warm skin, his heart beats hard and fast, matching the pained rhythm of mine. "I don't want to say goodbye," I admit quietly.

He kisses me then, as if he's drawing me into him, memorizing my taste. Despite his words, it's a kiss that feels like goodbye. He's breathing hard when he draws away to rest his forehead against mine. "So don't."

I stroke the sides of his neck. It's like trying to ease steel. "You're going on tour. How long is that? Four months? Five?"

He pulls me a little closer. "Counting practice and these pre-tour concerts, I'd say five and a half." He ducks his head to meet my eyes. "So what? Out of sight, out of mind? Is that how it is, Libs?"

My fingers curl. "I'm trying to be realistic. I know what goes on during those tours."

He huffs, his eyes narrowing to obsidian slits. "Do tell."

A flush of anger races over my skin. "Don't be thick. 'Sex, drugs, and rock and roll' is a cliché for a reason."

"Oh, I know better than anyone, honey." He lets me go with a sound of annoyance. "But if you think that's what will happen when I tour, you don't know me at all."

"I'm trying to do the grown-up thing here," I tell him, struggling not to yell, "and let you go without worrying about me."

"Oh, well, thanks for being so helpful. How about instead you give me some sign that what we have means more to you than a summer fling?" He tosses a hand up with a snort. "Fuck, you've got me sounding like a clinger."

I bite my lip. Even when I'm pissed at him, I love him. It scares the hell out of me.

"What do we have, Killian?" I ask softly.

His eyes meet mine. "I don't know. But it's real. It's the only real thing I have right now."

"You have the music—"

He cuts me off with a fierce look. "I don't want to walk out that door feeling like the second it closes it's the end of us. Because I won't do it, Liberty. As far as I'm concerned, we just started. No fucking way will I—"

I wrap my arms around his neck and tug him down to me. His words end in a muffled grunt as I kiss his lips. But he doesn't resist. He leans into me, opening my mouth with his, slipping his tongue in deep for a taste. With a moan, he grabs my butt and hauls me up. I wrap my legs around him and cling as he walks us backward, kissing me as we go.

We end up on the couch, Killian kneading my ass. He breathes into me, his lips sliding down to my neck, and a shudder runs over his big body. "Libby." Soft lips nuzzle that spot behind my ear that makes my body tighten. "This is not how I wanted this to go."

I kiss the crest of his cheek, the corner of his eye. "How did you picture it?"

He rubs my back as he continues to explore my neck and

shoulder with his mouth. "I've been thinking about it a lot, actually."

"You have?" I try to pull back to face him, but he won't let me.

His hands drift back to my butt and squeeze. With a sigh, I rest my head on his shoulder, and he gives my cheek a kiss. "Yeah, I have." For a long moment he stills, just cradling me against him as if he's reveling in the act. And I do too. He's strong and warm, his heart a comforting beat in my ear.

Its rhythm picks up as he takes a deep breath. "Libs... Come with me."

"What?" I sit up straight.

Killian's hands fall to my thighs, slowly rubbing them as he meets my gaze head-on. "Come with me on tour."

"No."

"No?" His short laugh is incredulous. "Not even a moment's thought? Just no?"

"You're reuniting with your band after a year. No way in hell am I showing up on your arm like some countrified Yoko."

He laughs again, this time with more humor, though his expression is strained. "You know, the whole Yoko thing was wildly exaggerated. The Beatles were already drifting apart."

"The fact that you called it a 'Yoko thing' proves my point. Truth doesn't really matter. Perception does. And your bandmates will not appreciate me showing up in tow."

His fingers grip my thighs. Not hard, but firmly enough to show his agitation. "You don't know that. You haven't even met them."

"I know people." Using his shoulders as leverage, I rise off him and sit on the couch at his side. "Mr. Scott looks at me like I'm a problem he needs to take care of."

"Call him Scottie, and he looks at everyone like that." Killian turns to face me. "Besides, I don't want you to come with me as arm candy. I want you to play with me."

I think my mouth falls open then. I know I can't do anything more than gurgle like a fish out of water as I stare back at Killian's expectant face. It takes me a minute to find my voice, and it's a pathetic squeak when I do. "Play? As in, go on stage with you?"

"Of course." A wrinkle forms between his straight brows. "What else would I be talking about? I've been writing those songs for us."

"Killian...I'm not..." I lift my arms, searching for the words. "Were you even listening when I told you about my spectacular failures? I am a stage fright queen."

"Lots of people have stage fright." He doesn't blink, doesn't waver. "And if I hadn't seen the regret in your eyes when you told me those stories, I might be inclined to let it go."

I ball my fists, wanting to stomp my foot. "Never mind I'm an amateur. I play music on my porch in my underwear, not in front of eighty-thousand people. People," I add, when he tries to talk, "who wouldn't be there to see *me* anyway."

Killian crosses his arms over his chest. It isn't fair that he hasn't put a shirt on. All that raw strength ripples under his golden skin and makes me want to cave just so I can touch him again.

"Are you finished?" he asks.

Ogling him? Never. But I realize he means my rant. I give him a sour look, which he returns with a raised brow.

"First," he says, "if you played in your underwear, eighty-thousand people would definitely be watching you."

He ignores my eye roll.

"Second, this is rock. All of our success is part talent, part luck, and crazy determination." His lip curls. "Jax used to joke that we're all amateurs up there. Lucky-ass dilettantes."

A sigh leaves me, and I slump against the couch. Outside,

Brenna is marching around, ordering moving men. Scottie stands on the porch across the way, his gaze on my house. I know he can't see me, but it feels like he can. It's a matter of time before he comes back over here.

Killian's deep voice is low, persuasive, pulling me back to him. "All I'm asking for is three songs: 'Broken Door', 'In Deep', and 'Outlier'."

The songs I've worked on with him. They're beautiful, relying on harmony and vocals over power. And they're nothing like Kill John's usual sound.

"How do you know the band will even like those songs?"

He won't meet my eyes. "They will."

"Which means you don't know."

"It's my band."

"It's theirs too."

The man actually growls. It would be kind of hot if I wasn't so annoyed with him. Killian surges to his feet and spreads his hands out wide. "Why are you fighting this? The truth. Not the excuses."

"Because I'm not impulsive like you! I need to think things through."

He rubs a hand over his face. "You tell me you dreamed of this life. You tell me you tried but were encouraged to walk away. You asked me how it felt to perform in front of an audience, to be adored. Let me show you. Let me give you the world, baby doll."

If anything, I feel worse now. A horrible, crawling sensation invades my belly, and I have the urge to run to my room to hide. I pick at the fray on my jean shorts. "That was just...pillow talk."

"Pillow talk?" He blanches.

I wince. "You know, *tell me about your life*. Getting to know you."

His cheeks flush. "You were humoring me?"

"No. I wanted to know you. What your life is like outside of here."

"But not see it for yourself?" His eyes narrow, that flush running down his neck.

"Exactly."

Silence grows so thick, the sounds of truck doors slamming ring out in the room. The movers are done. And I'm guessing we are too. A lump swells in my throat. But I don't move. I stare up at Killian, who looks back at me with disgust.

"Bullshit," he whispers.

Someone lays heavily on a car horn. I'm guessing Brenna.

"They're waiting for you," I say.

His nostrils flare. Then he's moving. I'm in his grip before I can blink. He hauls me up and gives me a hard, biting kiss. I welcome the sting, biting back. The idea that I won't get to feel him or taste him any more rips my heart apart. His kiss turns softer, but not sweet. No, he's molding and shaping my lips with his, savoring.

I try to put my arms around him, but he pulls away. He's breathing hard, his bottom lip swollen and wet. "I'm going now before I say something I'll regret."

Part of me regrets ever meeting him. Because this hurts too much. I could go with him. I could lose myself in him. Even as I think it, my entire body freezes in fear so violent, I swallow convulsively. I can't do it. I can't leave this house.

He searches my face for some sign. Whatever he sees has his jaw clenching. His fingers bite into my upper arms. "We aren't done. Do you hear me? Not even close to done."

"I don't want to be done," I whisper.

His teeth meet with a loud click. "Then stop being a coward and get your ass to New York."

When I don't say anything, he curses and strides away. The door slams in his wake. And he's gone.

KILLIAN

11

New York will always be my home. It has a strange effect on me: instantly relaxing and instantly energizing. Going to meet Jax, however, is another story. My fingers drum a beat against my thigh as I ride the private elevator up to his apartment. Scottie offered to arrange a meeting on neutral ground, but I rejected the idea. Jax isn't my enemy. He never was and never will be.

Doesn't mean I'm looking forward to this.

The elevator opens directly onto his foyer.

Two years ago, a magazine did a huge spread on Jax at home. Jax showing off his industrial loft, living the life of a young rock star. What they never knew is that it was all a lie. It wasn't even Jax's place; it was Scottie's.

Jax's real home looks like something an old New York society matron would live in: dark wood floors, crown molding, rich colors on the walls, classic artwork in ornate gold frames. It makes me laugh every time I visit because I half-expect Jax to greet me wearing a smoking jacket and clutching a pipe.

"Every time you walk in here, you're smirking."

Jax's voice halts my progress. I hadn't even noticed him.

He's leaning against the arm of a green velvet settee in his parlor—yeah, he has a parlor, for fuck's sake.

I stare at him for a second. He's bulkier than I've seen him, his color healthy, his light brown hair longer than usual, almost reaching his collar. I set my guitar case down. "It's because I'm expecting to be greeted by a butler. Or maybe find a little poodle yapping at my feet."

"I've been thinking of getting a dog." Jax stands. The corners of his eyes crease, his head cocking to the right. I know his face as well as my own. Better, because I've seen it since we were six years old. So I know he's tense and hating it.

That makes two of us.

I drop all pretense and move across the room to pull him into a guy hug, giving his shoulder a slap. "Fucking idiot," I say gruffly. "You look good."

He hugs me back before we break apart. "You look like shit. What the fuck did you do to your hair?"

I know he's bullshitting me, but my hand reflexively goes to my shorn hair. For an instant, I don't see Jax but Libby standing before me, her small breasts trying their hardest to poke through the thin tank she's wearing, her cheeks flushed, and her hands shaking as she cuts my hair. I can almost feel her fingers sliding along my scalp again, manipulating my head in the direction she wants it.

Christ, just thinking about her makes my chest hurt.

"Something I should have done a while ago," I say lightly, like I'm not fucked up inside.

Jax nods, but doesn't say anything else. We stand there, looking at each other, neither of us speaking. It's been this way since he woke up in the hospital. Me, because I couldn't think of anything to say that didn't end up with me shouting at his dumb ass, and Jax?

I used to know what he was thinking just by looking at him. Or I thought I did. I've realized I didn't know shit.

"Well," Jax says, breaking the silence. "You want a drink or something?"

"No. I'm good."

He nods again, then curses. "Fuck it, Kill, just get it out."

Get it out? I don't even know where to begin. Heat swamps my chest and pushes its way up my throat. My fist connects with his chin, and Jax hits the floor, knocking over a side table on his way down.

"Jesus." Jax rubs his face and gives a weak laugh. "I forgot how hard you hit."

I flex my fingers. "I didn't know I was going to do that."

"I did." He grunts and slowly rises to his feet, waving off my offer of help. Jax touches his lip where a bead of blood wells. "You feel better?"

"No." I head to the kitchen to get some ice. "My hand fucking hurts."

"Yeah, sorry my face got in the way." He catches the ice pack I toss him. "You gonna ice that hand?"

I want the pain. "I didn't hit you that hard."

Jax snorts and heads over to an old fashioned sidebar. His mini fridge is stocked with bottled waters and juices. A big change from the beer and vodka that used to fill it. "Want something?"

"A cranapple."

We drink our juice like good little boys until I can't take it any more. "It was the worst fucking moment of my life. Finding you." I swallow hard and stare down at my reddened knuckles. "I get that it was worse for you. Doesn't help. I...you scared the fuck out of me."

"I know." His expression is hollow, the ice pack lying limp in his hands. That day, his green eyes had been bloodshot and dull. They're glossy now, and he blinks, looking off. "I wasn't thinking about you. Or anyone."

"I was your best friend. And you just... You could have come to me."

He huffs, trying to smile but failing. "You would have tried to make it better."

"Damn fucking right I would." I push off the chair I've been leaning on and pace to a window half-obscured by red silk curtains.

"I didn't want to be fixed," he says. "Not then."

I can't even answer.

Jax sighs. "If I'd been in my right mind, I would have done things differently. But that's the problem; I wasn't."

My fingers dig into the silk. "You gonna do it again?"

It takes too long for him to answer. And when he does, his voice isn't strong. "I don't intend to."

I snort, anger racing hot through my veins. "That's comforting."

"I'm being honest. I'm getting help. That's all I can do."

Turning to face him is worse. He looks calm, composed, while I'm ready to jump out of my skin. "I don't know if I can do this again," I tell him. "If it's touring, the life, that set you off, I don't want to do it. I'll be worrying that I'll find you again, drowning in your own vomit."

A vivid image flashes in my mind. But it isn't of Jax. It's of me, of Libby hosing me down, putting me into a bed and ordering me not to mess it up. Guilt and loathing snake down my insides.

Jax glares at me. "I deserve that. But let's get one thing straight: You, Killian fucking James, aren't God. You can't fix everything or protect us all."

"The fuck?"

"Don't give me that. You've always been like this, taking all our shit on as your own. Thinking you can fix everyone's life and make it better. You can't. Just yours." He stands and slaps the ice pack on the table. "What I did was fucked up and shitty. I'm getting help. That's all I can say. Either you can deal with that or you can't. Your call."

He heads for the small studio he has in the apartment, not

looking back.

Left alone, I turn back to the window. Far below, traffic is a constant stream, people darting around on the sidewalks. Always trying to fix people's lives and make them better? Is there anything wrong with that?

I think of Liberty being here with me, what she would say right now. But she's silent in my head. Instead, I see the fear and frustration in her eyes when I tried to get her to agree to perform with me.

"Fuck," I whisper. Pulling out my phone, I text her. Her replies are stilted. Mine are too. Each exchange falls like a stone in my gut. I've damaged something between us. My thumb caresses the screen. I want to go to her. But I've got work to do here too.

Tucking the phone in my pocket, I grab my guitar and go to play with Jax.

LIBBY

HE'S GONE. And it's as if the sun has died. My orbit is off, everything dark and silent. It hurts to breathe, hurts to move. I knew he'd eventually go; I knew it would hurt. But I still wasn't ready for this. Nothing is right anymore.

I try to work. I have the creativity of wet cardboard. I kind of just sit, limp and staring. I finish up my projects—I won't be surprised if my clients complain about the uninspired work I've sent them—and turn away new jobs. I have enough money saved to take a vacation of my own.

Only what I'm really doing is walking from window to window, jumping at every little sound and catching my breath whenever a car drives along the road, which isn't often. Because I live in Nowhereville.

As soon as Killian left, I knew I'd made a mistake. I should have gone with him. I should have told my fears to shut up. But hindsight really is a bitch. Only now do I see what I've become.

A person can get...stuck, for lack a better word, in a life. It's surprisingly easy, really. Hours bleed into days; days fade into months. Before you know it, years have passed, and you're just this person, someone your younger self wouldn't even recognize.

My parents died, and somehow, so did I. Friends drifted away—no, I drifted away from friends. I can't pretend differently. I drifted away from everything—wrapped myself up in Grandmama's old house and a job that meant I never really had to leave home, and just hunkered down. It wasn't even a conscious decision. I simply retreated and never reemerged.

Killian wanted to drag me by my ankles back into the world of the living. Worse, he wanted to push me into its spotlight. Now he's gone.

And I let him walk away.

"I'm an asshole," I say to the room. Silence rings out.

I used to love silence. I hate it now. Hate. It.

"Fuck it." I'm not sure I like this development of talking out loud to myself. But I have bigger things to worry about.

I'm lying on the floor, wearing Killian's dirty Star Wars T-shirt like some lovelorn idiot, so I use my phone to open a search engine. I have no idea where Killian stays, but at least I can get to the correct city.

I'm scrolling through flights to New York when my phone vibrates with a text.

You were right. I needed to face Jax on my own.

I stare at the screen. Frozen. This is good. Why doesn't it feel good?

Little dots pulse at the bottom of the screen as he writes.

Another text pops up.

We're cool now. I actually want to get back to work.

Swallowing hard, I force myself to write.

I'm glad. Everything will be okay. You'll love it.

I don't know what else to say. I *am* happy for him.

He answers.

I miss you. Promise me you'll come to a concert.

No more requests to come play with him. Blinking hard, I stare out the window where the sun shines bright and hot. My vision blurs, and I blink again.

Of course I will.

A tear runs down my cheek. I ignore it.

He writes again.

I want to apologize. I tried to push you into something you weren't ready for. It was selfish. I'm sorry.

He's being sweet, and yet my throat hurts from trying not to sob.

It's okay, Killian. I know you meant well.

Jesus, we're texting like strangers. I try to think of something light, something that sounds like us. Anything. But then he texts.

Gotta go practice. Talk later?

Perhaps we will. But I know for sure what we had isn't the same anymore. My hand trembles as I type.

Sure. Have fun. :)

The little smile emoticon stares back at me like a mockery. I turn off my phone and toss it aside before Killian can answer. Lying on the floor in the sun, I close my eyes and cry. I missed my chance and only have myself to blame.

KILLIAN

12

The VIP section can either be an oasis of calm or a pulsing storm of frenetic energy. When you're famous, you quickly learn that it's your call how the night will go. You want privacy? You get it. You want a group of women willing to ride your dick and moan your name? Sure thing.

Tonight it's privacy. Jax and I wait in a room overlooking a crowded bar and an empty stage. Even though the club has a VIP room, it's not actually pretentious, serving beer and burgers rather than champagne and cocktails. Up-and-coming live acts perform nightly, and the crowd loves to dance for the fun of it, not just to be seen.

Music thumps and pulses from down below, but it's relatively quiet up here.

A waitress in worn jeans leads Whip and Rye in a moment later.

The second he sees us, Rye, our bass player, comes bounding over. And though I'm taller, he nearly hauls me off me feet as he gives me a squeeze that bruises my ribs. "About time you got here, fucker." When I laugh (wheeze) he sets me down, giving my head a slap. "Thought you might become a fucking hermit."

Rye is built like a linebacker with the energy of a puppy. A scary combination. He's grinning wide now, but there's caution in his eyes. His quick glance toward Jax tells me all I need to know. They're not sure of him either.

"I was on vacation, asshole."

"Out tanning his ass while we're working," Whip says, coming alongside of us. People often think we're related because we look a lot alike, only his eyes are blue. In school, we used to tell girls we were cousins, but it's bullshit. He's all Irish, with a faint accent to prove it.

He gives me a quick tap on the shoulder. "Tell me you found some hot girl to keep you occupied."

I've never hidden anything from them. But for some reason, I don't want to tell them about Libby just now. Not when I know they'll ask questions.

"According to Brenna," Rye says, "he had a cute little neighbor."

My back stiffens. "You gossiping with Brenna again?"

Rye's cheeks flush a little. It's well known to all of us that he has a thing for my oblivious cousin. And, yeah, I'm using it to my advantage just now.

But he quickly snorts. "I'm taking that evasion as a yes."

We join Jax at the table. "What's he evading?" Jax asks.

"Talking about the friend he made at summer camp," Whip says.

A waitress comes in and sets down the round of beers Jax ordered. Rye gives her a look, and she smiles wide. "I shouldn't ask...but are you JJ Watt?"

We all choke on our beers, trying to hide our laughter. Except Rye, who flushes again. His smile is easy. "Don't tell anyone I'm hanging out with One Direction here, 'kay? Might mess with my image."

"Okay." She frowns slightly as I give Rye the finger, and Whip kicks his shin under the table, making the bottles rattle.

"Jesus," Rye says when she leaves. "One year out of the press and I'm usurped by a linebacker."

"You do kind of look like him," Whip says, squinting at Rye. "Only shorter. Could get you a lot of sloppy-seconds action, though."

"My action has and always will be prime and all mine, fuck you very much." Rye sets his attention back on me. "So what about your summer crush?"

"Talk about evasion." I take a long drink of my beer before giving him a bland look. "Yes, there was a neighbor. No, she wasn't a summer crush." Libby is much more than that. "We hung out. She's cool. Her dad was a studio guitarist. George Bell."

"No shit?" Rye leans in, interested.

"You know him?" Whips asks.

"I didn't know him personally," Rye says. "But I've heard of him, sure."

It isn't a surprise that Rye knows about Libby's dad. Whenever we went on tour, Rye would have his nose in some music history book. There isn't an instrument he can't play or a musical tidbit he can't name. And we've tried to stump him. Many times. We always fail.

"You guys haven't?" he asks when we all kind of look blank.

"Not even a little," Jax says.

"He was a beast guitarist. Could have been a star on his own. But I guess he didn't want that. Sat in sessions for a lot of huge bands in the late eighties and nineties."

"That's what Libby said. He taught her to play." I glance around at their smirks. "Jesus, would you stop thinking with your dicks. She actually helped me come up with songs."

"Do tell," Jax drawls.

I don't appreciate the look in his eyes, as if Libby is already cheap entertainment. I might have gotten around to telling them about my relationship with her, but not now. Instead I lean back in the booth seat and shrug. "She sings and plays guitar. And frankly, she's fucking phenomenal." I pause, considering, but fuck it, these are my best friends. I can't hide everything. "I asked her to come play with us."

"What the fuck?" Jax looks at me as if I've sprouted a dick on my forehead.

"Don't worry, she said no." It still smarts. Because I know she was born to be out there. The same way I was.

"How about asking us first?" Jax says with another look of disgust. "Kill John doesn't need another member."

"It was to perform three songs with us as a guest. Shit, Jack White does it all the time, and it's brilliant."

"You're no Jack White."

"I'd say I'm better, but from where I'm sitting right now, I admire Jack's willingness to branch out and test his limits. We don't."

Rye laughs darkly. "He's right, man. We need new material."

Jax is still pouting like I peed in his Wheaties.

I shake my head. "If you want to know the truth, I had no interest in coming back until I heard her. She was inspiring."

They all look at me for a long moment, then slowly Whip nods. "Happened to me in Iceland. Was wandering around, not really into anything. Then I went to this club. There was this deejay, a mix master. His sounds were wicked hot, like nothing I've heard before. I hung out there all week and started working on some beats with him."

Jax frowns but doesn't say anything.

"Whip called me up," Rye puts in. "I flew out to meet him, and we started composing."

"Let me get this straight," Jax says slowly, his frown growing. "None of you wanted anything to do with music this past year?"

Heaviness settles over the table. I lean in, resting my forearms on the cold glass. "We might as well clear the air now. Yeah, Jax, we were fucked up." I gesture toward Whip and Rye with my chin. "What you did threw us all off. I'm not saying it to make you feel guilty—"

"Oh, well that's a comfort." He snorts and takes a drink.

"Too fucking bad," I snap. "It is what it is. And if it took branching out and roaming the world to find our way back, if we all found different sounds and inspirations, well, that's a fucking boon, not something to bitch about."

Jax glares at me while Whip and Rye sit quiet but tense. We all stare at each other for a long minute, the club pulsing and throbbing around us.

Then Jax sighs and runs a hand over his face. "You're right. I know you're right." His head hits the back of the booth with a thud, and he blinks up at the ceiling. "I haven't had some sort of musical epiphany." His green eyes cut to us. "But I want to play. I need to."

His urgency is palpable. It freaks me out that he wants to go on for the wrong reasons. But I'm not his dad. I can only support him and do what's best for the band. "That's why we're here," I say.

With the edge of his thumb, Jax picks at the soggy label on his beer bottle. "It means a lot." He glances up, faces us. "I'm serious. I know I've been an asshole. But… Thanks for coming back."

Thing is, Jax was never an asshole before. He was the happy one, the guy who got us motivated. I know Whip and Rye are thinking it too. The table goes silent again, and I wonder how we're ever going to get back to that easy place we lived in for so long, whether it's even possible.

"Aw, come on now," Whip blurts out in a plaintive whine better suited to a seven year old. "We've done the heavy. Can we just get over ourselves and drink our fucking beers?"

Jax laughs at that. "Yeah, man. We can do that."

Rye raises his hand to get the attendant who is quietly

standing far off in the corner of the room. He whispers something in the man's ear while the rest of us drink "our fucking beers" and look down at the action going on in the main room.

Not a minute passes before the door opens and a group of women enter.

Fuck.

"Thought we might like some company," Rye says. Musical genius, Rye might be, but he's also a total dog when it comes to sex. "You know, before all the bonding occurs."

The women are beautiful, well dressed, and very interested. A few months ago, I'd have been all over that. Now I'm annoyed that I can't hang out with my best friends for more than ten minutes without being interrupted. I don't even think about my dick. He's taken.

What I don't expect is Whip and Jax to be less than enthusiastic as well. Whip looks pained, his gaze darting down toward the dance floor and then to his hands fisted on the table. Jax just looks blank. But when he catches my eye, the look disappears and he sits back, parting his thighs to make room for the girl he grabs around the waist and pulls into his lap.

"Ladies," he says.

The girls giggle.

The sound crawls over my skin. When the rest of the women descend on the table, pushing themselves into the booth, I raise my hand. "Hold up," I say to a very pretty brunette in nearly sheer silk. "I gotta piss."

Classy. It has the effect I wanted. Her nose wrinkles, and she scurries out of my way. But her expression quickly smooths. "Hurry back. I can't believe I'm going to party with Killian James."

She's not. But I don't correct her.

I slide out and head for the exit.

"Wait up." Whip is at my side. "Wanna go down to the actual bar?"

I want to ask him why he's suddenly not interested, because he's a bigger player than Rye. But then I'd leave myself wide open for the same question. So I just nod.

The bar is crowded, people bumping into us. But there's anonymity here too. As long as we don't make eye contact with anyone, we'll be left alone for now.

"I got used to not being recognized," I tell him as we drink our beers.

"Me too." He glances at the empty stage. "Kind of liked it."

"But you want to get back to that."

"I must be a glutton for adoration." His eyes meet mine. "You?"

I think about it for a second. Did I miss the adoration too? There's a strange tension in my spine, along my arms. I look at the stage, and my heart beats faster. "I miss it."

I don't add that I fear it too. It would be so easy to let the need for it take over.

"Yep." He takes a drink. "As for the rest? I feel old now."

I have to laugh at that. "Old and boring."

"Maybe." He shakes his head. "I want something real. Get back to that place we were when we wrote 'Apathy'."

A place of truth. I had that with Libby. I felt it when we sang. I want it back. I want it with her at my side. Does that make me selfish? I don't know. But regret weighs on my shoulders. I backed off, gave her space. And it feels like a mistake.

I have made enough mistakes in my life. I set my bottle down on the bar, my stomach sour. "I want you to listen to the songs I wrote," I tell Whip. "I think they'll go with what you and Rye have been working on."

Whip slowly smiles. "We're gonna do this? Kill John rebooted?"

Anticipation licks over me like a good buzz. No more regrets. Forward action from here on out. "Yeah, man. We are."

LIBBY

I'M HAVING a pity party of one, lying on the couch and staring at the ceiling when someone knocks on the door. It sends my heart into instant overdrive, and I'm not ashamed to admit that I need it to be Killian.

Even so, I sit there for a long moment, trying to stop shaking.

Another knock gets me up. My legs wobble as I head for the porch. Outside, a town car sits in the drive. My mouth goes dry, my palms damp. They slip on the knob as I wrench open the door.

Disappointment sends my heart skydiving to my stomach.

"What the hell are you two doing here?"

Scottie gives me a dry look as he speaks to Brenna. "I thought Killian said she was shy."

Shy? Is that how Killian sees me? Knowing him, he probably called me a hermit, which isn't exactly wrong. I used to relish that, but now I realize how stupid it was, hiding away from life.

"Shy does not mean mute," I snap. "Or deaf. Try addressing me instead of your assistant."

"I love her more every time I see her," Brenna says with a bright smile. "She's like a little Kate Hudson. Only not as blond. Or as perky, thank God."

"Don't you two have an a cappella contest you should be commentating on?"

Scottie's perfect mouth twists. "A cappella? What are you

nattering about?"

Brenna snorts. "She's cute. No," she says to me in an overloud voice. "We've moved on to solo acts, kid." She bumps my hip with hers as she walks up into my house. She does it so easily, I don't even think to stop her.

Thankfully Scottie has some manners and inclines his head. "You really do not want to let her loose in your house unattended, Ms. Bell. May I come in?"

"If you can control Thing One, then you might as well."

Already Brenna has poured three glasses of ice tea and is rummaging through the kitchen for God knows what.

"Where are your cookies?" she mutters, opening a cabinet. "Kitchens like this always have cookies. I've seen it on TV."

"I have crackers, yogurt, and very sharp knives." I shoo her away.

"No cookies?" She lays a hand on her chest. "I've been waiting all day for some."

"Sorry to disappoint." I barely have any food in the house. I haven't felt like eating—I'm shocked too.

But because my hospitality gene kicks in, I put the drinks on a tray and take them out to my living room. Scottie and Brenna follow. For a minute, we sit sipping ice tea in heavy silence. Well, Brenna and I do. Scottie won't touch his glass, just eyes it suspiciously. I'm tempted to tell him it's not poisoned. Then again, part of me likes the idea of him fearing it just might be.

Setting my glass down, I get more comfortable in my chair. "All right, then. Why are you here?" Why isn't Killian here if they are? I miss him so much it hurts to breathe, and their presence makes it worse.

Scottie's expression begins to sour as if he's choking down something particularly distasteful. He can't blame my tea, at least. Brenna, on the other hand, starts to snicker. A lot.

Scottie shoots her an ugly look before leaning forward.

"Killian has a message for you."

"A message?" My heart kicks into high gear, but my mind skids to a halt. "What the hell is this? The fifth grade? Why can't he just call me?"

The corner of Scottie's eye twitches, and Brenna coughs loudly into her hand. Tears are forming beneath her cat glasses.

"Yes," Scottie grinds out through his teeth. "That would have been the logical choice." The twitching by his eye gets worse. "However, we're here to deliver it—"

"Is it a singing telegram? Because that might be worth it."

Brenna loses the fight and erupts with laughter, her slim form doubling over.

"Go search for cookies," Scottie snarls at her, though he hasn't really lost his cool. He's as contained as ever—well, aside from the eye tick thing.

Still hooting, Brenna staggers off, and Scottie turns his focus back to me. "There are days I truly hate my job." He pulls a folded piece of paper from his inner breast pocket and hands it to me. "Don't ask. Just read the bloody note."

Well then.

I hate that my fingers shake as I take it from him and open the smooth, creamy paper. Killian's penmanship is slanted and messy. And my heart instantly squeezes. Damn, I miss him.

Libs,

You gave Scottie shit about this, didn't you?

I pause, and part of me itches to look up to see if Killian is hiding somewhere in the room. It's silly, but Jesus, sometimes the man spooks me. I push aside the thought and keep reading.

You don't know how much it kills me to miss seeing Scottie choking on his disdain.

I fight a smile. He'd have loved the singing telegram part.

You don't know how much it kills me not seeing you, Liberty

Bell.

The note ends there, and I snort, not at all amused.

"If he wants to see me," I can't help but complain to a silent Scottie, "then why the hell isn't he here? And what the hell is this little—"

With a long-suffering sigh, he holds out another note. I pluck it from his grasp.

I can't be there. I've committed to practice and have been threatened with bodily harm if I try to sneak out. Have a little pity and read the damn notes, okay?

Lips twitching, I look up at Scottie. "Give me the next one."

Grumbling under his breath, Scottie pulls out a larger tri-folded paper.

I can't be there, Libby. But you can be here. You know you can. Come to me, Libby. Get on a plane and be with me. I miss you so much, I can't even call you. Because hearing your voice, hearing you say no, you won't join me, would rip my guts out.

So, like a coward, I sent Scottie and Brenna. (Plus payback's a bitch, and Scottie was due. He's dying right now, isn't he? Go on, laugh. It will make it worse for him.)

I do laugh, because I can hear Killian's voice in my head, cajoling and teasing. He wants me. A shuddering breath escapes me, and I blink to clear my vision.

These songs I wrote with you, they're our songs, not mine. I wrote them because of you. I'm not going to sing them with anyone else but you.

Come on tour with me. Meet the Animal firsthand. She'll purr for you, Libs, I promise.

Say yes, Liberty. Say it. Come on, just one little word. Part those pretty lips and say it. Y-E-S.

Okay. I'm not going to write any more. Except for one last thing.

The letter ends, but Scottie is already holding out another note, this one a bright, obnoxious yellow. I have to bite my lip at his pained expression, and I take it in silence.

Killian's scrawl is deep and thick in this one.

If you don't get your sweet butt on a plane, I'm going to send Scottie and Brenna to your house every other week until you or they crack. I'll do it, baby doll. Don't think I won't.

Yours,

K

"He's deranged," I mutter, lovingly folding up the paper and toying with the edges.

"As you say," Scottie deadpans. His gaze bores into me. "Well?"

A scattered stack of papers litters my lap. I rest my palm on their cool surface and sigh. "I'm calling him."

From the kitchen, I hear a long groan.

"Fucking hell," Brenna shouts. "If I have to keep coming back here, you'd better start making cookies!"

KILLIAN
13

"I miss fucking." With that little tidbit, Whip tosses a drumstick in the air, watches it twirl, and catches again.

"Not interested in helping you out there," I say, lounging against the couch as I down a bottle of ice-cold water. I don't tell him that I miss it too.

We've just finished an intense session, playing for a few hours. It felt good. Really good. Sweat slicks my skin, my blood is humming, and I'm keyed up. If Libby were here... But she isn't. Scottie has to be at Libby's by now. I shift in my seat, acid rising in my stomach.

"If you miss it so much," Rye says from his perch on a speaker, "go out and fuck someone and spare us your whining."

Whip gives him the finger while still tossing his drumstick. "Can't. I'm traumatized."

At this we all sit straighter.

"Holy shit," Rye drawls. "Sir Fucks-a-lot has gone cold? Say it ain't so."

Whip shrugs, concentrating on his stick. "Ran into some gritty kitty. Put things in perspective."

Rye and I shudder in sympathy.

"What the fuck is a gritty kitty?" Jax asks. He rarely talks now, but his brows raise in interest.

I wonder if that's why Whip brought this up, because it isn't like him to talk about personal stuff. And then I instantly resent the thought. We're trying to get back to that place where we aren't worrying about Jax and his moody ass—so different from the way he used to be—but it isn't easy. It sits on us like a stone.

I've got to guess it sits on Jax too.

Whip spins in his seat, neatly catching the falling stick. "How can you not know about those kitties? I refuse to believe that you, Mr. Jax-in-any-hole, hasn't encountered one."

Jax's lip curls, but his eyes are laughing. "Maybe because I don't use juvenile-ass language, so I don't know the term?"

We all snort at this.

"You shitting me?" I laugh. "You're the asshole who got everyone calling me Manwingo for a year."

"Manwingo!" Rye and Whip shout happily.

Jax almost smiles. "It was a compliment, chucklefuck."

I raise a brow.

Jax reads it well. "Yeah, okay, point made. Still don't know what gritty kitty is."

Rye shudders, and Whip's mouth puckers. "Dude, it's pretty self-explanatory. I went down to feast on what looked like it would be a pretty sweet kitty and it was all—"

We groan, cutting him off.

Jax shakes his head. "Shit, that's just wrong. I can't believe I forgot that one."

"It's like he's a born again cherry." Rye laughs.

"It was so unsavory," Whip goes on. "Realized I didn't know this girl's name or where the hell her pussy had been before. I got the fuck out of there. Figured enough was enough."

"Just because you encountered some grit doesn't mean you gotta quit." Rye wags his brows.

"Your rhymes give me heartburn, man," Whip says.

"Well, you're depressing the fuck out of me," Rye says as he stands and stretches his arms overhead. "Let's get the hell out of here and go to a club. Find some premium, well-maintained kitty."

When none of us say anything, he lets out a noise of disgust. "Come on. I swear, if you all start acting like old men, I'm going to kill my..." He trails off, going pale.

No one looks at Jax, but he laughs hollowly. "Word of advice: Stay away from OD-ing. Not as fun as it looks, man."

Heavy silence falls over the room, and Jax lifts his head to look at us. His expression twists with a smirk. "Too soon?"

It will always be too soon for me. But I'm saved from answering when my phone rings.

The familiar tune of "Hotel Yorba" plays, and I'm not embarrassed to admit my heart stops. Libby. I roll off the couch, striding toward the door as I pull out my phone. "Gotta take this." I might be running at this point.

Fuck. If she's calling to say no, I might punch a wall. I go into the padded sound booth so no one can hear me.

"Libby," I answer. Do I sound breathless? Shit, this girl has me acting like a preteen, and I don't even care.

"You have some interesting communication skills," she says by way of greeting.

I grin. Sending Scottie and Brenna to give her notes might be construed as juvenile and slightly corny, but there is some method to my madness. I knew it would either annoy her or throw her off guard before she could retreat behind her walls. I'm hoping for the latter. "I'd prefer talking face to face."

She huffs, but it doesn't sound angry. "I got that."

"Don't keep me in suspense, Elly May. I'm dying here."

"And you think calling me Elly May is going to help your cause?"

"Liberty Bell," I warn. Hell, I'm sweating. I lean against the wall. "Out with it, evil woman."

A sigh, and then her voice goes soft and small. "I miss you too. So much."

"You're killing me, babe." My eyes close. "You know what? I lied. If you don't come to me, I'm coming to you. And I'm not leaving empty handed."

"You'd forcibly haul me back with you?" she asks with a husky laugh.

"Yep. Might take you over my knee before I do, though."

I'm not going to lie; my dick gets hard at the thought. It twitches when she laughs again.

"You like living dangerously."

"You'd be well satisfied." I smile but it's weak. "Tell me, Libby. Tell me you're on your way."

She sighs. "You want me there to visit or to perform?"

I want her as my partner in all things. I know that now. But one issue at a time.

"Babe, I've made what I want very clear. Stop hiding away in that house."

"Killian, do you understand that the idea of getting on a stage and performing for a Kill John–sized crowd makes me want to vomit? As in, I'm eyeing the bathroom as we speak."

I want to hug her so badly. I clench my fist against my thigh. "Do you really hate the idea? Between you and me, without thinking about anything else, what does your heart say?"

Silence follows, highlighting the sound of her breathing. "I'm afraid…" Her voice is stark. "…that I'll lose myself."

"I won't let you." She has me now. Even if she doesn't fully realize it. I'll always be there for her. I just have to show her.

She speaks again, barely a whisper. "I'm afraid I'll look ridiculous up there."

I let out a breath. "Oh, baby doll. If you could just see yourself the way I see you. Your voice, the passion in the way you play—that brought me back to music. You belong out there. You said you wanted to fly. So fly with me."

"Why is this so important to you?" she rasps. "Why are you pushing it so much?" I can practically hear her brain whirring. "What aren't you telling me?"

I sigh and pinch the bridge of my nose. If I want her trust, I have to go all-in now. "The first time I told my parents I wanted a guitar, they sent an assistant out to buy me a six-thousand-dollar Telecaster."

She's silent for a beat. "Is that supposed to be bad?"

I snort in tired amusement. "They got me lessons from the best teacher in New York. Because, and I quote, 'Killian's finally found a little hobby.'"

I keep talking, exposing more. "When I told them I wanted to form a band, be a rock star, they asked me if I needed them to book a concert hall for me. They knew some people."

"I...ah...I don't understand. They sound more supportive than most parents. Maybe a little patronizing, but they clearly cared."

"Libs, I meant it when I said I had a good childhood, the best of everything. But I was also something akin to a pet. Interest in who I was or what I did with my life wasn't there. I wasn't missed or needed. And that isn't a poor-little-rich-me speech. Just the bald truth. To this day, they haven't heard a single song or gone to any of my concerts. Which is fine."

But it isn't.

She clearly picks up on that. "So you want to fix me because of what? Childhood angst?"

Something in me snaps. "I'm trying to show you how much I care, that your dreams mean something to me! They're not things to be swept under the rug or given lip service. They fucking matter, Libby. *You* matter." I stop there, my body tensing. I've said too much, exposed my underbelly. It isn't a comfortable sensation.

She draws a breath, the sound crackling through the

phone. "You matter too."

My eyes close. Maybe some of my motivation is selfish, because I miss her so badly right now it hurts. I'm so into this girl. She has no idea how much.

"I've always had my guys, the band. We pushed each other when one of us doubted. We were a team. I wouldn't be where I was without them. I want to be that for you, Libby. You're too talented not to at least try."

I swear, it feels like hours before I hear her response. Her laugh is tired and brief. "God. Am I going to do this?"

"Yes."

"That was rhetorical."

"I'm just moving the process along, babe."

She pauses for a second before speaking. "I have conditions."

"Name them." My heart pounds, adrenaline making me pace.

"I don't want anyone to know about us."

"Okay—Wait, what?" I halt, gripping the phone too tightly. Hide us? "What the hell? No. Why?" I'm sputtering now. "Is this that whole Yoko thing again?"

"It isn't a 'thing'," she says with annoying patience. "It's a legitimate concern—even more if I'm going to be on stage with you."

"Because your talent will suddenly disappear if people know my dick's been in you?"

"Don't be crude."

Oh, I'm being crude. I rest a fist against the wall. Just rest it. For now.

Her voice softens. "Please put yourself in my place. I'm an unknown, untried musician who you want to put on stage with the biggest band in the world. No one does that, unless they're getting themselves some."

"Which I am," I point out, stupidly.

"You trying to piss me off?" she snaps.

I sigh and thump my forehead against the wall. "No. I didn't mean it that way. Go on."

"You're right. People are probably going to think something like that regardless. But you go and tell your band that you want your girl on stage with you? They're going to think one thing: I fucked my way up there."

Wincing, I grind my teeth, trying to think of a retort.

I hear her voice catch. "I have my pride, Killian. Don't take it from me."

"Baby doll."

"Let me prove myself before they set their minds on who or what I am."

I'm silent for a long minute. "Fuck," I snarl, pushing off the wall. I sigh and the fight goes out of me. "All right. You're right. I know you're right. But they're going to know the second they see us together, Libs. I'm not good at hiding how I feel."

"Did you tell them about us?"

I stare through the glass. A sliver of the next room is visible, and with it Jax's profile. He looks relaxed. Solemn but okay.

"Brenna and Scottie know, obviously. But they won't say anything. The guys don't, though. Not details like that." I hadn't wanted to share, as if by telling them about it, I'd lose something private, something real. "Just that you helped me with my music and that you're talented as all fuck. They know I sent Scottie to coax you out here."

"And they don't mind?"

My teeth sink into my bottom lip. Truth? Or lie? But it isn't really even a question. "They thought I was cracked at first. Then I showed them the songs and played that recording we did of 'Artful Girl'."

I used my phone for that, and the sound quality was shit,

but Libby's talent shone through even then. It had been more than enough, for almost everyone. Jax is being a pain in the ass. But I'd expected as much.

I rub the back of my stiff neck. "They want to meet you."

It feels like an eternity before she talks. "Okay, I'll come. I'm not promising I'll go through with it. But I'll try."

Every tense muscle I have seems to release at once, and I lean on the console. I swallow hard before answering her. "I won't say anything about us. But once we're alone, all bets are off. That's my time, Libby. And I intend to use it well."

I swear I can feel her blush through the phone. But then her husky voice comes in strong. "Good. I've been left to using my imagination, so you'd better be creative."

This girl.

My dick is thick and demanding in my jeans now. Palming the head to ease its pain, I grind out the only thing I can. "Get here."

LIBBY

MY LEGS FEEL rubbery as I end my call with Killian. I'm going to do this. I'm going on tour with Kill John. I want to throw up. I want to see Killian so badly my teeth hurt. But performing on stage? That's another kettle.

I'd rather focus on his last words and the heated need in his voice. He'd been hurting—the same way I'm hurting now. I didn't know it was possible to feel empty between my legs, to actually want a cock in there so bad it aches. No, not just any cock. Killian's. It has to be his now. Damn the man, but he gets to me.

But I have guests camped out in my house, and I'm not walking around with hard nipples and flushed skin. So I take a deep breath and think of the time I walked in on Grandmama watching porn. Sufficiently horrified, I walk back into the living room.

"You look green around the gills," Brenna remarks. "Tell me that's because you're coming to New York."

Close enough. I nod.

Scottie goes…less stiff. "Very good." He looks me straight in the eye. It hits me anew how attractive this guy is. Not even sexually, though he has that too, but just the sheer force of his looks is enough to make me speechless. His crisp British accent doesn't hurt either. "You've made the right decision, Ms. Bell."

"Is that based on you not having to pass me any more notes in study hall, Mr. Scott?"

His eyes narrow. "Precisely."

While Brenna snickers, he stands and pulls his cuffs back into place. "I have a few calls to make."

The second Scottie is out of the room, I relax. I'm not proud of this. But damn.

"It's ridiculous, isn't it?" Brenna says in a whisper that carries all over the house. "How insanely gorgeous Scottie is?"

She's either too good at reading people or just as dazed in the man's presence as I am. I'm guessing a little of both by the way she seems to shake herself out of a trance.

"Are you and he…"

"God, no," she says with a snort.

"Flattering." Scottie's dry tone catches us red-handed as he walks back into the room. He really is unfairly man-pretty. All shiny and chiseled. Not my type, but a girl can admire.

"Obviously you heard me say you were hot," Brenna says. "You don't need any more of an inflated head."

Scottie takes a seat on my grandma's pink chintz armchair. Surrounded by flowers, he sits as regally as if it were a throne. "Looks are one thing. You insinuated that my character was faulty, which is far worse."

"Oh, stop fishing." Brenna turns to me. "He passes the first test but failed the second. And it has nothing to do with personality but basic chemistry. We have none."

"What are the tests?" I can't help but ask.

"Yes," Scottie urges. "Enlighten us, dear." He glances at me. "She's right, though. No sexual chemistry to speak of."

Brenna takes a sip of lemonade. "Whether you admit it or not, every person you meet, you assess for two basic things: hotness and fuckability." She nods and continues. "Test one: Hotness. How hot do you find a person? Obviously Scottie's hotness goes to eleven. He knows it. We all know it. Test two: Fuckability. Given the circumstances, would you want to do them?"

"This is true," I admit, holding up my hand. "Yes and no." Because I know she's going to ask if Scottie passes those for me. Of course he's hot. And though he acts like a snooty old man, he can't be much older than thirty. But no matter how good-looking he is, there's only Killian for me now.

She pouts, then goes and looks at Scottie, her gaze roving over him. He sits still, amusement in his eyes. She glances back at me. "Nope. There's still no spark. I could look at him all day, but that's about it."

I nod. Brenna and I are in total agreement.

"If you ladies are done dissecting my physical attractiveness," Scottie says, "I'd like to get going. Ms. Bell, I've booked you a flight to New York with Ms. James. It leaves in three hours, which means you'll have to get packing now."

"Aren't you coming?"

"No." He adjusts his already perfect cuffs yet again. "I've other business to attend to first. I'll be following later."

Brenna makes a noise that could mean anything, given her perfectly composed expression, but neither of them addresses it. She stands and heads toward my room. "Right then, on with the packing."

No way am I leaving Little Miss Bulldozer to pack for me. I hurry after her, excitement and anxiety thrumming through my veins.

LIBBY
14

New York City has a sort of silver tint to it—half of it in constant shadow, the other half shining in the sunlight slanting through the tall buildings. I crane my head, gaping up through the car window at those skyscrapers like the little yokel I am. I don't even care. It's a people-watching paradise, a constant rhythm and flow of human activity. There's an energy here that permeates the air and sinks into your skin. I have the urge to ask the car to pull over so I can walk.

"You want to roll down the window so you can pant like a dog?" Brenna's voice is full of humor.

I don't take my eyes off the scene rolling past. "I tried that earlier, and you complained about the hot wind mussing your hair. Remember?" We'd just come out of the Holland Tunnel, popping straight up in the middle of the Theater District, and I'd nearly jumped out of my seat from excitement.

Brenna makes a noise of smothered agreement. "We'll go exploring later. In fact, speaking of mussed hair, how do you feel about a makeover?"

The question pulls me from my window, and I sit back against the plush leather seat of our hired limo. "As in we have some sort of *Princess Diaries*, dude takes a pot of wax to my eyebrows and a weed whacker to my hair moment?" I laugh faintly. "Am I that bad?"

"No, of course not." Brenna's cool gaze travels over me as if she's inspecting a derelict house in need of rehab. "But every girl can do with a bit of sprucing up now and then. Especially if she's going to be in the press."

Press? My stomach takes an unruly tumble. "You don't need sprucing," I point out, ignoring the angry antics of my innards.

She shrugs, not even causing a wrinkle in the scarlet red suit painted on her. "I've had my makeover."

"If that's the result, sign me up."

"Really?" Her eyes glint, and it's only half evil.

It's my turn to shrug. "You think I'm going to complain about some shopping, a day in a hair salon, and a massage? Just because I don't usually do those things doesn't mean I don't like them."

"I never said anything about a massage."

"Oh, there will be massages. Mani-pedis, too."

"I like the way you think, Liberty."

We share a grin, and then she's on the phone making plans. When she finishes, she eyes me again.

I refuse to fidget. "You're looking at me like I'm a lump of clay."

"Just waiting for me to mold," she agrees with a nod. She arches a finely plucked brow.

"Nothing too outrageous. I still want to look like me. Only…better."

She chuckles. "I understand completely. We'll bring out the best version of you."

"And then get massages."

"That's the real carrot, isn't it?"

"Yep. I'm all over it like a starved bunny."

Even though she's smiling slightly, her gaze turns cool and cautious. "You realize Killian wants to pay for this."

"I figured. If he's offering, I'll accept."

Brenna sits back, crossing her legs. How she manages to make that look sexy and casual is beyond me. At this point I have a girl crush. "You know," she says, "I expected you to resist Killian footing the bill. Cry independent woman and all that."

"In the course of a month, Killian has torn apart my lawn with his bike, thrown up all over my favorite shirt, and eaten my food almost daily. I wasn't too happy about the first two, but feeding him was my pleasure. I'm guessing this is Killian's pleasure. Refusing a gift he's offering would be petulant. And I sure as hell don't have the money for what you have planned."

"You're slightly odd, you know that?"

"Says the pot to the kettle. Now tell me, is that your natural hair color or did you get it done at the salon we're going to?"

The limo turns up Fifth Avenue, and a shaft of sunlight slides through the windows. Brenna's red-gold hair gleams brightly. "Only my stylist knows, hon. But I do have some ideas for you."

"I'm all ears."

"I'm going to enjoy this," she says with satisfaction.

Five minutes later, the limo pulls up in front of a salon. We're whisked into a lounge area that is cordoned off from the main salon. There, a ridiculously gorgeous woman with brilliant pink hair, wearing what has to be the perfect little black dress, offers us a beverage.

I look around with wide eyes as I sip my chai-matcha tea—honestly, they must have a barista on staff. The space is all white, so pristine it seems to glow.

Lady Pink returns within a minute. "If you ladies will follow me."

"They're ready for me?" I slant Brenna a look. "Did you have an appointment already set up?"

Brenna matches my stride. "Of course I did. I'm a planner."

"And I am apparently predictable."

"Hardly." Brenna's sleek ponytail sways with a shake of her head. "Besides, if I needed to reschedule, they'd work around me. Even you have to realize the power Killian's name wields."

"At a salon?"

Brenna smirks. "Do you know how important that man's damn hair is? That close crop you did on him nearly broke the internet."

I can only gape.

"I know," she says, amused. "Young girls were crying over the loss of his beloved flowing locks, as if it signified the coming of the apocalypse."

"I was under the impression his hair was overgrown."

That snags her attention. "It was. But he usually wears it chin-length. You really didn't know who he was when you met?"

I resist the urge to squirm under her stare. She might not look very much like Killian, but clearly their interrogation skills were inherited from the same ancestors. "He was the last person I expected to find on my lawn. I guess my brain never connected any dots."

My sneakers slap against the concrete stairs as the salon hostess guides us up to the next level. She looks down her nose at my Chucks but apparently knows better than to risk more than that. I shake my head and pull my attention back to Brenna.

"But honestly, the only place I might have seen Killian is on an album, and he isn't on a single Kill John cover. None of them are. Why is that?"

"In the beginning, it was a statement. No pretense, just music. Now it's tradition." She waggles her perfect brows. "Of course it also helps add to their mystique and unattainability. But that was my doing."

I'd guess Killian doesn't care about that one whit, but she appears so proud that I nod.

My stylist is Lia, who immediately begins running her fingers through my hair while peering at me in the mirror. Until now, haircuts for me have been taking the scissors to my split ends. Who knew someone massaging my scalp and simply playing with my hair would be so relaxing. But my lack of styling clearly shows, because Lia and Brenna start discussing their plan of attack.

"We'll shape around your face and give your hair some movement," Lia explains.

"She's got great summer highlights," Brenna adds. "But maybe add a bit of richness to her base color?"

One hour later, my hair is wrapped in tin, and I'm stuck under a heater while two women do my nails. Brenna has been dancing around me, almost giddy.

"Next we're getting your brows tinted a shade darker and shaped. And then we'll go shopping for clothes. No, lunch first. Then clothes."

"Don't leave out my carrot," I remind her.

"Oh, the massages we save for last. We don't want to ruin our chill." She gives a happy sigh. "I might even throw in a facial. Yeah. That sounds heavenly."

It's hard to resist her enthusiasm. In lots of ways, she's a female version of Killian with her easy charm and bull-in-a-china-shop method of taking over. In some ways, that helps. It isn't in my nature to make easy friends or do small talk. With Brenna, I simply sit back and let her roll.

"Oh," she exclaims, "I forgot about the shoes! And—you think I'm crazy, don't you?"

Caught giving her a bemused smile, I can only shrug. "I kind of envy the way you enjoy your excitement. I'm more contained, and sometimes I'd rather not be."

The manicurists leave, setting my hands under mini dryers.

My nails are now a dusky, pale blue. After my hair is done, Brenna and I will get pedis to match. I've never had one, and suddenly I find that sad. Living under a rock was a waste of life.

Brenna toys with a hair clip. "I'm not always like this." She leans in, her eyes wide behind her retro glasses. "Most people think I'm a bitch."

"I get that from people too." Mainly because I have no idea how to talk to others without wanting to swallow my tongue.

Brenna's nose wrinkles. "Damned if you're too quiet, and damned if you're too confident."

"Sounds about right."

"My friends are all guys."

"I don't have any friends," I counter.

We both laugh, each of us almost shy.

"Killian is not only my cousin," Brenna tells me, her expression wide open. "He's one of my closest friends. He's clearly nuts about you. Honestly, I've never seen him write a girl notes before. The fact that he cajoled Scottie into delivering them is nothing short of miraculous. I swear, Kills must have some major dirt on him."

She's rambling, which is kind of sweet. But I won't say that; I'm pretty sure she'd be mortified.

At any rate, she keeps talking. "What I'm trying to say, rather badly, is that I hope we can be friends too."

Either it's a sign of how lonely I've been or I'm hormonal, because I damn near get weepy and have to blink a few times before answering. "I could use a good friend."

KILLIAN

TRUTH? I don't have to be playing for an audience to get a

hard-on over music. It just has to click, and I'm lit up.

That said, Scottie set up a gig at the Bowery Ballroom. It was our first time out in over a year. We'd grown used to stadiums, fifty-thousand fans at least. Singing for five hundred?

It's golden. My body throbs with the sound, sweat coating my skin. Lights burn my eyes, turning the crowd into a moving haze, limed in brilliant reds and blues.

I'm full-on pumped when we start playing "Apathy".

It isn't planned. I'm not even sure who decided to do it. One second we're playing random notes, the next we're a cohesive unit, hammering out the song that made us stars.

I lean into the mic, singing the lyrics, my guitar pick flying over the strings. In that place, there is no thought, no fear, nothing but rhythm and flow. Nothing but life.

I hit the high note in the song. Sound vibrates in my chest, throat. My guys are around me, supporting the song, elevating it to a new level. The Animal roars, cheering, a mass of bodies pulsing up and down. They're in it with us, feeding us love and energy.

And I'm home, back in that place where everything makes sense.

Until I look up, and I see her in the wings. Liberty. Watching me in my element. It's like I'm hit with an electric current. I sing for her, play for her.

Libby's eyes hold mine, a smile lingers on her lips. I can't help grinning back. Fucking hell, she's beautiful. I'm so happy to see her, it's all I can do not to walk off the stage and grab her.

We finish the song, and the Animal howls.

It wants more. Always more.

But we're done for now. Bowing, I toss my mic to a stage hand and jog off.

Whip gives a shout, twirling his sticks on his fingers.

"That's what I'm talking about."

The guys laugh and talk as they move on to the dressing room. Press waits, along with record execs and fan club members who won the meet-and-greet lottery. Someone hands me a bottle of water and a towel. I'm operating on auto, my body humming so hard my fingers shake.

Cold water goes down my burning throat. But I'm looking at Libby.

She hangs back with Brenna, about twenty feet from me, just inside the edge of the stage. The same push-pull I'm feeling is reflected in her eyes. The need for contact, the awareness that we can't do anything about it here because she won't let my guys know about us.

I resent the hell out of that. But she's here, and that overrides everything else.

And no one has noticed her. The only people left around us are the stage crew. Brenna gives me a wink and follows the guys backstage.

My entire body throbs, amped up and jittery. Holy hell, she's beautiful. Did I ever think of my Elly May as plain? Her skin is golden from endless summer days on the beach. Her hair, in shades of honey brown and pale blond, flows around her face like shining ribbons.

Then I notice her dress. And my brain skids to a halt. Fuck me sideways. My dick, who's already rising to his happy stance, jerks against my jeans.

The pale gray dress isn't short; it comes to her knees. It doesn't show cleavage, because it's one of those halter tops that exposes her arms but fastens around her neck. And yet it's fucking indecent. Because it's thin silk and shows the shape of her, clinging with loving care to the points of her perky tits. Everyone that looks at her knows exactly what she has to offer.

Mine. All mine.

I can't wait any longer. I stride toward her, loving the way she stands straighter, her pink lips parting, her eyes wide. I'm close enough to smell her scent, something warm and floral from her day at the spa. I lean down and give her a quick, impersonal kiss on the cheek, when I really want to claim her mouth.

"Killian." Her voice is breathless, happy. Eyes the color of blue-green frost shine up at me.

Emotion swamps me. It's like nothing I've felt before, both leaching me of strength and giving me a rush of pure lust.

My fingers tighten at my side. I want to touch her smooth skin, slide my hand underneath the edge of her top. "Come with me."

LIBBY
15

I don't know exactly what I expected when we finally came face to face. I'd purposely let myself get carried away by Brenna's exuberance when she dragged me all over the city so I wouldn't think of Killian. I lost track of the boutiques we visited, trying on endless outfits and buying so many things that I ended up closing my eyes as Killian's coveted black credit card swiped through machine after machine.

Now, my body is relaxed, my hair styled and highlighted, my brows plucked and shaped. I feel pampered and beautiful. And horny. Horribly, achingly horny.

Seeing Killian perform, his lean, muscular body glistening with sweat, his hands working his guitar with confidence, got to me. His voice, his energy, all that passion had me in utter thrall. I wasn't the only one. Everyone was under his spell, adoring him, wanting him.

And he is here with me, his eyes hot, his touch light on the small of my back as he guides me down a dark hall.

He pauses to grab a gray hoodie lying on a pair of old speakers and slips it on, covering his bare chest. I doubt the sweatshirt is his, as the word "Staff" is in bright yellow across the back of it. His brows waggle. "My master disguise."

Putting the hood over his head, he taps away at his phone before tucking it back in his pocket. Another glance my way, and he softly grins. "God, I missed you. I should have asked you to meet me at my place because it is fucking hard not touching you right now."

"Why didn't you?" My high-heel sandals clack on the concrete floors. I'm not used to wearing heels, but this dress doesn't work with anything else. Stupid dress. It's thin silk, and I'm braless. Every move I make sends the fabric dancing over my freshly rubbed and moisturized skin—agony because I can't help but think of Killian's hands, mouth, lips. I want them running over me instead.

At my side, he gives my shoulder a gentle nudge with his elbow. "Because I'm an arrogant bastard, and I wanted you to see me."

Those luscious eyelashes bat innocently, and his smile is cheeky.

"You were so pretty," I tell him truthfully but with a teasing tone.

He blushes. "Baby doll, you're tempting me to stop."

"No," I say, with exaggerated breathiness. "Don't stop, Killian. Don't stop."

I bite back a squeal as he suddenly spins, hooking me around the waist with his arm and tugging me behind a stack of crates. Our laughter mingles as he kisses me, quick, hot, playful, taking little nips of my lips. "Brat." His eyes are alight with happiness.

I steal my own kiss before pulling back. "Take me home, lawn bum."

Holding my hand in his, he jogs with me down the hall and into a back alley. A limo waits there.

"Michael." Killian tips his chin to the big, beefy man standing by the car. "You met Liberty today."

"I had the pleasure," Michael says, opening the back door for us. "Ms. Bell."

Michael had played the part of both chauffeur and

bodyguard for Brenna and me today. We hadn't talked much. Brenna assured me that was the norm, and shared her suspicions that Michael was actually a cyborg. Having read more than my fair share of sci-fi romance, I'd found myself wanting to agree.

Inside, the limo is cool and quiet, the windows darkly tinted to keep prying eyes out. A bucket is filled with ice-cold waters, and the privacy screen is up. I don't get to see much more, because the moment the door closes on us, Killian's hands cup my cheeks and his mouth is on mine. It's sweet relief.

I drink him in, kissing him back with a fervor that surprises me. I love his taste. I love the plush but firm feel of his lips. He breathes, and I take his air into me. Because I need that. I need to know he's alive and warm and right here. My lids prickle, the burn of tears threatening. I don't even know why.

"God," he groans, sucking on my bottom lip. "I needed to do that. You don't know how much I needed it."

"I'm pretty sure I do."

Somehow I've ended up sprawled across the seat with Killian half on top of me. He smells of clean sweat, his firm body damp and hot against mine. And when he moves, his hoodie clings to my arm. He glances down at himself and grimaces. "I should have showered."

"Babe, you are hot as fuck this way."

In the act of taking off the hoodies, he pauses. A shocked laugh bursts out of him. "'Babe?'"

"Yeah." I catch the cute little lobe of his ear and suckle it. "You're a total babe so…"

"I've never been anyone's babe. Kind of love being yours." Killian tosses the hoodie out of the way and kisses his way down my neck, pausing every now and then to touch each spot as if he needs to reassure himself that I'm really here. His warm breath gusts over my skin as he sighs into the hollow of my throat. "You smell edible."

"Pretty sure it's from being rubbed all over with oils."

I feel him smile against my neck. "You're giving me ideas, baby doll." A big warm hand runs up my calf and slides under my dress. "So soft. You have fun today, Libs?"

That hand moves higher, finding my butt like it's on a mission. I wiggle a little when he gives me a possessive squeeze. "Are you wearing a thong?" He goes to peek, lifting my skirt, but I swat his hand back down.

"Today was awesome. Thank you." Leaning back a little, I meet his heated gaze. "You haven't said anything about my makeover. Do you like it?"

Killian slowly blinks as if coming out of a daze. "You're beautiful. But you always are. I'd say something better, but... hell...I just see you."

Warmth floods my chest. "That's more than enough."

He hums a little, his gaze sliding over my face and wandering down. "Now, this dress..." The calloused tips of his fingers ease under the silky top and gently stroke my nipple. I catch my breath, molten heat pouring over me. "This dress," he murmurs, "is another story."

Back and forth he goes, caressing my breast, giving it a light squeeze, fondling my now-stiff nipple with a lazy sort of slowness. I can only bite my lip, close my eyes, and arch my back, trying to follow his touch, beg for more.

His other hand moves from under my skirt to reach around to the snap of my collar. One flick and the whisper soft silk slithers to my lap, leaving me exposed. My breasts tremble as the car bounces over a rut. My nipples stand stiff and swollen, waiting for him to give them attention.

Every inch of me tenses with a delicious tightness. No one can see through the glass. But the idea that someone might heightens my lust.

"Fuck, I've missed this sight," he rasps just before leaning down to suck a nipple into his mouth.

So good, the way he tugs at it—not too hard, but greedy, like he loves to torture me. I groan, my hands coming up to capture the back of his head and hold him.

"Damn it," he says, his lips teasing the aching tip. "Our first time is not going to be in the back of a limo."

I struggle to catch a breath. "Then why did you take my top down?"

"Couldn't resist. Needed to see the girls again." He kisses one nipple then the other, greeting them. "Ladies."

Between my legs, I'm swollen and tender. I shift my thighs and press into the hard lump of his cock where it's nudging me. "Tell me you have condoms."

The tip of his tongue runs down the small curve of my breast. "Are you kidding me? I've been walking around all day with a stack in my back pocket."

"Take one out and get in me." I wrap my legs around him and give him a glare. "Now."

"Ah, baby doll, I love how much you want it." He gives me a swift, deep kiss. "But I'm not caving. I'm gonna do you right. Naked and in my bed."

The evil tease. Thinking he's cute with that shit-eating grin, and looking so gorgeous I could cry. With a loud sigh, I lift one arm over my head, which brings my breasts up higher. His gaze follows the movement and grows slumberous.

"You asked if I was wearing a thong," I say, slowly parting my thighs. The action grabs his attention enough that he moves back to kneel on the limo floor before me. My skirt rides up. I reach down and ease it farther. Cool air kisses my skin. "I'm not."

An audible swallow, and then Killian's body does a full shudder as he grips the edges of the seat. "Fuck. Me."

"That's what I've been trying to do," I tell him as he stares like a man starved at my exposed sex.

"Oh, Libs," he says softly. "Look how wet you are. That pretty pussy all puffy and pouting for it." The tip of his finger slides along those swollen lips. "You hurting here?"

I shift my hips, heat licking up my thighs and pooling between my legs. "Yeah," I whisper.

He nods. "Yeah, you are." That finger runs back and forth, ghosting over my clit and sliding down to my opening. I moan, spreading my legs wider, and he nudges a rough fingertip in just enough to make me feel it. I rock my hips, trying to take him in. He has mercy and pushes that long finger into me. I moan in gratitude.

"I'm going to lose my mind when I fit myself in here," he murmurs in a dark voice. He doesn't touch any other part of me as he slowly fucks me with his finger. It only serves to draw all attention to the act. Another finger slips in, and he spreads them wide as he pumps. "You like that?"

I can't answer, only writhe and stare at the absorbed expression on his face. As if he feels my gaze, his eyes flick up. They gleam black in the dim interior. "Okay, baby doll," he tells me, "I'll make it better."

His free hand rips at the button of his jeans. And then his cock springs free. I haven't forgotten how big it is, but seeing it now, engorged and hugely erect, has my insides clenching in anticipation. Killian must feel my reaction because he makes a hungry sound and pushes another finger inside me.

I'm stretched wide, filled up. But I know his cock will feel like more.

He slips out of me and pulls a condom from his pocket. "Play with that clit while I do this."

My shaking fingers obey, sliding through my slickness. I want to be filled up so badly, my hips push restlessly against the seat as he rolls on the condom.

Killian's big palm rests on my hips, his fingers spread wide to hold on to me, his hot-coffee gaze rapt. "Now that's a pretty sight. Hold yourself open for me, baby."

I do as he asks. He makes a sound, low and guttural, almost a whimper but more needy, and all the muscles along his abs visibly clench. His free hand goes to his cock, giving it an idle stroke.

"Hell, I'm gonna have to get another taste of that." His breath is a warm sigh before his lips gently press to my swollen sex. It sends a jolt of heat through me. And when he hums his approvals against my pussy, I keen.

"Killian..." My hand cups the back of his head. I don't know if I want to push him away or shove him closer. He's slowly killing me, the way he peppers soft, lingering kisses between my legs, as if he's kissing my mouth. His tongue is lazy yet greedy, finding every hidden space and sensitive swell.

"Killian, please. Now." I tug his ear and he laughs—the fucker—sending more heat skittering between my thighs.

After a little goodbye flick to my clit with his tongue, he rises and takes a seat next to me. "Come here." His hands find my hips and he lifts me to straddle him.

Slouched back, he appears almost relaxed: rock and roll royalty lounging in his limo. But I don't miss the tension tightening the corners of his eyes, or the way his hand trembles slightly as he brushes a lock of hair back from my face. Between us, his cock lays like a steel bar against his defined abdomen. I want to wrap my hand around its girth and squeeze. I want to sink onto it and forget my name.

The man is so beautiful, his bold features stark, his eyes bright. My hands run over his smooth skin, hard muscles flexing at my touch. I trace a small, tight nipple, loving the way his nostrils flare in response.

Killian's rough fingertips trace my brow. "I want you so fucking much. Feels like I've always wanted you." He pulls me close, kisses my mouth. "It's taking all I have not to just plow into you, fuck the ever-loving hell out of you."

Our breaths hitch in unison, and I kiss him again, sucking his full lower lip. He groans a little, his hands bracketing my jaw. "We're taking it slow," he insists, and I half wonder if he's talking to me or to himself. "Slow. I don't want to hurt you."

The whole time he talks, he slowly rocks his hips, sliding his dick back and forth between my legs. He's so wide, my sex parts around him.

My breasts press against his chest as I lean forward and rise up on my knees. "Come into me, Killian."

"Fuck," he whispers, swallowing hard. His eyes hold mine as he reaches between us and guides the wide crown of his cock to my opening. I don't close my eyes, don't breathe, as I slowly sink down. The first breach pinches. I hold there as Killian pants, his fingers pressing into my jaw as if he's struggling to keep still.

The car goes over a bump, and he thrusts up into me. My breath hitches, my inner walls stretching and grasping. "Holy hell," I gasp.

"Babe." He kisses me, gently working his hips, easing his way farther in. All the time kissing me, like I'm his drug.

And I feel drunk on him, my senses swimming, my head heavy, and my body hot with pleasure. All I can think is that Killian is in me. He's part of me now. I feel him in the taut pull of my hips, deep in my body where the head of his cock pushes against some spot that lights me up.

I move with him now, meeting him thrust for thrust, our lips barely brushing, tongues almost idly touching. I take his air, and he takes mine.

"So good." He shivers, surging into me. "You feel so damn good. More. Give me more."

I grip his shoulders, bite his upper lip, lick it. Lust has made me feral.

His hands slide to my butt, gripping me there, and the tip of his finger toys with the entrance to my ass.

It's all too much. My forehead rests against his as I pant and ride him, claimed, owned. He has me.

My orgasm is a long roll, picking up speed and rushing over me with such force that I can only cling to him, cry out, and move against him in a messy, desperate way. I lose sight of everything but that feeling.

And then his arms are locked around me, crushing me to his chest as he thrusts into me hard, fast, frantic. I love the sounds of his cries, the way he groans like he's dying and somehow waking up all at once.

For a long moment, we lie limp—me against him, Killian against the seat. Deep within me, he still pulses, and my body squeezes him in response. Killian chokes out a weak laugh and snuggles me closer. His lips find my cheek; I'm too wrecked to turn my head and kiss him back.

"Holy hell, woman," he says against my damp skin. He lets out a shuddering breath. "Holy fucking hell."

"I know," I whisper. It's never been this way. And I know without doubt that Killian James isn't just an addiction, or a summer fling. He's becoming my everything. And that is both exhilarating and terrifying.

KILLIAN'S PLACE is about what I expected for a rock star who values his privacy. It's a penthouse in a converted church just south of Washington Square—a mix of sleek modern and old-world style with soaring ceilings, dark wood floors, glass walls, and massive stained-glass windows. The rooms are open and airy, a large terrace taking up the whole back. In his white kitchen, beneath a vaulted and beamed ceiling, he makes us *cubanos*, a sandwich of roasted pork, ham, swiss cheese, mustard, and dill pickles, grilled until it all gets hot and gooey.

"Why didn't I have you cooking for me before?" I muse before taking another huge bite.

He gives me a satisfied look around a mouthful of sandwich. "And miss out on your cooking? No way. I do make a mean *ropa vieja*, but that takes time."

"This is perfect."

We eat and drink icy beers. It's two in the morning, and everything is quiet and calm. His place is huge, but here with him, it feels cozy.

"Do your parents still live in New York?" I ask him.

"From October to December." Killian takes a swig of his beer. "Right now they're on their yacht, probably docked in Monaco or Ibiza depending on Mom's mood and Dad's business deals. If Mom wants to party, it's Ibiza. If Dad has a deal, it'll be Monaco."

"Wow. I mean, I've read about lifestyles like that but to actually live it..."

"My dad grew up with polo ponies. He went to Trinity at Cambridge. His 'chums' are royalty. It's his normal."

I can only stare at Killian. His shoulders are tight, his gaze distant. "It's your normal too."

He sets his beer down and meets my eyes. "I was always stuck between worlds. Staying with my *abuela*, traveling with my parents, the band. To be honest, Libs, I have no fucking idea what normal is. But I want it."

The intensity of his stare, the way his voice dips lower, makes me take his hand and squeeze it. I want to give him normal, but I don't know how. Not when I've left my normal behind to be with him.

I help him load the dishwasher when we're done. Though he had a quick shower before making dinner, he's still shirtless and wearing worn jeans that hang low on his slim hips. His bare feet are pale against the ebony floorboards.

I'm barefoot too, and, for some reason, that makes this feel more domestic. As if we both live here.

I tuck a strand of hair behind my neck as I put the last plate in place and catch him watching me. "What's that look?" I ask, because his expression isn't one I've seen before. It's light, and yet something is going on behind those dark eyes.

He shakes his head, biting his bottom lip. "Nothing. Just missed doing this with you."

"This" being the dishes. He always helped me with them when we were at my home. It became a ritual: Killian would watch me cook and keep me entertained with stories and anecdotes, we'd eat, then we'd clean up together.

"It feels right, you know?" he says, that soft smile still in his eyes.

Just like that, I need to hug him. I step close and wrap my arms around his waist. My lips press light kisses to his chest, because, really, I can't be this near and not kiss him.

Killian immediately melts into me, his arms coming up to squeeze me for a long moment, almost bruising but welcome. I want that strength. I want to feel as if nothing can come between us.

Long fingers comb through my hair, massaging my scalp. I snuggle in closer, my cheek pressed against him. The beat of his heart is steady and strong.

"When do we leave New York?" I ask.

His voice rumbles low in his chest. "Next week. We head north, then west."

My hands smooth along the valley of his back, where the flat slabs of muscle frame his spine. His skin is heated satin. "I need to find a place to stay."

The muscles beneath my palm bunch, and he pulls back. His dark brows lower on a frown. "You think I coaxed you all this way to send you off to a hotel? You're staying here, Libs."

Here is where I want to be. The idea of leaving him, even

for the night, makes my skin cold. "Won't…" I take a breath and forge on. "Won't the guys wonder why I'm at your place?"

That frown grows, but he shakes his head and gives me a quick kiss on the temple. "Nah. I have people stay here all the time. I invited you as my guest, so it would only be right."

"Right." I try to draw away but he won't let me.

Instead his lips slowly curl into a smile. "I like that you're jealous."

"Jealousy is not an admirable trait," I mutter, face flaming.

"Don't care." He rocks me ever so slightly. "Means you consider me yours."

He sounds way too smug. I give his side a poke, and he skitters away, giggling— which is *way* too cute—then cuddles me again.

"I might have had guests. But no one has ever stayed in my room, baby doll."

"Ever?" The question comes more like a snort.

That annoying smile of his grows. "If I hook up with someone, I take them to a hotel. Learned that lesson when pictures of my old apartment ended up on the Internet, and personal effects had a nasty habit of walking away without my permission."

"God, that's sleazy." I kiss his chest again. "I'm sorry they did that to you."

His fingers continue their massage along the back of my skull. "It should have been expected. They just wanted a piece of the fame or a souvenir. Like bragging rights."

He says it so matter-of-factly—as if it's no big deal to be treated like a thing instead of a person. He might not mind, but my stomach sours at the thought. But was I any better? Back home, I have a Univox Hi-Flier that was played and then subsequently smashed by Kurt Cobain; it's framed in a glass case in my upstairs office. Dad got it from some friend or another way back in 1989 before Cobain was a legend. A smashed and useless guitar, cherished because a rock idol played it.

I'd wanted to give it to Killian as a gift. But now I'm not so sure.

"So no," Killian goes on, unaware of my inner turmoil. "Only friends and fellow musicians get to stay here." He pauses. "And girlfriends. They get the full experience."

Warm to the core, I smile against his skin. "But you just said no one has stayed in your bed."

"No one has," he answers easily before his voice goes soft. "Until you."

Funny how some confessions can stop your heart and steal your breath, send everything spiraling. I close my eyes and hold him. He's never had a girlfriend? I wouldn't care if he had. Only here and now matter. But the idea that he's never let anyone else in sends the weight of responsibility settling heavy on my heart. I need to tread carefully here, keep him well and somehow find my place in this new world of his.

Killian slowly lets me go but holds my hand. His expression is tender, his eyes tired. "Let's go to bed." A quick smile. "I love saying that to you."

He's going to kill me. They'll find me lying on the floor, my heart burst wide open, too full of him to stay in my chest.

He guides me past a living area, a media room, and up a glass-and-steel staircase. We pass two more bedrooms and a reading nook, back-lit by another arched stained-glass window. His room is white, one wall taken up by a massive round stained-glass window. A king-size ebony wood canopy bed on a crimson rug dominates the space, though there's a sitting area with a black leather loveseat and a modern gas fireplace off to the side.

At his bedside, he helps me out of my dress with touches so tender, I'm in danger of bawling. My parents took care of me, of course. But this is different. I had boyfriends in high school, one in college. I've never felt *cared for,* as if I could do anything, say anything, and it wouldn't matter. I could fall apart, and Killian would be here to pick up the pieces and put me back together.

He kisses me on the shoulder and pulls back the cover so I can get into his luxurious bed. A second later, his jeans are off, and he's climbing in with me. The covers are cool and crisp, his pillows a cloud of perfection.

I smile wide. "You did buy my pillows."

He gathers me against him, warm skin to warm skin. Heaven. "Told you I was in love."

He says it lightly, but his dark eyes hold mine.

Everything feels both fragile and so much stronger now. I touch his cheek, trace a line along the shell of his ear before leaning in to kiss him. His hands cup my jaw and he kisses me back, lips tender, tongue delving in, tasting me as if I'm delicious.

The bed creaks as he rolls me over, settling between my spread thighs. The heat of his hardening cock presses against my belly. My hands explore the crests of his shoulders, the taut curves of his arms, and back up to his neck where his skin is baby-smooth and sensitive.

With a satisfied hum, he rocks his hips, that heavy cock sliding over my growing wetness. He kisses my top lip, the bottom one, angles his head and dips in for another taste. It's slow, drugging. I melt into the bed, my touches weak but hungry.

His scent. His skin. The powerful grace of his body. I need it all.

Killian is a magician. Somehow he's conjured a condom. Or maybe he had it all along. My mind is too hazy to remember. He leans to the side, exposing his flat abs and thick cock.

I take the condom from his hand and roll it over his length.

I go slow because the weight of his meaty cock in my hand is too good to ignore. He grunts as I squeeze him, give a little tug. And then he's settling back over me, his mouth hot on mine. Our kiss loses finesse.

"Libby," he whispers. And when he slowly sinks into me, that perfect intrusion of hot flesh, his eyes meet mine. "This is just the beginning," he says.

And I know he isn't talking about sex. He means our life.

My voice is breathless, tight with excitement. "I can't wait."

LIBBY
16

I ride to Whip's apartment with Killian. Michael drives as usual, and I learn that he's worked for Killian for five years. Today's car is a sleek silver Mercedes sedan with a cream leather interior that's butter soft beneath my roving palm. A palm that's damp. I'd rather the car turn around, but I have to face the rest of Kill John sooner or later.

"Why the limo yesterday?" I ask because I can't listen to my running thoughts any more.

Killian catches my hand and holds it in an easy clasp. If he feels how clammy I am, he's nice enough not to mention it. "It was your first time in New York, and you were having a *Pretty Woman* moment. That definitely calls for a limo."

"It would be smart not to mention *Pretty Woman* in that context," I tell him dryly.

His cheeks flush. "Shit. Right. You are a powerful, modern woman. If anything, I should be the prostitute here—"

"Not helping."

"Right. Right. No payment for sex of any kind." He lifts my hand and kisses my knuckles. "But lots of sex is still on the table. Hot, dirty, sweaty—"

I grab the back of his neck and haul him down to silence him with my mouth. He likes that, and practically climbs on top of me as he kisses me back.

Making out like teenagers in the backseat, this is what he does to me. We're both breathless when we pull apart. "If we keep this up," he murmurs, "I'm going to ask Michael to circle the block."

"No," I squeak out in horror. "He'd totally know what we were doing!"

He gives me a dry, slightly pained look. "I'm *sure* he had no clue what we were up to last night."

"Don't tell me that," I wail, covering my face. "God, I'll never be able to look him in the eye again."

Killian just laughs, pulls my hand away, and gives me a sweet kiss.

When we pull up, I keep my head down and mutter a quick "Thank you" to Michael as he holds the door for me.

Whip lives in a loft in Tribeca. According to Killian, half of it has been sound-proofed and converted into a stage and a small recording studio.

"Nothing too fancy," Killian had said as we got dressed to go. "Just convenient for when we want to mess around with new sounds or practice."

After Killian punches in a code, we take an old-fashioned service elevator to the top floor. It opens onto a light-filled space with worn wood floors and exposed brick walls.

I follow Killian farther into the loft on legs that feel like noodles, my pulse thrumming in my neck so hard I'm sure it's visible. When he stops short in the entrance and turns my way, I almost stumble into him.

Killian braces my shoulders, then ducks his head to meet my eyes. "Hey. Listen to me."

"I'm listening."

His dark eyes shine with emotion. "You are Liberty Bell. The woman whose guitar playing and voice brought me to my knees. You were born for music." His fingers squeeze just enough to hold my attention. "Nothing anyone says can take that away. You belong here."

My eyes smart. "Stop," I whisper. "You're going to make me cry."

His smile is tilted and brief. "Kick ass, Elly May."

A laugh bubbles in my chest. "Kick ass, lawn bum."

With a quick kiss to my forehead, Killian sets me back and walks on into the loft. "Yo!" he calls out, his voice echoing in the cavernous space. "Where's everyone at?"

We move past funky '50s modern furniture, a kitchen with navy cabinets and copper appliances, and through a pair of glass doors.

A group of guys stand around an open space with a small seating area and a low stage, set up with a drum kit and several guitars to the side.

They all turn when we enter, and I swear I'm about to stumble to my knees, I'm so nervous. Two of them are tall and lean like Killian—one with dark hair and blue eyes who looks like he could be related to Killian, and another with brown hair and green eyes. His expression is guarded, his body tense.

Another guy is built like a football player and has sandy hair and a big grin.

"Killian," says the big guy. "You brought a friend."

Killian's tone is easy. "Guys, meet Libby."

The one who looks a lot like Killian is Whip Dexter, the drummer. He shakes my hand in a bruising grip and gives me a friendly smile. "Heard your demo tape. You've got a great voice."

Blush. "Thanks."

The big guy, who is Rye Peterson, the bass player, nods in agreement. "I hear you play the guitar as well."

"Yep." I'm holding the case of my old Gibson, my palm so sweaty I'm in danger of dropping the damn thing.

"Glad to have you join us," Rye says. "It's gonna be fun, kid."

Kid. Okay. I can handle "kid."

Jax, the sullen one with brown hair, is the last to saunter over. All the guys are good looking. But Jax would be perfect in an Abercrombie and Fitch catalogue. He's got that all-American, pouty perfection about him. I suddenly remember that the press has called Jax a devil in an angel's body, and Killian an angel disguised as the devil.

I can see what they meant. Jax appears wholesome, polished—the kid you send to Harvard and he returns to run for office. Killian looks more like the guy waiting on his motorcycle down the street for your daughter to crawl out her window.

Personality wise, I know Killian is kind and honest. Apparently everyone else does too.

As for Jax?

He gives me a long look, and I'm clearly found wanting. "Liberty Bell, was it?"

"Pretty hard name to forget," I say, not liking his tone.

"True." He glances at Killian, and the ice in his gaze melts a little. "You ready?"

Like me, Killian is carrying his guitar. He sets the case down and rolls his shoulders. "Thought we'd show Libby how we do things, and then try a few songs with her first."

"Good plan," Whip says. "Show the newbie the ropes."

Jax's expression is a parody of confusion. And he makes his opinion perfectly clear. "We said we'd hear Liberty play, and then decide—not that she was automatically in."

A small shock ripples through me. At my side, Killian tenses. "No," he says patiently. "We agreed she was playing."

Whip frowns and glances from Jax to Killian and back again. "Man—"

"We always hold an audition," Jax snaps. "For every opening act. Always."

"She isn't an opening act," Killian shoots back through

gritted teeth. "She's playing with us."

"All the more reason she should fucking audition."

Rye holds up a massive hand. "Come on, now, assholes. I want to jam. Not listen—"

"Why are you afraid to let her do this?" Jax cuts in, not taking his eyes off Killian.

Killian's cheeks darken, and I know explosion is imminent. I step between them. "It's fine. I'm happy to try out."

A growl of protest sounds in Killian's throat, and I shoot him a look. "Seriously."

"Protective, are we?" Jax asks him.

"What do you want?" I ask Jax before Killian loses it.

Jax finally meets my eyes. I expect anger or dislike, but see none of that. If anything, his expression is perfectly polite, as if I truly was just another act trying to secure a place in their tour. But then it fades, and a glimmer of something—not hate, but something dark and unhappy—glints in his eyes.

"I heard you're a fan of grunge." He gives me a lazy, tilted smile that really isn't a smile at all. "Why don't you sing us 'Man in the Box'?"

The entire room seems to stutter to a halt. "Man in the Box" is a classic Alice in Chains song. Layne Staley owned that song with his intense, deep-throated growl, much the way Janis Joplin owned "Piece of My Heart" with her razor's-edge voice. To try to sing it is to risk looking like a total idiot.

Something everyone in the room clearly understands.

Killian slams his fist against his thigh. "What the fuck, Jax? Stop being such a dick and—"

"No," I cut in. "It's okay." I grab my guitar. If Jax wants to haze me, I'm not going to back down. "I'm good." I give Jax a level look. "Nice choice."

His gaze slides away as he crosses his arms over his chest. "Just get on with it."

"Dick," Whip mutters under his breath.

My hands shake a little as I walk up to the mic. Killian looks like he wants to take a swing at Jax, but he keeps his attention on me, and when our eyes meet, he gives me a small nod. I almost smile at his support, but neither one of us wants to give Jax ammunition.

Rye makes a noise of annoyance and moves to my side, picking up his bass.

"No helping her," Jax calls.

"Fuck you," Rye says blandly. "It's our band, J. Not yours. And I'm playing for Liberty."

I give him a small smile then move in close. "Let me get through the first refrain," I murmur. "I'll stop. Then we both start up."

Rye's hazel eyes brighten. "You got some ideas, don't you, sweets?"

"Yeah." I'll do the song my way, but I'm sure as shit not going to have Jax accuse me of punking out. Part of me wants to howl with laughter. It seems just yesterday, I was afraid to play in front of Killian. Now I'm going to sing in front of Kill John, and I'm not scared—much. I'm pissed.

Taking a cleansing breath, I start in on the opening lick. It isn't easy, and I haven't played this song. But I've heard it enough, and can feel my way through it. I don't go hard and fast like the original, but softer, slower, playing the opening riff over and over until I have the proper rhythm and feel. When I sing, it isn't with anger but with pain. I sing it my way, a lament.

I hear a noise of approval. I don't look. I don't look at anyone. My heart beats hard in my chest. I finish the first refrain of the song, then abruptly stop. Glancing at Rye, I nod, then my eyes meet Jax's.

I give him a big smile. He blinks.

And then I hit it hard, fairly screaming into the mic. Do I sound like Layne Staley? Not even close. But that isn't the point. The point is to act like I do. Fake it till you make it.

I see Killian begin to grin. Whip pops up and runs to his drums. He starts to play. Me, doing a song with Rye Peterson and Whip Dexter. Chills dance along my arms as I sing.

I close my eyes and lose myself to the music. My throat is raw, sweat running down my back.

Suddenly there's another guitar, the sound so strong and perfect, my eyes snap open. I expect to see Killian by my side, but it's Jax.

I stutter a lyric. And he gives me a look, a ghost of a smile twitching on his lips before it's gone. He sings backup, adding to the sound, making it better.

Killian jumps up and whoops, raising his fists.

We finish the set, and I'm left panting and feeling like I've swallowed razors.

Jax looks me over, his expression blasé as ever. "All right."

"That's it?" Rye says, giving my shoulder a hearty slap as Killian jogs over. "Naw, she killed it. Acknowledgment, Jax. Give it."

Jax snorts. "The point was to see if she'd try." He gives me a rare friendly look. "You did."

"You're still a dick," Killian says. A brief touch to the small of my back is all he gives me. It's more than enough right now, even if I want to turn and fling myself on him. His deep voice affects me as it always does. "She's in."

Jax nods, focusing on putting his guitar down. "Guess so."

A wave of dizziness threatens to topple me. Holy shit; I'm playing with Kill John. What the fuck am I doing?

LIBBY
17

Boston, Fenway Park. Full house. But don't worry, Killian told me earlier, it only seats about thirty-seven thousand people. *Only. Ha.*

Said people are now chanting something that sounds a lot like "Kill John." The floor beneath my knees vibrates with heavy bass as Not A Minion—the opening act—does their finale.

Where am I?

Crouched over a toilet, heaving my guts out.

I slump back, fairly disgusted that I'm on this nasty floor, but too weak to get up.

A faint knock sounds on the door.

"Go away. *Forever*," I add with emphasis.

But the door opens. Footsteps echo. A pair of worn, black boots appear on the opposite side of my stall. I would think it's Killian, but I know his stride. The man walks with a swagger, as if he's making room for that heavy, long dick he's packing in his pants. This walk is much cleaner, but just as confident.

However, the last person I expect to hear is Jax. "Do I need to throw you a life raft? Or is your head finally out of the toilet?"

"Har." I wipe my mouth and curse the gods that Jax, of all

people, has found me in such a low state.

Slowly, as if expecting another round of vomiting, he opens my stall door. I glare up at him, misery weighing me down. His expression, as usual, is placid. He hands me a frosty bottle of ginger ale. "Drink up, chuckles. You're on in twenty."

I take the proffered bottle with gratitude. The soda goes down cold and wonderfully refreshing.

"I want to die." I glance at him. "I don't even care if lobbing death jokes your way is in poor taste. That's how serious I am."

He laughs, short and dry. "I like you more for not curbing your jokes for me." He offers me a hand, and I take it, letting him pull me up.

I keep gulping the ginger ale as I make my way to the sink. Jesus. I look strung out—totally haggard and slightly green. Setting aside the soda, I wash my hands and pat cold water on my sweaty face. "So why are you here," I ask him. "You lose a bet? Draw straws?"

A soft snort echoes in the room. "I volunteered."

I stare at him in the mirror. "Well…that's new."

Jax's reflection shrugs. "The rest of them would just baby you. We don't have time for that."

Time. Right. My time is almost up. The sound of Not A Minion finishing up and the subsequent roar for Kill John is hard to ignore. The whole room hums with suppressed energy, as if a great beast is waiting to be let out of the gate. The Animal. That's what Killian calls the crowd. I understand that now. Too well.

Cold sweat breaks out along my back.

"I can't do it," I blurt out. "I'll barf on stage. I know it. I told Killian I was defective this way. Shit. Shit."

Jax leans a shoulder against the wall and watches me. After a moment, he pulls out a packet containing a tiny toothbrush and a little tube of toothpaste and hands it over. "You know why I have these things?"

"You've got magic wizard pants on? Is there a tent in that pocket too?"

"Not now," he says with a small smile, "but maybe later when a couple of eager female fans drop on my lap."

I wrinkle my nose. "Gah. I set myself up for that. Unclean!" I shove my new toothbrush in my mouth and brush with vigor.

He chuckles. "I have these things because I was just in the little boys' room doing the same."

I freeze. "You?" I squeak around the brush in my mouth, toothpaste foam bubbling on my bottom lip.

"Me," he says, frowning at my display. "Every freaking show."

I quickly rise and grab a paper towel to pat dry. "Seriously?" I mean, Jax Blackwood having stage fright?

He shakes his head as if I'm being ridiculous. "It happens to a lot of performers. Barbra Streisand quit doing live shows because she had it so bad."

"I have to pause here," I say. "You, Jax Blackwood, Mr. Too Cool Rocker, just referenced Barbra Streisand."

He pulls a face. "Smart ass. She's a legendary singer. Of course I know who she is." His lips twitch, but then he's calm again. "Would it be better if I'd said Adele? Because she's been known to puke beforehand too."

"Marginally," I grump.

He rolls his eyes. "If you go out there and hurl on stage, we'll talk. Until then, buck the fuck up, drink your soda, and be on cue. Got it?"

"No."

His eyes narrow to icy green slits. "Killian put his ass on the line for you. He believes in you, which means I have to too. Do not make him look the fool."

Of all the things Jax could have said to snap me out of my fear, that was it. I kind of hate him for finding my weak spot so easily. All I can do is salute, unable to resist sticking one finger up slightly higher than the others. "Got it."

"Good. Twenty minutes!"

Yep. I'm going to die.

KILLIAN

I LOVE PLAYING AT FENWAY. It's historic, filled with quirks. Legends have performed here, and it's imbued with the soul of baseball. Even though I'm standing under the burn of electric lights, I swear I can smell baseball—a faint aroma of hot dogs and beer, grass and sun. The stadium isn't huge, but it feels that way. Walls of fans rise almost straight up around us. The floor is a vast sea of writhing bodies. In the distance, I can just make out the baseball diamond, protected from fans by metal fencing.

My body vibrates as I finish singing and step back to take a drink of water. My hand shakes just a bit. I'm nervous. Not for me. For her.

Whip and Rye keep up the beat, doing a jam solo that will lead into the next song, "Outlier." It's Libby's first song with us.

I see her hovering in the wings, her face pale as death. My poor girl, torn up by stage fright. Jax offered to talk to her. Seeing as he's been a grumpy pain in the ass about her until now, I was more than happy to let him go. Maybe they can form a friendship. Something I'd love.

I catch her gaze and give her a slight nod and a smile. *You got this, baby doll.*

Like a good soldier, she straightens her spine, slips her

guitar strap over her head, and takes a visibly deep breath. God, but she glows with an inner light as she strides out on stage.

The Gibson L-1 open body practically dwarfs her small frame. She's wearing another silky sundress, this one white with big red poppies all over it. Chunky black boots grace her feet, just like the first time I met her.

Rye picks up a fiddle, and Jax switches out his Telecaster for a mandolin. Last week, we toyed with "Outlier" and "Broken Door," finessing the sound. Now it's perfect. John, who's in charge of all my equipment, hands me my Gretsch, and I walk to the mic.

"We're gonna do things a little different tonight. Get a little soulful."

The Animal howls its approval.

I grin into the mic. "And this lovely lady to my right," I say as Libby walks up to the mic next to mine, "is the talented Ms. Liberty Bell. Let's give her a proper welcome."

She trembles as the Animal screams, catcalls, and hollers, punctuating the night air. She doesn't look at me, doesn't do anything but stare out at the sea of humanity with wide eyes. And for a cold second, I fear for her. Have I pushed her too far? Have I fucked everything?

But then Jax starts picking on his mandolin, and Rye starts up on the violin: go time. Whip ticks out a one, two, three, and Liberty explodes into action, hitting her mark with perfect precision.

Her voice is clear and utterly beautiful. It breaks my heart and makes it swell all at once.

Jax sings backup. And then it's my turn to join in.

Libby and I harmonize. As she turns, the harsh stage lights set her aglow. She looks at me and smiles. Her joy is fucking incandescent. It sets me off, the surge of pure emotion stronger than anything I've ever felt on any stage.

Here is where she's meant to be.

The song ends too soon. My need to kiss her is so strong it hurts. A vibrating roar of approval surrounds us. She beams as she takes her bow and exits. I don't want her to go.

The rest of our show goes by in a blur until she returns for the last song. We'll do an encore later, but for now, we're ending with "In Deep." It's a love song with a sarcastic bent. Libby and I will play eighty percent of the song ourselves with the band coming in for the finale.

The second she's back by my side, my body tunes into hers. Looking more confident now, she plucks the opening tune—light, playful.

I don't face the crowd. I turn to her. I play and sing for her. And she sings back to me, her eyes shining bright. This. This is what it's supposed to be about.

We finish on a lingering note, and then Libby and I exit. The rest of the guys will play on for a few minutes. I need those minutes. I want to talk to her, find out if she feels as amped as I do.

But Libby apparently has other ideas. She doesn't look my way as she walks off stage, her pace so quick it's practically a jog. Her hair whips around her head as she wrenches off her guitar and thrusts it in John's waiting hand. I toss him my guitar as well, not slowing down. I'm so pumped, my heart races, my cock is a steel bar, bent painfully against my jeans. It wants out and in Libby.

But that's not going to happen now.

Past working crew, loitering execs, and God knows who else, she moves, never stopping, not making eye contact with anyone. I don't bother talking. She can't outrun me—my longer legs keep me in pace with her frantic strides—and eventually, she'll have to stop.

Right before she hits the ladies room, she announces in a loud voice, "I'm going to throw up."

Shit.

She storms into the restroom, and I follow—like hell am I going to leave her to deal with this alone again. The second I step through the doorway, I'm caught up in a tiny whirlwind of hot female flesh.

Libby slams into me, knocking me back against the door. Her mouth is on mine before I can take a breath. Hot and wet and demanding, she devours me.

My restraint shatters. On a groan, I kiss her back. It's a messy clash of lips, tongue, teeth. Fuck if my knees don't go weak. I slump down the wall, my hands grasping her plump ass. With an impatient, angry little sound, she climbs up my body, wrapping her legs around my waist.

Lust rages through me. I spin her round and her body thuds into the door. My hands are sliding up her thighs, pushing between us to get at her core. "Jesus," I grit out. She's fucking soaked, wet thighs, hot, swollen pussy.

Her underwear snaps in my hands.

Libby whimpers, thrusting her hips into mine. "Fuck." It's almost a sob. "Fuck... I'm...I need..." Another sob breaks free, and she sucks on my lower lip, licks my mouth.

"I know," I say, yanking at my jeans with clumsy hands. "I know."

I don't know how I manage to get a condom on. Blood rushes in my ears, and my heart is about to pound out of my chest. I'm in danger of coming. Our bodies, slick with sweat, slide against each other.

"Now, Killian. Now," she breathes into my mouth. Her body shudders. "Oh, fuck, I need you now."

"I got you."

One hard thrust, and I'm halfway inside heaven. She's hot as a furnace and so tight my eyes squeeze shut. Another thrust and she slides up the door with the force. Groaning, I grab her shoulders, pull her down onto me as I shove my dick all the way in. So fucking good.

Libby's panting hard, her head falling back with a thud as she wails. Her fingertips sink into the nape of my neck. "More." It's barely audible. But I hear it.

I pump into her, mindless and driven with the need to fuck. My balls slap against her ass. My head sinks down to rest on her shoulder as I brace my arms on the door and pin her to it with the force of my thrusts.

The instant she comes, her tight channel milking me, I lose it. An orgasm rips through me so hard everything goes white. I stay there, ass clenched, body bowed into hers, legs shaking for one long moment. And then I release on a sigh.

Exhausted, I press my cheek to hers, and she cups the back of my head.

"Fuck," I say, ragged.

She giggles, snorts, and turns her face into the crook of my neck. We both stand there, weakly laughing like loons, my dick still deep inside her.

The outside world returns too quickly, and I hear Jax's voice, amplified over the mic, saying, "Goodnight, Boston!" Time's up.

LIBBY
18

My little bedroom at the back of the tour bus is dark and cool, swaying slightly as we speed along toward Cleveland. Boneless and limp with exhaustion, I can only lie here and stare up at the ceiling. I'm too stirred up to sleep but can't seem to make myself move.

Every second of tonight plays like a movie in my head. The blinding light, the darkness beyond. The way the crowd moves like a living thing. And singing, playing my guitar. It had been...everything. The high of my life. Transcendent.

I had no idea.

And playing with Killian? That was pure joy. I could have laughed like a giddy kid riding a coaster. I want that feeling again and again. And I want that release of pure heat and lust that came afterward, Killian's thick cock driving in me, nailing me against the door. It was hard, fast, and everything I needed.

I want him now. But it isn't as if he can be in this room without raising questions. Hell, we were lucky to get away with screwing like jacked-up rabbits in the bathroom. He'd had to scramble, shoving his dick back in his pants and running out to meet the guys in their dressing room before doing two encores.

Now he's out in the main area of the bus, jamming with his

guys. It's three am, and they haven't slowed down. I can't blame them. Energy courses through my limbs and makes me twitchy.

"Fuck it." I wrench back the sheets and tug on my ratty sweats.

Music flows as I trudge down a narrow hall, flanked by four bunk spaces, and into the main sitting area. The guys stop playing as I enter. I probably look a sight with my overlarge Massive Attack concert tee and baggy pants.

"*Heligoland.*" Whip gestures to my shirt with his chin. "Fucking love that album."

I find space on the couch between him and the wall. Killian's dark eyes are on me, a smug, satisfied smile lingering there. I'd be annoyed, but my smug, satisfied lady bits refuse to be hypocritical.

"Can't sleep?" he asks me. His big hand is wrapped around the neck of his guitar, a gorgeous 1962 Gibson J-160E. John Lennon played that model. And now Killian James, capable of making that beautiful instrument sing, does too.

Those long fingers have played my body just as well. I press my knees together. "Too jittery."

"You'll get used to it," Rye says. He's holding a pair of maracas, which makes me smile. He smiles back. "You know, by staying up all night."

The guys laugh.

Jax peers at me. "Didn't hurl on stage."

"Yay me," I deadpan. "Thanks, by the way. You saved my bacon."

"Mainly, I saved the rest of us from having to smell your breath," he says with a shrug, but the corners of his eyes crinkle with humor. "I'll ask Jules to keep extra ginger ale and toothbrush kits in stock."

Jules is one of the assistants and is riding on another bus. So many buses. A bus for roadies. One for Brenna, Jules, wardrobe coordinators—that the guys have a wardrobe kind of made me snicker, but it's basically the shit job of doing their laundry—and press coordinators. One for the Not A Minion. And one for Scottie. Yes, he has his own bus. The guys, however, have always travelled together and stick with that tradition. And none of the other buses is as nice as ours with its black-and-cream leather interior, full kitchen, bath, and dozens of luxury perks—well, maybe Scottie's is too, but he won't let me in to check.

Killian hands me a bottled lemonade from the ice bucket at his side. There are also beers in it, but he knows me well. I take a long drink, refreshed by the sweet-tart flavor.

"So," Whips asks, tapping a quick beat on the small *djembe* drum he's holding. "How did it feel busting your rock concert cherry?"

I grin around my bottle and absolutely refuse to look at Killian. Memories of our bathroom visit are like handprints on my skin. "Once I got on stage, it was…perfection."

Whip laughs. "Yeah. It's something, isn't it? And you did good. Better than you think." His blue eyes crinkle with glee. "I remember our first big gig."

"Madison Square Garden," Rye puts in, chuckling.

"We'd done dozens of smaller clubs," Whip explains, "but finally we had hit our stride and were on a major tour. So there we were. Opening night. Jax is puking up a lung behind a set of speakers, sending roadies scattering like roaches in the light."

I laugh, and Jax shakes his head.

Whip continues with a big grin. "Rye's pacing back and forth, babbling about how he can't remember any of the music."

Killian flails his hands as if to mimic Rye, and his voice rises to a falsetto. "'What's the opening song?' 'What do we play after?' 'How do I fucking play my fucking bass?'"

Rye's cheeks pink. "Fuck, it's so true. I was a total blank."

"And you?" I ask Whip, because he's telling the story.

"Oh, I was a hot mess. Poked myself in the fucking eye with my stick."

"What?" I laugh.

"Seriously." His eyes gleam. "I don't even know how I did it. But the motherfucker was so swollen, I couldn't see out of it."

"Oh, God." I wipe my own eyes, now blurry with tears, then catch Killian's smiling gaze. "Where were you in all this?"

"Oh, Killian was right in the center of the storm," Whip says. "He just stands there, hands on hips, looking at us. And then yells…"

At once Jax, Rye, and Whip shout, "That's it, I want my mommy!"

Killian laughs, ducking his head.

The guys crack up.

"It was so fucking random," Rye says, practically choking. "We all stopped our shit and just gaped at him. Pulled us together in an instant."

Killian catches my eye, and I smile. Happiness and a tender, finer emotion swell in my chest. I adore this man. Everything about him. As if he reads this, his expressive eyes darken, and I feel his care, his need as clearly as if his arms were wrapped around me.

I blink and look away, not wanting the others to see what has to be clearly stamped on my face. "Well," I say, "I guess my vomit session wasn't so bad after all."

"You were golden, Libs," Killian tells me, his deep voice encouraging. "And it will only get easier."

"Says you," Jax retorts. But he turns his attention to the guitar in his hand and plucks out a familiar tune.

On cue, the guys follow suit and start to play The Beatles'

"Ob-La-Di, Ob-La-Da" with Killian and Jax harmonizing, Rye playing a small lap keyboard, and Whip beating on his *djembe*.

Whip nudges me with his elbow, and I join in singing.

We go like that all night, singing, playing, and trying to best each other with choosing obscure songs to perform. And the bus speeds down the endless dark highway. I have no idea where we are. But that's just geography. For the first time, I have some inkling of who I really am.

"LIKE SEX ON SUNDAY, sliding skin to skin," Killian growls to a crowd of sixty-thousand screaming fans, but his hot eyes are on me. "I'll sink into your grace, lick up your sweet sin."

Jesus. I was there when he wrote those lyrics, and it still makes me weak at the knees when he looks at me as though he's remembering every touch between us. Then he sings with his deep, raw voice, as if promising me more.

My words come out raspy, needy when I sing back, "You think you have me figured out. You think you want in, but that's not what love's about."

At my side, Rye bumps shoulders with me as we play, and Killian sings the refrain of "Broken Door." Stage lights turn everything into a white haze. Their heat caresses my skin. Energy flows through me on a wave, making the tiny hairs along my body stand on end. My nipples tighten, slick need swelling between my thighs.

If I hadn't already had sex with Killian, I'd think this was the most addictive thing in the world. Because, in this moment, I'm not Libby, the woman who has fears or doubts, who worries about where she's going in life or where she's been. In this moment, I'm just me, in my most basic version.

There is freedom in that. Joy.

It's the long crash down that sucks. Every time a concert ends, I'm disoriented, buzzing, and slightly dizzy. There's one thing that truly breaks the tension and brings me back to reality. Unfortunately, it's also the riskiest.

The risk doesn't stop me, though. Or Killian. We both need it too badly.

Minutes later, we're hidden in a storage closet that smells of Lysol, and I'm bent over a stack of old amps, Killian buried deep inside me. His big, rough hands cup my breasts as he thrusts hard and fast. Frantic, his hips meet my ass with a *slap, slap, slap*, the sound mixing with our muffled grunts.

The way he fills me, wide and thick, each thrust hits a spot within that I feel in my throat, in my toes. Cool heat ripples down my back, up my thighs. So good.

I push back, meeting halfway, needing the hard hit of him.

"Jesus," he grunts, his hips jerking. "That's it. Show me how much you fucking love this."

Faster, harder. It almost hurts. But it isn't enough.

We're too in tune for him not to notice my distress. He jerks a hand out from underneath my top, nearly tearing it. His fingers slide between my legs, find my clit. It doesn't take much. I'm so primed, my clit so swollen, that he merely has to tap it, give it a little flick like he's playing my body. And I go off.

I bite my lip, holding in my scream. He's in so deep, his cock so big, that I feel myself pulse around him. He feels it too, because he groans long and low, arching his hips into me as he comes. For a second, we're suspended there, straining against each other in search of our own pleasure. Then all that tension drains out in a mutual sigh.

Killian's body sprawls on top of mine, our panting in sync. Our fingers twine as we struggle to regain our breath. I come back to myself in stages, clarity of vision first, then the scent of our sweat mixing with cleaning supplies and must, the meaty girth of Killian's cock still lodged inside of me, and…

"There's a wet rag under my cheek." I wrench my head

away.

Killian peers over my shoulder and snorts. The sound of it sets me off, and we both start laughing. Well, I'm laughing and also a bit disgusted, because my face was in a dirty rag.

"You were on the rag," Killian snickers, his chest shaking against my back.

"Ugh, that was bad. Just bad. The worst joke ever." Still, I'm laughing. Part of it is the release, but most of it is as simple as the fact that Killian makes me happy.

He eases me to standing, his arms warping around my shoulders, his cock slipping out of me. "I have more where that came from."

"No doubt." I rest my head in the crook of his arm.

His breath is warm as he kisses my temple and gives me a squeeze, then steps back to tuck himself into his jeans. I don't know where he put the condom, but I'd rather keep that mystery and focus on the lean wall of his chest. Absently, I trace a line on his tattoo. "We better get back. This was crazy. Someone is going to notice."

"Naw," he says with a wink. "They're all off doing the same."

"They are? How do you know?"

"The need to fuck after a show is pretty common. It's what we all do. You know, find a willing..." His words end on a strangled cough, and he scratches the back of his neck, his cheeks flushing.

"Right. Of course." My fingers fumble with my top, smoothing out the rumpled lines from where his hands invaded.

Killian steps close, his hands clasping my upper arms. "Hey, stop."

I glance at him. "What?"

The corners of his eyes crease in agitation. "I shouldn't have brought that shit up. I did those things in my past. My present is all you."

"Believe me," I manage to get out, "I have no interest in thinking about your past. I know it has nothing to do with us."

He frowns, his gaze darting over my face. "Then why are you upset? And I can tell when you are, so don't deny it."

Killian, the mind reader. I roll my eyes, trying to shake him off. He won't let me go.

"I'm not jealous." Much. Okay, I hate thinking about him with other women. Sue me. "It's just...is that what we're doing? Using each other to get off?"

"No," he says calmly. "I'm making sweet, sweet love to you. In a supply closet." His dark eyes glint. "On a rag."

"You just had to get that in there, didn't you?" I sigh and push a hunk of my hair back from my face. "You know what? It's stupid. I'm the one who practically mauls you every time we end a set."

"I like it when you maul me." Killian waggles his brows.

Despite my mood, I snicker before sobering. "I just... It suddenly felt a little seedy when you said that. As if you'd be doing this regardless." Would I too? No, I can't imagine having sex with anyone else.

Killian's expression goes serious as he cups my cheeks. He doesn't say anything as he kisses me, no tongue, just his lips mapping mine with tender care. When he pulls back his gaze is intent. "We are never seedy. Dirty, kinky, hot, sweet, okay. But never seedy. And if I didn't have you tonight, I'd go jerk off somewhere."

"Lovely."

"I'm all class, babe." He gives me a happy smile and a kiss on the cheek. Then, checking to see if the hall is clear, he glances back at me. "I'll go first this time. The guys think you have an after-show vomiting problem, so we'll just go with that."

"Great. I'm known as Betty Barf. "

Killian laughs softly at my expression, then kisses me again. "*My* Betty Barf."

The second he's gone, my smile fades. I can't shake my unease. My attachment to Killian, my need for him, is in danger of consuming me. When I'm with him, it's as real as anything I've ever had. But if we weren't in each other's pockets, would it last?

KILLIAN
19

Anyone who tells you it's easy to go on tour is lying. Performing is basically your reward for constant travel, no sleep, fighting exhaustion, and making nice with endless people who view you as something not quite human. Idolized, adored, isolated. Worst of all are the long nights on a damn tiny bus where I can't crawl into bed with Libby. It makes me…twitchy.

I'm not sure I even like this dependence on another person. But, like any addict, I'm not looking to break the habit. If anything, I crave more.

Thank God for Chicago and two nights at a proper hotel—and the suite with an adjoining door to Libby's that Brenna booked me.

Unlike other tours, we're keeping the partying to a minimum. We have tonight off and have taken over the hotel's private movie theater. It's fairly small, about fifty seats, with a small lounge just outside.

While the staff loads up the movie, we hang out in the lounge and have drinks.

"I'm going to ask Libby out on a date," Whip announces, casual as fuck.

The beer I'm holding almost slips out of my hand before I clutch it tight. "What? Why?"

"What do you mean 'why'? She's hot in that girl-next-farm-over kind of way." He flicks his tongue against his teeth. I want to punch those teeth in.

"Lots of hot women on the road," Rye says, his attention half on a group of women he gave passes to last show. They're now walking into the lounge. One or all of them will get lucky tonight.

"Pick one of them," I say to Whip, trying to calm down. Honest to God. Because I'm having a hard time not launching myself at my friend.

Whip scowls. "I told you chuckleheads, I want a girl I know. No more groupies. And Libby is fun."

Fun. Yeah. I know exactly how fun Libby is, and I don't share. The thought of stomping my foot like a two year old and shouting "Mine!" runs through my head. That would go over well.

Jax gives Whip a long look. "We don't fuck the staff."

"Libby is not staff," I snap. Though why I point that out now, I don't know. *Stupid.* Let Whip think that if it means he'll back off.

"We pay her a lot of money to perform with us," Jax says in a bored tone. "So I'd say that makes her staff."

"She's an equal," Whip retorts. "Which makes it even better."

"And when shit goes south?" Jax asks. "What then? You're stuck with someone who hates you, and it brings us all down."

Whip rubs the back of his neck. "That would be awkward."

Thank fucking God. I might not have to kill him after all.

"Worse if she turns you down," Rye adds. "Then you have to face her knowing…" He trails off when Brenna bursts into the room with a loud laugh, stumbling on her sky-high heels. She's arm in arm with Jesse, one of our sound techs.

Whatever Jesse's telling her must be hilarious, because she's snorting and burrowing her face in his neck while his hand travels down to grab her ass.

At my side, Rye growls like a feral dog. The rest of us exchange a look. Here we go.

Brenna gives Jesse's ass a squeeze back before she heads to the bar, her hips moving in an exaggerated sway. Rye jerks to his feet, his eyes tracking her.

"Man," I say. "Don't do whatever it is you're thinking."

He either doesn't hear me or doesn't want to. Rye brushes off Whip's attempt to grab his wrist and stalks off. Heading for trouble.

"Should we stop him?" Whip asks.

"Too late for that," Jax mutters. "Years too late."

Rye's already in Jesse's face, his voice loud enough to carry over the din. "Man, we did not hire you to fuck around with our publicist."

"Are you kidding me?" Brenna all but screeches as she rushes over, getting in between Rye and Jesse. "You did not just say that."

"I'm pretty sure I just did," Rye snaps. "Seriously, Bren, have some self-respect."

Oh. Shit.

"You have some fucking nerve, *Ryland*. Can't keep your dick in your pants for five minutes, and you're lecturing me?"

"Yeah, well, I'm not the one in charge of PR." He's red in the face now too. "You set the example, honey."

"Don't you 'honey' me, asshat." She pokes his chest. "Or go around acting like some jealous—"

"Jealous? More like disgusted."

I push to my feet as Brenna goes bright red.

"You mother—"

"All right," I cut in. "Why don't we take it somewhere else?" I nod to the very interested crowd forming. Someone giggles, a few people duck their heads. But most stare.

Brenna blanches, her gaze darting around before zeroing in

on Rye, who doesn't appear to be bothered at all. "You are an asshole," she hisses beneath her breath.

It's the lowest she's kept her voice the whole time, but the force of her anger is enough to make Rye flinch. He opens his mouth like he's going to reply, but Brenna turns away from him, grabbing a mute Jesse by the hand and stalking off.

Jesse glances back, clearly fearful for his job.

I wave him off as Rye snorts.

"Little wuss didn't even stand up for her," Rye mutters.

He brushes past us, stealing a beer out of some guy's hand as he goes. The door slams on his way out.

"That right there." Jax shakes his head in disgust. "That's why you don't fuck with your *crew*."

LIBBY

"I BET they're doing it within the week," one woman says to another as they drink martinis and watch Brenna and Rye stomp off in different directions.

The other woman snorts. "They're probably already doing it. And can you blame her?" She sucks at her teeth. "Rye is hot as hell."

"Mmm...all those massive muscles."

"Personally, I'd rather do Killian. Tight and lean, with those sinful eyes. And that walk of his. You know he's loaded for bear."

"I have no idea what that means," her friend says with a laugh.

But I do. I turn away before I have to hear more speculation over Killian's equipment. Or the women who clearly want a chance to find out how big it actually is.

After-parties are a fact of touring life I never really

considered. Frankly, I think they blow. Oh, meeting true fans is fun. They practically vibrate with joy when they finally face one of the guys. It's cute. At least, those types of fans are. Then there are the groupies. Women whose job, it seems, is to put another notch on their proverbial bed posts. I shouldn't hate on them, and I try really hard not to. But watching them hang on Killian like he's a steak thrown into a pack of lionesses isn't easy.

And they will do anything—*anything*—to get attention. I've seen more tits in these past weeks than in the whole of my life. Tops coming off at the oddest times. Like, oh, hey, the music started? Let me rip off my top and shake what my mama gave me. Or my plastic surgeon. Same difference.

Doesn't matter if it's a room full of journalists, record execs, roadies, and other hangers on. In fact, that somehow appears to make a strip show more thrilling for them.

Killian doesn't encourage them. If anything, he always shoots me a pained look that says, "See what our hiding is making me do?" I love him for it. And hate myself a little more each time.

Oddly, Whip is also shying away from women. I'd wonder if he didn't fancy them, but his eyes always stay glued to the displays of female flesh as if he's hypnotized. Jax appears as apathetic about women as he is about everything. Oh, he goes off with a few, but the enthusiasm isn't there.

Rye is the only one who seems to enjoy it. At least he did until he blew up at Brenna. Now that they're gone, it's business as usual: overly loud and fake laughter, people looking around to see who's looking at them.

"Always something to talk about," says a female voice at my side as I lean against the bar and sip my drink. A pretty blonde who'd look right at home in a Southern sorority gives me a pleasant smile. "Or write about, as the case may be."

A press badge on her chest identifies her as Z. Smith.

Protective of both Rye and Brenna, I give the woman a quelling look. "Must be a slow day if a little argument is something to write about."

She shrugs, her gaze drifting over the room. "Depends on who's arguing." Her sharp blue eyes settle back on me. "I'm Zelda, by the way."

I take her offered hand. "I love that name."

"I hate it," she says with a nose wrinkle. "But it's mine, so what can I do? You're Liberty Bell."

"Which makes me an expert on oddball names," I say with a laugh.

"I don't envy the jokes you must have heard when you were younger."

Though she's simply chatting with me, I don't relax. Brenna and her assistant, Jules, have drilled into me the importance of watching your tongue with the press. They can take anything you say and twist it.

"The best response," I tell her lightly, "is to just yawn in the face of idiocy."

"I'll remember that." Her expression becomes a bit sharper. "So what do you think of being on tour? This is your first public experience, correct?"

Here we go. Interview time. "It's a learning curve, but I'm enjoying it. The guys have been very supportive."

"Killian James brought you in, right?"

"Yep."

"I heard some story that you were neighbors this summer."

Probably because that's what Brenna put in my press statement.

"That's right."

"Lucky you." Zelda nudges my shoulder with hers as if we're old friends. "Out of all the guys, there's something about Killian. He's delicious in that bad boy, charm-your-panties-off kind of way."

"I try not to think of the guys that way," I tell her, lying through my teeth, because her description is on point. "I have to work with them."

"Are you telling me you aren't fucking him?"

Her blunt question comes at me like a punch, and I recoil. "Excuse me?"

Zelda gives me a smile that's all teeth. "Sorry. I'm pretty blunt with my words after all these years in this business. But honestly? Killian James is infamous for being irresistible. And there are the facts. First you're neighbors, and then he's bringing you, a complete novice, on tour with him."

My heart thuds against my ribs. It's not like I should be shocked; she's saying everything I've warned Killian about. Almost verbatim. Expected observation or not, the humiliation I feel at being looked upon as nothing more than Killian's whore, is nearly crippling.

And then I get angry—at myself for predicting this, at her for thinking the same thing.

I give her a long look, watching her fight not to squirm. "You're kind of young to be a reporter assigned to Kill John."

"What are you talking about? I'm twenty-six, which is probably older than most of these groupies."

"Yeah, but they're here for one thing. Are you too? Because most of the other reporters I've met are men in their thirties, at the very least."

Zelda's eyes narrow. "It's a tough business."

"And a girl's got to use whatever assets she can to rise, is that it? Is that how you got here, Ms. Smith?"

"Oh, I get it. Shaming me, are you? It was a valid question, you know. You're linked with James. No one has ever heard of you before now. I have to wonder—"

"If I fucked my way in? Of course you do. Because that's what everyone wonders about attractive, successful women, don't they? Did we get here on talent or by spreading our legs? If I was a man, would you ask the same?"

"Killian hasn't been known to like men."

"And that's the reason you didn't ask."

Her mouth purses. "Point taken."

"Here's an exclusive for you, as honestly as I can put it." I lean close. "Killian had to talk me into doing this. Because I told him people would make ugly assumptions about him bringing an unknown on tour with Kill John. But if you truly do know anything about him, you'll know that he is stubborn as the day is long. And that for Killian, his love of music and what works for his band trumps any threat of stupid rumors."

"You're quite loyal to him, aren't you?"

"Of course I am. He gave me a chance few others would dare. Every member of Kill John did." I feed her the standard press line with a placid smile on my face. "Which is why it's a joy to work with them and contribute in any way I can." I stand and smooth my skirt. "Have a nice night. I hope you enjoy the movie."

She doesn't say anything but follows my progress with her beady eyes as I head for the movie theater. And I pretend that my insides aren't shaking from the cracks in my pride.

KILLIAN
20

One good thing about being a rock star? Diva moments are not only expected, they're never questioned. For once, I take full advantage of that as I enter the theater and make my way to the back row to claim a spot. My immense scowl wards off anyone who thinks of joining me.

I'm scrolling through my phone when someone plops down in the seat next to me. Whatever send-off I'd planned to say dies with I see it's Libby. She's carrying a big bag of caramel corn and a bottle of water.

"Libs," I say in greeting.

"I can't believe we're going to see *The Force Awakens*. I missed it when it first came out."

"My little hermit. When was the last time you actually saw a movie in a theater?"

She stuffs a handful of caramel corn in her mouth before muttering, "Shut up."

I help myself to some caramel corn...definitely better than movie quality. "You can thank Scottie for tonight's pick. He's a massive Star Wars geek."

"No," she breathes, scandalized. "That's so..."

"Human? Yeah, I was surprised too." I love Scottie. He's my rock in this business. But the dude is twenty-eight going on eighty. Half the time I expect him to wave a cane and shout at us to get off his lawn.

He's staked a claim in the middle of the middle row and, like me, is giving anyone who approaches a death glare.

Libby tucks her water bottle into the snack holder at her side.

"Can you believe this place?" With big eyes, she glances around at the fiber optic art on the walls and the massive crystal chandeliers, and at the rows of double seats that are basically meant for two. Her hands smooth over the wide leather armrest at her side. "I mean, reclining loveseats? Shut the front door." With a little "Whoop!" she hits the button that lifts our shared footrest.

My lips twitch.

"Calm down, Elly May." I mean it as a joke, but my voice doesn't quite get there.

Libby stops her gawking and narrows her eyes. "Why do you look all pissy?"

I give her an affronted look before leaning in a little to whisper under my breath. "Whip was considering asking you out on a date."

Pissy? Yeah, I'm pissy all right. What I don't expect is Libby's flush of pleasure.

"Isn't that sweet," she says, pleased as fucking punch.

"Sweet?" I hiss. "You like the idea?"

The corner of her mouth turns down. She pokes my side, and I barely manage to hold in my yelp.

"Stop thinking with your dick," she whispers.

Sadly, my dick isn't the one doing the thinking. It's the organ a little farther north, which is now pounding with agitation. I cross my arms over my chest and slump in the seat. Not exactly mature, but this is where she's led me.

Libby's pleased expression doesn't fade but grows. "It's just nice to be liked, you know? It means he accepts me being here. Besides," she says, looking out over the room as people finish taking their seats. "I don't think he was serious, anyway."

"I'm pretty sure he was." *The fucker.*

"Then why is he over there sticking his tongue down that reporter's throat?"

My head snaps up, and I'm greeted by the sweet sight of Whip making out with the pretty blonde who's been trying to get interviews all night. Okay, it's not a sweet sight, and I quickly avert my eyes. But my relief is palpable.

"You know," I say conversationally, as I kick back, "I want to fuck you right now."

Libby jerks as if she's been pinched and sits a little straighter, before getting a hold of herself and slouching as if she's completely chill. Cute.

She gives me a smirk and sips her water. "And what?" she drawls. "Mark your territory? Assert your manly dominance?"

"Yep." I slide my gaze to hers. "But mostly I just want to fuck you all the time."

God, I love the way her lips part as her body flushes with heat. So subtle, but there all the same. It makes me hard as steel, my balls squeezing tight. I don't look at her but pretend I'm observing the room. The lights are lowering for the movie now, the empty chairs in front of us obscuring our lower halves.

My hand falls to the space between us and smooths along her hip. She delicately shivers as my fingers trace her thigh.

"What about you?" I murmur, toying with her skirt in the darkening room. "You want to fuck me, baby doll?"

"Right now I want to kick you," she gets out between clenched teeth. "Keep your hands to yourself. There are nosy-ass people everywhere."

"They're all watching the movie, not us." Focusing on the screen, I keep my expression neutral as I ease my hand under her skirt. Her skin is smooth and warm. The movie starts in a blast of music and the familiar old logo as I trace over her knee and up her soft thigh. "And that wasn't a no."

She makes a cute growl in the back of her throat, but her legs part just enough to give me room to delve between them. Her inner thighs are hot and damp, and my cock twitches.

The storyline rolls along; my touch roams. Libby remains utterly still, but I can practically feel the tension vibrating within her. When the tip of my finger skims the crease where her thigh meets her hip, her breath catches, legs parting wider.

"Have I mentioned how much I appreciate this new skirt-filled wardrobe?" I whisper, drawing circles along her skin.

"Brenna's idea." Her hips shift just a bit, following my touch. "Right now I'm missing my shorts."

I smile, my eyes on the screen, my fingers drifting to the edge of her panties. "Later, you can put them on and we'll play Fuck the Farmer's Daughter."

She stifles a laugh, which turns to a strangled whimper when I pluck her panties. Her voice goes breathy. "I'm trying to watch the damn movie. I'm not interested in fooling around." She moves a tiny fraction, nudging against my finger.

In the dark, I grin, heat and lust pulling my abs tight. "I'm sorry," I say, not sorry at all. "But I don't believe you. I'm gonna have to check."

"Killi—oh, hell."

I'm thinking the same as my finger slides over slick, swollen skin. And it makes me feel like a fucking god. Because I did that to her. I'm the one who gets her this wet. The one she needs. I'm the one she's panting for right now, moving against my touch with a tiny whimper.

I'll make it better. It's my job now. My privilege. And I'll be damned if anyone tries to take that away.

LIBBY

I REALLY SHOULD STOP KILLIAN. We're playing with fire, fooling around in so many public places. A reporter just implied that I whored myself to him. And here he is fingering me in a movie theater.

I should protest, but the man is a damn musician; he plays my body like a master, never missing a beat. I can't resist that. I don't want to, not when each sure, sly touch sends heat and pleasure shimmering over my skin. Not when I can almost feel him holding in a grin, his shoulder pressed against mine, his eyes on the screen as he oh-so-gently circles my clit.

He plunges a finger into me, and it's all I can do not to moan and part my thighs wide, ride his hand. I struggle to keep still, keep my eyes on the fire fight playing out in some distant galaxy.

God, he's too good. Every time he pushes in, his finger crooks, hitting a spot that has me biting my lip. I can feel myself getting wetter, my flesh plumping. Beneath the sound effects and music of the movie, I can hear the sounds of him working me—wet and deep, slow and steady torture.

My head falls back against the seat, my breath coming in sharp bursts. Above the waist, I'm still, my hand only shaking a bit as I take a bite of caramel corn, pretending all is normal. But below, my thighs part wider—the simple act illicit and ratcheting up the tension in me—my hips make small movements, pushing each thrust of his finger in deeper.

Another whimper escapes me. Killian leans in, his lips close to my ear. "Shh…I'm trying to watch the movie."

The rat bastard gives my clit a flick with the tip of his thumb. I twitch, and he plunges two fingers in deep. My lids flutter, my heart pounding. I'm going to kill him. Soon.

"Mmm…" he says, his thumb continuing to fondle me. "I

love this part. Such a sweet movie."

My breaths are coming fast and light. Heat swarms my body. The fact that someone might see, that we could get caught, intensifies everything.

Maybe I should be ashamed of that, but I can't be. Not when an orgasm is stealing over me, creeping like a hot hand over my thighs, down my back, along my breasts.

It catches and holds, taking my breath. I stiffen against the seat, practically vibrating.

Killian's deep voice, barely a whisper in the dark, is at my ear. "This one is mine. Give me what's mine, baby doll." Teeth nip my lobe, his fingers pushing up into that spot. "Come."

And I do. All shuddering, repressed breaths, body shaking, my thighs squeezing against his hand. I come so hard I see stars behind my closed eyes. As I sag into the soft seat, he leaves me with a last, lingering caress—a gentle tap as if rewarding me for a job well done.

I should kick him for that. But I can't move. He's destroyed me.

"Jerk," I whisper without heat.

His shoulder nudges mine. "You can take your revenge later."

I glance at him then, only when I can finally meet his gaze without showing how much he affects me. His dark eyes glitter in the flickering light. When I try my best to reprimand him with a look, he grins wide. Impossible to resist. I don't know why I even try.

Taking a quick glance around to see if anyone is watching, I lean in and give the hard swell of Killian's biceps a soft kiss. His muscles twitch in surprise, but then he sighs, his long body slouching down in the seat.

His hand finds mine in the darkness between us. In a low voice only for me, he speaks one last time. "Baby doll, I *could* assert my manly dominance, thump my chest, and declare you're mine. But it wouldn't mean a damn thing if I'm not yours in return."

KILLIAN
21

My mood is mellow now. Getting Libby off will do that for me. I take my time heading out when the movie's over. Eventually I'll meet her in the suite. She'll draw us a bath, insisting that we have a nice, hot soak to end the day. She always does. Libby is a creature of habit, and I find that oddly soothing. Whatever craziness life throws my way, I want her there, calm and steady.

Scottie is standing by the exit door, arms crossed, feet planted. His expression is granite. In other words, he's ticked. Why he's glaring at me instead of Brenna and Rye, or even Whip and that reporter, I don't know.

"What's up?" I ask. "Someone talk during the movie? Or are you still pissed Han died?"

His eyes narrow. "Some things we don't joke about, Killian."

Right. Brenna had told me she was almost one-hundred-percent sure Scottie cried when they first went to see the movie. I didn't know the man could produce tears.

"Maybe it was a fake-out," I tell him. "You know, he's really hanging on some scaffolding, waiting for Billy Dee to pick him up... Right. No more talking about Han."

Scottie grunts and walks with me out to the lobby. It's fairly empty now, hangers on and crew having gone off to the next party.

"You're not as circumspect as you'd like to believe," he tells me.

Confused, I glance at him. He glares right back.

"Eventually people will notice you and Ms. Bell getting cozy."

My steps slow. "Say what you're going to say, Scottie."

He stops and faces me. "You saw what happened with Rye and Brenna tonight."

"Everyone saw. Your point?" My mellow is heading toward pissed off.

"The longer you draw this out, the worse it will be when people learn the truth." He sets his hands low on his hips. Lecture stance. "There's a saying: Shit or get off the pot."

"That's classy for you, Scottie."

"You two want to be together, make it known. Brenna and I will find a way to deal with it."

"We're not a problem for you to deal with," I snap, keeping my voice low.

"You are. And if you can't see that, you're being deliberately blind."

For a second, I have to look away.

Scottie takes the moment to go in for the kill. "I want her, Killian."

I reel back as if punched in the gut, and he rolls his eyes.

"To manage, you git." For the first time, humor lights his expression.

I take a bit longer to calm. "Jesus, say it another way then. I already had to deal with Whip tonight, for fuck's sake."

"I've never seen you so territorial." He's quietly laughing at me. Ass.

"Get used to it." I run my hand over my tight neck. I definitely need a soak now. "Seriously, though? You want to take Libby under your wing?" I know what that means. It's something anyone who knows anything about the industry dreams of. Scottie is a legend.

He started off with us, convincing four eighteen-year-old punks to take a chance on him, never mind he was basically our age with absolutely no true experience at the time. We took that gamble and never looked back. As for Scottie, he's picked up a select number of other clients along the way, all of them going platinum.

The man is a business and marketing genius with a killer instinct. If he says someone has It, the music industry listens.

"You were right to ask her on the tour," he says. "She is exceptional. Brenna tells me she's getting an increasing number of interview requests for Liberty, fan mail by the dozens. We haven't said anything to her because we don't want to overwhelm her at the moment."

"Good plan." Because Libby would freak. And not in a good way. "But why are you talking to me and not her?"

"I plan to discuss this with her. Perhaps suggest we start once the tour is over." His eyes narrow as he studies my face. "I want to know how you'll take it."

And then I remember how it was in the beginning. I didn't own a second of my life. She does this, and our time together will whittle down to nothing. Absently, I rub my abs, where my stomach squeezes in protest. Really not feeling mellow anymore.

"I don't know how Libby will handle going full tilt," I tell Scottie. "Or if she'll even want to. But I won't stand in her way." I'd never do that, even if it means that, one day, she's gone.

LIBBY

SCOTTIE MAKES ME NERVOUS. I can admit that. I'm not attracted to him, but I won't deny his effect. The combination of his stunning looks, hard eyes, and crisp voice acts like an avalanche on the nerves. You're pinned in place, and even if you look away, he's trapped you with his voice.

So when he approaches me during the sound check at the stadium, I tense, keeping my eyes on Killian singing as long as I can.

A low chuckle washes over me. "Avoiding eye contact won't make me go away, Ms. Bell."

Bracing myself, I turn. "Prolonging the inevitable is a thing with me, I guess."

He's not smiling—he rarely does. But his eyes are soft—well, for him. "Intelligent move. I want to discuss something with you. Have you a moment?" He inclines his dark head toward the right wing row of seats, just far enough away that we can hear each other while Kill John runs through an older song.

I'd rather stay here and not discuss anything. But I nod and lead the way.

He waits until I'm seated to fold himself into a nearby seat. And then he looks me over as if inspecting a bug. "You are not backup material."

Instantly I tense, steel coming into my spine. "Seriously? Is this some fucking cliché shakedown? Because we can skip to the end right now where I tell you to fuck your mother."

"Colorful," Scottie murmurs, looking amused. "No, Ms. Bell, this is not a shakedown." He peers at me. "You do have a vivid imagination, however. And I now see why you're so compatible with Killian. Same descriptive vocabulary." He leans in, resting his hands on his knees. "You are a headliner, Ms. Bell. Front and center stage."

"I...ah... What?"

He keeps his tone even and patient, as if he's talking to a

distracted child. "Your sound, the quality of your voice, is unique. More importantly, when you get on stage, you are compelling. I want to represent you, Ms. Bell. Develop you."

My ears ring faintly. "Hold on. First, please stop calling me Ms. Bell. It reminds me of being sent to the principal's office."

"Fair enough." His expression says I'm insane.

"Second. I'm...well, I'm not an entertainer. I came for Killian."

I glance in Killian's direction, and our gazes clash. Even now, he's aware of where I am. His dark eyes crinkle, as if he's trying to encourage me, even as he sings and plays his guitar. I break eye contact and face Scottie again.

"I'm not a star."

Scottie's brows draw together. "There are many things you are not, Ms.—Liberty. But you *are* star material. More importantly, when you get on a stage, you come alive." He gestures toward the band with his chin. "Just as they do. Tell me you do not feel that."

"I do." My insides being to tremble. "I love it, but..."

"The worst thing you can do in life is ignore an opportunity out of fear."

"I'm not afraid."

His dry expression makes a mockery out of that statement. I cringe. "Okay, a little. It's just... I do love it. But the rest? The public side? No, thanks."

Scottie sits back, resting his ankle on his bent knee in that way men have of crossing their legs. "I am afraid to fly," he tells me.

"Okay..."

"Utterly and completely," he continues, his body stiff. "Every time I get on one of those death contraptions called a jet, I want to vomit."

"But you fly all the time."

"My job demands that I do." Another brow quirk. "You

understand my meaning?"

My head feels heavy as I nod.

Maybe Scottie notices that I'm on the verge of panic, because his voice goes soft as Kill John ends their set and the music stops.

"Killian believes in you."

I refuse to look in Killian's direction again.

"He brought you here, put you on that stage, because he believes," Scottie murmurs.

A shuddery breath leaves me.

"You had to know this," Scottie says.

"Yes." I knew. But I'd never allowed myself to think too deeply on what was behind all his support. Had he pushed Scottie on me too?

As if reading my mind, Scottie makes a noise of disagreement. "No one in this group does something against their will. Including me." He leans in, forcing me to meet his eyes. His expression is hard, serious. "I have little interest in managing a reluctant singer. You have to be all-in or you will fail."

"Then why approach me at all? When you knew I'd be reluctant?"

"There's a difference between snapping out of a fear and being unwilling to do a thing at all. I wanted to discover which scenario I was dealing with."

"And now you know?"

Scottie gives me one of his quick, tight smiles. "Only you can tell me that. I've merely opened the door for contemplation." He rises, crisp and fresh as ever in his perfect three-piece suit. "You know where to find me when you have an answer."

KILLIAN
22

"Where the hell are you going?"

Jax's question stops me short. So close to the exit, and yet so far. I turn and adopt what I hope is a bland expression. "To bed. Catch a nap."

Yeah, that goes about as well as expected. The guys look at me as if I'd just said I wanted one of them to put a diaper on me. Once they get over their horror, the questions start flying.

"Bed? There had better be a woman waiting in that bed."

"More like three," Whip adds. "It's freaking four o'clock. You don't go up to bed at four for anything other than three women."

"Is that a new rule?" I deadpan.

"It ought to be," Rye retorts, disgust still riding high on his face.

"Seriously, Kills?" Jax shakes his head. "Are we old men now?"

I can't tell them the truth. That I do have a woman waiting for me. Or that Libby is better than three women, better than any amount of women. So I have to stand here looking like a killjoy and a dick. "I'm just tired." Lame. Lame. Lame.

"Fucking lame, man." Rye shakes his head.

I keep my mouth shut.

"Next thing you'll be telling us you have a headache,"

Whip says, his nose wrinkling like he's scenting something ripe.

"Now that you mention it," I start with a forced grin.

They all roll their eyes and groan. Jax tosses a water bottle at my head. I catch it mid-air.

"Take some aspirin and buck up," he says, chucking a small pill bottle next.

I catch that too and clutch it in my hand. Fucking hell. I'm stuck. We have a rare night off. After we wrapped up our run-through and initial sound check, Libby went upstairs, saying she was taking some time for herself. None of the guys questioned that. Why should they? She's entitled to some personal space.

I am not given the same leeway. No, they want to hang out, go to a bar and check out the local scene—which means women. Ordinarily, I'd be down with spending time with the guys. They're my best friends; we've been apart for nearly a year. But having to push off advances from women without the guys figuring out why? Not easy. And not fun.

Neither is continuing to pretend that Libby is just my friend. I can't touch her the way I want to, which is pretty much all the time and all over. I practically have to sit on my hands to keep from reaching for her. Makes me damn grumpy.

Worse? Libby has been sliding me looks all day. And they were not sexy, when-are-you-going-to-be-inside-of-me-again looks. She's thinking things. Never a good sign when it's accompanied by frowns.

Scottie talked to her earlier, so it's a pretty good bet that's what it's about. But I can't figure if she's mad or not. And I want to know. Now. When she cut out on the evening early, it wasn't like I could say, "Oh, hey, I'm leaving with Libby too." I'm stuck biding my time.

I might have channeled my inner toddler and fucking pouted were it not for the fact that the guys would wonder about that too. Fuck it.

Frustration claws its way up my throat, and I blurt out the one thing I know will make them back off, even if it humiliates me in the process. "I have the shits, all right?"

Three sets of shocked faces stare back at me.

"Now can I go, or is there anything else you wanted?"

Rye clears his throat. "Dude, just go. I mean, take care of you and all that."

"Grab some Pepto or something," Whip adds helpfully.

"Didn't you just use that bathroom?" Jax darts a glare toward the bathroom in question. "You better not have befouled it—"

I ping the water bottle back at him. "Shut the hell up."

I'm never living this down. I'll be Senõr Shitpants for the whole tour. But it sets me free. "I'll meet up with you later," I tell them as I head for the door.

"Not if you're still Crappy McGee," Rye calls out.

"Maybe we'd better have Jules order a box of Depends just in case."

Yep. The whole tour.

When I finally let myself into her room, I'm tense, irritable, and ready to climb the damn walls.

Libby is in the bedroom and calls out a faint "hey" as I set the keycard down on the console and toe off my shoes. My insides are still jumpy, but I can't ignore the simple fact that walking into a space that contains Liberty is like stepping into a hot shower after a long show. My muscles release. I can breathe. I feel like myself again.

Her disembodied voice comes from the bedroom. "You know what sucks?"

"When cable networks decided to split TV seasons in half?" I peel my shirt off and toss it aside, heading her way. "I mean, what is that shit? Don't make us pay just because you have a slow-as-fuck production schedule."

"Don't really watch TV."

Halting in the doorway, I press a hand to my heart with a pained groan. "That's it; we can't be together anymore. And what the hell are you doing?"

Liberty stands on her tiptoes at the top of the bed, her sweet ass peeking out from under the edge of one of my T-shirts while she tries to reach something on the ceiling. "What I wouldn't give for a broom. I'm trying to get this moth—"

My yelp effectively cuts her off. I scramble back to the edge of the door. "Moth? Where is the fucking moth!"

Libby turns, her mouth hanging open. "What on Earth?"

A cold sweat breaks out over my skin as I eye the tiny hell devil fluttering around the pot light over the bed. Jesus, did I miss that? It makes a move my way, and I shout, jumping farther back. "Kill it, woman! Kill. It!"

Libby sputters out a laugh then does a double-take when I fall onto the arm chair. "You're serious."

I don't take my eyes of Mothra. "Are you going to kill it, or am I calling security?"

Snickering, she picks up a pillow.

Horror arcs through my gut. "Not the pillow—" She smashes it into the moth. And I shudder. "Damn it, I'm not using that pillow. Ever again."

"We'll wash the case."

"Not good enough. Put the pillow in the hall."

Libby gives me a side-long look as she grabs a tissue and cleans up the little moth carcass. Or I think that's what she's doing. I can't watch.

"Is it gone?"

Libby's warm thighs slide over mine, and her weight settles on me. Even though I'm still creeped out by the moth previously hanging out above my bed—just fucking waiting to get me when I slept—my hands immediately seek her, smoothing over her soft skin and grabbing hold of her ass.

God, I love her ass, plump yet toned. I could squeeze it all day.

She makes a little throaty noise, her arms coming up to wrap around my neck, and heat flares up my thighs. I tug her closer, wanting her over my dick. She doesn't resist, but she's definitely distracted.

"What's with the moths?" she asks, placing a soft kiss at the corner of my eye.

It's weird to shiver with both the pleasure of her kiss and revulsion for the moth. As good as she feels, an intruder moth has the power to send me running. I grimace and concentrate on her scent, her warm skin. "I hate them."

Libby makes a soft sound. "I got that. Why?" Her fingers trace patterns through my shorn hair.

"It's stupid." I kiss my way up her neck. "I was nine. At summer camp. A moth flew in my ear, started fluttering around..." A full-body shudder threatens to dislodge Libby from my lap, and I squeeze her tight, pressing my face into her hair. "Let's not talk about it."

She chuckles, her hands roaming over my shoulders, my nape. "Poor Killian. Don't worry; you're safe now."

I grunt, nudging her with my hips. "I'm not convinced. Kiss it and make it better, Libs."

I can almost feel her smile. "Where does it hurt, baby?"

"The tip of my dick."

Libby hums, rocking against said dick. "Hmm... So a moth crawled up your—"

With a yell, I leap up, sending her butt to the floor, where she cracks up as I jump away. I glare as my chest lifts and falls. "You are fucking evil. *Evil.*"

I try not to notice that her shirt is around her waist and her legs are spread wide as she lays there laughing her ass off. Libby wipes her eyes. "You walked right into that one."

No, I won't smile. Growling like I mean it, I swoop down and haul her up. She squeals as I throw her over my shoulder and toss her onto the bed, landing on top of her before she can get away. Caging her between my arms, I frown down at her. She just smiles and laughs.

"You're supposed to be repentant," I say.

She responds by craning her neck and kissing the tip of my nose. "Okay."

I settle more comfortably between her legs. "Don't give me that cute smile." My lips brush her cheek. "I'm mad at you."

"Uh-huh." Her hands find my neck, her fingers digging into the tense muscles there. She snickers again.

"Keep laughing," I say. "See where that gets you."

"Did you know you can laugh yourself to death?"

"What? Fuck, don't tell me that." I kiss the crook of her neck, lingering there. "I'll end up living in fear that one of us will die laughing."

My hands bracket her delicate jaw, and I kiss her again, just to feel the shape of her smile. Libby melts beneath me, her lips opening. But I'm not the one doing the taking. She kisses me like I'm her favorite flavor.

Her lips curve against mine. Another smile. I'd have all of them if I could. This is why going out no longer means anything. If the guys had this, they'd get it.

"Don't worry," she says, playing with the short ends of my hair. "I'll protect you."

"Protect me from laughing? I don't see how since you're the one who usually makes me laugh."

"Whenever you're in danger of losing your breath with laughter…" She suckles my earlobe, brining me in close, her voice a soft tickle on my skin. "I'll mention moths."

I yelp, a jolt of ear-to-moth-induced terror lighting through me. Libby tosses her head back, cackling. I launch myself on top of her, my fingers finding her sensitive spots. "You evil pixie. Cruel, evil…"

Words dissolve. I'm done for with this girl. I sink against

her with a sigh, careful not to crush her, but letting her feel my weight. My eyes close as I wrap myself around her. "I missed you today."

My voice is muffled in her hair but she goes still, clearly hearing me.

"I was right there with you," she says in a low voice.

"Were you?" My back tenses, and I remember her earlier distance, the coldness of being shut out. "Felt like you were somewhere else."

She tenses too, her body squirming. I don't let her go. She'll run, and I hate that.

"Killian, let me breathe."

"Breathing's overrated," I mutter but roll off her.

Libby sits and swings her feet over the side of the bed, giving me her back. Fuck it. I'm not letting her hide. I push up and sit next to her.

"Scottie talked to me today," she says, staring at the floor.

"I saw." I'd been waiting for her to tell me. For any word. Instead I'd gotten silence.

An exasperated sound tears from her throat. "You could have warned me."

"Yeah, I could have." I run a hand along the back of my neck. "I didn't want to."

She turns toward me so fast, her hair slaps my shoulder. "Are you fucking kidding me?"

I snort, holding her glare. "So you could run from it? Talk yourself out of things before you heard what he had to say? No, Libs, I'm not kidding."

"You don't know that—"

"I do. I know you. Whether you want to admit that or not." I lean closer. "I. Know. You."

I hear her teeth clack. "If you know me so well," she grinds out, "you should know I don't want or need you to plot my life."

"And if you knew me at all, you'd never accuse me of that." I lurch to my feet and pace away, my face going hot. "Shit. I mean, you seriously think that's what I did?"

She crosses her arms over her chest. "You just admitted to talking to him!"

"Talking, Libs. That's all. Jesus." I clamp my hands to the back of my aching head. "He asked my opinion. I gave it. Don't turn this into some wild conspiracy."

Libby stands, her fists balling at her sides. "Are you telling me you didn't bring me here thinking this would happen? That you didn't, for one second, think about Scottie trying to make me something I'm not?"

"You think I'm going to deny that the second I played with you I knew you'd be great on a stage? I'm not." I laugh without humor. "And you shouldn't either."

She blows out a breath. "I'm not a star."

Something in me softens, and I take a step closer. "You're already halfway there. You just don't see it yet."

Panic flares in her eyes, and she backs up, her lips parting as the struggles to breathe. "I want this."

The crazy thing? I'm the one who lights up inside. Her successes have become mine. "Babe, you'll have it."

But she shakes her head as if I'm not getting it. "A few months ago, I was living by the sea. The only people I talked to were Mrs. Nellwood and old George at the gas station."

"And did you like it?"

"I hated it," she hisses, her eyes going glassy. "You took me out of that. I never dreamed this life would happen. But it's here. And now..." A furious blush stains her cheeks. God, my girl has pride by the boatload. But her confidence has been kicked hard. Libby brushes back a lock of her hair and lifts her chin like she's squaring off for a hit. "You agree with Scottie that I should do something that will take me away."

The implication hits me like a brick. My heart squeezes in

my chest. She's so fucking wrong. How can she be so right for me and so wrong about herself? I close the gap between us and draw her into my arms. She struggles, trying to break free as I "shhh" her under my breath and rub her arms.

"It's not about sending you away, baby doll. It's about setting you free."

Her back stiffens. "Free? I'm sorry, but that's just semantics, Killian."

"No way," I say against her cheek, still holding fast. "You want the truth? When Scottie told me he was going to ask to represent you, a part of me hated the idea." My fingers grip her silky hair. "A big part of me. Because I want you here. With me. Always."

She sucks in a breath, like she's going to respond, probably tear into me. So I kiss her, soft, searching, then hard and a little desperate. We're both panting when I pull away. My chest hurts, and when I rest my forehead against hers, I'm suddenly so weary I have to close my eyes.

"But that's selfish, Libby. And I can't do that to you. Never to you. Because you deserve that chance, even if it pulls you away from me for a time. So I told him to go for it."

"Killian." She sighs and rubs her hands along my chest, almost as if it soothes her more than me. "Not everyone has your confidence. Some of us need to feel our way around a little."

My lips press against her forehead, and I breathe her in before speaking. "Babe, if I've learned anything about opportunity, it's that you make it happen. Fear will only hold you back. You can have the world. Just reach for it."

"I don't need the world," she whispers.

"What do you need?" I ask just as softly.

Her hands slide up to my neck, her lips nuzzling my jaw. "You."

I swear my knees go weak. I have to lock it up, suck in a

breath. I hug her tight, unwilling to let go even to find her mouth. Not yet. "Fuck, Libby." I snuggle her closer. "We need to stop hiding. I fucking hate it."

I feel her tense and cup her cheeks. Her eyes are wide and panicked. It pisses me off and makes me want to cuddle her, protect her from the world. Only I'm the source of her pain. Which is a kick in the gut. It turns my voice raw. "You want me, but you want to hide us?"

"When you put it that way, you make it sound petty."

"Well, excuse me for stating the facts." Irritation crawls up my spine.

She flinches, her fingers wrapping around my wrists. She holds me there. "Words are simple, Killian. Real life is a bit more messy."

"Bullshit. Why are you resisting this? Because I gotta tell you, it hurts."

"Jax is just starting to respect me."

"Jax can go fuck himself," I snap, then sigh. "Baby doll, you have his respect. It's not going to go because we're together."

"You sure of that?" She doesn't sound remotely convinced.

I open my mouth to answer, but it gets lodged in my throat. Because who the fuck knows with Jax anymore? Libby's eyes narrow.

"You can't even deny it," she points out.

"Look, maybe I don't know exactly how he'll react."

"And the reporter who asked me if I was fucking you?"

"What?" A lick of anger flicks against my neck. "Who the fuck asked you that?"

"A reporter in Chicago. She asked me flat out if I was fucking you. She wondered why else I—'a nobody'—would be on tour with you."

"All right, what's this chick's name, because I'm not having that shit." In fact, I'm rethinking having any fucking reporters at our after parties. Not if they're going to harass Libby.

"It doesn't matter," she says in a weary voice.

"Of course it does—"

"No, Killian. It doesn't. Not if that's what they're all thinking. Getting them fired or cussing them out will only fan the flames."

"Shit." I pace in front of her, grasping the back of my neck. "It's a bunch of bullshit, you know. Anyone who hears you knows you're talented. Scottie wouldn't want you as a client if you weren't. Trust me on that one."

"I do." Libby approaches, eyes wide and pained. Her palm rests on my chest a second before she wraps her arms around my waist, and because I can't stand not touching her, I hug her close. She nips at my neck then sighs. "I hate it, you know. You think it's easy for me to hide how I feel?" She laughs but it doesn't sound happy. "God, it's the worst kind of torture. Even worse than back when we first meet and I was trying to keep my cool and not jump your hot bones."

My eyes close again, and I rest my cheek on her head. "That so?"

"Mmm-hmmm... Because now, I know what I'm missing." Her fingers steal under my shirt and stroke. "You are the best part of my day, Killian."

My throat locks up with embarrassing swiftness, and I hold her tighter.

Delicate fingers run along my back. "Nothing would make me happier than being able to claim you in public. But that joy would be blackened if, in return, we have to deal with ugly speculation."

I think about how I would have reacted if I'd heard the reporter ask Libby those questions. I would have lost my shit. I know it. And the knowledge sinks like a stone in my gut. Gone are the days of wild, out-of-control rocker behavior. You cause a scene, you're gonna pay. Record label lawyers breathing down your neck about breach of contract and behavior clauses, press replaying your actions in slow motion over and over. It isn't pretty.

One of the absolute worst parts of Jax's suicide attempt were the clips of him being wheeled into an ambulance, which played on a seemingly endless loop, along with the smug-as-fuck reporters discussing why he did it and whether he'd ever recover his career. Was it the band's fault, or was he was just trying to get attention?

Turning away from the life was the only recourse any of us had to maintain our sanity and dignity.

I take a heavy breath and let it out slow. "Okay, we don't have to make it public yet. But the guys? They can keep secrets. Hell, we're trained to close ranks. No one will know shit unless we let them. And I'm tired of hiding this from my friends. I'm tired of lying. It isn't exactly admirable, either."

She lets me go and runs her hand through her hair. "I know. But the guys won't look at me the same way."

"I disagree. But, hell, it shouldn't matter what they think."

She snorts, her lips twisting. "No, it shouldn't. But it does. And I've yet to come across anyone who truly doesn't care what the people they work with think about them."

"I don't."

"Yes, you do." She rests a hand on my chest. "You have more confidence than any one man has a right to, but you want your friends' good opinions. You wanted it for me. Otherwise, you wouldn't have done all that you did to smooth my way."

Pressure tightens against my ribs, and I grunt. "Okay, fine. I want them to like you. I want us to get along. But—"

"Right now it's just us in our own private little bubble. Everything changes when we tell them, for better or worse. If we could just wait..." She bites her lip. "Please, Killian? Please, just a little longer?"

My chest tightens even more. Sure, she has a point, but when will that ever change? And if she doesn't want this now, when will she? I swallow hard against the lump in my throat. "I hate this. All day I wanted to touch you. It's not even sex, Lib. I have to fight the impulse to hold your damn hand. I'm cut off at the balls."

Her mouth quirks, but it only fuels my anger.

"I can't do this much longer." The words hang there, sounding harder than I intended.

"Do what?" she asks, her face paling.

I stare at her, realizing I could give an ultimatum. I could force the issue. I'm not used to feeling helpless or hurt. Fuck. I take a breath past the ache in my ribs. "You've had a lot heaped on you today. I'm taking a shower." I back away from her, heading toward the bathroom. "Figure out your shit, Libby. I'll be here when you do."

LIBBY

I'VE HURT HIM. I know this. I knew it when I asked Killian to keep our relationship quiet, and when I asked him to continue doing it. I hate hurting him. But I see what he either can't or refuses to acknowledge. The world isn't black and white. And the band isn't all right. They're walking wounded right now. The love between them is clear. They're brothers. But Jax leveled a blow they're still reeling from. And the idea of adding more drama, more uncertainty makes me feel ill.

At first, it was pride that had motivated me to keep my relationship with Killian a secret. But now it's something more. I care about these guys, as individuals and as a group. I don't want to get between them when they're obviously still fragile.

I tell myself all of this. But it doesn't help when we climb into a limo and head out for the night. The guys want to relax, let off some steam by going to clubs. I should have stayed in, but when Whip called to ask, the look on Killian's face—as if he expected I'd keep away from him—hurt too.

So here I am, crammed in between Whip and Rye, who are trading jokes over my head: most of them about Killian's supposed intestinal distress. Putting the pieces together, it sounds as if Killian made an excuse to return to me at the expense of his pride. I feel even lower.

Not that Killian appears bothered by their teasing. He sits across the way, his long body lounging against the seat, his thighs spread wide as if he means to take up as much space as possible. As we drive along, the lights of the city slip in and out of the darkened car, illuminating his face, then throwing it into shadow.

He doesn't say much, only stares out of the window and occasionally snorts at a shit joke. But then, as if he feels my stare, he glances my way. Our gazes clash, and it's as if someone's pulled a rug from under my feet. My insides swoop, heat prickles over my skin. And on the heels of that comes a rush of emotion, squeezing at my heart, catching me by the throat.

It's always this way. He looks at me, I fall. I have an awful feeling it will be this way my entire life. Killian James wakes me up, makes me whole.

I want to tell him this, to put my hand in his and ask that he never let go. But he glances off, leaning over to say something to Jax. I can't hear what—my heart is thundering in my ears.

The car halts, the door opens. I'm ushered out to follow the flow of the guys into a club. We head up to a VIP section at the top of a massive circular steel staircase. People watch as we go.

Gazes crawl over my skin. For years the guys have lived

this way. I don't know how they manage. Perhaps they love it. They're all smiling, clasping hands with people they know, pausing to hear someone whisper in their ears.

Killian is ahead of me, walking with Jax. They're practically mobbed by women, until just their heads are visible above the swarm. I set my jaw and follow. This is part of Killian's life. There isn't a thing I can say here because, in the world's eyes, I'm just his friend. This hasn't bothered me before now. It felt more like a secret we shared between us. Women could hover, but they'd never go home with him.

Now it just hurts. Because it suddenly seems as though I'm glimpsing a future where I'm not there. I can't even pinpoint why I feel this way. Only that Killian and I have been moving along at full-tilt and the slightest knock might push us off course. Or maybe it's because I know that Killian doesn't need me as much as I need him. Why would he? He has the world. And I am completely out of my element when it comes to this life.

"I need a pity party cocktail," I say in Brenna's ear as she comes alongside me.

Her gold eye shadow glints in the light. "Extra strength?"

"And fruity," I add. "Pity cocktails should always be fruity."

She grabs my elbow and leads me to a somewhat quiet little booth in the far corner of the room before she goes off to get us drinks. There are times when the band requests a small room just for them. This is not one of those nights. People flow in and out—mostly in—like cattle through a gate. The music isn't as loud in here, but it's enough that conversation isn't going to be on the agenda. Whip is already standing on one of the tables, dancing with a brunette in a tiny silver dress.

I regret not putting on a little dress as well. In a sea of itty-bitty dresses, I'm the conservative one in black skinny jeans, heeled boots, and a green silk camisole. I'm comfortable, but I don't feel sexy. There are times when a girl needs sexy. That's the thing no one ever tells you. Sexy can be both a weapon and a wall of defense.

The booth I'm sitting in wiggles as Rye plops down next to me. He drapes an arm along the back of my shoulders and leans in. "What's shakin', bacon?"

My lips pull in a reluctant smile. "Nothin', stuffin'."

He takes a sip of what appears to be a gin and tonic—because of course he's already been served. There's probably a waitress on standby for him. "You look like you've swallowed a goat."

"A goat?" I laugh. "How the hell does that look?"

"Faintly ill and fighting a gag."

"You really know how to make a girl feel good about herself, Rye."

He sticks the tip of his tongue between his teeth in a lewd gesture, but then his expression turns gentle. "I'm serious, Buttercup. You all right?"

"Buttercup?"

"Yeah, you kind of look like Princess Buttercup."

"That's about as far a stretch as saying you look like the Dread Pirate Roberts."

"I could totally rock a mask. It'd be kinky as fuck." He takes another sip, his eyes roaming before coming back to me. "So, what's going on? Someone being mean to you?"

"What? No. It's nothing."

"You sure? Because I don't have these massive biceps just for show. I'll gladly put on the hurt for you."

"You're sweet. But it's really nothing. This is just not my scene."

"It's no one's scene. You have to own it to make it yours."

"Well, I'm not interested."

A glance across the room and find Killian's familiar form. He has two women clinging to his arms, though he doesn't seem to notice them as he talks to John, one of our sound engineers. The blonde on his left clearly doesn't like being ignored and begins to stroke his chest. My own chest tightens, and I look away.

"Right there," Rye points to my face. "Goat look."

"Argh, would you stop using goat? I'm going to develop a complex." My laugh feels forced. "I'm fine."

"Here we are," Brenna announces brightly as she sets down two martini glasses, filled with lime green liquid. "One fruity, pity-party cocktail—industrial strength."

Rye gives me a look. "You were saying?"

"What was she saying?" Brenna asks, sitting down and taking a sip of her drink.

At this point it's a miracle she's including Rye in the conversation, so even though I'd rather not talk about it, I answer. "That I do not look like I swallowed a goat."

One finely plucked brow rises. "Of course you don't, darling. It's more like you sucked a lemon."

I roll my eyes and grab my drink. It's tart, sweet, and burns a little going down. Perfect.

"She's in a mood," Rye says. Without warning, he wraps a beefy arm around me and pulls me in for a hug, sloshing my drink all over the table. "There, there, Buttercup, tell me who put the frown on your face, and I'll best them with my sword."

A weak laugh breaks free, and I rest my head on his shoulder. I'm an only child, but I know Rye would have made an excellent big brother.

It's almost strange how I can feel Killian when he comes near. One second, I'm grinning, feeling a bit heartsore but cared for. The next, my body tenses, my heart rate picking up. I know it's because of him, and it's not a surprise to look up and see him standing in front of our table.

The blonde is still on his arm. The woman hasn't done anything remotely wrong, and I hate her.

Everything inside me plummets. I feel like I've swallowed a goat.

His gaze flicks to me, then settles on Rye. Tension lines his mouth as he bends forward to be heard. "Hey, man, Jenny here wanted to meet you."

Rye instantly untangles himself from me and gestures for Jenny to scoot in on his opposite side. "By all means. Meet me, adore me, buy me a drink. I'm good with all the above."

A barely veiled gagging noise comes from Brenna's direction. Rye ignores it and tugs Jenny down on his lap.

While she giggles and snuggles close to Rye, Killian glances back at me. His eyes are hard, and I want to laugh. Does he really think I'm cozying up to Rye? The twitch at his jaw tells me he does. I glare back, annoyance plucking at my skin.

"I was going to ask if you two needed anything," he says, overloud to compensate for the music. "But it looks like you're taken care of."

I'd like to tell him where he can take his snide tone. But Brenna cuts in. "Hang out with us." She sounds almost desperate, her body stiff and her gaze resolutely *not* on Rye and his new friend.

Killian doesn't look at me as he shakes his head. "Jax has been giving me shit about being a *hermit*," he emphasizes the word like a whip in my direction. "Hiding away in a booth isn't going to help."

Ass. I'm not a hermit. Not since he dragged me into this life and made me see what I was missing. And I don't hide. Okay, right now I have the urge to crawl back into my shell. But I've grown out of it. I'd be miserable there too.

A lump rises in my throat, loneliness washing over me like a wave. But then Killian turns to me, leaning in a little. Even in the cold, musty air of the club, I catch his scent, spicy and warm. His coffee eyes soften. "You good?"

The lump in my throat grows. He's giving me what I asked for. Anonymity. If I don't want our relationship public, this is how it has to be. But he's still mine. I can see it now in the way his eyes suddenly look pained.

"I'm good," I croak.

He peers at me for another second, then nods. "See you."

As soon as he's gone, I deflate in my seat.

"Trouble in paradise?" Brenna murmurs in my ear.

I down the rest of my cocktail before answering. "He doesn't like hiding."

I don't worry about Rye overhearing. He already has his tongue down Jenny's throat, and they're slowly listing to the right.

Brenna ignores them, her expression so smoothed out, I know it's costing her. She takes a sip of her cocktail. "My cousin is surprisingly forthright."

"You think I'm a jerk, don't you?" I need another drink.

"God, no." She leans against my shoulder in a show of support. "You're protecting yourself in a shit world. Doesn't mean he'll like it."

"I thought I was protecting myself," I tell her, misery swamping me faster than the alcohol can numb it. "But thinking back on how I felt when that reporter questioned me, I think I'd rather tell the world to fuck themselves than cower."

Brenna knows all about my run in with Ms. Zelda Smith. "Yeah, well, Zelda didn't seem to have a problem fucking a band member, so she can't exactly throw stones."

"Honestly, I don't want the public in my business. Ever. But that's more about being a private person in general."

"They don't have to be. Famous people hide their relationships all the time. Well..." She gives me an apologetic smile. "For as long as they can, anyway."

Famous. I want to laugh. I'm not famous. But Killian is.

And his life is just coming back into focus.

"If it were just me and him? I might not mind so much. But the guys are getting back together. Jax clearly didn't want me joining them."

"You're protecting them." She sounds genuinely surprised.

"Is that so wrong?"

A frown works over her face, and she turns her attention toward the part of the room where the guys are now laughing in a group—well, except for Rye, who is making noises so lewd I really don't want to look.

Brenna's expression softens as she watches Killian and Whip do some weird sort of hip bump, as if they're demonstrating a dance move to a bunch of starry-eyed women. "You should have seen them before Jax... They were like a bunch of puppies." She laughs, takes a drink. "We all were, really. Even Scottie. It was this wild ride, never coming down, party, play, party."

Emptiness fills me. I can't be that girl. I don't want to be.

Brenna glances at me. "It was all bullshit, though. Nothing real. When Jax tried to— It broke us all."

"Killian said as much—about it shaking them up."

"He's right. Yanked us out of childhood." She shakes her head, pursing her glossy red lips. "It's not a bad thing, Libby. Living like that wasn't healthy. These boys, they had nothing to ground them. Nothing that meant anything."

The music changes to "Right Now" by Mary J. Blige, and a woman pulls Killian out to dance. He lets her. He's not doing anything lewd. Just dancing. Doesn't change the fact that another woman has her hands on him, swaying and grinding with the beat.

Brenna talks quietly in my ear. "Life moves forward, Libby. Trying to stop it or rewind is a waste of energy."

Watching Killian dance cuts into my heart. I can't breathe. I have never been a jealous person. I can safely say it's the worst emotion on earth. And now it writhes inside me until I want to throw up just to get rid of the feeling.

All the things I've said to him, all the things he's said to me, the things we've done—all of it—whirl around in my brain. I think about that day I first saw him sprawled on my lawn. If I had picked up the phone and called the police instead of engaging with him, I'd be blissfully ignorant right now. Safely hidden away from the world. From life. A life without Killian.

When the woman's hand drifts to Killian's butt, I stand, knocking into the table. Drinks slosh, the table screeches.

"Excuse me," I mutter to Brenna, who wisely scrambles out of my way.

My exit from the table is far from graceful, more like a bulldozer pushing everything out of its way. And Killian's head jerks up, his eyes finding mine. A worried look works across his face.

I can only stare back, drinking in the sight of him.

His dark hair, cropped close to his well-shaped skull, highlights the sharp curve of his cheek bones, the slashes of his brows, and the soft curl of his lips. He is a beautiful man. Dressed in a black button-down shirt and black slacks, he also looks nothing like the man I found drunk on my lawn. Here, he is the slick millionaire, the effortlessly cool rocker, an untouchable idol everyone wants a piece of.

People surround him, a wall of human flesh between him and me. I ignore it all. This isn't what's real.

His frown grows as I walk, my steps determined. Inside, my heart is pounding. I don't know what he sees in my face, but his careful expression shatters. Dark eyes fill with purpose, his body standing taller. He excuses himself and moves, liquid grace, powerful strides.

I start to shake, deep within me. Desire I can handle. But the emotion in his face, as if he knows—*he knows*—I'm breaking apart, and he is too, blurs my vision. I blink twice and go to him, shouldering people aside.

He meets me halfway, stopping before me, his height blocking out everything around us. He gazes down at me, searching my face. "Elly May?"

My head tilts back to meet his gaze. "Lawn bum." I reach up, cup his cheek, sandy with stubble, and tug him close. Our lips meet, his questioning, mine demanding. And then he lets out a low sound, like a sigh, but rougher, needy. His arms wrap around me, hauling my body against his as he angles his head and sinks into a kiss that takes the strength from my knees. But Killian has me secure.

There, on the dance floor, we kiss, and it's messy, dirty, and filled with silent confessions: *I'm sorry. I know. I need you. I need you more.*

When we finally pull back, his lips curve in a half smile, and his fingers lace with mine. "All right, then."

I touch his cheek again. "I adore you, Killian James. Whatever may come of it, I'm no longer willing to hide you away like you're something to be ashamed of. Everyone should know that."

His smile grows, and he rests his forehead on mine. "Pretty sure everyone does now."

I snuggle into his embrace. "Good. Then I won't have to take out an ad."

A half-laugh rumbles out of him. His hand slides up to my neck and gives me a squeeze. I close my eyes.

"Time to go," he whispers. "Before I take you right here."

I can't stop grinning. "Move your things to my room. Or I'll move to yours."

"Baby doll." He kisses me again, softly this time, then presses his cheek to mine. "I do, too, you know. So much it hurts."

"Are you two done?"

Jax's irritated tone erases our glow in an instant. Killian straightens to his full height and turns. Jax's look of utter disgust actually hurts to see. I'm not sure I even like the guy, but he's Killian's closest friend and important to him.

"Yeah," Killian says slowly, ice in his voice. "We're done."

Jax snorts. "I fucking knew it. Thinking with your dick."

I twitch, and Killian's grip on my hand firms as he pulls me closer to his side.

The room stirs, and I realize Brenna and Scottie are directing people out. Bouncers do a great job of helping them clear the room in what seems like seconds.

"Jax, man," Killian says. "Don't go there."

"Why not? We're all thinking it."

Whip draws near. "We're not *all* thinking that."

"Definitely not what I'm thinking," Rye adds. "About time, is more like it." He gives me a happy smile. "No more swallowing goats."

"No," I say, giving him a small smile back.

The rest of the guys are clearly confused by that one.

But Jax snorts. "And yet you all know exactly what I'm thinking."

"Why don't you lay it out for me?" Killian asks. There is a silky, dark note in his voice that I've never heard before. A definite warning.

Jax either doesn't hear it or doesn't care. "If you wanted your side piece to come on tour, you should have just said so. You didn't have to drag her on stage and mess with the band."

Killian sucks in a sharp breath and lets it out slowly. "I'm not gonna hit you," he finally says. "You deserve it. But I'm not. Get this now. That is the last time you disrespect Libby. You got me?"

Jax glances at me, and for a second I see a wince of regret, then it's gone. "You disrespected yourself," he says, "hiding and pretending this was about performing."

"You're right," I say before Killian can respond. "Which is why I'm no longer hiding."

"But you're still going to pretend like you belong here?"

Okay, that hurt.

Killian snarls, taking a step toward Jax. "What the fuck is your problem?"

"My problem? You fucking lied. To all of us."

"Dude," Rye says, shaking his head at Jax. "It was obvious they were together."

"Seriously. Take your head out of your ass, man," Whip adds, giving Killian a cheeky smile. "I knew he was gone on her the moment he started waxing lyrical about her voice. And it's not like they're very good at hiding those moony looks they keep throwing each other."

Killian's eyes narrow. "You knew and you were going to ask her out?"

"Naw, I was just fucking with you, Big K. You should have seen your face. I thought you were going to bust something." Whip laughs.

"I was about to bust *your* face," Killian mutters, but he doesn't look truly pissed. Not at Whip, anyway. He sets his attention back on Jax. "You used to be better than this."

"And you used to be straight with me."

Killian's brows lift. "You get the hypocrisy you're throwing my way, right?"

The corners of Jax's mouth go white. "Nice."

"Jax," Whip begins, but Jax gives him a quelling look.

"We didn't need this bullshit right now," Jax says. He walks off without another word.

KILLIAN

23

"Libs?" My voice is barely above a whisper in the dark hotel bedroom.

Hers comes back just as soft. "Yeah?"

"When I told you I'd never had a girlfriend, it wasn't to score points. It was a warning."

Sheets rustle as she lifts up on her elbow. The soft fall of her hair slides over her shoulder, the silky tips tickling my arm. "Warning?"

I roll on my side and pick up a lock of her hair. "That I have no idea what I'm doing. That I'll probably do stupid shit."

"Killian, what the hell are you talking about?" She doesn't sound annoyed, more amused.

My eyes have adjusted to the dark enough that I can make out her features. Naked and mussed after hours of sex, she's also so beautiful, I'm having a hard time concentrating. But her brows lift a little as if to prompt me to speak.

"I'm sorry," I tell her.

"Sorry? Why?" She shakes her head. "I'm the one who should be sorry. I hurt you. And it hurts me too."

I'm pretty sure if I kiss her now, I'm not going to stop. So I give the ends of her hair a gentle tug in acknowledgment. "Same goes, baby doll." A sigh escapes me before I can rein it in. "You were right. I push too hard to get what I believe is best, and I don't think things through. Tonight was a shit show. Just as you predicted."

Already, the press is going crazy. I haven't told her about the social media frenzy and the way the world is now demanding our story—and to know everything about her. I don't want that nonsense invading this space.

She doesn't say anything for a second, then her warm palm finds my chest. I close my eyes as she smooths her hand over my skin. "We were both wrong. And both right."

I blow out a breath and look up at her. "I'm going to have Brenna put out a statement that we fell for each other during the tour, and that's all we're giving them."

Libby's brows draw together. "Why?"

"Because your happiness is more important to me than anything else." A dark, ugly slide of regret goes down my insides. "And I'll be damned if anyone treats you the way Jax did tonight. I'm sorry about that too, Libs. So fucking sorry."

Her hand slides up to my neck as she leans down and kisses my chest, right over my heart. Soft lips brush over my nipple before her little teeth nip it. My abs tighten in response, and a familiar heat surges up my tired, but clearly still eager, cock. Libby gives me one more tender kiss, then braces her arms on my chest. "Promise me something."

"Anything." My arms come around her waist, tugging her closer.

She smiles. "You might regret answering so easily."

"Never." I kiss the crook of her neck, stroke her hair.

"Don't be mad at Jax."

Well, hell. I draw back enough to meet her gaze. "Feelings are a little hard to ignore, Libs. And I'm fucking pissed."

The tip of her finger traces my eyebrow. "I know you are. I'm asking you not to be. You need each other."

I want to argue, but she talks over me.

"And you aren't happy when you're pissed at him."

"There are times when I truly dislike that you read me so well," I tell her.

"He has a right to be mad. I was wrong to ask you to hide it from your friends, and I plan to apologize in the morning."

My back teeth clench. "He had better apologize in return. That shit was uncalled for—"

"Killian," she chides. "Let it go. I don't want to regret what I did tonight."

"Regret it?" I scoff, dragging her fully on top of me where she belongs. Her soft tits pillow on my chest, and I grunt with contentment. "You'd better not. That was hot as hell. Very *Officer and a Gentleman.*"

She giggles. I love when my girl giggles. She needs more lightness in her life. "What are you on?"

"It was," I protest, kissing the tip of her nose. "I half expected you to pick me up and carry me out of there."

Her laugh is full-out now. "Nerd."

I nod. "And I loved seeing you jealous."

"I was not," she protests, her nose wrinkling in disgust.

"Was too."

"Not even."

"So much. Your skin had a green tint. Pretty, but not as pretty as it is now, all sex-flushed and wanting more. It's okay, you know. I'll give it to you. I'm easy that way."

Her laughter shakes her body, the smooth curve of her belly pressing into my hard dick. She shakes her head again. "Good. I'll always want it from you." Her eyes glint in the dim light. "And I was jealous."

"That's it." I roll over, pinning her to the bed. "No sleep tonight. Because I need to make a few things clear, and it might take some time."

LIBBY

KILLIAN MAKES himself at home on top of me, bracing himself on his forearms.

"I'm not going to be jealous anymore," I tell him before he can speak. A counterstrike, because jealous is a petty emotion I don't want any part of, if I can help it. "That was a rare anomaly."

"Okay." He answers so easily, as if content with whatever I say. I think he's just humoring me. His brows lift a touch, and there's a smile in his eyes. "Did you stake your claim on me tonight because you were jealous?"

"You know I did." I poke his side, finding the spot that makes him yelp before I grow serious. "Actually, I thought of how my life would be if I'd never met you, and didn't have you in it. That is unacceptable."

"You'll never have to know how it would be," he whispers. "Because I'm not letting you go."

Cupping the back of his neck, I kiss him. And he sighs, sinking into it.

"Seeing you pawed by other women did suck, however." I give him that honesty because he deserves it.

"I hate being pawed by other women," he breathes against my lips. "Kiss me and make it all better."

I do, practically eating at his mouth because Killian tastes so good, and because no matter how many times I touch him, I always want more. My body trembles, my legs twining around his waist, pulling him closer.

He undulates against me, rocking his hips into mine, clinging like he'll never get enough either.

One of his hands slides to my neck, stroking it, the other dips between us. His fingers find mine, guiding them down. I wrap my hand around his hot flesh, and he groans.

"This is yours," he says, thrusting a little in my grip. "As his owner you have an obligation to take good care of him."

I smile against his mouth. "Oh, yeah?"

"Mmm…" He nips my chin, makes his way down my neck. "Pet him, kiss him, keep him warm at night, entertained during the day."

I stroke along his length, squeezing the tip. Killian hums in approval.

"Like that, yeah." He sucks at the crook of my neck. "So you know, he'll also need plenty of quality time with his new best friend, Pretty Pussy."

A soft laugh escapes me, but my body heats. I'm bone-tired and sore. We've been at it all night, and still I want him inside of me again, pushing his way in with that low, greedy grunt he always makes. The thought makes me lightheaded. My thumb circles the broad head of his cock, where it weeps. For me.

"If he's mine," I whisper, nibbling at his ear, "maybe he doesn't have to get all dressed up when he comes in for a visit."

Killian stills, his breath warm and damp at my neck. "Are you saying you want me to fuck you bare?"

I can't tell if surprise or caution tightens his voice. I've never asked a guy to go without. I've never wanted to. But I do with Killian. "Do you not want to?" I ask, cautious now too. "Because it's okay if you—"

"I want it," he cuts in, husky and insistent. His gaze darts over my face. "You on the pill now?"

"Had a shot. Three months of clear sailing. So to speak."

A familiar, cocky grin spreads over his face. "You know, going without, this speaks of long-term commitment, doesn't it? You don't say, 'Fuck me bare,' unless you're thinking it's just you and me for a long time."

I still, lifting my head up. "You're pulling me out of my

happy place, Killian James."

His chuckle vibrates along my skin. "And here I am about to sink right into my happiest place." My noise of annoyance only serves to make his eyes crinkle. "Babe, it's just you and me." With that, his too thick, too hard, too fucking perfect cock pushes in.

That first thrust of his is always a shock to the system, my body reacting to the invasion with a ripple of pure heat and a pinch of sweet pain. But it's that feeling of connection, our bodies finding each other again in the most elemental way that clutches my heart.

Killian enters me, and I am whole. It is that simple.

I know he feels it too, because his body trembles on a gusty sigh. He doesn't stop until he's made his way fully inside— big, bold, and undeniable.

"Hey," he says softly, holding himself there. "Look at me."

My lids flutter open, that lazy, languid feeling coursing through my body like liquid golden heat.

His eyes shine with emotion. "You and me, Libby. We stick together, and everything will be okay."

I believe him. There in the dark, surrounded by his strength, I believe that nothing will ever tear us apart.

LIBBY
24

Seattle. It's cold. It's rainy. It's beautiful. It's also the last stop on the US leg of the tour. From here we go overseas—, to Berlin first. I have no idea why we're jumping all over the place, but Brenna has explained it has to do with concert promoters and venue schedules. I really don't care; going to Europe is exciting, and I can't wait.

For now, though, it's Seattle. Once we check into our hotel, the guys and I pile into a van Whip rented. He's driving, and for once, it's just the five of us. No crew, no managers, assistants, or journalists. It's kind of nice.

First stop is Caffe Ladro, where I'm served a latte so pretty with its little stacked hearts on the foam that I almost don't want to sip it. But I do, because the roasted-coffee scent is making my mouth water. It's rich, creamy, dark, and damn delicious. I don't feel even a little embarrassed when I moan.

The guys chuckle, but are equally engrossed with their own drinks.

A couple of scones and a second round—this time in to-go cups because, damn, that's good coffee—and we head out to Aberdeen and Kurt Cobain Memorial Park. Cobain's ashes were scattered, so this is the closest thing the guys can get to a grave site, and they want to pay their respects.

A soft mist falls when we finally find the park. It's tiny and forlorn, not much to it. Frankly, the place depresses me. A homeless man shuffles by, headed for the bridge by the river as we stand in silence around a stone guitar memorial marker.

Killian's arm wraps around my shoulders, tucking me close, with Jax on my other side, huddled up as we all are. I'm fairly certain Killian finds the place equally sad. But it's Jax's expression that catches my attention. He appears haunted and faintly green around the mouth.

I know Cobain was his idol. There are similarities between them—both left handed guitar players, both shot to fame with dizzying speed, and both unable to handle it. Unfortunately Cobain, unlike Jax, succeeded in ending his life.

I have no idea what Jax is thinking, but I can't stop myself from taking his hand in mine. He stiffens at the contact, sucking in a swift breath. I'm not surprised. We haven't spoken much since he found out about my relationship with Killian. He hasn't been rude or shunned me, but he's definitely retreated further into his shell.

Not looking up, I give his hand a squeeze, try to tell him I'm here, that I'm his friend if he'll have me.

His cold fingers lay still for a moment, then slowly, he squeezes back.

"'Love Buzz' was the first song I learned to play on bass," Rye says suddenly. He laughs. "Didn't even realize Nirvana was doing a cover until years later."

"If they loved a song, they'd play it," Killian says. "No pretension about only doing their own songs. It was all about the music."

Jax's smile is barely a curl of his lips. "Remember that phase when we tried to sing like Kurt?" He glances at Killian. "And you lost your voice?"

They all laugh as Killian winces. "Ah, man. I sounded like a bull being castrated."

I snicker at that. Especially since Killian's voice is closer to

Chris Cornell's. "In college, someone fed me 'special brownies'" I tell them. "I had no idea what they were. I ended up dancing around the dorm, singing 'Heart-Shaped Box.'"

"I'd pay money to have seen that," Killian says. "Big money."

"Apparently, I had food on the brain, since I kept singing, 'Hey, Blaine, I've got a blue corn plate! Falling deeper in depth on piles of black rice.'"

The guys crack up. I join them until our laughter drifts off.

We stand silent for a minute more, lost in our thoughts. Then Jax lets me go, and we head back to the van. On the way I notice Killian's bloodshot eyes. I'd been so worried about Jax, I hadn't thought about how it would be for the rest of them. They very well could have done what I did for their friend.

But Killian gives me a small, quiet smile. "Thank you," he says, glancing at Jax, then kissing me softly. "He needed that."

Hours later, my subdued mood hasn't lifted as we attend Kill John's record label party at the hotel's rooftop pool area. The views of Puget Sound are breathtaking, the food excellent. The people? Loud and plastic comes to mind.

"You're with me tonight, kid." Whip appears at my side and pulls me into a hard half hug. I almost choke on my salmon puff.

"To what do I owe this honor?" I ask as I wipe a crumb from my lip.

His pretty profile is stern as he surveys the crowd. "The piranhas are out in full force tonight. A guy could get eaten alive."

There *are* a lot of gorgeous women here, and a lot of suits, as Killian calls the record label execs. I don't know which makes Whip more wary. I'm definitely not liking the way the suits keep looking at me as if I'm a stray that wandered into the party uninvited. Though it's probably all in my head.

"You need to be my beard," Whip tells me for clarification.

"You're bi?" I ask, because I really don't know.

He glances at me, blue eyes twinkling. "Well, as a teen, I thought a little variety would add to my sexual mystique. But, alas, dicks do nothing for me. I'm all about the kitty."

I'm rolling my eyes when another male hand wraps around my wrist. This touch I know well.

Killian gives Whip a look. "Dude, get your own woman."

"I tried. You cockblocked me." Whip winks at me.

"What happened to that reporter you were all over at the movies?" I ask.

"You saw that?"

"Everyone saw that," Killian and I say in unison.

Whip makes a face. "Turns out she thought the best way to get info out of me was to suck it through my dick."

"Sounds labor-intensive," Killian says with a laugh.

"More like a lost cause." Whip's nostrils flare then his expression clears. "But she had great technique."

"*La-la-la,*" I sing. "I can't hear you."

Laughing, Whip lets go as Killian fits himself behind me, wrapping his arms around my shoulders.

"See," Whip quips. "Cockblocker."

Killian's cheek rests against mine for a second before he gives my temple a kiss. "He thinks because we're faux cousins I won't kick his ass. He's wrong."

They're grinning, so I ignore the boast. "Faux cousins?" I ask.

"Chicks used to think we were related because we look so much alike," Whip tells me. "We said we were cousins. For some weird-ass reason, that got us a lot of play." He frowns. "Women are strange creatures."

I laugh, snuggling back into Killian's embrace. He's warm, solid, and all mine. "If you say so. Though I think it probably had more to do with you both being hot, as opposed to related."

"See?" Whip says brightly. "She thinks I'm hot."

"She thinks I'm hotter," Killian counters. "Don't you, babe?"

"Scottie's really the hottest of you all," I tell them.

Killian chuckles darkly, and his hand slips down just a bit. Under the cover of his bent arm, his fingers graze the side of my breast, his warm palm giving me a gentle squeeze. I squirm a little and feel his grin against my neck. "If you say so, baby doll."

Cheeky ass.

Whip rolls his eyes, but leans in and gives me a quick kiss on the cheek. "Any time you want to dump this bum, you know where to find me."

He gives Killian a tap on the shoulder as he heads into the crowd.

"Can we leave now?" Killian murmurs. His hand is still busy, slowly fondling me, each touch getting heavier, more direct. I squirm again, my butt pushing against his rising interest. He grunts low, nudges me back.

"We can't," I whisper, though I really want to agree. "You promised Scottie you'd make nice with those journalists."

Killian sighs, grinding his dick against my bottom one last time before letting me go. "Okay, fine. But we're not staying long."

I watch him walk away, because his ass in those well-worn jeans is a thing of beauty. I'm already regretting being good tonight.

"Wow," says a male voice in the dark. "You've got Whip Dexter and Killian James wrapped around your finger. You must be good."

The bar table next to me is tucked in the shadows, away from the bulk of the party. I hadn't seen the guy until now.

He steps my way, clearly thinking he's the shit. Tight black, leather pants, flowing white silk shirt. I want to ask him which

'80s hair band's wardrobe he raided. He's extremely good looking, in a slick, pretty boy way—dark hair falling over his brow, pouty lips, fine, almost girlish features.

I stare at him, unimpressed with the way he casually flicks his hair back from his face. "Good at what?" I mean, I know what. I just want him to say it.

"You doing them both?" He shows his teeth. "Or maybe taking the whole band on?"

"Let me ask you something. Do you actually think that's acceptable to say to someone?"

Pretty Boy gives me an innocent smile. "Aw, come on. I'm just kidding around. Seriously. I know the score. We newbies don't get anywhere without a little persuasion." He offers me his hand. "I'm Marlow."

I glance at the offered hand. "Marlow, I don't care if you sucked dick to get invited here or not. But do not disrespect women as an opening line." I push off from the table. "If you'll excuse me."

A hard hand slaps down on my shoulder, and I'm wrenched around. The guy is scary strong—something I didn't anticipate because he looks all of a hundred twenty pounds. Angry grey eyes glare down at me. "You've got a some nerve," he snarls, his fingers biting into my skin. "I'm a signed artist. Who are you? Killian James' fucking whore."

"Get the hell off—"

He invades my space, my back hitting the edge of the bar table. "Why don't you play nice? Be a little friendly."

It's then I see how glassy his eyes are, the pupils wide. It distracts me. Without warning, he grabs my breast and squeezes. Hard.

Revulsion, rage, shock—all of it floods me. For a bright, hot second I can't move. And then the rage takes control. My hand flies up, fingers punching into his eye sockets.

He rears back, stumbling, and I knee him between the legs.

Unfortunately, my hit glances off his thigh. But he's stunned and blinking frantically, snarling out curses.

I know when to run. My heels grind into the pavement as I pivot, my heart in my throat, flight taking over fight. I hear him coming for me.

"Fucking bitch!" Nails scratch my exposed back, catching on my halter. It rips, the sound loud against the buzzing in my ears.

My hands fly to my top, grasping my breasts to keep the fabric from falling down farther. I think I cry out. I don't know for sure because another shout drowns out all sound.

And then Killian is there, bearing down on us like death. I sob. His expression actually scares me, even though I know it isn't directed my way. He brushes by me, and with another enraged bellow, grabs Marlow by his neck.

The guy doesn't stand a chance. Killian slams him to the patio pavement. He doesn't talk, doesn't hesitate, just starts whaling on the guy with his fists. It's terrifying, brutal.

Around me, a crowd gathers. Phone camera flashes go off, others held up to record it all. Three more guys blow past me. Whip, Rye, and Jax.

They're trying to pull Killian off a struggling Marlow, who gets a hit in. Not that Killian feels it. He strains against Whip and Jax's hold. "Get the fuck off. You mother fucker…" And with that, he kicks Marlow. A security guard rushes into the fray.

I bite back another sob. Something soft and warm settles over my shoulders: a tiny beaded shrug jacket. At my side, a woman with heavy gold eye makeup gives me a small smile. "It's all I have." She puts an arm around me, drawing the shrug farther over my exposed shoulders. "You okay, hon?"

She's a groupie. I know her on sight. And her kindness breaks me. I start to cry again. Two other women join us, closing ranks, protecting me from the cameras.

Maybe Killian's rage has run its course. Maybe he hears me. Whatever the reason, he throws off Jax and Whip with a snarled "I'm good."

His gaze finds me, and the ugly expression on his face crumples as he comes. "Libs."

I clutch his shirt as he hugs me hard, his body damp with sweat. The rest is a blur as we're ushered back to our room. But not before I see Scottie's expression. Shit has clearly hit the fan.

"WHAT THE BLOODY hell was that?"

Killian looks up from his spot on the couch and gives Scottie a cold look. "That was me kicking a shitbag's ass."

He hasn't stopped shaking, and he hasn't let me go. Even when a doctor looked at his swollen and bruised hand—and suggested Killian should have an X-ray for broken bones—he had an arm around me, squeezing me tight. The only time he released me was to pull off his shirt and put it on me.

Scottie snorts now. "That shitbag was Marlow. The label's newest and hottest young star, for fuck's sake."

Lovely. The sick feeling in my stomach intensifies.

"He's going to be singing through a feeding tube if I see him again," Killian snaps.

"At any rate," Scottie retorts, "I was asking Libby, not you."

All eyes turn to me, except for Killian's. He just cuddles me closer. "Leave her the fuck alone. She's been through enough."

"It's okay, Killian." I rub my hand down his forearm, trying to calm him. He grunts but relaxes a little.

Scottie, Jax, Whip, Rye, and Brenna are all waiting. I take a deep breath, because remembering makes me shake as well. "He came out of nowhere," I say. "Said that I should..." I glance at Killian.

He exhales a hard breath. "Just say it, baby doll. I'm not going to hunt him down or anything."

This doesn't sound remotely sincere.

"He suggested that since I was servicing all the members of Kill John, I should do the same with him."

"Mother fucker," snarls Killian.

"Dicknozzle," Whip mutters.

The rest are silent. Waiting for me to continue.

"I...ah...told him what I thought about that, then I tried to leave." Cold fear trickles down my spine. I'm safe. I know this. But I don't feel it. At my side I feel Killian tense more and more. He's practically twitching.

I blink several times. "He...ah...grabbed my breast."

Killian makes a sound I can't even interpret, and I'm suddenly on his lap, wrapped up tight. I breathe for a couple of seconds before I finish the story. "This blow-up was my fault."

"No fucking way," hisses Killian.

"It's never your fault," Brenna cuts in. She's been silent until now. But I see the way she trembles. "Never."

"I just meant, when he did that, I poked him in the eyes, tried to ball him. That's what really set him off. He deserved it, but I should have handled it quietly, left sooner."

"And I would have just beat the shit out of him sooner," Killian says, pressing his face into the crook of my neck. "Baby doll, I'm so sorry."

"It's okay." But my eyes tear up. I've never been physically attacked before. I took self-defense courses during college because it seemed the safe thing to do. But reality is different, and not so easy to let go.

Scottie sighs and runs a hand through his hair. "Nothing is 'okay.'" He pins me with an icy stare. "Are you all right?"

"Yes."

"Good. Then get some rest." He turns his attention to

Killian. "You. I want those fingers in the splint the doctor left. Don't give me shit, or so help me..." He holds up a hand and appears to be doing a mental countdown.

"I'll splint the damn fingers," Killian says, exasperated. He already has them wrapped in ice. I'm afraid to look. His whole hand was swollen, the knuckles split and bleeding, before they treated it.

Finally Scottie blows out a breath. "We need to fix this."

"It won't be easy," Brenna says somberly. "The entire fight was filmed from multiple angles and is already being played on numerous outlets."

"Fuck," sneers Jax. He doesn't look at me, though I feel the weight of his disappointment in the air.

It doesn't matter that we're here because a self-centered prick thought it was okay to put his hands on me, or that I defended myself the best way I could. Guilt still rides me. I'm the one who was involved. Everyone here knows Killian wouldn't have lost his shit if it hadn't been in my honor.

I can't bring myself to look at anyone.

LIBBY

25

Late at night, when we finally slip into bed, Killian holds me for a long time, his chest to my back. I drift in the warmth of him, body and soul at peace. And he breathes me in, slow and deep as if he's memorizing my scent.

"I could have killed him," he whispers in my hair.

In the dark, my hand finds his forearm, pressed across my chest, and I stroke his skin, tracing the muscles beneath it. "But you didn't."

His breath is soft and low. "I totally lost my shit. Didn't think of anything but beating his ass."

"It's over now." Under the cool of the covers, with his heat along my skin, I'm safe. And though Killian is more than capable of protecting himself, I wish he felt safe as well.

His fingers curl around the curve of my shoulder. "I've never been needed by anyone but the guys. We became each other's family. I watch out for them."

I don't say anything, simply run my fingers over the strong bones of his wrist, along his inner arm where his skin is like silk over stone.

"I failed them, Libs. I should have known Jax was losing his grip."

"Killian—"

"I should have kept us together after he tried to end it

instead of drifting away."

The covers rustle as I turn to face him. "Almost every night for a year, I went to bed thinking I should have tried to get my dad into rehab. I should have said something instead of looking the other way." I cup Killian's cheek, rough with the day's growth. "Half the time I couldn't look in the mirror because I thought, would my dad have been happier, would he have drank less, if he'd never given up the life to have me?"

Killian's eyes widen as if he's in pain. "No, Libby. No one who knows you would ever consider you a regret."

I sigh, my thumb touching the corner of his mouth. "That's the problem, though. Logic tells you one thing, but you still feel another. You can tell me I'm wrong about my dad. I can tell you you're wrong about failing the guys. But believing is harder, isn't it?"

His lips press against my brow. "I don't want to fail you, Libs. And right now, I don't know how avoid doing that."

"I feel the same," I whisper.

He moves over me then, settling his body on mine. There, in the dark, he makes love to me. It's almost desperate, the way we touch—searching kisses, fumbling caresses. And it's heartbreakingly tender. Every touch counts, feels like the end of something, the beginning of something else.

I'm terrified, and I don't know why. Maybe he is too, because he doesn't let me go. Not when we reach our climax, and not when we drift off to sleep in the waning hours of the night.

In the morning, I'm alone. Killian has gone to get his hand X-rayed just in case there are fractures.

I eat breakfast in my room and don't expect visitors. When Jax shows up, I'm wary. He barely looked my way last night, as if he couldn't stand the sight of me.

"You want some coffee?" I ask as he follows me into the suite's living room where the room service cart is set up.

"Yeah, sure." He taps his thumb against his thigh.

We've been traveling together for a while now, but we've never really been alone except for that first night when he came to check on me and my sad case of stage fright. We're not friends, but I've never considered him my enemy. Unfortunately, I have no idea if that's true for him or not.

In silence we sip lukewarm coffee until I can't take it anymore. "You here to bawl me out or something?"

Jax smirks. "You have a bit of a dramatic side, don't you?"

"Oh, please, you looked like you wanted to spit nails last night."

His mouth twitches. "Last night was fucked up. On all counts."

I run a thumb around the thick edge of my cup. "It was at that."

Jax sets his cup down. "Despite what you may think, I like you, Libby. You're talented as hell. You belong in this world as much as any of us do." Shock courses through me, but he doesn't stop there. "And I'm sorry as hell that dickhead put his hands on you. He deserved a beat down."

"Why do I feel there's a 'but' coming along?"

His green eyes lock on mine. "The record label is going to give Killian hell. Right or wrong, what he did looks bad for the band. And for you."

"I know this."

"I know you know. But do you understand the power you have over Killian? It's pretty apparent, he'll always choose you over anything else."

"What do you want me to say?" I ask. "I'm sorry this happened. I wish it hadn't. But I can't change Killian's reaction."

Jax rubs his fingers over his forehead then peers at me. "And in the future? When other assholes come out of the woodwork? Because they will. Half the public already blames you. For the simple fact that you're a woman, and Killian's now acting unhinged."

"Great." Though I'm not surprised. Victim-blaming is alive and well in modern society.

"Yeah, great," he repeats with a sigh. "He cannot handle it —not when the spotlight of judgment is on someone he cares about. He couldn't handle it on me, and he absolutely won't be able to take it on you." Jax kneels next to me, his eyes tired but intense. "There isn't a day that goes by that I don't feel the repercussions of what I did. I feel guilty as all fuck for the way I hurt them. But especially for the way it caused Killian to break down. Because he was the one who tried to shield me from the press and take it all on his shoulders."

After last night's confession, I know more than anyone how much it still hurts Killian. My throat clicks as I swallow. "This is why you didn't want me here?"

Jax nods. "I didn't know what would happen. But I knew there'd be something." He laughs sadly. "There always is on a tour. And I knew Killian wasn't ready. He doesn't have his walls up anymore."

No, he doesn't. I don't either. Both of us are walking around exposed and vulnerable. I feel naked enough as it is. But the idea that I'm also Killian's weakness is intolerable. You're supposed to protect the ones you love, not leave them open to pain.

"Promise me something," I whisper, because my voice is fast fading. "Be...kind to him. Take care of him. He needs it."

Jax nods, tension working between his brows. When Jax leaves, I head to another room.

Scottie answers on the second knock. It's a betrayal, what I'm about to do. But it doesn't stop me. "Can I come in?"

‑KILLIAN

"WE ARE NOT AMUSED, **Mr. James.**"

Sitting at a glossy conference table in a cold hotel meeting room is not my idea of fun. Listening to the duo I like to call Smith One and Smith Two is giving me heartburn. My two least favorite record label execs sit across from me, both of them in identical black Armani suits and sharing the same reproachful expression. They only need sunglasses and ear pieces to complete the Agent Smith look.

As soon as I calmed down last night, I knew this meeting was coming. You cause a scene at an industry party, you will be hearing about it.

Back when Kill John first started, we'd been their bitch—attending parties and functions when they wanted us to, touring when they demanded it, every damn aspect of our lives under their control. Those days are gone. You put out a diamond-status album like we did with *Apathy*, and the tables turn. Kill John no longer kisses ass, we get our cocks sucked.

Doesn't mean certain execs don't forget that once in a while, especially when they smell blood in the water—something Smith One clearly has been waiting for. "First we had to deal with John Blackwood's drug habit—"

"He didn't have a fucking drug habit," I snap. "He was clinically depressed, and I'll thank you to shut the fu—"

Scottie holds up a hand. "What happened with Jax isn't pertinent to yesterday's events."

"I beg to differ," Smith One says. "It is yet another pileup in the car wreck that is Kill John lately."

A red haze swarms over my vision. "Metal Death left a bathtub full of actual shit in a hotel room, but you've got a problem with me defending a woman?"

"Property damage can be quietly taken care of," Smith One

retorts. "You, on the other hand, attacked a man in a room full of reporters."

"Details."

"You damaged our newest talent, breaking his nose and busting open his lip, because you can't keep your dick in your pants."

"No," I say with exaggerated care, "I beat the little turd because he couldn't keep his hands to himself." I give Smith One a smile with teeth. "You see the difference? Because it's an important one. You go after an unwilling woman—my woman in particular—and you're going to get hurt."

He doesn't miss the warning. His eyes narrow. "We've had to hold off our promotional plans until Marlow's face heals. Thousands of dollars wasted in cancelled appearances."

"You should probably talk to him about his behavior. Assign him community service so he can think about his sins."

"You think this is funny, Mr. James?" Smith Two taps his gold pen on the table as if to get my attention. "Because I assure you the label isn't laughing."

"No," I agree. "They're sweeping an attempted sexual assault under the table. Bravo for that."

"Not to mention," Smith One puts in, "that you damaged *your* hand."

I refuse to move my wrapped fingers from their gaze. "It's fine."

"It's insured for a million dollars, Mr. James." Smith One shoves a stack of papers toward me as if I'm going to read them. "Premiums just went up."

I laugh, a short bark of annoyance, and then catch Scottie's eye. Up until now, he's been sitting back, almost lounging in his chair. Although the Smiths are wearing Armani, Scottie's sharp tailoring makes them look like slobs, because his charcoal-grey bespoke three-piece suit is straight up Gieves & Hawkes out of Savile Row. My father shops there, and his standards are only slightly less particular than Scottie's.

Scottie's appearance is its own form of intimidation. The fact that nothing scares him is another.

"Marlow is a flash in the pan," Scottie says, bored. "And yet here you are insulting your highest-earning client. I suggest you make amends for wasting his time with this meeting and direct your efforts to putting a better spin on the story."

Smith and Smith blink in unison, and Smith One sneers. "Mr. James is under contract—"

"Mr. James has fifty-million followers on Twitter alone."

News to me. But I join Scottie in leveling them a long *How you like me now, bitches?* stare. Whatever it takes to get them off my back and away from Libby.

Scottie rises. "None of whom would appreciate him being mistreated. Never underestimate the power of social media or fanatical fans. Now if you'll excuse us, gentlemen. My client has a concert to perform."

Smith Two's cold eyes follow our movements. "Make all the veiled threats you want, Mr. Scott. But we will have order. No more running off the rails, or there will be repercussions."

"THOSE TWO ARE a pain in my ass," I grumble as we walk back to my suite.

"They're right, you know." Scottie's laser gaze slashes my way. "What you did was stupid. On all counts."

"What the hell?" I glare at him. "You're actually taking their side?"

He stops short, turning to face me. We're of a similar height and stand eye to eye. "You *are* under contract. They *can* make your life difficult, and they most certainly can blackball Liberty from gaining a foothold in this industry, if they so choose. They were interested in signing her. But now they have concerns over PR issues created by your blowup."

My heart skips a beat, cold flooding my veins. I'm as untouchable as I'm going to get. But I cringe with regret at the thought of putting Liberty's future in jeopardy.

"Setting that aside," he continues, "you've managed to bring Kill John back into the limelight, though not as a band united, but as the butt of a sad joke where Killian James flies into a jealous rage because Marlow, the new hot—younger—rising star, got handsy with some tart."

"Hey." I step closer. "Don't call Libby that."

"I'm not calling her that. They are."

"You think I should have just let that shithead off?"

"No. If it were me, I'd have done the same. I'd like to rip the tosser's tiny balls off and cram them down his throat. But it doesn't change the fact that we have to fix this. And quickly."

"Shit." Hands on hips, I duck my head and try to calm my breathing. "How?"

Scottie doesn't miss a beat. "Take her off the tour."

"No." My loud reply echoes in the hall. "She'll think we're punishing her."

"That's merely a matter of your fear and her ego at risk. The reality is she'll be miserable with all this added speculation, the two of you constantly under the microscope. However, if she were on her own…"

"On her own?"

"People already love her. Brenna's staff is fielding hundreds of requests a day for more Liberty. It's her moment to break out. So let me break her out while she's hot."

I don't want to agree. Everything in me screams in protest. If she goes, I'll lose her. My fear is that simple. But it isn't my call to make. It isn't even Scottie's; it's Libby's.

I know this, and yet the idea of sending her out to the wolves suddenly chills me. I want her to shine, *and* I want to wrap her up and tuck her into my side.

"This morning, she sought me out to talk," Scottie says. "She agreed to let me manage her. She also asked me what I thought she could do to make things easier for you."

It shouldn't feel like a betrayal, but it does. Not that she wants to try or that she was looking out for me, but that she discussed these things with Scottie first, not me. I don't have any experience in relationships, but I'm fairly certain confiding in the other about life-altering decisions is a key component.

My head aches something fierce; my guts are rolling like I'm hungover. I want more time alone with Libby, away from the world. But that's not going to happen. I want to do right by her, but I'm bumbling my way through. "What did you tell her?"

"I told her to get off the tour."

"Jesus, be a dick, why don't you?"

"I'm being realistic. And I think she understands that."

My jaw aches from grinding my teeth. "If she wants to do this, I'm not going to hold her back. I've already told you that."

"Yes, I know. The problem is, mate, she doesn't *want* to leave you."

I'd be happy about that, except I have a bad feeling she's holding on out of misplaced loyalty. The whole situation is a shit cracker on top of a shit day. And it isn't even noon. "She's tough, Scottie. But not hardened. I don't want her crushed before she has a chance to bloom."

"I'm planning to stick with her, if that makes you more comfortable." Scottie's gaze is level, calm. "Jules can manage the day-to-day tour details here."

Jules, Scottie's assistant, is great. But I really don't give a fuck about the tour at this moment. Clearing the thickness out of my throat, I search for words. "Protect her." I press my hand to my eyes to ease the hot throb of pain behind them. "That's all I care about."

Silence follows. For once, the ice man is gone. In his place is the Scottie I met years ago as a young punk hungry for fame, the one who looked after Jax when he tried to take his life. This Scottie is the man you'll follow anywhere because you know he'll have your back.

Those eerie blue eyes of his seem to burn with determination. "There are no guarantees in life. I cannot promise you the world won't try to chew Liberty up and spit her out. But the woman gives me shit on a continuous basis. And I've made grown men cry."

Despite my crap mood, I feel a smile forming. "My favorite was when the owner of The Lime House blubbered."

Scottie's eyes narrow with remembered glee. "Complete tosser." His expression evens out. "As you say, she is tough. And she'll have me on her side."

Which in Scottie terms is to say she'll have the best in the business at all points. It still sits heavy in my gut that she won't have *me*. Not if I do what needs to be done to get her to go.

My headache threatens to crush my skull. I'm going to have to let Libby go. Set her free.

I swallow hard and nod. "I'll talk to her."

LIBBY
26

I'm curled up on the couch in our suite, playing the guitar, when Killian finally returns. He leans against the door for a long minute, head tilted back, gaze on some distant point. The lines of his body are tight with tension, making him appear almost gaunt. I want to go to him, hold him close. But he pushes off and heads my way.

"Everything all right?" I ask, setting the guitar aside as he hunkers down before me, sitting on the low coffee table. Bluish smudges mar the skin beneath his eyes. There's a scrape along his jaw, presumably where Marlow punched him, and his hand is splinted. Guilt is a punch in the heart.

Killian sighs and leans forward to rest his head on my shoulder, his hands going to my hips. Immediately, I wrap my arms around his back and stroke him. We sit in quiet until he takes a deep breath and lets it out slowly. "Shit day, baby doll."

"Yeah," I agree, my throat thick.

He kisses the side of my neck, a soft press of lips, then sits up straight. His face is somber. "Talked to the record execs."

I sit up straighter. "They're giving you trouble, aren't they?"

"They tried." He shrugs. "They were pissed about the fight. But that's to be expected."

"I'm so sorry—"

"No," he cuts in. "Don't start that again. We both know who is to blame, and that fucker isn't coming anywhere near you again."

"Doesn't make it any better, though, does it?"

Killian's sigh is tired and low. "Guess not." He snorts with disgust. "They want me on my best behavior from now on."

My fingers feel cold, and I rub my damp palms along my thighs. "Killian—"

"You talked to Scottie." Pain shadows his eyes, making them dull. He doesn't ask about what. It's obvious he knows.

I clear my throat. "You're upset."

He smiles, but it isn't with humor. "No, Libby. I'm proud. This is huge. It's the next logical step, and you're taking it." His big hands curl around my knees, giving a small squeeze. "It's huge. I'm happy for you."

"You don't exactly look happy," I point out. My heart begins to pound with a sick dread, and I don't even know why.

Killian's gaze slides to the side, his teeth catching his lower lip. "I just wish you had come to me instead of him."

"I know. I'm sorry." I touch his hand and find it cold. "I wanted a different perspective. And you kept telling me everything was fine, not to worry. But it isn't fine. And I do worry. I want to help you."

Killian takes that in with an expression I can't fully read. Regret, maybe? Hurt, definitely. But his voice is even when he finally speaks. "Scottie told me he thought you should start working with him now. Said it was your time to break out."

"He did," I say slowly. "But the tour is still going."

Killian grips the back of his neck, his arm flexing. He won't meet my eyes. "The tour is moving to Europe. No one will question if you aren't there."

No one will care. Because I am not really a part of Kill John anyway. I know this. I never wanted to push my way into their band. It still doesn't stop the shards of pain from stabbing their way into my chest.

I need to get a grip. I am the one who went to Scottie. He told me that leaving the tour was best. But for some ridiculous reason, I thought Killian would put up a fight. That he wouldn't want me to go. Pride. Stupid pride.

"No, I suppose not." I hate that my voice breaks.

He nods, the action slow, as if it's taking effort. "Scottie can get you set up in L.A. By tomorrow."

My insides swoop. "Tomorrow?"

Holy hell, I'm being handled, a problem swept under the rug. It's one thing to take control of the problem, but to have Killian actually agree with Scottie is unsettling.

Still, I have to ask. "Is that what you want?"

Killian looks at me sharply. "It isn't about what I want anymore." He lets his hand fall, and for a moment, I think he'll reach for me. But he rests it on his thigh. "It's about what's best for you. For the band. It would be better for you if you do this now."

"But is it what you want?" I snap, unable to let it go.

Killian seems to brace himself. When he lifts his head, his eyes are clear. "Yeah, Libby, it's what I want. I think you should go."

Nausea rolls in my belly. God, how many times had my mama warned me? Musicians don't stick when life gets hard. And if they do, they regret it. I lurch to my feet.

He tries to grab my wrist. "Libs—"

I brush him off with a tight smile. "I'm okay. I have to stand. My legs are falling asleep." I pace to the window where rain streaks down in rivers, the landscape blurry and gray. "It's a good plan," I manage. "The best plan."

He's silent, and I risk a look. I wish I hadn't. Pity etches hi' features. Fuck that. My fingers curl around the heavy drape

He's sending me away. After all his cajoling, after outright ordering me to join him, when the shit hits the fan, he fucking sends me away.

"I could come with you for a bit," he says. "Help you get set up."

Jax's warning runs through my mind. Killian will put me first. Even though it's clear he wants me gone, his loyalty will always drive him into doing the noble thing. I'm the problem here. I refuse to add more to it by tearing him away from his life, his obligations.

Killian had the courage to push me toward a life I didn't want to admit I craved. I can do this for him now and walk away with dignity. The lump in my throat reaches epic proportions. I swallow convulsively, willing myself not to cry. "And leave the tour?" I choke on a sharp laugh. "No. That's ridiculous."

He frowns. "Libby, if you need me—"

"I don't." I know he cares. But I'm done being his problem to solve.

He recoils as if I've slapped him. That burns too. I'm not the one backing off. He promised everything would be okay if we stuck together. And now this.

"Okay, then," he says slowly, the frown growing deeper.

I want to rage and fight. But pride forces me to remain calm. I refuse to be any man's regret. I sigh and run a hand through my hair. My head hurts. My heart aches. "Killian, I'll be fine. It's like you said; this is just the next step." *Where I leave you. I don't want to leave you.*

"And your tour won't last forever. I'll just wait in L.A...." I trail off, not really knowing what else to say. Everything is jumbled and stuck in my chest.

His body is stiff as he stands, setting his hands low on his hips. "Look...You'll be busy. I'll be busy." He takes a breath, like he's trying to force his words out. "You can take this time to settle down, see what you really want."

"What I really want?" My lips feel numb. He's not just sending me away. He's letting me go. And here I was worried about setting *him* free. I want to laugh. Or cry. It's a toss-up.

"Yeah," he croaks. "Without me hovering or holding you back. You can... You can figure out if this is the way you really want to live."

Somehow I find the strength to nod. "Yeah, you're right. Everything has been going full-tilt. Half the time, it didn't even seem real."

He blanches at that but makes a noise of agreement. It's so stiff, his manner so impersonal.

I find myself babbling on, making excuses for both of us. "And it would be stupid to hold each other back when we don't know where we'll end up."

Lie. Lie. Lie. I want to beg him to just hold me, tell the world to fuck off. But he's already backing up.

His gaze is clear. "This is good, Libs," he tells me, his voice flat. "You'll see. You can take the time now and find out if this is the life you want, without me interfering. And I can..." He shrugs. "I can do the tour like a good little rocker and stay out of the news."

I flinch. It's my fault he was in the news. "So, that's it then."

Killian's dark eyes hold mine. "Yeah, I guess it is."

KILLIAN

I LET HER GO. It needed to be done. For her sake. I tell myself these things as I make an excuse to get the hell out of the room, claiming I need to do a sound check. She doesn't stop me. That hurts just as much as anything. Maybe I expected her to tell me it was all a mistake, that she was only saying what she thought I wanted to hear, that she needed me.

But she let me leave. Are we broken up? I'm not even sure. I was trying to be supportive, to get her away from this mess. But if feels like something else. Like we're done.

Taking the elevator down, I can't look at myself in the door's reflection. My entire body hurts, my heart screaming at me to get the hell back in that room and stake my claim.

She doesn't need me.

She made that clear.

No one in my life has. Not my family, not Jax when he was hurting so badly he'd rather end things than reach out to me, and not Libby.

What the hell is wrong with me that I need to be needed?

By the time I reach our practice space, set up in some conference room, rage pumps through my blood. I said what I had to say to get Libby to go. Only now do I realize I'd wanted her to fight me with the same conviction she fights everything else. I wanted her to choose me. How fucking selfish is that?

I did the right thing here. She'll be out of the tour's harsh glare. People won't see her as my girl, but a talent in her own right.

I plug in my guitar. I'm shaking so hard, I drop my pick twice.

"Fuck it," I snarl.

"Someone is in a mood," Whip says from the door. He walks in and takes a seat at his kit. "What crawled up your butt?"

"Libby isn't going to Europe with us."

"Why? Because of last night?" He shakes his head and taps on his cymbal. "That's bullshit. And you're okay with this?"

No, I'm not fucking okay. I'm barely holding it together.

"She wants it. Scottie's taking her under his wing." The words taste like ash in my mouth.

Whip gapes at me. "And she said this? She said, 'Killian, I want to ditch your ass and go off with Scottie to find my fame.'"

"No," I mutter. "She didn't say it like that." I turn away from him and grab a fresh pick. "She...I gave her a push."

"Man, I don't think—"

"It's done." I turn on an amp and flick the volume up to full. "You gonna play or continue to piss me off with questions?"

"By all means," Whip says, twirling his drumsticks. "Let's play."

But it's no fucking good. I don't get further than a few chords before the rage surges up once more. My fingers fumble on the strings. I can't play. I don't *want* to fucking play. This time, the rage chokes me. I can't breathe. I can't think. I'm barely aware of ripping the guitar strap off over my head. The Telecaster in my hand smashes into the floor with a satisfying crack and a deafening buzz of reverb.

Guitar destroyed, chest heaving, I don't feel better. Not even a little bit.

Whip comes to stand by my side, surveying the damage. "Guess we aren't playing today. Come on. We'll medicate with single malt like proper rock stars."

Libby wouldn't like drinking. But Libby won't be around by tomorrow. I press my fingers to my aching forehead. "Yeah, a drink sounds about right."

I COME BACK to Libby in the middle of the night, and she's asleep. I curl myself around her anyway; she feels so good I almost can't stand to touch her anymore, not when she's leaving.

The thought hits me like a comet, and my insides flare. I must make a noise because she stirs, her voice soft and muffled with sleep. "Killian?"

She turns in my arms, her body warm, her fingers tracing my brow. I was going to let her sleep, but I can't. My hand slides to her cheek.

"Give me this," I whisper. "Before you go. I need this."

I find her mouth. I'd say kissing her is like coming home, but I've never had a true home. I don't know if the sense of rightness I feel with her means home or not. Right now it's something stronger, tinged with desperation. I'm desperate for her. The way she tastes, the way she moves, the little sounds and sighs that only she makes.

There's no one else like her. There never will be. I know that now. Maybe I've always known that, but now it feels like I've discovered something too late.

Libby moves against me, waking up in my arms, and she kisses me back, her hands roaming over my arms, neck, back, like she can't find a place to land. We go slow, lingering, memorizing each other. I angle my head and open her mouth wider with mine, get deeper, take more. I need it all.

The bed creaks as I roll over and fit myself between her willing thighs. She gasps in my mouth, and I swallow her breath. I want it all, and it isn't enough right now by half. Breaking away from her lips, I lean back so I can pull the shirt over her head. It's my shirt. The ratty old thing I wore at the beach when we first met. It has to mean something that she's always wearing it.

I'm pulling at straws. And she's naked beneath me. My hands ghost over her satin skin. Perfect.

In the dark, I trace the topography of her body with my fingers and lips, kissing my way down her graceful neck, along her collarbone. I take my time on the little places I've often overlooked—the center of her chest where I can feel her heart beating, the soft, fragrant curve along the side of her breast.

The skin on her inner arm is like fine silk; she shivers as I run the tip of my tongue in patterns down to her elbow. Libby sighs my name, her fingers combing through my hair and massaging the tight spots on my nape. Beneath me, her thighs are parted wide, her body pliant. The wet heat of her sex press against my chest, calling my attention.

I slide farther down, licking and nipping my way along. I love the way she squirms. I know how much she gets off on the anticipation of me reaching my destination. It's a little game we've played many times: how long can we draw it out, touch each other and yet not touch those places we want it the most.

I press my lips against the hard curve of her hipbone, my arms wrapped tight around her waist. Fuck. No one knows me better than this woman. And I'd bet my life I know her better than anyone on Earth. And I'm sending her away. She's going. It's so fucking wrong, it's choking me.

I try not let it show. But I can't stop the tremor running through me.

"Killian?" her vanilla cream voice slides through the dark.

Tell her. Tell her what she is to you. She's your lodestone. You have a fucking map inked on your body, but you are completely lost without her right next to you. Tell her.

I suck in a breath and surge down. My mouth finds her slick, swollen flesh, and I latch on, feasting like it's my last meal.

Libby gasps, her body arching off the bed. In the gloom, her skin is a pearly cream, her sweet little tits pointing up and shaking as she writhes. I hold her hips down and eat her out with no finesse, just greed. And she whimpers and cries.

Good. Remember that. Need it. Crave it. I know I will.

I don't let her come. Not yet. When she quivers against my tongue, her clit swelling, I lift away. Libby cries out, her arms reaching for me.

"Shhh," I whisper, crawling over her. "I got you."

Her damp breasts cushion my chest as I settle over her, needing that skin-to-skin contact. The throbbing tip of my cock finds the slick notch of her pussy, and I push in, no hesitation —a little mean about it, even. We both need that.

The first thrust is always the most painful. Because it never fails to punch me in the heart, the fucking perfection of her, the tight, hot, wet clasp. Like home. Yeah, she's my home. My everything.

She never shies away from me, but raises her hips, spreads herself wider, as if she needs to take every inch I can offer. Her legs wrap around me, her hands grasping my shoulders. "Killian."

We move as one, pulling apart, sliding back together. It's slow torture. Every time I ease back, I feel cold. Every thrust in, I want to grind myself there, imprint myself from the inside.

My arms bracket her slim shoulders. In the dark, I find her. Her eyes glint as she stares up at me, and we slowly undulate. Her air becomes mine.

Tell her. Beg her not to go.

I dip my head and kiss her, kiss her until I don't feel anything but her mouth, her body. Kiss her until I can't think about tomorrow.

I'm probably crushing her. There isn't any space between us. But she's wrapped tight around me, not letting go. Her lips consume me, her sweet pussy milking my dick as she comes. And I want to shout. It can't end. Not yet.

But then I'm coming too, so hard my body shakes. I don't make a sound. I can't. I'll be begging her if I do.

I fall asleep wrapped up in her, my fingers clinging so hard to her shoulders that my knuckles ache.

In the morning, she's packed before I'm out of bed. The sight of her bags settles like lead in my gut as I pull on a pair of jeans.

"You're leaving now?" I ask, stating the obvious. But, Jesus, she's fast.

Libby shifts on her feet, as if she's already imagining walking out the door. "Your plane leaves tonight, anyway. Scottie got us a flight out early."

Right. Because he's now the one she plans things with. He's her manager. He *should* be planning her life right now. He does the same for me. A green tinge of jealousy clouds my vision.

"Okay, then. I guess you gotta go."

Libby nods and grips her rolling suitcase. "Have a safe flight."

"Yeah, you too." Fuck, we're already talking like strangers.

She glances at the door and a small smile tugs at her pretty lips. "Seems we're destined to always be leaving each other."

So stay. Tell me you can't live without me the way I can't live without you. But she doesn't. And I don't either. I should. My heart tells me I'm a fool not to tell her how I feel. But I've pushed and cajoled Libby too much already. She needs this, and I refuse to stand in her way just because I'm hurting.

If you love someone, you set them free. Isn't that how the saying goes? That, if it was meant to be, they'll come back. Doesn't help me for shit right now, though.

"Well…" I make an abortive move to go to her just as she leans in to hug me. We meet in the middle, our lips brushing, her nose bumping into mine. It's quick, almost impersonal. It fucking sucks.

"Call me," I tell her.

Her gaze is on the floor. "I will."

One last awkward hug, and then I step back, stuffing my hands into my pockets. I'm not proud of that, but I know I won't be able to let her go if I don't distance myself first. I don't watch her leave, just turn away and head for the bathroom. But I hear the door click and the hollow sound of an empty room loud and clear just the same.

LIBBY
27

As I board my plane, I've realized two things: I let Killian go without a fight. And he did the same with me.

At the time it all felt very self-sacrificing. Now I feel as though I've swallowed razor blades. Why didn't we just talk to each other? Why did't I put up a fight? Why didn't he?

Self-doubt is not my friend, and it's whispering in my ear. Did Killian regret putting so much on the line for me? Getting his band and himself in hot water again because of me?

I lean my head against the small plane window and close my eyes. When has taking a break ever resulted in something good? Isn't it just another way of saying goodbye?

The plane takes off, and I feel like I've left a large chunk of myself behind.

LA is...not what I expected. Oh, I thought there would be sun, sea, and palm trees. And LA has that in spades. What I did not realize is that a good chunk of LA is made of long, slightly downtrodden strip malls.

That all changes when Scottie checks us into the Hotel Bel-Air. The place is gorgeous with its fragrant gardens, soaring stucco architecture, and swank black-and-white color scheme. It has to be expensive as hell, but Scottie made clear that he's footing the bill until we sign a deal with a record company. And Scottie does *not* stay in dumps. Or so he tells me when we part ways to settle into our rooms.

My room has its own garden terrace with a Jacuzzi plunge pool, living room, and a fireplace. Instantly, I want to take a picture and show Killian. He'd love this place. It occurs to me that he's probably stayed here many times.

But I don't. I need to make a clean break with this. Go cold turkey. If I keep calling him, I'm going to want to be with him even more. I'm going to end up saying something stupid like, "please take me back!"

I put my phone away and take a long bath. I decide then and there that if I ever have the money to build a dream house, I'm designing it just like this place. I'm just not entirely sold on the location.

After room service of a spectacular lobster Cobb salad, I meet Scottie in the lobby.

The man looks right at home here in his cream-colored three-piece suit, gray silk tie, and sky blue shirt. He's wearing loafers and sunglasses. All of this would look ridiculous on a mere mortal, but not Scottie.

"Are you sure you've never modeled for Dolce & Gabbana? Because you look exactly like that model—"

"Don't say his name," Scottie snaps, glaring at me over his shades. "Ever."

"You're just giving me ammunition," I reply in a sing-song voice as he guides me out to a waiting Mercedes sedan.

"I've filled an entire cemetery with musicians who have tried to tease me, Ms. Bell."

He doesn't appear serious. Of course with the sunglasses on, it's hard to tell.

Our destination is a recording studio, and I try not to gape as I spy not only a few famous movie stars walking by but two of my favorite singers chatting in a glass-and-steel break room inside.

"This way." Scottie ushers me into a smaller, private booth

where a man waits for us.

He looks to be in his mid-forties, balding (with gray frosting what hair is left) and icy blue eyes. Those eyes lock on me, and I can see their keen intelligence. He stands as we enter.

"Scottie. Good to see you."

They exchange handshakes, and then the man turns his attention to me.

"This is Ms. Liberty Bell," Scottie tells him.

"Love the name." He shakes my hand. His grip is fast and brutal. His smile is genuine. "Did you two come up with it?"

"No, sir. My parents had that honor."

"Honey-sweet voice as well. Excellent."

I might be offended if it wasn't clear he was figuring out how to market me.

Scottie gestures for me to take a seat, and the two men follow suit as soon as I do.

"This is Hardy," Scottie says to me.

"As in 'Hardy Jenns. With two Ns'?" God help me, I flipped him off. Wincing. I lower my finger. "I'm sorry—"

"Let me guess," Hardy interrupts with a wry smile. "You hate when it does that."

I smile too. "It's bad form to mix movie quotes."

Scottie looks at us with his usual put-out expression. "When you're done with your '80s movies fun, I'd like to get on with this."

Both Hardy and I blink in shock.

"Hell, Scottie," Hardy says with a laugh, "I had no idea you'd lower yourself to watching '80s movies."

"Mmm…" Scottie hums, deadpan. "And sometimes I listen to rock music. Fancy that."

Hardy leans closer to me. "Warning: taunt the tiger too much and he'll swipe."

I like Hardy, with his easy humor and kind eyes. He's

nothing like what I'd heard from my parents about record producers being egotistical artists who liked to browbeat musicians.

The thought amuses me, and I actually turn my head, some deep-seated part of me expecting Killian to be at my side so I can share a look with him. But he isn't here. His absence is a cold blast against my skin, and my smile dies.

Thankfully neither of the men who actually are in the room seems to notice.

"Hardy is an excellent producer, and we've been discussing your options."

"I've seen clips of you with Kill John, Liberty—"

"Call me Libby. Please."

"Well, Libby, you have a voice and natural sound that guys like me dream of developing." His icy eyes light with excitement. "I've got a few ideas I'd like to run by you."

"I'm game if you are." That sounded all right, didn't it? On the inside I'm shaking like a leaf in a storm. If I can get through this without giggling like a fool, I'll be happy.

Scottie is texting, but he glances at the door when it opens, and three more men enter.

"Ah, yes." Scottie puts away his phone. "Your backup band. Tom plays guitar, Murphy on bass, and Jefferson on the drums."

The guys file in. They're all older than me, clearly seasoned musicians. Guys like my dad, who worked the industry but never tried to make a bid for stardom. Instantly, I feel a measure of comfort. Glancing at Scottie, I'm guessing he knew exactly what he was doing when he hired them. And I have the urge to kiss his handsome cheek. If I didn't know it would make him uncomfortable as hell, I would.

"You look like your mother," Tom says as he sits down.

Surprise tingles over my skin. "You knew her?"

Of the three men, he's the oldest, probably in his forties. "I knew both your mom and your dad. Marcy and George were true talents." His brown eyes grow solemn. "I was sorry to hear of their passing."

"Thank you."

Murphy and Jefferson take a seat as well.

"Marcy and George," Jefferson says. "And your name is Liberty. That some sort of George and Martha Washington joke?"

"You know, you're the first person who actually got that," I say with a laugh. "Most people focus on the whole Liberty Bell thing."

"I'm named after Thomas Jefferson," he says. "So I get the torture too."

"Shit, at least you weren't named after the place where you were conceived," Murphy adds. The tall, wiry guy grins at me from behind a mop of blond hair.

We all think about it for a second, and then I groan in horror. "Oh my God, they didn't name you after a Murphy bed, did they?"

His cheeks go ruddy. "Fuck yeah, they did. Why they had to share that little factoid with me is the real question."

"And yet you shared it with us," Hardy says.

"My pain is now yours."

Laughing, we move on to discussing Scottie's grand plans for me, which include developing some new songs, recording, and, in the meantime, doing the publicity circuit with appearances in small clubs and on talk shows.

It sounds exhausting and exhilarating. The guys Scottie's hired are supportive and clearly talented. It's a dream come true. But the hole in my heart still bleeds steady and cold. I tell myself I'll get over it, but it feels like a lie.

KILLIAN

THE ANIMAL IS GONE. In its place is an ocean of people. And endless sea of writhing bodies, screaming for Kill John, screaming my name. I have to answer. They're waiting for it.

"Hello, London." My voice echoes into the sea, and the sea roars back

They want me, adore me. For the first time in my life, I don't care.

"HEY, *it's Killian. Apparently, my mother hen tendencies are strong. You said you'd call. You didn't. Let me know you're okay. That's all I want, and I'll get out of your hair.*"

"HEY. *It's Libby. You didn't answer, so here goes. My backup band is great. The guys are nice. Not as great as your guys, but I like them. I did my first talk show appearance. Felt like a complete fake. Then again, the actress who went on before me was so out of it, an intern literally had to snap his fingers in her face to get her to react. Once on, though, she was on. Host's breath smelled like tapioca. Which is weird. I've never even had tapioca. How do I know what it smells like? But it was the first thought that popped into my mind when I caught a whiff. Anyway, going to bed.*"

"DAMN AFTER PARTIES *are too loud. Sorry I missed your call, Libs. Had my volume up full blast and still didn't hear it. Whip recorded your show on the bus DVR. You were awesome. Don't like how Tapioca Breath was staring at your tits, though. Next time I'm on that show I might have to accidentally step on his balls. Libby, I really...*"

"YOUR CONNECTION IS SHITTY. *All I heard was something about Whip, awesome, and balls. Then it went dead. I'm not sure I want to know. Lie. I do. Tell me you haven't moved on to balls. Oh, and say hi to the guys. I've got to go.*"

"SERVICE *to the US sucks here. I can't get a call through half the time. And—would you guys shut the fuck up? I'm on the phone. Sorry. I'm trying to find a private place here. I'd call you when I get back in my room, but the time difference sucks too. I'm pretty sure you're asleep right now. Shit. It's breaking up...I...*"

"IT'S *a lost cause trying to connect, isn't it? Why don't we try to talk when things calm down? And...well, if we're really taking time to figure things out, maybe we shouldn't be talking so much right now, anyway. Not that I don't want to talk to you. I just...we're both busy. I'm babbling so I'm going to hang up now. Take care, Killian.*"

I LISTEN to her final message three times. It doesn't get any easier to hear. I've lost her. What I don't know is if it's because I sent her away or if she simply realized that she doesn't feel as strongly for me as I do for her.

I want to ask—no, demand—that she tell me. I want to lay it all down and hash this shit out. But I can't do that over the phone. And I can't leave the tour. I can't do that to the guys.

My thumb taps the edge of my phone as I think of what to say.

I'll let you go for now. But text me if you need anything. K?

When she doesn't answer my text, I chuck my phone

across the room. The door to the dressing room opens before impact, and the phone smacks the center of Jax's chest. He frowns down at the phone that's clattered to the floor before looking back up at me. "Fans are waiting for the meet and greet."

As if to punctuate his words, a group of women bursts in behind him on a wave of giggles. Their smiles are eager and all for me. All blonde, all gorgeous, they're whispering in a language I don't understand. Norwegian. We're in Norway.

I rub the aching spot over my chest. Fuck. I need to let this thing with chasing Libby go. She's busy building her life. The life I sent her to lead. My life is here. Doing what I've always done. I've survived just fine for twenty-six years without her. I can survive now.

"Right." I find a smile and paste it on. I won't touch them. The idea makes me ill. But I can play host. I can do that much for the guys. "Welcome, ladies."

I'm tired. So tired I don't remember where I am half the time. Everything is nebulous. I'm living in this strange cloud filled with too many strangers and too many fake smiles—my fake smiles. I hand them out like a politician passes out buttons. And I feel just as slick doing it.

I have been completely on my own for a while now. But not since my parents died have I felt so utterly lonely. It doesn't matter that I'm surrounded by people, my schedule full. I don't have the one person I want at my side. Hell, I even miss the guys. A lot.

My backup band is great. But they aren't true friends. When the job is done, they head home to family. And Scottie is a man unto himself. In a strange way, he's a lot like me. Not shy, not antisocial exactly, just self-contained and private. I certainly can't throw stones his way. But he doesn't make for an ideal companion.

"Is it always like this?" I ask him as we leave yet another party in the Hills. The house was breathtaking, the people there even more so. I met actors I'd watched since childhood and those who are just now hot commodities. So many gorgeous creatures, I hadn't known what to do with myself or what to say. Not that I had to say much of anything. Most of these people love to hear themselves talk.

All night, I had to check myself from turning to whisper a comment in Killian's ear. Because he wasn't there. Why can't my brain and body seem to get that message?

"Is what 'always like this'?" Scottie answers, nose deep in his phone calendar.

"The endless pushing." I ease my shoes off my feet, wincing. Thanks to Brenna, I now own my own Louboutins. My appreciation for them died the first time I put them on. "Two months we've been at it. At this point, I feel like a snake oil salesman."

Scottie's lip twitches. "I do so love your expressions. Don't change them. They add color to your persona."

"Good to know," I mutter, then nudge his arm with my elbow. "I'm talking to you. Get your nose out of that thing. It's indecent."

Good lord, Killian must have learned that imperious brow quirk of his from Scottie. This man's is downright glacial. But he does put his phone down.

"What is the problem, Ms. Bell?"

"I go to these things you and Brenna book for me, and the parties y'all seem to think I need to attend, and I feel…I don't know. Fake. Like I'm faking it."

Scottie stares at me as our hired car snakes down the twisting mountain road. When he speaks, his tone is softer than I expected. "You are faking it."

"Excuse me?"

"Calm down." Scottie leans back, resting one ankle on his bent knee. "In here, we are simply Libby and Gabriel—"

"That's your name? How did I not even know your name?"

He pinches the bridge of his nose. "Back to the point—"

"How old are you, anyway?"

He glares ice chips. "Twenty-eight."

"Back the truck up. Really? I thought you were in your thirties."

"We see what we want to see. And if you're good, you make people see what *you* want them to see. For my job, if I skew slightly older I'll garner more respect and credibility. All bullshit, but appearances matter in this world." He pins me with a look. "Which is precisely my point. Stardom is an illusion, an ideal carefully cultivated by persons like myself and Brenna. In private, you can be yourself. But the moment you step in the public eye, you become Liberty Bell, talented ingénue—"

"Hey! I can be sophisticated."

"Who," he says over me, "is taking the music world by storm with her unique sound. That is all they'll know. Because that is all you'll show them."

"I just want to be me."

"You misunderstand. You are being you. Merely another version of you. It is armor, Libby. If you give them all of yourself, the world will drain you dry. But if you go to these events and act a part—something they're all doing as well—you have a certain freedom. It isn't real. Therefore it isn't really you who's constantly being watched and judged."

I get what he's saying. It still deepens the pit of loneliness that's been haunting my insides. "Is that what Killian does?"

Scottie's gaze goes sharp. "Not with you. Or his inner circle. But you have to have seen the difference in how he acts with the rest of the world." Scottie's hand drifts toward his phone, left lying on the seat cushion. "And he's had years of practice. He knows just how much to give without losing himself."

I'm not so sure. He was lost when I found him on my lawn. I saw him come back to his own, saw the shadows leave his eyes. Together we were happy, solid, alive. And I left him. Just as surely as he left me.

Suddenly, I don't want to talk anymore. I just want to crawl in bed and burrow under the covers, pretending that I'm not constantly reaching for someone who isn't there.

SCOTTIE'S RIGHT. As days pass, it does get easier. It's not exactly fun, but it isn't the torture I made it out to be. And when I perform, even on my own, the adoration of the audience is a beautiful thing. Killian had it right: it *is* addictive, almost as good as sex with him. But I've known that bit for a while. And though I feel myself getting into a groove, finding my place, it's still all wrong. I can't shake the emptiness inside me—an emptiness I've never experienced before now.

A week later, Scottie leaves me to check on Kill John in London. It takes all I have not to beg him to let me go with him. Brenna will remain with me in his place now. And though I've missed her and love her company, her presence is another thorn in my side. She's been with the guys—with Killian—all this time. I constantly want to ask her about him. And I constantly refrain from doing so. Call it pride, but I don't want to hear about him from second-hand sources.

Tonight, Brenna has taken me to a club. I don't blame her. That's the way the guys relaxed after "work." Me? I'd rather play my guitar in my room.

The place beats with music so loud the floor rattles. Bodies writhe, laughter breaking out in disjointed bursts. Beautiful people, impeccably dressed and with perfectly capped smiles, wide and fake, are everywhere—eyes on everyone else. Watch and be watched.

I hate it. Longing for my porch hits me so hard that I struggle to catch my breath.

"I can't stay here," I tell Brenna at my side.

She nods. "Thank God. I'm really beginning to hate this shit."

We make an about face, and Brenna calls our car service.

Back in my suite, I take a long, hot shower. It doesn't seem to wash the fug off my skin. I'm imbued with an ugly feeling: time of my life, and it's a void. I dress myself in my beloved Star Wars shirt that used to be Killian's. The soft cotton caresses my skin as I pull on sweats and go back to the living room.

Brenna greets me with a cocktail. She's been serving me way too many of these Pity Party of One drinks. I reach out to take it from her, my fingertips brushing the icy glass, when a wave of nausea hits me so hard I double over.

"I can't do this," I wail, hunching on the ground.

In an instant, Brenna is kneeling by my side. Her hand rubs gentle circles over my back as I try to catch my breath. "What is it, Libs?"

"God, don't call me that." I can't hear Killian's nickname for me right now.

"Okay. Okay." She continues to pet me as if I'm not totally off my nut.

Taking a deep breath, I push my hair out of my face and sit on the floor. The carpet has a scummy film over it, the way most hotel carpets do. I wrap my arms around my knees. "I'm sorry. I didn't mean to freak out."

Brenna copies my position, her sky-high heels snagging on the carpet. "Freaking out doesn't bother me. It's *why* you are that's my concern."

"I don't know." I wipe my watery eyes. "I just saw myself taking drink after drink. The same way my father did—so casual, like it's no big deal…"

"You are not your father," Brenna insists. "And far from an alcoholic. Trust me, I've seen my share of them."

I try to smile but can't.

"What's wrong, Libby? Talk to me."

Absently, I rub my thumb over my knee. "I had a guitar in my hands before I learned to write. I never tell anyone that. But it's true. Music was our family's way of communicating.

My parents died, and I just let it go. Until Killian."

I glance up at Brenna. "My mom didn't want this life for me. She thought it was too hard, soulless. My dad didn't either. But because he thought it was too addictive. And I told myself I resisted being here because I was afraid or shy. But it was them and their constant warnings that if I tried to live this way, I'd lose myself."

"Libby," Brenna says quietly. "Your parents' experiences don't have to be yours. What do you want? If you want to quit and go back to your farmhouse, you can."

Closing my eyes, I can see the golden coastal light slanting through the old glass of my grandmother's house, the worn floorboards, the battered farm table where I served Killian biscuits. The echo of his laughter haunts my memories.

"I was on vacation there," I tell Brenna. "That wasn't real life."

"What is for you?"

"I love singing, making music, performing. Killian saw that in me when I couldn't see it myself. But this life right now? It's empty. It doesn't…it doesn't have him."

I miss Killian with a force that's nearly crippling. We haven't spoken in a while, and that's on me and my pride. It still hurts that he sent me away. Find myself, my ass. I'd found myself with him. But I let him go too. The fact that we both just seemed to give up depresses me. Maybe we weren't meant to be.

Silence ticks.

"You have to know Killian is crazy about you," Brenna finally says.

"I thought so," I say thickly. "But if he really was, he wouldn't have told me to go live my life without him. Would he?"

"What?" she sounds shocked.

My chest clenches, and I have to force myself to tell her the rest. "He could have said we'd met up at the end of his tour. But he didn't. Instead he tells me that we should take this time to reevaluate what we want."

It isn't until I say the words that I really feel how badly he'd cut me. "He pushed me away."

Brenna looks at me for a long minute. "I know my cousin. He has never been this way about a woman. Ever. If he said that, he was probably trying to do something noble and set you free."

I laugh without humor. "Oh, he certainly did that."

"No," she says gently. "I mean, he told you what he thought you needed to hear to go because he thought it was best for you. Not because he didn't want you anymore. That's typical of my big-hearted but ham-handed cousin." She gives my arm a nudge. "Come on, Libby, he'd be here in a heartbeat if you asked him to, and you know it.

"Brenna, my dad drank to escape the reality of life with me and my mom. I cannot be any man's burden. I can't. I want Killian to know I'm okay on my own too. That I can manage without him holding my hand."

"But you aren't okay." Brenna's pretty face pinches. "You're miserable."

I stand and dust myself off. "You know what? I am. I miss Killian so much it's eating me alive. But worse than that, I've been feeling sorry for myself. Moping like a sadsack."

Brenna's face changes. "Okay..."

"We doing the Late Night Show tomorrow?"

"Yeah."

"Can you make sure Killian sees me on it?" I know she can. Between her and Scottie, they could take over the world if they wanted to.

"Sure thing."

"All right, then. I have to practice a song." I head for my room. One thing is certain: the tight band I've kept around my emotions has snapped. And now broken, nothing can hold back the tide. I need to find my way back to happy.

KILLIAN
29

I have no idea where the fuck we are. I don't really care. Jax can shout the customary, "Hello, insert whatever the hell town," for once. Our dressing room is like all the rest: stark and filled with people who don't need to be here.

A shrill laugh stabs at my nerves. I don't bother looking to see who it is. Scottie's brought in a small TV. Libby is going to perform on the Late Night Show. She's in L.A. Right, I'm in New York. Hours behind her.

Scottie gives me a nod, turns on the TV, and sits in the chair beside me, crossing one leg over the other like the elegant bastard he is.

On the screen, the audience claps, Libby having already been announced. And there she is, walking on to the tiny soundstage with that determined stride I know so well. Brenna has developed a signature look for her: flowing, almost bohemian knee-length sundresses and big, chunky combat boots. Pure Libby.

My chest clenches at the sight of her, a pang of longing shooting through my heart. It hurts seeing her. Agitated, I turn the volume up high as she gives the audience a nod of acknowledgment.

Libby plucks a few strings on her Martin, then leans closer to the mic. Her pretty lips are glossy and pink, and the ghost of their touch tickles along my neck.

"My best friend in the world taught me this lesson," she says in that sweet vanilla cream voice of hers. "Just took me a while to believe it."

And my heart pounds. Am I that friend? I hate that I have to ask myself. God, please let it be me.

Libby starts singing Prince's "Cream." Perfect tune, perfect delivery. There's a little smile about her mouth, almost wry, a bit bittersweet. And she looks at the camera—directly at it, as if she finally owns her talent. Her song choice confirms it, the lyrics about taking your chance, reaching for what you want in life.

The hairs on the back of my neck stand on end. A frisson runs over me, just as powerful as when I first stepped on stage. I can actually feel the world shifting gears, changing her life and mine into something new once again.

A girl tries to hang on my arm. I brush her off without taking my eyes from the screen. "Do you see her?" I say to no one in particular. "Right there, that's my girl. Isn't she fucking luminous?"

Whip stares down at the TV with a proud smile. "That she is, man."

I turn to Jax. "And I made her feel like I didn't want her when I sent her away. Because I'm an idiot."

Jax sighs and runs a hand through his hair. "And I'm an asshole. Kills, man, I encouraged her to leave the tour. Said you'd be distracted by her. But that was my own shit talking, me trying to put things back the way they were before."

I should be pissed. But mostly I'm just tired of struggling to pretend everything is normal. "We broke, Jax," I tell him while watching the TV. "We're gluing ourselves back together, but it's never going to be the same."

"Fuck. I know."

The defeat in his voice makes me bump his shoulder with

mine. "We're not who we were. We're better. Evolution, Jax. Not regression."

He shakes his head, but he's fighting a smile. "I'm sorry, though. I miss her too."

Libby's smoky voice snags my attention again. "She's it for me. It's a done deal." I've been hers since the second she hosed me down and woke me up. "My life doesn't work anymore without her in it."

"I know, man. We all know it." Jax puts a hand on my shoulder. "Do this show, and then you go get your girl."

LIBBY

IT TAKES FOREVER to wash the makeup off my face. By the time I'm done, my skin is pink and angry at me. But I feel better. Freer. Sometimes all it takes in life is to decide to own it. And everything changes. Would Killian understand? I sang that song for him as much as for myself—to tell him I finally got it. Life is what you make of it. I know that now. Because of him.

I hear Brenna enter the suite and go out to meet her. She has a box of pizza in one hand.

"Your performance was totally awesome." She does a little victory dance that makes me laugh.

"You've told me that three times now."

"You have to give reinforcement in threes," she says, sticking out her tongue. "Otherwise it doesn't stick."

"Consider it stuck, then." I accept a piece of pizza and take a big bite. So good. I'm starved tonight.

Brenna scarfs down her own slice. "The guys are in New York now."

I pause mid-bite. "I thought they were in London."

"They were. They got into New York this morning for their final concert of the tour. They always like to end things on their home turf."

"Right. I'd forgotten that." Longing falls like a heavy blanket on my shoulders. I actually roll them as if I could shrug the feeling off. Doesn't work, though. I set my piece of pizza aside and search for a water in the mini fridge.

"They're on stage now," Brenna says, watching me with wary eyes. "Scottie has a recording of it he wanted you to see."

"Scottie does?" I can't keep the skepticism out of my voice.

Brenna gives a cheeky grin. "Pretty sure he was ordered to."

"Hmmm..." I can't say more. The idea that Killian is passing me yet another proverbial note sends me a flash of hope and an ache of nostalgia.

We curl up on the couch, and Brenna plays the video. God, it hurts seeing him. Bare chest glistening with sweat, ratty old jeans hanging low and lovingly outlining that nearly obscene bulge of his—he's a hot rock star at his finest. And the way he holds that white and black Telecaster in his big hands is like music porn.

His deep, rich voice sends a shiver down my spine as he dips his head to the mic. "We'd like to play a tribute tonight. If you know the words, sing along."

I don't know what I expected, but it wasn't "Darling Nikki." Oh, but it's so good. Killian's voice is pure sex, dripping with sticky sin. And watching him work his guitar? Jesus. Heat washes up my thighs, pools between my legs.

Killian's beloved Animal goes wild. Women scream; men hold their hands up in solidarity. They all join him, shouting the words.

He absolutely shreds the guitar on the solo, his hips thrusting, his back bowed. Emotion pulls the slashes of his brows together, has him biting his lip. I've seen that face before—when he's over me, coming, giving in to lust.

In my periphery, I catch a glimpse of Brenna gawking at the screen and then back at me.

I don't know what to say. A lump closes my throat. I swallow hard against it, but the pain doesn't go away. My hands start to shake.

Killian's shouting how he wants another grind.

A song about a freaky whore? About a deal with the devil? An unforgettable woman? It could be all and any of those things. A tribute? To whom? Prince? Or me? I sang "Cream." Now he's singing this.

"Libs—" Brenna starts to say.

I hold up my hand. "I...ah...I'm going to bed. I need to think..." I don't say anything more. But I do leave my phone on the table as I walk away. Because I have a feeling he'll call, and I have nothing I can say to him over the phone.

KILLIAN
30

I'm on my phone the second I get back to the dressing room. My blood is pumping, my body humming. I have to pace to cool down. People flow around me, laughing, staring, trying to get close. I want to order them out, but I'm too busy trying to call Libby. I keep getting her voicemail.

I don't leave a message. I want to talk to her.

Sitting my ass in a chair, I start to text her, only to see one from Brenna.

What the fuck was that? Idiot. (!!!!) >:-(

I read it twice before holding up the phone to the guys. "Why the hell is she yelling at me?"

"Dude." Rye shakes his head. "I told you not to choose that song."

"What's wrong with 'Darling Nikki'? It's my favorite song on *Purple Rain*—an album we talked about when we first bonded over music. She played Prince tonight. I played Prince tonight. I'm supporting her. How can it be more clear?"

"A." Rye holds up a finger. "That is way too esoteric."

"It's supposed to be," I protest. "It's a message to her, not the rest of the world."

"B," he says over me. "'Darling Nikki' is what Prince sings to Apollonia when he's basically calling her a whore."

Whip nods. "Yeah, the lyrics pretty much say she's only

good for freaky sex."

I stare at them, incredulous. "Why didn't you all tell me this *before* we did the fucking song?"

"You were pretty insistent," Rye says with a shrug.

"And you knew the lyrics," Whip points out calmly. "You just sang them."

"Of course I know the lyrics. It's the *context* I didn't get."

"Context is everything, man."

I press the heels of my hands against my eyes and try not to shout. "Shit. Shit. Shit."

Jax hands me a water. "Relax. If she knows you as well as I think she does, she'll get your message." He fights a smile. "Convoluted as it was."

"Shit."

"LIBS, if you get this message, call me. Please. Baby doll. Please. I need to talk to you. I...ah...that song was for you. Shit. Not to call you a whore— I mean, never! Okay? It was because I am so proud of you. I wanted to tell you— Just call me, okay? Please."

"LIBS. I'm getting a little concerned. Where are you? Pick up your phone."

NO TEXTS EITHER**? You're killing me here.**

"ELLY MAY, pick up the damn phone. Call me back. I'm getting on a plane and tracking you down. Or I would if I could fucking find you. Damn it, I told you I'd get shit wrong. I want to make them right. Please let me."

"I NEED YOU, all right? That's what it comes down to. You're it. My present, my future, my everything. Not my whore. I haven't even seen the damn movie! Okay, just… yeah. Call me."

LIBBY

NEW YORK CITY. One redeye flight, and I'm here. I feel like I've been run over with a sand truck. Gritty-eyed and sore, I sit passive as a makeup artist works on my face. Someone else is blowdrying my hair, attempting to give it some waves around my face. Good luck with that.

I'd rather be anywhere but here. But Brenna, now crowned Official Pain in My Ass, booked an interview with *Vanity Fair*. I *could* cancel, she told me. But it would look bad. Especially considering the little gossip column that showed up on TNV last night.

I don't have to look at it again to remember it. The fucking thing is burned in my brain:

Last night on the Late Night Show, *the new darling of the music world, Liberty Bell, performed an absolutely cheeky rendition of Prince's "Cream." Not much by way of news unless you consider that, only an hour later, rock god and rumored boyfriend of Ms. Bell, Killian James, countered with a cover of "Darling Nikki" during Kill John's concert in Madison Square Garden.*

One must speculate, is James declaring their supposed fling officially over? Thanking Bell for a good time? Or is he asking her for another go? Whatever the case, we are certain Killian's loyal fan base is waiting with bated breath to find out if their sexy idol is once again single and free.

Well, I can't exactly blame them for interpreting Killian's

message that way. But it stings to know people are all up in our business, judging us. I feel naked down to my soul.

It will be over soon. I haven't turned on my phone yet. I know Killian has been trying to contact me. But the conversation we need to have can't happen over the phone.

Frankly, I'm sick of phones and texts. I avoided social media and casual texting all these years for a reason. I don't want cold and impersonal. I don't want to hide behind a screen. I need personal contact, face-to-face communication.

The makeup artist finishes, and an assistant with a Bluetooth headset has me sit on a chrome-and-leather chair.

"There's water just here," he tells me as if I can't see the ice bucket at my side. "The green one is excellent. Imported from Japan at over four hundred dollars a bottle."

I refrain from pointing out how crass it is to tell me that, and choose the slightly less ostentatious bottle of Bling H2O with the logo bedazzled onto it.

A reporter comes in, her hair brilliant blue, her smile welcoming. I steel my spine and grit my teeth. *Just get through this, and you'll be free to go. Get through this.*

"There's been so much written about your involvement with Killian James. But you and James have been rather closed-mouthed about the topic." The reporter gives me a slight but encouraging smile, her blue hair slipping over one eye. "Given last night's performance, would you care to offer us a little bite?"

"There isn't much to tell that the world doesn't already know." Not really true. But true enough.

The reporter's smile has an edge to it now—a barracuda searching for blood in the water. "Oh, now, I'm not so sure about that. After all, we don't know your side of the story."

Nothing to lose. And everything to gain. "What do you want to know?"

KILLIAN
31

"You ever think about it?" I whisper. She sits before me, skin gilded in the evening light, eyes glazed, frosted jewels. So fucking beautiful it breaks my heart. "What it would be like? You and me?"

"Yeah."

I breathe in her scent. Touch her skin. "You can have the world. Just reach for it."

"I don't need the world," she whispers in my ear.

"What do you need?" I'll give her anything. Everything.

Soft hands on my neck, gentle lips mapping my skin. "You."

"Dude, we have to get out there." Rye's voice comes to me at a distance.

I stare down at my phone, rubbing my thumb over the screen.

"Dude?"

"Killian," Jax says, sharper. "Snap out of it."

I run a hand through my hair. It's longer now, in need of a trim. "She isn't answering me. I don't know where she is. Brenna won't tell me." We're back at the Bowery Ballroom where we started our tour. Memories of Libby flood in, and I swallow hard.

A hand lands on my shoulder. Jax's eyes meet mine in the mirror. "As soon as the show is done, we'll pile up on Scottie and make him cry uncle."

"Yeah," Whip agrees behind me. "That shithead definitely knows where she is."

I'm pretty sure we could break Scottie's legs, and the man still wouldn't talk. He's like ice that way. From outside the dressing room door comes a steady chant for Kill John. The air hums, but I don't feel the familiar crackle of anticipation.

"Come on, man." Rye slaps my other shoulder. "Get off your ass. Moping is a destructive and unattractive quality."

This from the guy who stayed in bed for a week when John Entwistle died, crying that The Who would never be the same again. But he's right. I pull myself together because my guys need me.

One more show and I'm free. Just get through this.

LIBBY

THE LAST TIME I saw Kill John perform, I was in the wings, watching them from behind. Being in the audience is an entirely different experience. On stage, the crowd's energy comes at you like a wave. In the audience, I feel the full force of Kill John's power. And it is awe inspiring.

Killian's deep, luscious vocals blend with Jax's brutal melody. Together they are rage and yearning. Whip beats on his drums with perfect timing and rhythm, while Rye's funky base supports it all. That is the technical aspect. But the real truth of their music cannot be defined. You have to feel it.

I'm swept up by it and find myself dancing with the crowd. Scottie assigned me protection in the form of a massive bodyguard named Joe. He's at my side now, blocking people from crushing too close or stepping on my toes. It's sweet, but not necessary. The club is small and not so overcrowded that I can't move.

Kill John finishes up "Oceans," and a sweaty Killian pulls off his damp shirt. Predictably, whistles of approval break out all over. His lips twist but he doesn't acknowledge them as he gulps down some water.

Standing midway to the stage, I can see him clearly enough to note the shadows under his eyes and the lines of strain around his mouth. And though no one else would notice, I can tell the guys are concerned. It's in the way they watch him, Rye and Jax's bodies angled slightly toward him like shields.

While the crowd shouts requests, the guys make a few adjustments, Jax and Killian getting different guitars and Whip picking up a new set of sticks. Killian's movements are unhurried, almost languid.

"Play 'Oceans' again," a guy right behind me yells loud enough to blow my hair forward.

The request is ridiculous enough to grab Killian's attention. He lifts his head, a smirk on his face as if he's going to say something, but then our gazes clash. I know the second he realizes it's me. Because everything freezes. His expression wipes totally blank, then shatters, his lips parting on a breath, his eyes going wide.

I feel that look down to my toes. It wrenches my heart. I know there and then that he's hurting as much as I am. It's all there in those coffee dark eyes. Everything that's passed between us—every look, word, touch—is all there. Tears blur my vision, and I offer him a watery smile.

He twitches as if he's fighting not to hop off the stage. But then a slow smile spreads. He barely nods. I wonder if he's having as hard a time functioning as I am.

When he turns toward his guys, his movements are jerky. One by one, three sets of eyes focus on me. Whip's expression is one of relief. Rye's smile is wide and bright. Jax stares at me for a long moment and then gives me a small chin tip.

My heart thuds as Killian turns back to the mic. His gaze

locks onto me. "I met my best friend on the lawn of a farmhouse. I'd lost my way, my music. She helped me find it again." I choke back a sob, clutching my arms around my chest, as Killian keeps talking. "Back then, she asked me to sing one of my songs for her. I wouldn't do it. Truth is, I wanted her to like me more than she liked my music."

The crowd *awws*, and he gives them his cheeky smile. "I know. I'm pathetic, aren't I?"

"I love you, Killian," shouts a woman at the back. "Have my babies!"

"No," cries a man near the stage, "have mine!"

Killian chuckles low in the mic. "Sorry, guys. I'm taken." While the crowd moans, he grins and switches out his Telecaster for a big acoustic Gibson J-200, plucking a few chords. "Thing is, I still want her to like me. So I'm not gonna play a Kill John song right now. I'm gonna play an old favorite of mine. And maybe I'll get the message right this time."

There's a wolf whistle in the crowd.

Jax leans close to his mic. "You'd better, or we're benching you for the rest of the game."

People laugh again, but I'm stuck on the happy grins Jax and Killian exchange. Gone is the underlying tension that's seemed to ride them, replaced by an easy joy and appreciation for each other that brings a lump to my throat. The band is in perfect sync as they start to play "Trying To Break Your Heart" by Wilco.

A half-laugh, half-sob breaks free. His choice is quintessential Killian; he'd never go for a straightforward, saccharine love song. But this song, with its twisted lyrics and gently teasing remorse, makes perfect sense to me. The music is lilting and bittersweet and full of possibility.

Tears blur my vision, and I'm laughing again. Laughing and crying.

He catches my gaze, and his eyes soften. Through the

lyrics, he tells me how much it hurt to let me go. How much I hurt him. How much he wants me back.

My feet start moving. I weave through the swaying crowd, Joe helping to clear a path. Killian watches me come, his whole heart shining in his eyes. He's calling to me, singing that he's the man who loves me.

By the time I reach the stage, it's apparent to the audience that something's going on. People make room, their smiles wide. But not as wide as Killian's.

Setting his guitar down, he strides over and holds out his arms. The second our hands clasp, something inside me relaxes. He hauls me up with ease, and then I'm in his arms. Holding tight, his long, lean body surrounds me, a shelter from all things.

He's sweat-slicked and trembling. My nose is crushed against his pec. I don't ever want to let go.

"Libby," he breathes into my hair. "You're here."

If anything, he holds me tighter. It's okay. I don't need air. Just him.

I turn my head and find his jaw with my lips. "You asked me to come. In the song. You asked me to come back to you."

He bursts out in a broken laugh that makes his chest hitch. "You got that? No one else did."

I close my eyes, let him support me. "No one else matters."

He shivers harder. "Only you, Libs."

Suddenly I hear the crowd again, hooting and shouting. Killian must hear them too because he lifts his head, giving them a wave and a smile. I see the blur of stage lights, dozens of phones held overhead, and Jax's wink. Then Killian hurries me off the stage, refusing to let me go.

He doesn't stop until we're alone in a small dressing room.

I don't know who moves first, but the door closes, and I'm wrapped in him. I've missed the way he feels, his taste, the scent of him. His hands bracket my cheeks, his mouth moving over mine.

"I missed you," he says between frantic kisses. "I missed you so fucking much. I shouldn't have let you go." He kisses my eyes, my cheeks, the corner of my ear. "I thought I was setting you free. But it killed me. I need you, Libs. So much."

"I know." I cup the back of his neck and squeeze as I meet his gaze. "It was the same for me. I was just...empty."

Dark, pained eyes search mine. "And then that stupid song. You wouldn't answer me. I thought—"

"I'm sorry," I cut in. "I didn't mean to upset you. I just needed to think things through. And I wanted to talk in person."

He nods before dipping down to rest his forehead against mine. "What are you thinking, baby doll? What do you want?"

"You." When he jerks, I grip his hard biceps. "I just want to be with you."

"Good. Because I don't think I can function anymore unless you're here."

"I missed you," I tell him. I don't think I can express it enough.

For a long moment he just looks at me. "I made a career off writing songs. They've given me awards for my lyrics. And never can I get the message right with you."

"I don't need you to—"

"I love you."

My breath catches in my throat as my heart stops. I exhale in a burst, and he kisses my lips softly. So softly. The tenderness in it breaks me. I nearly sob when he does it again.

"That's what I've been trying to say all this time." He smiles, the barest curve of his lips. "I used to think those were just words. Something I could put in a song. They didn't mean anything. I get it now. I get it."

"Killian..."

The tip of his thumb caresses my cheek. "Love breaks your

heart, fucks you up—perfect, all-consuming chaos. I didn't know what to do with that. It felt safer to walk." He wraps me up in his arms, his eyes on mine. "But it's also this. Peace, and warmth, and so fucking beautiful, you'll risk anything to keep it."

"Killian…" I cup his cheek, run my fingers into his hair. Just hold him. "You do just fine getting your message across. I love you too, you know. So much."

Oh, God, that smile—it's pure happiness. "I need you to understand, Libby. You're my reason, the answer to all questions."

"And you, my sweet lawn bum, are my home. I'm just wandering unless I'm with you. And I'm so tired, Killian. I need to be home now."

He takes a deep breath, pressing his lips against my forehead as if he has to ground himself. "I'm here. You're here." He ghosts a kiss over my cheek. "We'll make it work. I'll take time off and travel with you—"

"I've realized something," I cut in. "I don't want to be a star. Not at this level. It isn't me."

He frowns down at me. "Were you that miserable?"

"No, honey. It was an experience of a lifetime. I wouldn't change the opportunities you gave me for the world. But these past few months?" I shrug. "Maybe I am my parents' daughter. All I know is that it isn't the stardom that lights me up. It's playing, singing. It's being with you. Those things matter to me. The rest is just…air."

Killian's soft laugh is wry, the corner of his mouth kicking up. "Funny thing, I realized that too."

I still. "You want to quit?"

"No. But I do want to slow down. I want time with you. Time to enjoy life." He shakes his head. "Kill John will always be part of me, but I've changed. We all have. I don't know what will happen, but I'm not afraid of it anymore."

I take a deep breath, press my cheek against his jaw. "You pulled me out of my shell. All that I am now is because of you."

His fingers thread in my hair, giving the strands a gentle tug. "And you woke me up again. Let's make a life together, Liberty. It'll be good. So fucking good."

I meet his eyes, those coffee dark eyes that always hold promise of sin and sweetness. Excitement tingles over my skin, pulls at my breath. "I can't wait."

Epilogue
KILLIAN

The winter grass is the color of toasted sand, stretching toward a slate gray sky. It's windy these days, the air wet with salt and sea. But on Libby's farmhouse porch, with the cast-iron stove going, it's warm enough for me to hang out in jeans and a T-shirt, my bare toes tapping on the worn floorboards.

I'm sitting in a rocker, drinking coffee and inhaling a heaping plate of the best damn biscuits in the world. Looking back on it, I probably fell in love with Libby the first time I ate one of her biscuits.

I tell her this now, and she gives me a look. The kind that says she finds me amusing but doesn't want to admit it.

"Mama always said a man was led by his stomach and his cock," she says from the rocking chair at my side, while she idly strums her guitar. "It was just a matter of figuring out which one needs the most appeasing at the moment."

I take another bite of heavenly baked goodness. "After we eat, you can appease my cock."

She hums. "Good thing it's so cute, or I'd take exception to that."

"Cute? My cock is no longer appeased."

Libby fights a smile. But her attention is on the Gibson in her hands. It's my guitar, but she plays it so well. A sweet melody rings out, old-fashioned and happy but nostalgic. Her honey-soft voice joins in as she sings "Sea of Love."

The sound of her wraps itself around my heart. Her sound is home and hope all rolled in one. It always was. It always will be.

When she finishes, I turn to her. "Was that for me?"

Her smile is soft, beautiful. "They all are."

It's a good thing the guys aren't around to see me welling up. Just yesterday, Rye texted to say it was only a matter of time before Libby and I started looking like the couple in *American Gothic*, that all I needed was a pitchfork. We sent him a picture of us standing in front of the house, me with pitchfork in hand, both of us flipping him the bird.

We haven't been completely idle. For the past month, Libby and I have been writing songs. A couple of them are for Kill John, a couple are for Libby's album. She still doesn't want the limelight, but Jax, of all people, pointed out that she can have a career on her own terms. So that's what she's going to do: write, record, and perform in small venues.

Next week we're going back to New York. I'll start trying out the new songs with the guys, and Libby will go to the recording studio. But for now, I'm making the most of our semi-vacation.

I set down my plate and grab my Martin, making a few adjustments. "I've got a song. But you have to sing with me."

"I will if you tell me what you're playing," she says.

Grinning, I bite my lip, a thrill of anticipation going through me. "You'll get it."

I start the White Stripes' "Hotel Yorba." By the end of the opening riff, she's playing along, her rhythm framing my lead. We sing the refrain laughing, playing our guitars double time.

Her eyes are bright when the song ends. "You have that as my ringtone."

"Yep." I lay my guitar down. "Set it the second I left this house and you behind."

"Why that one?"

"Lyrics fit my mood. I, too, just wanted to be back on this porch, alone with you."

Her expression softens. "Well, here we are."

"And what about the rest of it, Libs?" I ask, my chest growing tight. "Am I the man you love the most?"

A flush rises over her cheeks as she looks at me, the little spot where her pulse beats on her neck visibly fluttering. She knows the lyrics. She knows what I'm asking. "Yes," she says, almost shyly.

I've had this planned. Doesn't stop my heart from trying to pound its way out of my chest. Slowly I kneel in front of her, my hands settling on her lush hips. "I'll love you my whole life, and it won't feel like enough. So what do you say, Libs? Want to go get married?"

Her smile is my sun. She wraps her arms around my neck and kisses me. "Where's my ring, lawn bum?"

I smile against her lips. "Look in my pocket, Elly May."

Her little jolt of surprise is cute. Did she think I wouldn't have it? The way her hand shakes as she pulls out the small box tells me she's as nervous as I am. For a long moment she looks at the vintage gold-and-emerald ring. Then her eyes well up, and she flings her arm around my neck, putting me out of my misery. "Oh, hell. I'm marrying a musician."

I hold her close, breathe her in. "We're gonna have so much fun."

Her laughter is a warm breath against my neck. "Yes, we are. And I'll love you forever, Killian James. That much I know for certain."

Thank You!
Thank you for reading *IDOL*!
I hope you enjoyed it!

Reviews help other readers find books.
I appreciate all reviews, whether positive or
negative or somewhere in between.

I like to hang out in these places.
Come and hang out with me. Callihan's VIP Lounge,
The Locker Room, Kristen Callihan FB author page,
and @Kris10Callihan on Twitter.

Sneak peek of MANAGED *
book 2 in the VIP Series
Preview of Scottie's book—subject to change

SOPHIE

YOU KNOW those people who Lady Luck always seems to be kissing on the cheek? The ones who get a promotion just for showing up to work? Who win that awesome raffle prize? The person who finds a hundred-dollar bill on the ground? Yeah, that's not me. And it's probably not most of us. Lady Luck is a selective bitch.

But today? Lady Luck has finally turned her gaze upon me. And I want to bow down in gratitude. Because today, I've been upgraded to first class for my flight to London. It's due to overbooking, and who knows why they picked me, but they did. First fucking class, baby. I'm so giddy, I practically dance to my seat.

And, oh, what a beautiful seat it is, all plush cream leather and burled wood paneling—though I'm guessing it's fake wood for safety reasons. Not that it matters. It's a little self-contained pod, complete with a cubby for my bag and shoes, a bar, an actual reading lamp, and a widescreen TV.

I sink into the seat with a sigh. It's a window seat, sectioned off from my neighbor with a frosted glass panel I can lower with the touch of a button. Or the two seats can become one cozy cabin by closing the glossy panel that sections off the aisle. It reminds me of an old-fashioned luxury train cabin.

I'm one of the first people on board, so I give in to temptation and rifle through all the little goodies they've left me: mints, fuzzy socks, sleep mask, and—*ooh*—a little bag of skin care products. Next I play around with my seat, raising and lowering my privacy screen—that is until it makes an ominous-sounding *click*. The screen freezes an inch above the divider and refuses to rise again.

Cringing, I snatch my hand away and busy myself with removing my shoes and flipping through the first class menu. It's long, and everything looks delicious. Oh man, how am I supposed to go back to the cattle-roundup, meat-or-chicken-in-a-tin hell that is economy class after this?

I'm debating whether to get a preflight champagne cocktail or glass of white wine when I hear the man's voice. It's deep, crisply British, and very annoyed.

"What is that woman doing in my seat?"

My neck tenses, but I don't lift my head. I'm assuming he means me. His voice is coming from somewhere over my head, and there are only male passengers in here aside from me.

And he is wrong, wrong, wrong. I'm in *my* seat. I checked twice, pinched myself, checked again, and then finally sat down. I know I'm where I'm supposed to be—just not how I got away with it. My fingers grip the menu as I make a pretense of flipping through it. I'm really eavesdropping at this point. The flight attendant's response is too low to hear, but his isn't.

"I expressly purchased two seats on this flight. Two. So that I would not be seated next to anyone else."

Well, that's...decadent? Whacked? I struggle not to make a face. Who does that? Is it really so awful to sit next to someone? Has this guy *seen* economy? We can count each other's nose hairs back there. Here, my chair is so wide, I'm a good foot away from his stupid chair.

"I'm so sorry, sir," the flight attendant answers in a near purr, which is weird. She should be annoyed. Maybe it's all part of the kiss-the-first-class-passengers'-asses-because-they-paid-a-shit-ton-to-be-here program. "The flight is overbooked, and all seats are spoken for."

"Which is why I purchased two seats," he snaps.

She murmurs something soothing again. I can't hear because two men walking past me to get to their seats are talking about stock options. They pass, and I hear Mr. Snooty again.

"This is unacceptable."

A movement to my right, and I nearly jump. I see the red suit coat of the flight attendant as she bends close, her arm at the man's screen button. Heat invades my cheeks, even as she starts to explain, "There's a screen for privacy..."

She stops because the screen isn't rising.

I burrow my nose in the menu.

"It doesn't bloody work?" This from Snooty.

The rest goes just about as well as you'd expect. He rants, she placates, I hide between page one and two of the menu.

"Perhaps I can persuade someone to exchange seats?" The helpful flight attendant offers.

Yes, please. Fob him off on someone else.

"What difference does it make?" Snooty snaps. "The point was to have an empty seat next to mine."

I'd love to suggest he wait for the next flight and save us all a headache, but that's not in the cards. The standoff ends with the jerk plopping into his seat with an exasperated huff. He must be big, because I feel the whoosh of air as he does it.

And I feel the heat of his glare just before he turns away.

Fucker.

Slapping my menu down, I decide, Fuck it; I'm having some fun with this. What can they do? They're loading the plane; my seat is secure.

I find a stick of gum in my purse and pop it in my mouth. A few chews and I have some superior gum-smacking going on. Only then do I turn his way.

And freeze mid-chew, momentarily stunned by the sight

sitting next to me. Because, good God, no one has the right to be this hot and this much of a jerk. This guy is one-hundred-percent the most gorgeous man I've ever seen. And it's strange because his features aren't perfect or gentle. No, they're bold and strong—a jaw sharp enough to cut steel, firm chin, high cheekbones, and a bold nose that's almost too big but fits his face perfectly.

I'd expected a whey-faced, graying aristocrat, but he's tanned, his coal back hair falling over his brow. Sculpted, pouty lips are compressed in irritation as he scowls down at the magazine in his hand.

But he just as clearly feels my stare—the fact that I'm gaping like a speared fish probably doesn't help—and he turns to glare. I'm hit with the full force of all that masculine beauty.

His eyes are aqua blue. His thick, dark brows draw together, a storm brewing on his face. He's about to blast me. The thought hits along with another: I'd better make this good.

"Jesus," I blurt out, lifting my hand as if to shield my eyes. "It's like looking into the sun."

"What?" he snaps, those laser-bright eyes narrowing.

Oh, this will be fun.

"Just stop, will you?" I squint at him. "You're too hot. It's too much to take." This is true, though I'd never have the guts to say so in normal circumstances.

"Are you quite well?" he intones, as if he thinks the opposite.

"No, you've nearly rendered me blind." I flap a hand. "Do you have an off switch? Maybe put it on low?"

His nostrils flare, his skin going a shade darker. "Lovely. I'm stuck next to a mad woman."

"Don't tell me you're unaware of the dazzling effect you have on the world." I give him a look of wide-eyed wonder. At least I hope that's what I'm doing.

He flinches when I grasp the divider between us and lean in a bit. Hell, he smells good—like expensive cologne and fine wool. "You probably have women dropping at your feet like flies."

"At least dropped flies are silent," he mutters, furiously flipping through his magazine. "Madam, do me the favor of refraining from speaking to me for the remainder of the flight."

"Are you a duke? You talk like a duke."

His head jerks as if he wants to look my way but he manages to keep his gaze forward, his lips compressed so tightly they're turning white at the edges. A travesty.

"Oh, or maybe a prince. I know!" I snap my fingers. "Prince Charming!"

A blast of air escapes him, as if he's caught between a laugh and outrage but really wants to go with outrage. Then he stills. And I feel a moment's trepidation, because he's obviously realized that I'm making fun of him. I hadn't noticed how well-built this guy was until now.

He's probably over six feet, his legs long and strong, encased in deep blue slacks.

Jesus, he's wearing a sweater vest: dove gray and hugging his trim torso. He should look like an utter dork in it, but no... It only highlights the strength in his arms, those muscles stretching the limits of his white button-down shirt. Unfair.

His shoulders are so broad they make the massive first class seats look small. But he's long and lean. I'm guessing the muscle definition under those fine and proper clothes is drool-worthy too, damn it all.

I take it all in, including the way his big hands clench. Not that I think he'll use his strength against me. His behavior screams pompous prick, but he doesn't seem like a bully. He never truly raised his voice with the flight attendant.

Even so, my heart beats harder as he slowly turns to face

me. An evil smile twists his lush mouth.

Don't look at it. He'll suck you into a vortex of hot, and there will be no return.

"You found me out," he confides in a low voice that's warm butter over toast. "Prince Charming, at your service. Do forgive me for being short with you, madam, but I am on a mission of the utmost import." He leans closer, his gaze darting around before returning to me. "I'm looking for my bride, you see. Alas, you are not wearing a glass slipper, so you cannot be her."

I glance at my bare feet and the red Chucks lying on the floor as he does. He shakes his head. "You'll understand that I need to keep my focus on the search."

He flashes a wide—albeit fake—smile, revealing a dimple on one cheek, and I'm breathless. Double damn it.

"Wow." I give a dreamy sigh. "It's even worse when you smile. You really should come with a warning, sunshine."

His smile drops like a hot potato, and he opens his mouth to retort, but the flight attendant is suddenly by his side.

"Mr. Scott, would you like a preflight beverage? Champagne? Pellegrino, perhaps?"

I'm half surprised she didn't offer herself. But the implication is there in the way she leans over him, her hand resting on the seat near his shoulder, her back arched enough to thrust out her breasts. I can't blame the woman. Dude is potent.

He barely glances her way. "No, thank you."

"Are you sure? Maybe a coffee? Tea?"

One brow rises in that haughty way only a Brit can truly pull off. "Nothing for me."

"Champagne sounds great," I say.

But the flight attendant never takes her eyes from her prey. "I really do apologize for the mix-up, Mr. Scott. I've alerted my superiors, and they shall do everything in their power to accommodate you."

"Moot at this point, but thank you." He's already picking up his magazine, the cover showcasing a sleek sports car. Typical.

"Well, then, if there's anything you need…"

"I don't know about him," I butt in, "but I'd love a—hey! Hello?" I wave a hand as she saunters away, an extra sway to her hips. "Bueller?"

I can feel him smirking and give him a look. "This is your fault, you know."

"My fault?" His brows lift, but he doesn't look away from his magazine. "How on Earth did you come to that conclusion?"

"Your freaky good looks made her blind to all but you, sunshine."

His expression is blank, though his lips twitch. "If only I could strike women speechless."

I can't help it, I have to grin at that. "Oh, I bet you'd find that marvelous; all of us helpless women just smiling and nodding. Though I'm afraid it would never work on me."

"Of course not," he deadpans. "I'm stuck next to one afflicted with an apparently incurable case of verbal diarrhea."

"Says the man who is socially constipated."

He stills again, his eyes widening. And then a strangled snort breaks free, escalating into a choked laugh. "Jesus." He pinches the bridge of his nose as he struggles to contain himself. "I'm doomed."

I smile, wanting to laugh too, but holding it in. "There, there." I pat his forearm. "It will all be over in about seven hours."

He groans, his head lifting. The smile he wears now is genuine, and a lot more deadly because of it. "I won't survive it—"

The plane gives a little shudder as it begins to pull out

from the gate. And Mr. Sunshine blanches, turning a lovely shade of green before fading into gray. A terrified flyer. But one who clearly would rather the plane actually crash than admit this.

Great. He'll probably be hyperventilating before we level out.

Maybe it's because my little sister is terrified to fly as well, or maybe because I'd like to think Mr. Sunshine's horrible behavior is fear-based and not because he's a massive dickweasel, but I decide to help him. And, of course, have a little more fun while I'm doing it.

END

WANT to learn more?
Sign up for my newsletter at
www.kristencallihan.com

PLAYLIST

Django Reinhardt, Limehouse Blues
Nirvana, Smells Like Teen Spirit
The Black Keys, You're The One
Sinead O'Connor, The Last Day of Our Acquaintance
The Beatles, In My Life
Bon Jovi, Wanted Dead or Alive
Pearl Jam, Indifference
Alice in Chains, Man in the Box
The Beatles, Ob-La-Di, Ob-La-Da
Mary J. Blige, Right Now
Nirvana, Heart Shaped Box
Prince, Cream
Prince, Darling Nikki
Wilco, I Am Trying to Break Your Heart
Cat Power, Sea of Love
The White Stripes, Hotel Yorba

ACKNOWLEDGMENTS

Huge thank you to my go-to beta readers Kati, Sahara, Tessa, Elyssa, and Monica. Copy editors Dana Waganer and Jessica Royer Ocken. My awesome cover designer Sarah Hansen. To Dani for her PR excellence and all around hand-holding. And Natasha for...you know what. ;-)

And a special thank you to all the bloggers and readers who help spread the word about my books and for being so supportive.

All my love!

CPSIA information can be obtained
at www.ICGtesting.com
Printed in the USA
LVOW12s1519061216
516056LV00002B/207/P